T0063389

The Patmos Paradigm

James Hendershot

Order this book online at www.trafford.com
or email orders@trafford.com

Most Trafford titles are also available at major online book retailers.

Printed in the United States of America.

ISBN: 978-1-4907-1822-4 (sc)
ISBN: 978-1-4907-1823-1 (e)

Trafford rev. 10/25/2013

www.trafford.com

North America & international
toll-free: 1 888 232 4444 (USA & Canada)
fax: 812 355 4082

Dedicated to my wife Younghee, with many thanks for financially providing for our family throughout my writing days and to my sons, Josh & John and daughters, Nellie & Mia.

par·a·digm

: example, pattern; especially : an outstandingly clear or typical example or archetype

: an example of a conjugation or declension showing a word in all its inflectional forms

: a philosophical and theoretical framework of a scientific school or discipline within which theories, laws, and generalizations and the experiments performed in support of them are formulated ; broadly : a philosophical or theoretical framework of any kind

Synonyms, archetype, beau ideal, ensample, example, exemplar, ideal, mirror, pattern, standard

Disclaimer: This book is fantasy and fiction. It is not based on personal experiences or some mystical insight into the unknown. It is not intended as a theological source for religious debate. Read it for your entertainment.

I will not be held liable for any losses due to psychologically damaging nightmares, to lost sleep, increased physical dysfunctions, or mental breakdowns, hearing enigmatic voices or complaints about furniture floating in your homes.

CONTENTS

CHAPTER 01

Emos

The great admiral of the Empire Halitus yells out to his spellbound crew, “Okay, troops; it is time to switch off; your replacements are crystallizing now.” Then senior direction team chief Tacenda yells out, “pol jot steady.” The admiral, Admiral Nidificate now yells, “Where is the translator chief, everyone else, keep it steady and calm. No time for any mistakes now in this cosmos of emptiness.” Then a young ensign reports, Translator Technician Quab, his translator is not working. The Space Ray Jumper Specialist Melomania speaks out, “Ghu’vam amaze, action ‘op tagha’ wIghaj.” Quab then looks at the Admiral and says, “Sir, I got it.” He rushes over to Melomania and runs his adjusting tool over his suit and says, “Got it Sir” Then Melomania repeats, “This is amazing; we finally had some action, okay it works now.” The Admiral then says, “Relief team, report back in four hours. I think our adrenaline has recharged. Then Quab asks the Admiral, “Sir, our translators have not reported any malfunctions in almost one million years, why now?” The Admiral answers back, “Quan, in my forty years of zapping in and out of universes and so many ages in time, this is the first malfunction that I have ever seen.” He then looks at the Direction Pilots and says, “Colonel Balatron and Colonel Halitus, I need you women to slow us down. Chief Tacenda, give me a detailed scan of everything within one million light years. How long will that take?” Chief Tacenda reports back, “Sir, it’s coming in now. There is something about 900 thousand light years at 300 degrees, at Tajvaj mark 77945220." Colonel Halitus asks, "Sir; we have been at warp 10^{108} powers for over one year now and seen nothing, not even a speck of dust. How can something be out here?" The Admiral now pushes the Red alert button and calls for his senior advisors to report to the mission room. As he enters the mission room he orders, "All non-senior advisors out currently." It had been so long since the room had been used, a crew was bringing the room back to the Empire's standard for a sitting Admiral. Chief Exploration Advisor Callow reports, "Sir, we are carefully analyzing what appears to be a dated spheroid made from materials that are not listed in our database." The Admiral now shakes his head and orders, "Double-check that check that again, because we both know that it is impossible to have materials that are not in our database. By the way, is that an Azurian accent you have?" Advisor Callow replies, "Yes Sir, you are the first one I have ever met that could pinpoint as most people take it for a Feuilletian accent." The Admiral now laughed and said, "I made that mistake once and found myself playing Jutty by myself as my Azurian date left me standing alone with a black eye." Then Advisor Callow laughed and said, "I do not think as an Admiral on one of our greatest flag ships you will ever have to worry about getting a black eye; however, the Azurian women are feisty, so I would recommend you wear your uniform on your first meeting." The Admiral answers back, "Advice well noted." Now three other senior advisors report that this object, which is at the present time in full view of this space world, "This unknown object has over 500 unfamiliar elements. Recommend we do not bring it aboard and go to war alert." The Admiral pushes his worldwide communicator, "Citizens; we are now in contact with an object that may have up to 500 unknown elements, thus we do not know what to expect. We will go into high war alert. Any abnormality shall be reported and investigated immediately. I want Star Fleets 17,000 through 43,000 deployed in our immediate space." Now another senior advisor says, "Sir, please, our Empire has not discovered a new element since the days of Absquatulate, over one billion years ago. We are in a death trap. We need to get our world out of here as fast as possible." The admiral now pushes his command button and tells the deck crew, "We need to move back mark 740002345 and 310 degrees." This world, which has over one billion inhabitants, at this moment in time, starts to retreat with 1000's of star fleets providing cover. The admiral now tells his advisors to release all the collected data to the world scientists and orders, "We must discover where this spheroid is from, for this is the discovery of our Empire. Could we actually be in the days of absquatulate?" The station intercom at present reports, "High Governors arriving at station x4332." The Admiral now orders, "Elite team 445 reports with me at x4332." The Admiral takes one of his special flash lines and arrives waiting for the High Governors as they are now crystallizing. The first Governor asks the Admiral's group, "Has Emos been notified?" One of the Colonel's answers, "Yes, one of my staff was scheduled for recycling today, so he took this knowledge with him into Emos's eternal pool." They then ask this Colonel if Emos had answered yet. He responded, "He told the Admiral to retreat this world until more data is processed." Then Governor Nihilarian answers, "We had better had a seat and think this through, for we may have stumbled upon the greatest mystery ever known, especially if the all-knowing Emos does not know. Have we had any word back on our request to have the recycling terms extended?" The admiral answered, "Sir; we would not know about things such as that, for that is between Emos and his priests. Just to feed my curiosity how long of an extension are you asking that Emos give those he created?" Governor Nihilarian replied, "Another seven 365's." Admiral then smiles saying, "That would give me an extra three 365's with my family in retirement, unless we keep finding these synonymities. I have my Chief Exploration Advisor Callow with his Azurian accent to update us, to include me on our status. Subsequently Governor Nihilarian starts laughing, saying, "Another Azurian accent; I thought you swore no more after your wife." Then Admiral Nidificate, also laughing, answers, "What can I say Sir, she turned out to be a good bottle of wine and just got better over time." Afterwards Governor Nihilarian shook his head yes, and fired back, "She must have, because I see that you are not wearing your dark glasses, or maybe she lost her ability to aim so effectively." The Admiral next finished this off with, "Or, perchance I got better at ducking, Callow what do you have for us?" Callow adds, "Gentlemen, this could be a discovery greater than Emos's race. We have run every possible analysis from every database that Emos has, and we still have no idea what this thing is made of or where it came. Emos says the structure and technology predates his earliest memories, so we are easily considering that this little mystery ball could be around 100 billion years old." Governor Limerance of the Mesonoxian asks, "How can that be possible and how could Emos even suggest such a thing?" Callow answers, "Sorry Sir, if I am going at least to make it to my recycle date, I must not question the infallibility of

Emos." Limerance now answers quickly, "Oh no gentlemen, I in no way would ever question the infallibility of Emos, and I am just trying to conceive how something could have been before Emos's ancestors." Callow at the moment complements this by saying, "Believe me Sir, so is Emos. Oh, hold on, some more information from Emos. He is reporting that we are in no danger from this 'Paradigm." Admiral Nidificate at the present time yells, "What is a Paradigm?" Emos currently talks, "I am still trying to figure that one out boys. The device is identifying itself as 'The Patmos Paradigm.' It claims to have been deployed for information purposes only from a place called the 'Milky Way.' This place has never appeared on any of our space charts and must have merged through many other galaxies since after that. Even the material that it is made from has since afterwards been erased from all known universes, although some of the basic atoms have some dangerous characteristics in that they are not split." Then Governor Limerance of the Mesonoxian asked Emos, "Are we supposed to believe that atoms exist that have never been split? That is like having the death in a cage with no door. Do you feel we are safe at such hazardous material?" Emos then continues, "I can see no evidence where any of its atoms had ever seen a split attempted." The Admiral now questions, "Oh great Emos, every new child whom you give us has the knowledge of the ease in splitting an atom." Emos then added, "That is true Admiral; however, that has always been a theory as we have yet to find a united atom, yet before us in that small ball could be trillions of them, enough to build millions of worlds we are now on." The group just sat around in amazement and shock. The greatest treasure from a past before maybe that time began was in front of them. Emos now added, "We can no longer scan it for the shell may be unstable, nevertheless, it wants to communicate with us. My systems will not allow me any more contact with it. Please update me after you have taken all precautionary measures." A chill, at present froze this meeting room, for they were now to contact and work as an object that even had Emos removing himself from it. The Admiral at this moment in time asked the governors, "What do you think we should do at this point?" Currently Governor of Security Widdiful recommended, "We need to put this device in a secure cylinder so that it would not be harmed by anything accidentally." They all agreed and it was so. The device would still control its destiny, however if it were to approach another civilization it would be slowly diverted. Although where it was now located, it would most likely take another billion years to approach the first star, stray objects could cause dangers such as loose meteors. The governors currently asked to have this conference in a larger room with more department heads available. They had to decide on the parameters of this object. They then would decide how to approach this new form of life, if it were indeed life. The group continued to debate as brand new information was constantly being processed. They soon could verify that this was not a military device, but a time capsule of some sort. The amount of data stored in it was impressive for its age, which did predate Emos's ancestors. They could project an estimate of where it originated from, although the projections were poor since the input ranges were even beyond any known parts of existence in any age. This primitive device created marvel in its history alone. No one risked physical contact of any part of the device since it was made from whole atoms. Therefore, they developed a series of scan sequences, which would slowly combine numerous scans in manifold layers only to combine them in another layer. The information they were receiving, once it had a few periods to consolidate, it revealed that it was reporting information from a minute planet, about one-fourth the size of this world ship. Everyone wondered why one such small world would be important, until the data kept reporting a mass variety of material. This minuscule world had over seventy-two parent languages, which within themselves offered a wealth of variations and modifications. How could such a tiny place ever function with so much constriction? The Halitus Empire and all known contacts throughout history only had one language. No one ever considered that other languages could exist. Even stranger was how they were made with the same basic organs of the animals which survived with them. Nevertheless, these animals could survive from the environment with no accessories, yet the dominant ones on the planet needed extra wrappings to survive in their environment. The group was shocked when they saw how these beings killed each other and fought great wars over such foolish things. They also could not understand why all these creatures had constantly to consume material from their environment only to expel it. Another strange factor was how the ruling species existed in two stages, the first like animals, and the second like the invisible ones. Even the unseen ones were always fighting. The Halitus Empire had never had a murder, nor had to kill anyone in a battle. No one died in this Empire; he or she was simply recycled, which at birth, Emos would give a part of himself to a new shell that it operates. When the shell reaches a certain number of 365 cycles, it is returned to Emos takes back the part that he gave and blends that experience in his being, so the next shell he makes will have those experiences. There are no differences between the males and females; he only separated them so as not to look different from the creations of the other Emoses. There was no greed or selfishness because everyone returned what he or she had in the world when recycled. There was no reproduction since Emos made all, and the laws determined the recycle periods. Life was good and no one again questioned it since no other form of existence ever was. This is why this Patmos now represented a danger, and its knowledge would not be made available to the public. Emos would receive it and control it, is he was known to make changes and try new things. The evidence was clear; all these differences and freedoms were causing pain, and misery, not happiness as the data would predict. The Empire had a creation that did not comply with all known physical laws. They could see that when objects approached each other, they did not stop automatically and would sometimes crash into each other causing the lives inside to stop functioning. The deadliest forces on this planet were the smaller ones who, as viruses and bacteria invade the large creatures and destroy some of their tasks causing them to stop their host. The researchers had never known about viruses and bacteria and now declared the alien ball quarantined and only accessible by Emos. They also could not understand why these beings did not merge back into their creator, but remained as separate creations. This meant that each one had to learn all of its ways from scratch, which made no sense. The difficult process for this creation was that of trying to unite all the separate beings. They wondered how something so old and outdated now had deadlier features that could destroy all known life. Something was missing, and that was the purpose of this cancer. Was it to destroy all future life or did it have a message? Now the alarms sounded as parts from the beginning, and the ending spoke their language. This civilization or existence did have some link with reality. They now discovered that this device was to be a time capsule and recording of one of the most chaotic civilizations ever to exist. They were the bed of both evil and righteousness, and this was the recording of the end times with righteousness was forced to terminate the evil. The pre-historic Emos of this world fairly selected non-biased reporters while still in stage one of their existences to collect the visions for this report. The group now took a recess and agreed to meet first thing the next day and review this end-time vision created by a world that stopped functioning over 100 billion years earlier, which was far earlier than ever before believed imaginable. The subsequent morning when they awoke, and after congregating, they beheld the most bizarre vision over before even known likely.

CHAPTER 02

Summer days shall always plays

June is now upon us as the days begin to get a tab it hot and summer is here, which means the school is out. I have a few extra tablets this year, so I decide to begin keeping my diary. Oh, wow, I get to talk to myself. This should be fun. The western place is famous for bears and a few mountain lions, so maybe this summer I may compete with Daniel Boone. It is in the mid seventy degrees this afternoon as the sun is high above, and we have to be careful not to lose our baseball as it makes its journey from my friend's bat to its new resting place, the pocket of my baseball glove. All three of my brothers, Emery, Floyd and Harry plus one sister, surprisingly the old one, Jennifer will spend most of the summer on this nice baseball diamond with our two friends Don and Jeff. We took some of grandpa's cycles and cut down the weeds to open the diamond up on a field beside Townsend Airport, off Broadway Street, opposite side of Cemetery Lane. We use Broadway Street as our third base foul line, so we are not tempted to foul too many over into Cemetery Lane, because we and stay clear of that place. Additionally, with the way the sun sets, this gives us extra time to find lost balls on our way home. For some peculiar reason, Jeff always fouls the ball over towards the Lane, and we sit back and watch him find it, while naturally making some strange noises. I am excited about this summer ball because more neighborhood kids will be drifting out to play with us during the days. They only play for about five or six hours and then switch off. They are not dedicated like we are. In addition, I read some books in the library last winter that displayed how to throw sliders, forkballs, and curve balls. Even though my pitched ball may not have many movements, I believe my strange body movements can psyche them. Since we do not have an umpire or a catcher, I must get them to swing and miss, for if they do not swing, then someone has to get the ball, which if they are winning they will get it, and if we are winning, we end up chasing it down. Sandlot mountain baseball, there is nothing like it.

When I said winter earlier, we get some winter here, staying below freezing for the first three months during the year. Thus, when baseball season hits, we play outside. I am glad that our oldest sister is playing with us this summer. She is a tough girl. She caught her boyfriend kissing another girl; well actually, my younger brother Harry caught them. Harry was signing the k I s s I n g song and our oldest sister yelled at him to tell him she had not kissed Daniel. She was afraid daddy would find out. Daddy is a mountain man, and mountain men do not take too kindly to others messing with the clan girls. Anyway, Harry told her he knew she did not; Daniel was kissing Sam, her best friend. Therefore, she said no best friend or boyfriend this summer. I still do not know what the big fuss is all about, after all kissing is almost slobbering, and daddy told us to kiss girls is always the beginning of headaches for boys. Nevertheless, a new girl just moved in over on third and North Cedar Street which we call four barrels. She is very pretty, and all the boys say her carburetor is built for speed. Either way, she promised to watch some games this summer so that should be nice.

Lucky for me, the baseball landed in my glove, so this dandelion picker can head on in and bat. Don's dad got him a new baseball bat he brought here today. It feels like it swings very well, so perhaps I can shoot for the fences between us, and the Townsend Airport landing strips, which receive maybe one plane a week. City people like to take the planes and go hunting deeper in the mountains. Our first day was not very bad; we won six and lost five, so I cannot complain. I just need to soak my catching hand, as with the rusty winter between last summer, and me, I caught too many balls today with my palm and not with the open part of my glove. I will be able to remedy this quickly I hope. Jennifer says we all have to take a bath to clean up tonight, so we jump to it. She is so much better than a mommy is, because she only tells us to do things when she knows mom and dad will catch us, and she does not help us as mom does. The other kids will tease us if they catch mom helping us. In view of that, this is fair. Don and Jeff rush home to see what fate awaits them. Nighttime offers us some hot dogs, macaroni, and cheese than Dorothy made for us. She and Lisa like to cook, and we like to eat. Mom is usually very busy in the summer time, as are most of the mountain moms, so we kids fend for ourselves. Dad is always at work. He works nonstop in the summer and gets many days off in the winter. That is when he does all the things mom wants him to do. I do not know what sort of a job he has, in that he does what all the other dads do, thus in that manner, everyone is pretty much the same. Don told me once that his uncle told him the people within the city areas think they are so smart, yet they cannot skin a rabbit. I would not have believed what he said was true; however, he told me when we were at church, and I asked his uncle, and he said it was true. My brothers and I were so shocked that a boy would not know how to skin a rabbit. We have now been a feared that the city folks may all be retarded. My brothers and I, after taking our baths and putting on our pajama's we hear some serious screaming downstairs. Jennifer, while crying yells for everyone to come downstairs for a talk with dad. I bet this is not going to be good. When we all arrive in the living room, Jennifer tells us that Dorothy is still outside. Mom is calling from the phone checking with other people in town. Finally, she receives word that someone saw her getting in a truck with some of the high school boys. I feel sorry for the kid that told on Dorothy. Dad calls the sheriff, who thinks he knows someone who has a truck that fits that description. While dad was with the sheriff, I asked mom how she found out that Dorothy got in a truck considering my butt is on the line also for this, as when dad whips he lines us up applies his board of education to the seats for our knowledge. Mom says that old Ms. Wilson, saw them and was so worried about Dorothy, not wanting anything bad to happen to her. I thought to myself, 'Ms. Wilson was not worried; she was just stirring up trouble; I mean if Dorothy was screaming for help Ms. Wilson would have run away, yet she had to have seen Dorothy happily joining her friends.' I guess we will have to start up our neighborhood patrol for one more special mission. Our time reflecting was ended abruptly as dad is currently bringing Dorothy home, and she does not look happy. The sheriff is rushing back to his car like a tog with his tail tucked between his legs. Around here, the law stays out of the affairs of family discipline. We all were punished and rather betray Dorothy; we all joined in our brother-sister circle. It is not that we are ganging against our parents; as such, things are unheard of around here. We just always hang tight together as we know our blood is thicker than water, and that we need each other to be ourselves. That may be one reason why Jennifer is playing baseball with her brothers this summer, knowing how we will idolize her for doing so. One thing is for sure at present, now baseball tomorrow is canceled at the present time as Floyd has a black eye. He always makes dad angry during our whippings, pushing him beyond his control. Floyd only understands the considerable lashings, as he is so stubborn in any fight. I have almost ended up as hamburger a couple of times at school when he tells some great beast that I am going to defend him and seek revenge. We put up with him, since he is a part of our family. Now that darkness has covered our small wonderland in this big world, mom rings the dinner bell. Let me tell you, we are all hungry as our bodies surrendered everything today trying to control that ludicrous torn baseball. Mom has a considerable meal for us tonight, with a big roast from one of our cattle we processed last fall. Mom made some noodles and Lisa helped her with the mashed potatoes, biscuits, beans, and gravy. After our meal, all is forgiven and our family retires to the family room to sing a few gospel songs. Mom holds this time dear, and our family has undergone this bedtime ritual all the days of our lives. We have no TV as our parents are so set against it. Dad always says that we will look for a TV after everyone in this house has read every book in the county library. Very few families have a TV in our small town, and none of the farmers has them. Everyone holds true to the ways to the west on this subject, even though Hollywood is in the west. Try to explain that to an adult in this town or to the Sunday minister that has them all scared to death. All of us boys head to our room, and our sisters head to theirs. The first day of summer has ended, as we go to bed with sore legs, sore buts, filled bellies and everyone we woke up with in the morning. The morning wakes us up with some rosters crowing from the nearby farms. I often think that they want to ensure that we all hear them. Today is my turn to run over to granny's farm in the morning. As I go in her back door, she welcomes me in and hands me our morning basket. I kiss her cheek, and tell her was all love her and run back to our house. Granny always has a basket waiting for us in the morning. Today she put the normal eggs, bacon, homemade bread, berries, and apple juice. This is truly as scrumptious as possible as mommy gives daddy his morning coffee, creamed with some homemade cream. The aroma of the bacon and coffee blends in with heavy morning mountain air as all in the house are soon rushing around our table in the kitchen. Jennifer waits until our parents are gone and shows us a tree that dad pulled in with his tractor last night and revealed to her this morning. She now pulls out the axes and hands them out one to each of us. In cutting fire wood, there is no difference between boy and girl. The important thing is that we all give Lisa and Harry, the youngest ones; extra room since their swings can, at times, is erratic, and we have no hospitals nearby. Either way, Dorothy teaches us some songs that we have to keep a secret from the minister and all the adults. This is her way of making up for getting us in trouble last night. By lunchtime, we have finished chopping the wood, as Don and Jeff joined us for the fun. Anything is worth the high status of learning these new suggestive songs. We will be the heroes among our friends now, which are those who do not have high school siblings. We currently put the wood in one of our sheds and decide to take a trip in the woods today. Dorothy has been promising to show us the old family's homestead that Uncle Earl cares for. It will take us an hour to walk over the hills to get there. Our young bodies are packed with all that energy from granny's breakfast, so we can trek these hills as the Indians did a few short centuries ago. As I feast my eyes upon this old house, I am bewildered by its size. Dorothy tells me that Uncle Earl made a lot of money from selling oil produced from some wells in his far back acres. In those days, things cost a lot more in these remote parts of the mountains and as such; this mansion was at one time the pride of the area. Uncle Earl lost our aunt to a rare Indian virus, the only documented case of this virus in over three hundred years, and that case survives through legends of their medicine men. He has refused to let any go inside the house since those personal losses and had metal fence built in the yard that encloses his home. Any products he purchases from the markets are delivered here, and he unpacks them when all are gone. I have yet to see his face nor have any of my siblings. Jennifer claimed to see a curtain blocking the window to his upstairs small porch as we were coming over the hill. We were sure to make noise as we approached, as Uncle Earl has been known to shoot at the intruders who startled him. I would bet that this house would take over one hundred gallons of paint to make the exterior presentable once more. The front right outside his house has a Victorian four windows each floor tower. I am saddened that the outside boards that fall below the two extra upper windows are now exposed. I can currently just speculate about the grandeur that it once had. I am puzzled about the slate holding on the roof as some parts beside the simple visible chimney on this side. I believe he spends most of his time in the attic in the wintertime trying not to freeze to death. We could never determine exactly why he decided to spend his days as a hermit, although I have heard some tales from our cousins around campfires at night. These tales claim that he feels there is something evil outside his house. I may only be a kid, yet I know that there is something evil outside my house, and I deduct this as follows, there is evil from this world and there is no evil in our house, so that evil must be in the world. This does not mean that I am going to spend my entire life dying a prisoner in my house. I think he may have smoked too many peace pipes. I have always noticed how the old timers all act differently around the Native Americans, even though we have so few of them around here, having five times more African American than Native American. I have a very good Indian friend at school, and even though he has invited me to visit his family, I have yet to enjoy that pleasure. I will when I am permitted to walk toward his house or dad takes me. He has suggested that someday I ride the bus home with him. I believe I will do that next year. I can almost feel the prison this has been for Uncle Earl. He is in prison by choice or according to him escaping from evil, yet Uncle Brice has to live in prison not by his choice. Many people are angry because Uncle Brice is in prison saying all he did was make people happy. I think he may have messed around with some magic because Jennifer once told me that Uncle Brice could make the moonshine. That is why I am careful never to point my flashlight at the moon and make it shine, because I do not want to be beside Uncle Brice for making the moonshine. I have heard that girls like to kiss boys under the light from the moon. That must be how Uncle Brice made the people happy. They must not allow flashlights in prison because Jennifer said Uncle Brice does not make moonshine in prison. She also told me that they told you when you can play baseball, and that you can have no guns. I want to play baseball during the summer and want to have guns when I go hunting. Daddy teaches all his sons how to hunt. He said it is the way through the hills. We are now all sitting on a line outside the fence and trying to figure the story about this house. We can feel it saying something; however, it is talking either too quiet or furthermore fast. Something is stirring inside me, as if a hunger for my family's ancestry. I am pretentious of a better day gone by that is too hard to ignore. The desire for our past is crying out for the house to take us back to it. Coupled with this is the helplessness of not being able to save a part of us. We can see the tears slowly flowing from our eyes since the understanding of such foolishness from an adult; especially an uncle in our family is burdensome to say the least. Mom is always yelling at us to take care of the things she gives us. I can understand the rationale behind her words now. Jennifer tells us we are seeing a death that is slow in coming. She scared Lisa thus she is crying now, so we need to start back to our house. Jennifer will take us through as many open fields as possible so Lisa will not get more anxious. Our fields are tinier than those of the Midwest area are, and by such, cut with considerably smaller equipment, with many farmers still using horses, which are actually much more practical on our steep hills. Dorothy has elected to start singing some of her spicy songs again, as we all join along as if to be uncovering great secret words unknown by humanity. The thrill of being special and uncovering mysteries adds a joyous touch to our rhythm. We now all stop our cadences instantly as we see approaching us Ms. Black. Everyone says she is a witch. Her family name really is not Black; it is a strange European name, and we all call her Ms. Black because she only wears black and never change her clothes. I think she sleeps in her clothes, as the dry brown of the dirt has absorbed itself merging her skin and the fabric as one. She always walks around chatting weird words. She lives in a cabin that is probably the oldest house in this area that has no doors and only one boarded window she climbs in and out. No one has ever seen her talk to anyone else, even in the grocery store, as she always communicates in writing using her little notebook. She has been around here for the ages and is now just a thing that is in our world, no threat only abnormal. Another thing that helps makes our community different. We just walked past the old woman shunning her so as not to take any chance in making her angry or crazy. Once we were past her, Dorothy, who appears to be our recreational coordinator today suggests that we play tag on the way home. We all agree and of course; Lisa is the first one to be it. Even though she is the smallest she does have some sneaking tricks, such as today falling down on a rock that cuts her skin producing a small amount of blood and crying as if approaching death. Jennifer rushes to her, tears flowing from her eyes and body trembling as little Lisa revives from near death to scream, you are it, and run like wild. The youngest got older and we are all now scattered, because we know Jennifer can get anyone, nevertheless, she usually goes after one of her brothers, continuously somewhat being protective of her sisters. We must be careful where we run so as not to step on any bees as none of us wears shoes during the summer time. We all enjoy the freedom our feet enjoy, especially the opposite of the deep cold winter months when we wear multiple layers of socks, shoes, and heavy boots. In order to get some joy out of our lives in the summer time, we must completely remove any thoughts about winter, because winter will come, like it or not. We all arrived home before mom and dad, thus split up and did our chores. We like the way Jennifer compliments us, so we try extra hard to keep her happy, after all she is a big girl who plays baseball and any girl who plays baseball will be liked by boys. This is the natural way of things. We all helped to get our supper ready. Now, Dorothy is yelling from the basement. We all rush to her, and she is screaming because there are worms all over our potatoes, so Jennifer tells us to bring all the potatoes outside and put them in the open yard. They do this, and it the meantime birds are swooping down and eating the worms. After they carefully inspect the potatoes, and separate the potatoes with worms from the ones that do not have worms, during which time I have been in the basement killing all the remaining worms and cleaning up our potato bin. We put the good ones back downstairs and the ones with worms in our old washbasin, which we filled with water. Everyone in town is complaining about extra insects this year, so we figured might as well get used to it and be prepared to do a lot of insect cleaning this year. It is not the quantity of the insects that people are complaining about; it is the excessive amount of the often dormant or rare ones. I have noticed so many different kinds of bees this year, and there are always wasps and yellow jackets. The wasps this year appear to behave as if attack helicopters, and once they lock on come in for the sting. We are all sitting on our front porch, which is painted unless Uncle Earl's house, with our wasp spray cans that can shoot for twenty-five feet and knocking them off one by one. Weird how as fast as one goes down another appears. Jennifer tells us we will have to be careful about leaving food in our house uncovered, as those along with a garbage can excite them. Mom is now coming home from her day in town. She works at one of the stores, and then goes around with the other women helping those who are having trouble. We are all big on helping each other since we need each other to survive, or at least our tradition tells us we do. Any ways, for the most part, it is better to help each other than depend upon some government people to help us. They always give too much also late. Any way you figure it, they will be passing through our house soon, as they do rotate between each other's houses also. Dad is now pulling and parking his truck. We can see a used bike in the truck bed, thus we all get excited and go in the truck. Dad now tells us not to get excited; he needs that bike for his work. He is going to start riding his bike to work and around town for basic marketing. Jennifer asks him if there is something wrong with the truck, and he tells her that gas just went up to $8.25 a gallon today so he is going to keep the truck pretty well parked and start working more overtime at work. He is worried over the impact it will have in the grocery stores and other stores, especially since we only have small stores this far up in the mountains. I know we cannot be that remote, after all route 287 connects with twelve, fifteen, and ninety, so we, weather permitting can get around to some big towns, yet Butte and Helena about the biggest places in this area. The way dad is talking today; it could be seldom that we visit anyplace just for fun in our truck, which is always a hassle on the big roads, since all of us kids, except Jennifer rides in the truck bed. After our supper, we all pitch in and clean up the kitchen and Jennifer rewards us by showing us some constellations. We must clean our dishes after each meal as we only have a few dishes. We do not mind, as we know that each time we are eating from a clean plate. Jennifer shows us; Cancer, Mensa, Monoceros, Musca, Norma, Octans, Ophiuchus, Orion, Pavo, Pegasus, Perseus, and Phoenix. We stop her now, and even though this is fun, it could be mistaken for summer school, and we do not want anyone seeing us would think we are foolish. We have currently finished cleaning ourselves, and head into the family room to sing our nightly gospel songs. Mommy now asks us, "Do you know the legend of the Cherokee Indian youth's rite of Passage?" We never heard this one, so we ask her to tell it to us. She continues, "His father takes him into the forest, blindfolds him and leaves him alone. He is required to sit on a stump the whole night and not remove the blindfold until the rays of the morning sun will shine through it. He cannot cry out for help to anyone. Once he survives the night, he is a Man. He cannot tell the other boys of this experience, because each lad must come into manhood on his own. The boy is naturally horrified and can hear all sorts of noises. Wild beasts must surely be all around him. Maybe even some human might harm him. The wind blew the grass and earth, and shook his stump, but he sat stalwartly, never removing the blindfold. This is the only way he could become a man! Finally, after a horrific night, the sun appeared, and he removed his blindfold. It was then that he discovered his father sitting upon the stump next to him. He was at watch the entire night, protecting his son from harm. We, too, are never alone. Even when we do not know it, God is watching over us, sitting upon the stump beside us. When trouble comes, all we have to do is reach out to Him." My brothers and I were now asking our dad if we could take that test. My dad said we had better not do it tonight, since the yard still might have many worms in it from the ones, we took out of the potatoes today, and that some big snakes might be in the area looking for those worms and mistakenly think we were dead and try to eat us. We agreed that daddy might be right on this one. Dorothy, who is trying to rebuild her position with our parents after last nights 'boy' disaster asks mommy, "Why do you not tell Uncle Earl that story?" She tells us that Uncle Earl has a disease or maybe even worms in his head, and that we are to stay away from his house. She growls at Jennifer when she discovers that she took us there today for a short visit, yet then finally surmises, "Well at least they went there with you Jennifer and not on their own. Just be careful where you take your little brothers and sisters, for they can hit you with their charm, and you will be helpless." They both laugh as we exchange our good nights and head off to dream land. The next morning, after Lisa brings our breakfast from grandma's the day starts off with a big bang. One of Dorothy's friends comes running up and knocking at our door. Hank Bradly and Grant Hart are going to fight over behind the State Bank of Townsend off Broadway Street. The fight is going to start when they see the sheriff's car head out 287 for his morning patrols. All the kids are hiding in that area now or pretending to play. Soon the sheriff heads off on his morning ritual, although today about three minutes later than normal. When he is gone, we all make our way to the small picnic table behind the bank, which does not open until eleven A.M. today as the money truck is always late on Thursdays. We listen to Dorothy's friend tell her why they are fighting. Hank went out with Grant's sister Marsha and told everyone that he and she had sex in the back in his truck. Marsha eulogizes that is a lie, and thus Hank is fighting for her honor. Marsha needs no honor now, because Dorothy's friend told her, she already received ten phone calls this morning from boys wanting to take her out on a date in their trucks. No one has cars in this area because the snow gets so high in the winter. When Hank discovered all the calls, he really got angry. Any way you slice it, the fists will be flying in one minute. Soon the fight was in full force as Hank came out swinging and Grant came out ducking, yet soon he got his chance and landed a few hard ones right on Hank's face bloodying his nose. He got three more punches in and went down. Grant got on him and demanded he yell uncle, which he did. This fight was over too fast. I was glad we did not have to pay any money to see it, for if so, I would have been angry. Now Grant made Marsha tell everyone the truth and when she did, the fight was over as Hank apologized to Grant. Marsha went to go home; however, so many boys are forming a circle around her singing songs to her and begging for a date. Dorothy and her friend are bewildered, "Marsha confessed to lying, nevertheless all the boys are forgiving her and willing to give her a chance. They ask Jennifer who tells them, "Someday you will understand." Now the hot news comes out, "There has been a car crash in front of Lucky Lil's Casinos." We are all laughing because of a few people, that place was not blessed with good luck today. Subsequently, we become serious when we hear the ambulance and fire trucks. When we get there, I can hear a couple of the big boys say, "It was just a small fender bender." I go over to the fire truck driver and ask him why he is here. He tells me that by the state and federal safety and insurance laws, they must be nearby, just in case our lives could be in danger. Seems to me, that if someone was hurt someone else would call however, I guess it is the timing in such a situation, which is important. Anyways, it is baseball time now, so we all prepare to head to our baseball diamond down the street to play some ball. Jennifer takes Dorothy off to the side to have a talk to her about Marsha. She is asking Dorothy not to be like Marsha. I can only deduct that Jennifer does not want Dorothy to tell lies, which would get her into trouble with mom. Anyway, all this excitement made me strike out my first at bat and of course, Holly was watching. Maybe that is the way of sports with women. When I want to impress them, I cannot hit a thing. I will have to focus on the ball. The next time, Jeff got a hit, and I smacked the ball extremely well, landing just over the fence we use as the home run fence that is on the other side of the running track that we use as our warning track. It does feel so excellent with Holly cheering; we shake hands as I round third base, and head home as the game continues. How excellent it feels to have someone actually cheering for me. Holly is a pretty girl, although her older sister is more popular amongst the boys. That does not matter to me, because Holly is the one that is here cheering me. As we prepare to take the field, I stay in left field since the extra two runs give us an eight-run lead, so defense will be more important now. Holly stands behind the home run fence, so we make some small chat between batters. At first, I thought this was great, until someone hit a routine fly ball to me, and I tried to catch it basket style and misjudged it. The stupid thing hit me in my nose as I can feel the blood splashing everywhere. I can hear everyone laughing, except for Holly as I look over she is crying and rushing to me to begin my nursing. Holly tells Jennifer that she will rush me to her house since North Cedar Street is closer than our house on North Oak Street. Once again, one of her sister's rushes ahead to help her mother gets everything ready. When we get her mother uses some old wet rags and cleans my face, feels around my nose, which does hurt; however, I will show no pain in front of Holly stays right beside me as her mother suggests I lay down on her bed and rest after a while. She guides straight to her room as her mother tells her, "Holly, keep the door open because he must have fresh air to help his nose heal." How is it that a mother can destroy all hope with one fast blow? Little boys have no chance around mothers. Notwithstanding, I think mommies are so worried about the plans of boys; they forget the creativity of their daughters. Holly just causally positioned me where she would be able to block the view of her mother, because she had something, she wanted to share with me, and this was the view of the largest breasts of any girl at our school, and she was only a freshman. When I saw them, my heart stopped, and she actually had to push down on my chest to start me breathing again. How could something be so beautiful and why did she want to share this with me? I know I talk a lot of big talk around girls; however, my bark was light-years ahead of my bite. I looked into her eyes as she started laughing and for the sake of my life lowered her shirt back to its normal position. I was glad that she kept her bra on; because we all knew, the blessings that she was endowed with bounced everywhere. I subsequently had to have some saving grace strategy, so I told her, "Holly, sorry for getting choked over what you just shared with me, as you know, I have been with so many girls and none of them are as blessed as you." Holly then told me, "That is strange, because only a few girls confess to being with you, my older sister being one of those." I then told her, "That is because I make them promise to keep it a secret, so they do not end up like Marsha did this morning. Yes, I was with your older sister, Anne, because I wanted to find a way to attract you. I wanted you to know about my excellent skills, which I hope she rendered in her testimony to you. Anyway, Holly, why were you laughing at me a minute ago?" She then handed me a little mirror, as all girls have in their possession. I looked into the mirror and saw a monster. My nose was completely swollen over twice its normal size and yes; it hurt. I then wondered what would happen if I looked like this forever. Fortunately, her mother came in to look at me. I do believe she had no worry about her daughter and me, with the way I looked. She felt around and put those big mommy eyes that when they look at you make you confess everything. I could feel my tongue starting to move. Oh my God, what if I confess. By the time her dad finished with me, I would make Frankenstein look like Ms. Universe. Pepper came in and looked at me; beginning to laugh and Anne looked at me and began to cry. Her mother then said, "Anne, I take it that you know George." Holly currently told her mommy, "She used to know him; however, he is mine now." I thought, 'Oh my god; I god, I was never going to make it from this room with four girls alive, three chicks, and the mother hen.' That mother hen is going to roast this little rooster. Her mother was cool about his saying, "Well Pepper, come with me and let your sisters fight over who takes George home." I was thinking, 'Yes, get me out of here before the big dog comes home." Anne looked at Holly and after that at me and said, "George, please be nice to my little sister and do not hurt her." I then said, "Sure thing, Anne." I was actually serious this time, because I now only had a lonely future of looking like Frankenstein ahead of me. As Holly was guiding me home, being the perfect cursory nurse worrying about every short-lived step, I was talking; my mother came running up behind us yelling for me. We both stopped and turned around. Holly held her position in a supportive way without regard to her comfort or outward appearance, which was starting to impress me. I think my mother was impressed with Holly's style as she began the conversation, 'Good afternoon Ms. Holly. I want to thank you for your excellent care rendered to George." Mommy, then moved over to my other side, to help walk me home, as it was apparent, the Ms. Holly was not going to relinquish her position. On our way home, we stopped into Dr. Vinson's office, and he took me back and examined me. His verdict had both decent and bad news. The good news was that I would be pretty much healed in one month, considering the nose has cartilage and not a lot of bones where I was hit. The bad news is no baseball for one month. Dr. Vinson told me that if I was hit again, the damage could actually be fatal. When I looked over and saw that Holly had heard this, I knew baseball was out for one month. She had that look in her eyes and Dr. Vinson saw it also remarking, "George; I can see that you are in good hands." I had so many things going through my mind now. I somewhat always felt sorry for Holly, as since she was different in the extreme good way; all the girls treated her like a freak.

If Holly talked with you, it was like the kiss of death with the other girls. This time, I did not care. Why should I treat someone wrongly, just because of other people's insecurities? I had a situation today, and she stood by me, and in the mountain world that was important. We now held hands on our way back to the ball diamond, this time I would be on the disabled list. When we returned the game was winding down as Jennifer declared today to be a washday. That meant that we are all going to Canyon Ferry Lake, the official shower room and washing machine for our town during the summer months. I did not dive in as, I usually and poor Holly would not be able to go around her waist today with so many people here since she forgot to bring another shirt. The tee shirt she had on, if it were to get wet would literally send this town is a shock wave. Notwithstanding, she waded in waist deep and carefully cleaned us both as best she could. I noticed people were acting different for us now, not teasing us as before. Jennifer was treated Holly nice also, asking her if she needed any help working on me. They treated each other with respect. I have never seen girls behave like this before and especially and older sister to step aside working on one of her injured brothers had to hurt her as much as it did mine. I think our baseball clan was discovering something new. A bond was formed, where two people were going to go separate and care for each other, no matter what others said or would do. If any wanted to continue throughout their lives, the former two would now be as one. I felt special and asked Jennifer what happened to us and she just causally laughed and said, "Cupid shot you two." Everyone is acting as if this is so normal, yet none can see how scared I am. I wonder if Holly is also scared. The reasons I am scared are, first I do not understand what is happening, second, I am afraid that I could hurt someone who is giving so much to me and third; I think I still have a lot of growing up to do. I never actually cared for a girl before. I just enjoyed sowing my wild oats, yet now my future only has 'no trespassing signs over these fields. I will talk to Jennifer and dad about it tonight. Jennifer tells me not to worry about it but "To count myself lucky that someone cares for me and to show her that what she saw is existent." I, however, wonder what she sees and what is real. Dad pretty much says the same thing and also added, "Do not trust your friends around her and remember you are to protect her, not hurt her." I just want to go back to where baseball is everything in the summer, yet even if I go there, I must realize that I am on the disabled list for one more month. Henceforward, my world will not see much baseball this summer. I will do some umpiring and coaching or whatever. Nevertheless, Jennifer suggests that I just spend some time with Holly. She tells me in a joking fashion, "You are not going to find much more female in what your girl has." She is true concerning that. I guess we can start taking some walks and maybe do some fishing. I kind of like the way we can precisely walk right down the middle of town and out to the worlds, and everyone ignore us. Don says that is because, ordinarily, everyone is worried about the girl; however, when she is the one leading the way, she only sits back and envy the boy. Right now with a Frankenstein face, I can use some envy instead of pity. Jennifer recommends that Holly and I will take a good walk tomorrow and just talk with each other. The time away from people will do me decent also, because I hate the way, everyone stares at my nose. I tell Holly about Jennifer's recommendation the next morning, and she thinks it is a great idea. She tells me it has been a long time since she has been on her Aunt Rita's farm, which is about a day's walk away. I ask Jennifer if it is okay, and she gives us permission, as mom and dad always agree with her decisions. Their biggest thing is to know about it and having some justification for the decision. Jennifer tells me she will tell our parents that with my nose, she felt it would be good to get away for a few days and could think of no one better for me to go with, a chance to meet some of the family kind of thing. Consequently, we stopped back to her house to get her mother's approval then my house to pick up a rifle, as in these mountain forests, it is suicide to go without one. Holly's mother also gave her a pistol, so we should be safe. We each grabbed an extra shirt in case the weather changed on us and off, we went down the railroad tracks to just out of town and at the fork on the road, took the high road or Indian Creek Road. It was a nice day, even though the gravel roads we walked on liked to bite at us with an occasional sharp rock. As we held hands, most of the time we acted stupid laughing at every little thing as love stricken lovebirds often do. We both knew how important this trip was for today, and tomorrow we would know if we were compatible and should dedicate our lives to each other. I did not try to seduce her, as she did not try to seduce me. Everyone knew we would, so by not doing it, for now, or as long as we could hold out, we would know something that no one else knew. Anyway, we had excessively much on our plates at the moment. We were not each other's enemy, so we should not act as such. We would either be able to work together, or we would not, that is just the way things turn out. I believe we both want something from the other, which I guess is the basis of relationships. We have spent most our time today discussing what we liked and what we did not like. There really was not that much different both belonging to such a small tight nipped community. While we continued to walk, we passed a minuscule group of Indian tepees, and as I looked after the children playing in the front yard, I recognized one and yelled out, "Hey Little Running Eagle." He looked up and yelled back, "Hey George." We up to shake each other's hands when his dad came running out and asked us, "Where are you two going today?" Holly said, "To my Aunt Rita's house as she lives over in Helena National Forest." Little Running Eagle's dad then told Holly, "Oh your aunt must be an Indian afterwards, for only Indians may remain in the government parks." Holly then told him, "Yes our ancestors were Northern Cheyenne." His father, Flying Eagle now told us to be, "Careful on our journey for the spirits have been acting strangely lately." We said ok and that we had to keep moving so we could be there by nightfall. Back to the road we went. The sun was now in the middle of the sky, and the birds were getting ready for their afternoon naps. We will be depending on the birds a lot for our security as when a bear moves the birds will get excited. Holly wants to bathe some when we find the next stream. She can do that today as we have some privacy, and she has an extra shirt. I will make her put it on if she gets her chest wet, since this area does have some strange mountain people who, for the most part, keep to themselves. I just, as a precautionary measure does not want to get them too excited, because Holly is furthermore innocent to know what a great blessing mother nature has made her for men. Either way, we are going to enjoy some play on the water and soak our tired feet. We need to relax ourselves some as Flying Eagle's words shook us some. Who wants to be in a deserted forest only to know the spirits are uneasy? Anyway, I got us a turtle for our lunch, so we should be good until late this evening. I just saw some deer run pass us. I did not shoot, because that is too much meat for us to eat, and it would only excite the taste buds of the carnivores in this area as the smell of blood floods the valleys and even the caves. I soon get us back on our chosen path, as fortunate for us most of the afternoon paths are close to trees as we are moving deeper into Helena National Forest. The thing that bugs me at present is how the squirrels love to jump from branch to branch shaking up the sky. The winds are starting to pick up some now, making strange eerie sounds. Even the animals are uneasy now. Holly says we have a few more hours to her aunt's house. This is getting difficult for me, because I must act very calm and not even let my palms sweet for she will feel it and get scared. This is a lot of responsibility for me; however, I am willing to accept this because Holly has in such a short time grown under my skin. I got her out here, and I will get her back to Townsend safe, which is, even if we are in danger. There is no way of knowing if we are in danger, or if we are over reacting to nothing. The hours of darkness shall quickly come upon us, and yet before me is another mystery I cannot believe, it is snowing. There is snow flooding upon us. As I look into Holly's scared eyes, remaining calm, I ask, "My new love, I do believe we may have picked the wrong day to visit your family, yet, even so, how far is your lovely Aunt Rita's home?" She moves her mouth to my ear and after kissing my ear, she whispers, "About a twenty-minute run." I currently must say the magic words that shall surface the first time in our new relationship. I had planned to tell her this after the end of the summer; however, it appears that the summer is now ending with the snow turning us into white, and our legs into a strange shade of red. I now, while petting her face surrender, making her the victor, "Holly, I love you." I expect her to begin laughing or giving me her ten commandments. My daddy told me when you meet a girl, they charm you with great freedoms, yet once you tell them you love them; they shall give you their commandments and when you say I do at the chapel, they will say to you, "I did" upon being carried over the threshold." I wonder what commandments she is going to give me." Strangely, she wraps her arms around me and gives me a nice long kiss. I think, maybe her mother has not taught her the laws yet. How could a mother not teach a daughter with such great man traps the laws? Either way, I might as well find out now and ask her, for someday she will discover them. I ask, even though it is so painful to pull my lips away from hers, "Holly, do you not know the great commandments you are to levy upon me?" She answers, "Yes, my mother told me, but she also declared that I have the power to love you instead. I am lucky in that the one I love furthermore loves me. The only thing I ask from you is that you stay faithful to me, as I shall to you, and that you not abandon me, and the children I shall give you. Worry not about providing for us, for I shall work beside you." I then held her tight and promised, "That I shall do, my Holly." I now almost feel guilty, for I wonder am I hugging her for love or for that furnace of heat that is flooding from her body. I recognize it is for love, yet the warmth is keeping the hug alive. I at present realize that she must be taken to safety fast, so I ask her again, "A twenty minute run?"

She then says, "Yes, we should start now," as she breaks away and starts running. I immediately follow my partner and soon catch up with her. We are felicitous that the path is wide. I am fortunate that she can see the real question I am asking. It may not be so dreadful being in a relationship. We run through the woods zigzagging. After thirty minutes, I ask Holly, "Holly, do you know where we are?" She tells me, "George, we are not far; I just need to keep those hills in a straight line, so I can hit her cabin perfectly. It will only be a few more minutes." Moreover, off we go again, and after another ten minutes, she stops and says to me, "Practically here George, we are almost nearby." I can see the calm in her eyes, so I know she believes what she is saying. Nevertheless, the snow is at the moment so deep that we must avoid any openings in the forest, so we do not freeze our bare feet. It is hard now to determine the hour, because the snow has blocked out the sun, which sets much later in the mountains. I always thought that to be strange, in how the sun sets earlier in the evening for the Midwest and eastern states, yet for us who are in the mountains and thus, technically, closer than the sun; it sets later in the evening. My young life is now starting to get used to strange things as they occur even more frequently. How could I think when I was eating grandma's food this morning for breakfast that this evening, I would be lost in Helena National Forest after declaring my first love in a snow storm? This is strange, yet very true, a wonderful delight so early in our summer vacation. All those times I prayed for snow during the school year, only to have my prayer answered during the play days of summer. Sometimes strange is not good. Once again, Holly says, "Come on George, we are nearly there." I wonder, are we really almost there?"

CHAPTER 03

Aunt Rita

"George, we are almost there; we have to go across this clearing." I tell her to stop, and after that, I rip my shirt into four strips and tie them to each of our feet. This is a onetime shot, because after that clearing the shirt will be freezing wet and then start to freeze our feet. I trust what she has told me this time to be true, because I know a mountain girl would only cross a clearing in the snow with no shoes if she knew it to be the truth. As we cross the clearing, she stops and looks around. I am taking the rags off our feet and waiting for something from her mouth. Are we in trouble or if our destination in sight? She then breaks the silence from the cold eerie taciturnity that the forest is giving us in the early darkness of our night. "George, right there, can you see the smoke from her chimney?" I look over and see some smoke from the forest. I do not see a house, which is concealed by the forest, nor do I care now if it is her aunt's house, because if it is not, I will do enough begging to get us in front of that fire. She currently flashes like a bullet down this hill, and I follow suit, more out of not wanting to lose her in this darkness, then a thought of seeing Aunt Rita. Soon, we are at the front door of a cabin, and she is beating at the door, crying out, "Aunt Rita, please open the door." I sense of peace now floods my heart, as this was the initial time I trusted her with our lives, and she came through. We have crossed the first bridge on our road to our new future. Now, joyfully the silence in the cabin is broken as an old crackling scared voice answers back, "Who is there?" Holly quickly answers, "It is Holly and George." The voice says, "Who is George?" Holly then answers, "He has been my greatest new lifetime forever love Aunt Rita."The door now slowly opens as we enter and cautiously stand in a straight line waiting for Aunt Rita and her double-barreled shotgun to give us permission to go at ease. Aunt Rita closes the door and then says, "You stupid kids get in front of that fire at this moment in time." "Holly and I, holding hands, sit in front of the fire trying to bring life back into our red-skinned cold flesh. I massage her as she massages me. Then Aunt Rita says, "Lovers, stop massaging each other and massage yourselves instead, for only you know what needs tending to first." We do as she and that shotgun command, although she has now put the shotgun down and is bringing some food and drink to her table that is beside us. For the first time in hours, I can start smelling again, for in the forest as the cold hit all smells retreated to their safe havens. A rich forest filled with new life turned into a lifeless, motionless, empty world so quickly. That nice fire in front of us is flashing with its own world of movement. I look around, and see her loft filled with firewood. That is strange, for I never heard of one keeping their loft bursting with firewood this early in the summertime, thus I asked her, "Aunt Rita, why do you have so much firewood in your house this time during the year?" "She answers, "Does not your family store their firewood in a warm place during the times of snow?" I then said, "Yes, we do, yet summer time is not a month of snow." Aunt Rita subsequently said, "As you watch your calendar, I listen to Nonoma, who told me one moon before that a great snow would fill our lands this summer, and that Holly would bring a stranger to dwell with me for one year." I next looked at her and asked, "For one year, why would be staying here for one year?" Aunt Rita then said, "After you have warmed up, rested and eaten tomorrow I will show you the visions. You shall, of course, be free to leave whenever you wish to do so." We then dined, as she brought out to us a nice thick fur blanket to wrap ourselves in while we sleep. I afterwards confessed to Aunt Rita, "Aunt Rita, Holly, and I are not married." Aunt Rita then said, "Children, in my house I am the law and the law now weds you, currently sleep together as you shall for the remainder of your days." Holly then ran over and hugged her aunt shouting for joy. She then pulled me to the floor saying, "Prepare our blanket my love." I knew enough to do as she said, for her man bombs were eager to take me prisoner, and I had no desire to deny them their due to victory. I knew that the heat her body produced is trapped in this fur would render unto us a nice of great warmth to drive away the cold during the winter that now ruled these national forests. Our first night sleeping together was awkward at times, as our bodies would need time to be adjusted to another within our private zones. My arms ached and wanted to fall asleep on me a few times, as I had to wrestle it loose from beneath Holly's head and shake it to return the blood flow. I usually sleep on my belly; however, with Holly beside me; I now slept on my back, wanting to assume a more protector type position. With all the strange surprises we experienced today, neither had an urge to consummate our relationship. I remember reading somewhere that when bad times are ahead, people naturally slow down their reproducing, yet when good times are ahead, many daughters are given in marriage. I wonder which one rules when the future may hold uncertainty. I knew that tonight, my nightmares would not curse me with baseballs crashing into my face or hearing "Strike three" repeatedly throughout the night. I had, at no time slept this close to a fire before. My father not at any time let his children sleep close to a fire as one of his brothers was burned by a fire when he was a child. He always said, "An extra blanket and a safe distance from the fire will give you all the warmth you need to stay existent." He must be right, because we all are still alive. When the morning hours approached, I saw Aunt Rita putting out our fire. I asked her, "Aunt Rita, why are you taking away that which is keeping us alive?" She then told me, "I do as the Winter Wind commands me." She currently handed me some batteries and asked me to put them in her radio. Aunt Rita now told us, "We can have no fire by day, as the smoke will lead death to our doorsteps. We shall listen over the radio later this morning. Now we must wrap in many furs to keep our lives." As we sat at her table, preparing to eat, a white horse with a spider wearing a crown on its back, and many bows in its arm-legs came running through her cabin. He would run through the walls entering and leaving. He did this twelve times before entering no more. We all sit stunned at her table. I thought to myself, 'how could I have thought yesterday was peculiar, for now within only the first hour, all things before that I thought to be strange are currently normal. I have now seen strange. I never saw a giant spider riding a horse before, nor have I ever seen horses that ride through walls. Where have I been all my life? Is Townsend really that far removed from what is normal?' I now asked Aunt Rita, "What was that?" She answered, "That was Maheo riding a white horse, yet I at no time remember him riding a white horse previously." I agreed with her,

"I do believe I have never seen him riding a white horse before . . . As I have never seen him before." Aunt Rita then told me, "This is the first time that Maheo has revealed himself to me also. I heard him say that, 'the times of old are forever gone." The way she said this, put Holly at my side and a sense of fear in my heart. Without shoes, I knew we would not make it far outside, so fore Holly's protection we would stay here until the snow melted away. We finished our breakfast without saying a word. Then Aunt Rita fetched the radio and turned it on. We heard a special news report saying that the entire Earth was now being covered in deep snow. All the crops and fruits throughout the Earth were at present brought destroyed. I wondered if this was not the greenhouse effect, which we had heard in warnings about throughout our whole lives. The news channel now, as if reading my mind, reported that this had nothing to do with the greenhouse effect, as the Polar Regions continued to be frozen. No one could explain why it happened nor how long it would continue. Any predictions would only be wild guesses. Major cities now, such as New York City, Rome, Beijing, which entertained already more than four feet of snow. Some parts of Africa and the Far East had seven feet of snow, as these were their normal winter months. Rita currently turned off the radio, telling us that she only had one more box of batteries, and that we may need to know the news for many days in our future. She now told us that with this much snow, and snow still falling, any wind would create such large snow shifts that no roads would be passible. Aunt Rita now told us that the next twelve years would have a new season cycle of three moons freezing, three moons burning, three suns six months perfect than followed by three times, and six moons terrible. I wonder where she gets this crazy stuff from, yet as I look at all the wood, she has in the loft of this cabin and the four feet of snow outside, I become conscious that she may actually not be crazy after all.

Aunt Rita now calls us to her table, as Holly and I unwrap ourselves and proceed to her table as she has requested. Aunt Rita at present lights a candle, and we have some light before us now. She currently tells us about her fresh visions, "My children, Maheo now rides a white horse to introduce a modern transformation that is driven from the face of the Earth. This change has been driven by those who have broken the laws of the spirits. Old ways shall be forever gone, as those who survive shall survive with the spirits. Those who resist this change do so with the sword, which shall cut both ways, destroying both the defender and offender. We now looked as appeared before us a pregnant woman clothed in the sun and the moon as her feet. She then spoke out saying, "My male child will be given power over the nations around the world and destroy his enemies with the rule with a rod of iron. He shall give those who follow him the morning star." Then she slowly vanished. I asked Aunt Rita, "What does this mean?" She told us, "Say no more, but watch, for another vision is upon us." We now looked to the past at where last night's fire burned. I saw the spider run back, this time with no horse and lay on his back shooting many arrows into the sky. A great eagle dropped through our roof crashing onto the floor. I looked up at our roof, yet it had no hole. I heard the spider laugh and say, "The whore Eagle, who in the entire world fostered sexual debauchery is no more. The Eagle has fallen." I currently saw demons coming from within the earth bringing greater supplies of food, saying, "He who eats shall eat our food, which has been given up by dark deities." The visions now departed as we could feel the Earth tremble as never before. It would tremble for about five minutes, stop in an hour, and then tremble again. In the second round, we turned on our radio. We caught and emergency broadcast, which said, "We warn all to seek emergency shelter, for a new round of nuclear weapons will be released soon. The United States and China are no more as World War III is now at hand. This second round of bombings is coming from third world nations as Iran and Iraq are being bombed by Israel, and Pakistan is at full-scale war with India. The Korean peninsula is also at war, as the Russians are fighting with the Japanese. Africa is not fighting as each nation is fighting all the other nations, creating mass confusion, yet many casualties. The loss of wartime communications is adding to the mass hysteria, as even neighbors are now attacking their neighbors. All fight as if tomorrow shall never be." At this, I turned on the radio. Is this true, can a world at peace now be killing each other? Has the value of life been discounted so much? Aunt Rita sits there so calmly. I ask her, "How can you be so calm, when all we have is now being lost?" She answers sluggishly, "My son; I gave up that world before Holly received her first breath?" I looked around and surmised that what she had said to be true? I now tried to block the opening of our fireplace from the rest of the cabin, hoping to save what warm air or I guess not freezing air inside our living space. One fur handled the trick. Aunt Rita once again went to her bedroom as Holly, and I snuggled up in our furs in a corner of the cabin. We both were too restless to sleep and furthermore anxious to love thus only stared into each other's eyes. I asked her, "Holly, what do you think is going on?" She answered, "The joy of being your woman is that I do not have to think, for I can say, 'George, tell me what is going on,' and you tell me what we should think." I told her, "Holly, I have three sisters who talk ceaselessly, so I know you can think. Have you recognized that I may be afraid in you knowing what that radio just told us?" Holly then said, "It told us the world was destroying itself; however, it did not start to destroy itself until, Nonoma blew in the cold winds, so ask me, who is the one with the power?" I let her logic rest upon my mind, a thing my father warned me about, for he said if you let the thinking about a woman invade your mind, you would find yourself in deep danger. Well, the only thing I can ask my father is, "Does that apply when the Earth is destroying itself?" The reality is that since I listened to her, I am now snuggled up in a hidden cabin away from whatever is out there. I do realize that things are probably not that bad in Townsend, as we are a somewhat remote community and as such, everyone still relies on the local farms for produce to can, and meat to butcher, and orchards for fruit. Therefore, they will be okay for a little while and with the tremendous amount of snow, no people from the big cities should be invading them soon. The radio did not mention the snow today, as I guess World War III would take precedence. This World War is different in that there is no solid one group fighting the others, as the winner of one group attacks the others, such as China now fighting the Russians and the fallen Eagle fighting Canada and Mexico. It appears as a fear that the blood level will drop below a certain line. I decide not to worry about this and now to concentrate on Holly, for we have to grow up fast. She was wise not to speculate as to what is going on in the world today. We have plenty of time to worry about that. I now move my lips to her still receptive lips, and we slowly kiss each other as our worries float away in all that snow that is outside. I will wonder on a way to get outside later, for at present it is time to enjoy the love that is beside me. Subsequently in the afternoon, I look over at the eating table, which is loaded with food as Aunt Rita yells to us, "Time to eat you love birds." It is still strange for me not only to be permitted, but also to be expected to love my lover in this new world we are living. Holy and I are treated as one now. I guess all of us kids constantly think about our parents as one, unless we are denied a request from the first parent and receive a yes from the second parent, a skill which children who want to do many things learns to master early in their lives. I invariably asked Jennifer, because if she said no, I would just start to cry. That got her every time. A little boy must stick with what works. Now that little boy is a big boy currently, so the things I did, as a child, is to be no more. I now wonder how we will ever be able to tell our children about things such as a passenger car, TVs, considering Holy, and I have never been in such. Our rides were in the beds of trucks and tales about TV's in the books we saw at the school library. I now glance over to the table as my legs lift me up the table becomes larger as I get closer to it. I can see fresh juice, hot fresh bread, a nice roast and steam escaping from gravy and the buttery smell of soft mash potatoes. I set down as we load our plates, Aunt Rita tells us to give thanks onto whomever you wish before you eat. Holly and Aunt Rita give thanks to Maheo, as I give thanks the way, my mother always did before each meal we ate. I then looked at Aunt Rita and asked, "Do I offend you by giving thanks to my God?" Aunt Rita said, "I care not young man; I only give thanks to the one who truly gave us this food." I looked after the food again, and then I started to wonder; we had no fire in this cabin, yet this food is all cooked. I saw no storage area for food, yet it is all here fresh and ready to eat. Then I thought it wise to eat first and ask questions later. This food tastes as pleasant as it looks; the roast is especially excellent having a new rich and spicy taste to it. I ask Aunt Rita, "This roast is absolutely remarkable, tell me how you prepared it" Holly and her both started chuckling as Holly finally answered, "It is an old family secret, and you may only enjoy these treats if you marry me." I subsequently looked at Holly and said, "Good taste, or not, I shall marry you and be the most envied man in town." Holly then told me, "You will not be envied in our town." I afterwards told her, "After that, we will move to a new town, for you are me, and I am you. Anyway, Holly, please do not let this bother you, for the things that they mock you for now the girls will beg God for later, you are just different in a good way, a way that only those who have aged in their eyes can appreciate and desire." Then Aunt Rita added, "He is right Holly; the angels blessed you, and as such you need to thank them for giving you such a great blessing. Later, those who mocked you, if not already dead shall desire you with a fire that will burn them into madness." As I looked at Holly's man bombs, I knew that Aunt Rita spoke the truth. I then said to Holly, "Many men will try to make you hate me and wish to destroy me, so they may have you. Your love for me shall be tested too many times, as I now fear the burden will be as well great for you." Holly next began to cry and then told me, "I promise never to betray you, if only you have me as yours." I then told her, "As a mortal man, I cannot refuse such a promise from the most beautiful of all heaven's angels." Aunt Rita then added, "My visions tell me that you both shall remain as one until the spirits take you to your eternal homes." This was one time, which is enjoyed Aunt Rita's input, because I felt a new hope burning inside of me. I could now only see so many in the world today whose lives were forever changed in a bad way, yet ours was changed in a good way. As we went to clear the snow out of our chimney, so we could start our nightly fire, I noticed the snow had a lot of murky dust in it. Rita gave me a small shovel and told me to dig a hole at the corner of her spare room and to bury this black dust in that hole. She further added that this gloomy dust was deadly and to have a rag wrapped around my mouth when working with it. She at the moment told us that we could keep the fire burning currently, since the dark clouds would camouflage the smoke. I now asked Aunt Rita, "What is this black dust?" She told me it was, "The dust of death, the death of destruction, the destruction of life." It sometimes bugs me when she answers my question by creating a million new questions in my head. After contemplating this, I decide she can no more know what this is then can me." One moon passed as each day now we just sat around in this life capsule between dead worlds. I now wondered how Aunt Rita could keep everything so clean inside our cabin, when we were sealed with no way out. The food kept coming, as I now realized that no one could have this much food in storage. Another piece to this puzzle was how each night she tossed down enough wood for another day, yet the wood is not dwindling. Something is strange here, and even though it is keeping us alive, I wonder now even if we should be living. The radio news is of no value anymore as each week fewer stations remain broadcasting and the news continues to be local in nature, as if there is no purpose to tell of life beyond what they call the New World. Today, I decide to do some exploring within this cabin, and walk over to Rita's private room and open the door. The room is empty, with only a box at the corner. No one is in this room. I now am lost as to knowing where Aunt Rita is. I know I saw her come into this room. I feel all the logs along her walls to ensure that so special exits exist. I then leave the room and go back over to where Holly is sleeping, and myself went fast to asleep. Upon hearing a strange noise, I woke up and saw our fresh food for the next couple of days on our table, although this time there was much more food as if we were going to have a feast. Aunt Rita is walking towards me with a shovel. She tells me, "It is time for us to make clear our front door, for tomorrow we shall receive two more to our family here in the cabin." I asked her, "Do you know who they are?" She tells me, "I have never seen them before, yet they claim to know Holly and you." With this news, Holly and I both rush to where the sealed door is and slowly work at breaking away the ice that has us sealed within. We both work throughout the night, and early the next morning chiseled steps from our new opening creating a tunnel beneath the surface. Later in the morning, we finally reach daylight. I notice that the black dust layer is currently about four feet from the surface. Aunt Rita tells us the air is now clean. We break through to the surface, as a new world at present opens above us. We crawl out onto the frozen snow, having at the moment two months of isolation what feels like inside the earth. I now can only that marvel at how Noah lasted so long in his ark, although his world was filled flooded with water; this world is flooded with ice. Both worlds could be voided of life. I chill at the thought of being the modern Adam and Holly being the modern Eve. Take away an L from her name; and she could be the new mother of the brand new Holy. I know beyond every fabric within my mind that there is plenty life still on this Earth. I must be careful not to listen to all those tales from Aunt Rita. Sometimes I do not know if what she says is true, yet every day we eat well and stay warm in front of a fire that continually burns. Holly is my main reason to stay here, for I have it not in my heart to place her in any sort of danger and with her Aunt Rita caring for us, I know that Holly is in her heart so at least she is safe. I never dreamed of being in such a way as this, exploring the Earth as it now new. I can only guess which beasts could survive. I looked around, and for the first-time notice that the trees have no leaves and what leaves it did have are at the moment far below the ice. The sages of green, which adds any possible apparition of life, which the evergreens now apportion, gives more exultation than that of gold. The white is fighting so hard to make these trees invisible, yet cannot win. I knew we had many pines in my area; however, they have much more in this remote protected place as if to say with a loud voice; this is how mother earth wants her surface to look. I can see some wide clear paths that travel through this forest and the large metal electric towers that carry the heavy wires. We have not heard much on the news about electricity, except to know that if there were no electricity, there would be no news. The electricity itself could be harboring other sanctuaries of life. I at no time actually visualized that while down in our cabin. I can never remember the sky looking as clean, since no fresh jet streams are adding their marks to our firmaments.

I almost feel as being on top of a new world. What humankind has tried to kill, is, and I hope shall once again, come to life. I know we have one more month of freezing; afterwards all this shall be roasted by the hot sun drying everything. Holly and I now rub some snow on our faces, as they are rather dried out by the cabin's fireplace and then Holly descend back into our special haven from all this death. The death we do not see, we only see the absence of men, which implies the presence of the genuine world. The sole true thing we are missing would be a rare set of tracks from an ATV, which would most likely be illegal hunters' hunting on government land. We looked around and saw no tracks, not even from animals. The sky has no birds, which is not strange for winter months. They must have received a big surprise when the winter havens were also covered with snow. The brisk wind can spread the smoke from our chimney quickly, which is another added security for our new home. I now drop down into our cordial cabin and close the door. Aunt Rita invites me to our table as I slowly eat this delicious food, which is still as warm as it was when she put it on the table last night. I had to ask her now, "Aunt Rita, how can you be able to contradict all the laws of Mother Nature?" She answered, "I wondered how long it would take you to answer this question. That secret shall be revealed to you when the spirits allow me." I then thought to myself for a minute afterwards asked her, "Are these spirits decent or wicked?" She quickly answered, "At most the good one's son, for do you see evil in me?" I could sense her anger and thus went over and gave her a hug, the first since we have been here and told her, "Only good my Aunt Rita." I next wiped away some tears she was fighting so hard to hold back and then gave her another hug. I felt so guilty now, for she has done nothing but good for us and whole-heartedly shared everything she has. Holly at present joined us, as we both worked hard to console her. Aunt Rita now told me, "Do you think you just came here by some random choice? You were brought nearby by these spirits for they have called you. The two proofs that they called you shall be given within the hour." I subsequently told Aunt Rita, "If you say it, then I need no proof." Aunt Rita currently argued with me by saying, "You will only believe the words from one mouth, which shall be here within the hour." I currently told her, "Since neither Holly, nor I slept last night, we shall rest for this hour if you allow us." Aunt Rita then told me, "You will need your rest, now rest children, and I shall open the door to allow your evidence to enter within." As we lay down, we both fell into a very deep sleep. When I awoke, I immediately ran to our door and up to the ice steps and looked outside to see the dark. What happened to our new guests? Had I slept through it? I rushed back downstairs and looked across the table to see less food, and then I looked over at the fireplace and saw two furs with wrinkles under them. That might be our new guests. I rushed over and pulled down the furs to receive that greatest shock in my life. I could now see one who I always believed all she had ever told me. I always hid under her powerful wing. It was my new hope. I woke them up by screaming with joy, "Wake up Jennifer! Wake up Floyd!" This must be a miracle indeed. As my voice flooded our cabin, Holly came rushing over to join us. Jennifer and Floyd both had their hair chopped succinct. I asked Jennifer why her hair was so short. She told me, "So the raiders would not rape me, thinking me to be a boy." I then told her, "We never heard about any rapes on the news." Floyd told me, "This was to pretend as it was not, for if they reported the rapes, those who were worse would come in sensing this area to be weak. Do you know what has happened? Where have you been?" I told them, "Holly and I have been here with Aunt Rita." Jennifer looked at Aunt Rita and said, "You are the woman in my dreams." Aunt Rita then told her, "You are the only ones from your family that I could find. George spoke of three brothers and three sisters." Jenifer said, "Many things have happened since you have been gone George." Something came through our towns and many of those who went to church on Sundays. Whatever it was; it took them during the Sunday morning services. Some churches suffered few losses while other churches suffered greater losses. Our parents and the remainder of our sisters and brothers vanished that Sunday morning. An airplane crashed into the mountains not far from our house a few weeks later. It was an airplane that carried mail, although none on board had postal uniforms on as all mail stopped after the nuclear bombs destroyed all the big cities. On this plane, we discovered many letters, newspapers, and magazines. Through them, we learned about the terrible things happening around our old nation. We no longer have any freedom of the press, so these were all underground papers written by rebels who want to rebuild a new nation. They blame aliens for stealing so many people from the churches. Apparently, the churches were not the only place to suffer these losses. Some airplane pilots vanished as the planes they were flying crashed into the Earth. Some large trucks lost their drivers. So many strange disappearances, notwithstanding, this was only the beginning of our sorrows, as no evil people were taken. Those in the prisons had to be released since they were imprisoned by governments, which no longer existed." I subsequently looked at Jennifer and asked, "Why did not you and Floyd go to church that Sunday morning, because I can never remember our parents allowing any to stay home?" Jennifer then confessed that she did. She told me, "Floyd and I were angry because we lost you. Do you not know what this was, for mom always warned us through so many of her stories?" I now asked my sister, "Are you talking of the times of Jacob's trouble? In addition, why would Holly and I be left behind, for we have no sin, only love, in our relationship? We were joined by Aunt Rita, who has favorable spirits that bless her. Furthermore, explain why only the people at our church would be taken during the Sunday morning service, as we are on Mountain Time, and everyone else has their own time zones?" Jennifer now said, "I did not say all the people were taken from different times; they were taken at the same time, which for us was during church time. I still cannot figure why Floyd and I were left behind and to suffer as we have the last few months. I too am searching for answers, for you know that I served the Lord with the same fever as our mother." Then Rita told us not to worry why we were not taken, for we have yet another mission. We all looked at her and then wondered what her words were regarding. Rita now asked Jennifer and Floyd to tell them what they saw during the last few months. Jennifer started by saying with a firm posture, "The rapture did take place and all the truly righteous were taken away. That turned out not to be as many as we always thought, for so many false doctrines had caused so many to fall to one side. All the new pleasures that our great age held, most of which never made it to Townsend, except for the video games, caused so many churches to be empty most of the time. However, that was the way when you were with us; it just became magnified as the news raved about it for a few days, and then went on to another news. Russia attacked Israel. The Chinese marched a 200 million-soldier army towards Israel. China had to obey the Russians, because we completely crippled their defenses and production. They had so many mouths that had to be fed. The Russians pushed them towards Israel, promising to share in the booty of the Arab oil, which Israel now controlled. One nuclear bomb destroyed that pronounced army. Following that, an extreme army from a new united Europe destroyed Moscow and rushed to Israel's defense. As a ploy to play off old doctrines, they named themselves the Roman Empire and afterwards causally attacked the remaining naval yards and airplanes in our fallen nation. Each day, we could see hundreds of planes flew over our remote area and then bodies started parachuting out of them. These looters went house to house torturing all the men and raping all the women. Then when all were dead, they would search for all things that were of value and kill of the animals they could not load on their planes. They ensured that no food remains. They also put poison in the water supplies. They burned so many bodies that the sun turned black, and the moon turned red at night. The scientist said this was caused by the human ashes in the clouds. Now, only those who have the implant of the American Romans may live. This implant triggers a special sensor when in stores or passing any police or soldiers. If the 'Yes' button does not flash, you are killed on the spot. They are supposed to be able to detect people anywhere on the Earth. I wonder why they have not detected you here as of yet?" Aunt Rita then told her, "Greater is he that protects us than he who tries to kill us." Jennifer continued by saying, "Other scientists claim that the sun turned black because of a great comet that crashed into the Black Sea. That is one of the reasons the Russians attacked Israel, blaming them for this inordinate disaster on top of all the hail fire and bloodshed. I do know that this new attacking Empire is granting immunity to all Jews and taking them back to Israel, which for the first time now enjoys peace as the Arabs have been relocated to the Sahara Desert. They have destroyed the temple mound and removed anything, which could be Muslim. He is now working with the Israeli government to rebuild the temple. He has told them that the United States protected the Arabs, and was planning to destroy Israel before the Russians. Thus, when China and the United States literally crippled each other, and the Israeli's gained control over the Arab oil, the time was ripe for now with all the oil, the Romans can control the entire earth. Each day, we heard of people starving and new diseases spreading. Then one day, the news changed to the official Roman News, which reported how many people they killed throughout the world and the success of their new church, the United Roman church, which combines all three of the Abraham religions. The Jews now can worship under the open with freedom. Israel and this new empire have a seven-year pact for world freedom as the Romans search hard to bring all the Jews home. Do you remember Hank Bradly then told Jennifer, "Yes, there were in a fight just before Holly, and I came here?" Jennifer after that said, "The invaders were raping Marsha, and he came charging out from behind a tree with a pitchfork and killed one of the soldiers. As he turned to unchain Marsha, the invaders swooped in on them and taking them to the center of town where all could see they burned Marsha in from to Hank then tailed his arms to a cross, with five nails in each arm. No one dared to free him. Floyd and I could hear him cry from our hiding place but knew we could not save him. It took him three days to die. All buildings in our town were destroyed. These beasts will allow nothing to remain that could support life. George, the world you left a few short months ago is now gone. The Earth has seen at least three out of each four people destroyed, when adding the wars, famine, earthquakes, and diseases. Even though this new Roman Empire has, three times the land it once had it still has fewer people than its original Empire at its height. Floyd and I thought we would die soon also, except your friend; Little Running Eagle found us and took us to a cave he and his sister Flying Dove were living. We have been eating pinecones since the Earth died. We were lucky that since his father never liked fireplaces they always slept under many fur blankets at night, thus this deep freeze was nothing for them." I then looked at Jennifer and asked, "Why did you not bring them?" Jennifer said, "I wanted to get permission from Aunt Rita first." Aunt Rita then said, "Of course they can, for they are Indian." I now got excited and asked, "How soon before they are here?" Aunt Rita currently said, "So you may know the power of our hosting spirits, and that they are for the righteous, they both shall be in the front within the hour. Therefore, you must work hard to reopen our door, so they may enter, for they shall be cold and hungry as Little Running Eagle has a serious wound that our spirits will heal." Holly now tells Aunt Rita, "George is only excited because Flying Dove is coming here." I look at Holly and say, "Holly, why would I want Flying Dove? Your blessings are every man's dream." Then Floyd said, "He is telling you the truth Holly, anyway, Flying Dove was my girl for the last three years." Holly afterwards said, "That is strange, for I never heard of that before." Floyd next told her, "That is because you were not a member of the secret lover's circle." Subsequently I looked at Floyd and said, "I have never heard of that club." Then Jennifer told us, "It is only for couples who have been together for more than two years. And they are sworn to secrecy." I then asked Floyd, "Why did you break the secrecy?" He answered, "Because those who I promised to keep it a secret is no longer alive." Jennifer now took command of this conversation, "It does not matter, the thing that is important that we must all get along, or we cannot stay together. If Holly is to be jealous of Flying Dove, then we shall kill her when she arrives." Holly now started crying and begging Aunt Rita to spare Flying Dove's life. Aunt Rita supported Jennifer by saying, “If there is one once of jealousy or any form of rivalry between you and Flying Dove, then she will have to die.” Holly now swore her allegiance Flying Dove. Aunt Rita and Jennifer examined her as poor Holly stood straight and seriously taking very few breaths. Then Jennifer asked Aunt Rita, “Should we trust her?” Aunt Rita said, “We will put her on probation, for any sign of hatred will lead to Flying Dove’s death.” Now we heard a thump as Little Running Eagle came sliding in. Holly immediately rushed past him and as Flying Dove came sliding in, grabbed her kissing her non-stop saying, I love you repeatedly. Flying Dove currently stood up and said, “I love you also Holly; however, I was hoping that Floyd will welcome me such as you have.” Floyd now creaked between Holly and Flying Dove and started kissing her. I at the moment am pulling Holly away and said to her, “Give them some space and save your kisses for me, or I will also become jealous of Flying Dove. Holly currently looked at me in shock and stuttered repetitively, “Oh no; I am not such as that, for I am your woman, please believe me.” I next told her I was teasing her. I then looked at Little Running Eagle, and saw he had two gunshot wounds, one in a leg and the other in his stomach. Aunt Rita now told him to follow her into her room. However, first she told everyone to examine in wounds and for Flying Dove to tell us what happened. Flying Dove said, “We were gathering some pine cones when raiders attacked us. They shot Little Running Eagle in his leg and stomach. When I saw him fall, I called for our horses, and we tried to escape. They shot the horse that he was on, so I pulled him onto my horse, and we circled the bottom of the hill looking for an open drift created by the wind. We found one and quickly ran up the hill; however, their machine guns killed my horse. We now fell to the ground as the winds shifted directions, burying the killers deep under the snow. I tied a branch to his wounded leg and helped him to this place. The journey took us four days.” Aunt Rita took Little Running Eagle into her room and about ten minutes later brought him back out. His wounds were gone. He was as good as new. We all looked at each other. Then Jennifer asked Aunt Rita, “How did you do that?” Aunt Rita now told her, “Only a fool would think I did something like this, nevertheless, how can I, for I am merely a human as are you? Have no fear, for it is not yet time for you to know these things.” She now gave Floyd, Little Running Eagle and me each two pistols with a matching holster. They were nice pistols, long and light. She told us to sleep with these pistols and never remove them for the hour of our deaths are not known. We all prepared to sleep, as Floyd and Flying Dove paired off leaving Jennifer and Little Running Eagle separate. I then told them, "We may be here for a long time, so you might as well snuggle up. We only think you strange for not doing so." They looked at each other, and Jennifer remarked, "You could do worse, you know." Little Running Eagle contradicted her by saying, "I cannot agree with what you say, for you are truly a very beautiful and strong woman." Jennifer enjoyed this as they snuggled together. I could hear them whisper throughout the night. Then in the middle of the night, I heard the door slam open and men sliding inside. I jumped up, and with a pistol in each hand shot two of them. Floyd also jumped up and shot two and Little Running Eagle cast his knife into the fifth one. Aunt Rita came out and told us to carry the bodies into her room. She then closed the door. We could now hear the wind blowing very assiduously. Holly asked her, "Why is the wind blowing so hard?" Aunt Rita told her, "To hide our location and to destroy the two helicopters that are watching us. There now shall come more snow, for the succeeding twenty-nine days before our dry summer arrives." We spent the next few days chatting about our previous lives and adventures during the dull days of school. I could sense a special hurt in Jennifer and Floyd's eyes when I looked at them. It was as if the others from our family were calling out for us. This hurt was not going away, and we had to discover what the purposes of our lives were now. I, therefore, approached Aunt Rita in private and asked her, "Why do we still live, when we should have gone like the others? We have the right to know what the spirits wish from us, for is it not wrong to treat us as cattle, feed us, and then lead us to our butcher?" Aunt Rita now called us together and explained, "Children soon we shall visit the spirits and receive their will. We may not enter yet, for more dangers abounds above. Once that danger is removed then we shall descend, never again to ascend. I ask that we all remain patient while we wait." I then asked, "If danger is to be among us, can you at least accompany the girls to safety with you?" The three girls began to refuse such an offer, as Holly leading the group said, "No Aunt Rita, we wish to be with our men." Jennifer and Flying Dove also agreed. Aunt Rita then looked at me as I told her, "I understand." Aunt Rita now told us, "One of the invaders last night had a virus on him. I need to know who touched him and may have touched his blood. Then Little Running Eagle confessed that he had some of their blood on him, for he was hot and removed his jacket to unload them in Rita's room. After that Floyd also confessed doing the same before returning into our main room and putting out the fire. We had all placed our blood-soaked furs in front of the dead fireplace to help reduce the smoke that went out into the cabin, and then bundled up with some unused furs. Rita now looked at the furs and them. She called Floyd and Little Running Eagle into her private room and reemerged without them. When we only saw her return, we all became unglued and demanded to know where they were. Aunt Rita finally consented and invited us all into her room. As we entered therein, we heard some new booms and felt a series of fresh Earthquakes and shakes. Aunt Rita now told us, "It is time to meet our spirits." We all went to her bedroom. Her floor lowered itself as an elevator would as we fell into a large open cavern within the Earth. As we walked out into the opening, we saw appearing many spirits no two the same. Aunt Rita told us, these were the spirits of the Earth, for they no longer live above as mankind now shall exist only as long as possible on their own free wills, which days are few. We currently saw seven chairs arise as twenty-four old spirits descended each wearing a crown. They at present sat dispersed on the marble benched before us. An angel at this moment in time appeared, walked over to the elders, and collected a box from them. The angel now came before us, sat down the box, and then vanished. One of the elders rose and began to speak, "Fear not our children for we mean no harm unto you, except for the joy which one receives in suffering for the Lord." Jennifer now raised her hand, and the speaker for the elders acknowledged her. She at present asked, "I have counted twenty-four in your numbers, what do you represent, for my Bible told me to question all things during the end times least a false profit deceived me?" The elder now told her, "Jennifer, your words are wise, and now I understand why the Lord has given this group unto us so his word my live throughout the ages. We are the twenty four elders, twelve from the tribes of Israel and twelve from the apostles." Flying Dove, raised her hand, and after being acknowledged asked, "Had not one of the apostles betrayed our Lord?" Then another spirit arose and said, "How many times are we to forgive those who transgress against us?" Flying Dove answered, "Seventy times seven." The elder said, "You are very wise, yet how can those who say Judas betrayed the Lord not understand that the Lord commanded him to do so. Judas, however, because of his suicide was replaced by another who rules in his place. Be it for you to know that he was forgiven for obeying the Lord, as the Pharisee's were only able to capture him by his will, so that he could offer himself as a sacrifice for his saints. The Lord had to have twelve apostles in order for this prophesies to be fulfilled." Jennifer continued, based upon so many teachings that our mother gave us, "There are many theories about who the twenty-four elders are. How can I know you speak the truth?" The elder is now answering, "This is not a mystery for our Bible tells us so, straight from the mouth of our Lord. Listen to his words from Mathew 19:28 "And Jesus said unto them, Verily I say unto you, that ye which have followed me, in the regeneration when the Son of man shall sit on the throne of his glory, ye also shall sit on twelve thrones, judging the twelve tribes of Israel." How can this be a mystery?" Jenifer then thanked the senior elder as he now turned for the purpose of his presentation. Within the days of the next generation following the Generation of our Lord, the Heavens saw that the word as given created a following that was too weak and passive to survive. The word needed some power and some punch. The Lord decided to give his Patmos to another Saint named John." Jennifer interrupted, "I was always taught that Patmos was a place, an island." The elder then continued, "There is an island named Patmos, and the Lord did give John this revelation while there. As many places are named for their purpose, Patmos was named for the Patmos which John received." Then Holly asked, "What is a Patmos?" The elder now told us, "It is the visions that John saw and was commanded to write thereof. You shall also eat from the Patmos, so that the visions may be in your souls as we protect these visions from the wicked ones, who if knowing their defeat at Armageddon, may avoid that battle." Flying Dove now asked, "Cannot the sinful ones read the Bible?" The elder then complimented the girls for their questions and asked, "Why do you boys not ask questions. To answer Flying Dove's question, the evil ones can read the Bible; however, they can never believe it. It is with their heart that if the Lord says it, it can be changed. If they saw it, then they would believe it. That is why your Patmos is the most guarded item on this Earth, and your stewardship of it attests to your eternal life with the Lord." I then asked, "Is that the reason we were left behind?" The elder now said, "Yes, my wise son." Each of you shall look into the Patmos and see a vision. With that vision, you will record what you see through your soul, which will return here and place it in the eternal Patmos that shall be the closing chapters on the life of the human on Earth." Floyd subsequently asked, "Will we suffer also?" The elder afterwards said, "It will never be a burden greater than you can bear? We shall now show you what has already begun according to the Patmos. Here you see that a scroll with seven seals is presented to the Lord. The Lord, currently having seven horns and seven eyes accepted the scrolls, as all in heaven bowed and all the wild beasts upon the heart died. The Lord at the moment calls home his saints, which he saves in a special place beyond the heavens. He releases the first three seals. A white horse with its crowned rider begins the nuclear wars, which shake the foundations of the earth, and free some very wicked demons who have been trapped within the earth for so many ages. All nations desire now to conquer and destroy each other. They appear and keep the wars going by serving the red horse. Israel does extremely well as your news has told you during these wars and making an ally with one who has brought so much great pain for the Jews throughout history. The pronounced bear on the north cannot resist the urge to capture the new rich oil fields in the Middle East that they have lusted for so long. All this destruction and killing as made the work of the black horse so easy, as the World Wide Web is destroyed and international trade and all banking has all but stopped. Nations no more have access to the bounty of the Middle East oils and thus cars, which few are remaining, are no longer of value. The markets cannot sell, and the buyers cannot buy. Inflation is ramped, and the people starve. As a hungry man has no laws, great rebellions break out throughout the world, except in Europe and Israel. One out of each two humans is now dead or has been taken in the rapture. The rapture produced for too few saints, as all in heaven was filled with grief, for so much work and signs had been given to humanity, yet they believed them not. Those who lived in the bucolic areas fared better than those from the urban areas did. This may be that the rural areas are closer to nature and have less worldly temptation. Arising, as if almost by overnight came forth from Europe a unknown mighty Roman Empire, which had actually been formed in secret for many years. Currently with the world in chaos, she only needed to ensure that China, Russia, and the eagles of the New World were destroyed. Russia at present believed Israel would now attack them in great revenge and that this new Europe Empire would destroy them. As such, Russia and China signed a pact to work as one. China gave to Russia a 200 million-soldier army that marched towards the Middle East. They would march through the old Babylonian Empire, at the present time under Jewish rule and regain the oil fields for their pact. To this great surprise, the army being tired and many soldiers not fed for weeks, the Romans easily destroyed them with their air power, which now ruled the Earth. As Russia currently attacked Israel, the Romans came in from behind them and working together with the Jewish nation destroyed this last bite from the great bear. The fourth seal was at the present time granted to take one out of each four still remaining person. The pale horse thus worked through the Romans, who were determined to rule the Earth. They now destroyed all that they could touch in Africa, the Americas, and Asia. These initial raids were by their air power only. It would take time to flush all the nations on the ground, which would see another one out of three die. The new ruler of the Roman Empire believed his success rested upon the blessings of the God of Israel, such as the United States once enjoyed until she betrayed Israel in secret. He now visited Jerusalem and asked the rabbi's, "How can I reward your God?" They then said, "Build us a new temple for the Arabs bombed and destroyed our previous one, for they wanted never that the Judaic nation worship here." The ruler saw this as a way to please everyone, so he immediately ordered the rebuilding of the temple and within one month the Jewish nation, since the times of Christ now worshiped and sacrificed at the temple. The Roman leader, not giving preference to any religion wanted to make sure that all followed one religion. He feared that too many wars had been fought over differences, so he had to keep the differences to a minimum. He, therefore, had declared the Jewish religion as the official world religion and as a sign of goodwill, gathered all the Jews from around the world once again to settle in the holy land. They flocked like fools into his trap. I now say unto you, our Patmos Saints you shall go forth in a vision. Your entry point will be very random as we are not to be bound by time and space. We shall now leave and allow you to decide who will receive the first vision tomorrow. Tonight, enjoy the richness of your special blessed group." With this, they could be seen no more.

Silence now filled our room as we looked at each other. One would have difficulty in knowing we are blessed ones. Notwithstanding, we all knew that blessings have a price. I now realized, that I should go first, having here a good friend, a brother, a sister and my lover. It was time that I learned more about responsibility and the loving of others more than I learned about myself. I can see the resistance from Jennifer and Holly, yet there can be no way that I can allow my lover or my sister to proceed before me. Even though Jennifer is older than I am, that does not matter. Jennifer came here for me, not to die for me, but to live for me. I now stood up as only Holly's whispers of 'no, no, no," and both arms pulling at my arm made the ascension harder. Either way I was getting up, so I slowly moved away from her as she at present began to cry. I now told the group,

"It is I who must go first." Holly then screamed out, "Why?" I looked at her and answered, "To be the man you think I am." Holly afterwards said, "George, it does not matter; you promised to stay with me." I next told her, "Holly, we must all go, to include yourself. I hope that by me going first, I can tell you things you can do to increase your chance of returning." Jennifer looked at me and said, "George; we know that I should go, so go ahead, and sit back down." I then told her, "Not this time Jennifer, it is time that I grew up the way you always wanted me to." Jennifer now sat back down with a rich smile on her face and said, "I am proud of my strong brothers. I always felt safer with you boys beside me." Then Aunt Rita invited us to join her at her new table. Thus, we, all sat down she began by saying, "Children, why do you fear, for what you have seen if harm was the desired outcome for you, would you all not be dead now? You must have faith in the great blessing that you are currently to receive. You shall have visions that shall forever be a part of the Patmos. All who are here now are vested under my care, for if a thing were to happen to George, Holly would have me; and if a thing were to happen to Floyd, Flying Dove would have me; and finally if a thing were to happen to either George or Jennifer, both Little Running Eagle and Holly would hate me. You must now learn to have faith in the bonds of this special group. For you shall be blessed with the Lord for eternity." I then asked her, "Will not you also be blessed with us?" She answered, "Yes, for Little Running Eagle, Flying Dove and I shall rest with our master, Maheo." Jennifer then asked, "Is that allowed?" Aunt Rita now told us, "The place we are at present eating is an earthly home of Maheo, and did not you just speak to the twenty four crowned elders? The spirits of love and righteousness are all united, only some speaking and acting different to satisfy the needs of their family. After eating, Floyd and Flying Dove went to walk among the many tunnels that were here. Aunt Rita gave them a bell to ring if they got lost. Holly and I elected to explore the tunnels in the opposite direction while Little Running Eagle, Jennifer, and Aunt Rita remained on the table discussing things that were dear to their hearts. Aunt Rita told Jennifer not to make a relationship with Little Running Eagle too difficult to achieve, as a lifetime alone is a long and sad lifetime. Jennifer then began to relax with Little Running Eagle as soon they also began to walk. Holly and I decided to follow a tunnel that ran next to a small underground river. We actually saw a few tiny fish zipping around in the water. We started carefully to collect some golden rocks, until I told her, we must discard these stones, for gold has no value in the heavens and having it here on Earth during these times would only invite evil and death. We now both began to complain about currently having our life on Earth and having no children. I then told her, "We will also escape so many deaths and sufferings as they seem to take away from the blessings. At least, we know our future, if we stay strong as the faith. We now sat down on a rock and let our feet cool in the warm water. My mind was not comfortable on the water being amiable, for it should be freezing cold, as this tunnel still had a chill to it. If the water had been following genial for a long period, this tunnel would be genial. I would have to ask Aunt Rita about this when we return, however, Holly now wants to kiss for a while. I guess this is only right, as she must be the first to see her lover enter the unknown portal. In secret, I wonder how our life would have turned out. Her man bombs would cause us much grief, yet I can feel the sincerity of her love. To see our world being destroyed has a way of cementing a bomb. I do feel sad that I was never capable to give her some flowers or write a love poem, or take her to a dance ball at our school. Even though there were many things that we were not able to do, there were many things that we were gifted to enjoy. Our stories are very far from over, as we will still be able to meet some exciting challenges only offered by Patmos. We now slowly make our way back to our main group. As we approached our group, all have returned. I do believe we are all too uneasy to be away from our main group. I now ask Aunt Rita about the warm water into the streams we were wading. She tells us, "The days of freezing our finishes as the days of burning are now upon us. The cabin above us has been washed away be the floods. Great floods cover many parts of the Earth, as we now just wait until the heat from the sun to give us back so much land." We all just now looked at each other, knowing the pains of a burning sun. Jennifer now calls us together and starts telling some famous tales to us. We have all heard the tales many times, yet now surmises that we all trying to relive where we heard these tales. The tales are adding some grounded amalgamated memories to our currently turbulent world and potential evolving features. Jennifer now began some hymns, which added a special touch and flooded life back into these open tunnels. Aunt Rita now puts the hammer to the hymn by saying, "You all need some rest for tomorrow shall be a busy day for you." Floyd now asked her, "What do you mean by tomorrow we all have a busy day?" Aunt Rita looked at each of us as, if we were all fools and then said, "Do you all not know that tomorrow all of you shall go into the Patmos." Flying Dove now asked, “Oh, so that way we all return somewhat in sequence?” Aunt Rita at present explained, “My children, the time in the Patmos and here are different, one second here can be many years in the Patmos.” As the last one leaves here in the future, the first shall be returning to giving his or her visions to the Patmos. Now, we all need to rest so that tomorrow you all will get a nice jump into our future.” That is when I hit us, we will go into the tomorrow. Like it or not, we are going to take the adventure of our lives. Time will not tell, for time does not yet know, the road we shall go.

CHAPTER 04

First half of Daniel's seventieth week

I woke up earlier the next morning than the others did. I suspect I was somewhat nervous about my day before me, as I would now have to face my greatest fears face on, not as a victim, but instead as a silent messenger, rendering my message through the ages. My mother had always told so terrible things about this period. After Rita broke her fast with us, I stood in front of all and only knew one way to enter, the same way in which a diver dives into a pool. The diver had the advantage over me by seeing some of what was about to swallow him or her. I had to be brave as poor little Holly's eyes were beginning to flow with tears, as was also Jennifer's eyes. To my surprise so was, Flying Dove's and she clinched hard to both her brother's hands and Floyd's hands. This was too much for me so off I rushed into this blinding light. That few seconds would make no difference for me the next few years. As the lights flashed and did that entire gambit of psychotic crap to impress me, I landed before a giant beast. This beast looked like none I have ever seen before. He spoke unto me saying, "Record not my appearance, for I are many things combined and after Daniel's seventieth week is no more nor shall I be. You should have no fear in your heart for you are among the chosen one." I then asked, "What is a chosen one?" The beast now revealed to me, "You have been chosen to do a work for the kingdom of Jehovah, and as such none can harm you. As you approach death, smile, for you shall be spared all harm. However, your faith must believe this to be so. We shall not always tell you where to go or what to do; these are decisions for you, for you must decide how to share this message for it shall happen no more for the times of the Earthmen." I then asked him, "Am I the only chosen one to be here today?" The beast said, "All seven of the chosen ones are in the world to this time, with different missions." I then asked, "Seven, for I thought there only to be six." The beast said, "There are seven in your group are there not?" I afterwards said, "If we count Aunt Rita." He then answered, "And why would we not count her?" I thought about it yet could give no answer. He now opened up the Holy word of God, and the book began to read its words aloud from Daniel 7:23-24, "He gave me this explanation: 'The fourth beast is a fourth kingdom that will appear on earth. It will be different from all the other kingdoms and will devour the whole earth, trampling it down and crushing it. The ten horns are ten kings who will come from this kingdom. After them, another king will arise, different from the earlier ones; he will subdue three kings."

The book then jumped to its end reading from Revelation 17:12: "The ten horns you saw are ten kings who have not yet received a kingdom, but who for one hour will receive authority as kings along with the beast."

I looked and now saw the power of the new Roman Empire as it controlled all of Europe and stung the entire Earth. With the power of her wings, none could escape her claws of death. When the Eagle fell, it took with it much of the Dragon, which then gave itself to the Bear and fell to its death in the wastelands of Babylon, which would still have one more day. These ten horns, who were yet small, would receive their kingdoms before the great battle to end this age. The Eagle, Bear, and Dragon fell to the beast who crumbled the entire Earth with death as his breath. He only spared one nation, not wanting to make the mistake the Eagle had earlier made, in denying the protection of the Jews. I saw the name of the great one, who came forth from this powerhouse of Europe, yet Patmos forbid any others to know his name, for his name is the name of evil and death, and Patmos feared that the name could cause vulnerability among the righteous. Even now, I feared to say its name. His power was too great, for none could refuse him. He was the master of all history, learning why things had gone wrong and using this knowledge. He cited the fall of Hitler to his holocaust of the Jews and not controlling whom many, he went to war with at a time. That is why he first let the Dragon, and Eagle weakens themselves, and then watched the Dragon fall to the power into the mighty one in the decay of Babylon. Once all had been weakened, with his powerbase controlled he leveled the remains of the Eagle, Bear, and Dragon. Now one could ever stop him. He chose to let Israel share in the revenge against the Bear, offering them freedom from the evil bear through their union. Israel gave them all the oil they needed from Babylon, as the oil from the other nations was more than they needed. The Great One, as all call him, knew about the history of the old pronounced empires, had religion to bind them and the only religion, he could see that could unite the remnants of a world without Christianity was Judaism. His parents were Jewish and seemed to have the business philosophies and attitudes that gave him the determination to be where he was today. No other human ever to live now had the power that he had, and he would never it up. Any who rebelled against him saw not only they suffer but all in their immediate area. Judaism supported his denial of any supernatural involvement glorifying the validity of their now quickly dying faith. He also knew that the Jews could not be controlled, and completely destroyed if needed to be, they had to all be put into one place, and what better place than in the new Arab free middle east. He decided that one thing would be the extra magnet that would pull them to their ancient homelands, and that would be a rebuilt temple. He destroyed the old one since it had too much of a history of oppression as laid forth by the Muslims. Upon completion, he made Judaism the official world religion, and ordered the beginning of the daily sacrifices again. He made sure that all in the Holy lands knew whom he was. When he entered into Jerusalem to make the first sacrifice, the nation went hysterical over all he said and all he did. He promised peace to all you supported the union. He promised Israel a time of great peace and an evolution into a future as never before seen in history. All who saw him knew that none would dare to ever stand before, even fearing that Jehovah himself stood beside him. Why else would they collaborate to give this new Earth for the Jews? Many currently claimed that the messiah was now among us. The book now reappeared before me, just in time for my mind to continue to become completely become embalmed in something that had to be not only lifeless, but also straight from the pits of every snare to bring down a fool. The book once again opened yet this time an army of powerful creatures as never before seen by those from the earth stood. I heard them cry to the book, "Oh great book let us destroy he who is deceiving the sons of Jacob." The book spoke back and said, "You cannot do this, for it is not written in the word of our God. Your time has not come, for you shall be among those who cast him into the bottomless pit with those who have his mark. The book now read from Daniel 11:36-38, "Then the king will do as he pleases, and he will exalt and magnify himself above every god and will speak monstrous things against the God of gods; and he will prosper until the indignation is finished, for that which is decreed will be done. He will show no regard to the gods of his fathers or for the desire of women, nor will he show regard for any other god; for he will magnify himself above them all. Nevertheless, instead he will honor a god of fortresses, a god whom his fathers did not know; he will honor him with gold, silver, costly stones and treasures." The beast returned to Rome only to show his great power by ordering the massacres throughout the world. The Earth shacked as mountains began to fall in the sea. The Earth's crust had now shifted as so many places currently were in danger of dropping deep within the Earth. The Great One at present solitary feared in losing the land that his war machines cleared of human life. He now returned to Jerusalem to face the only thing that was greater than he upon his world was, and that was a foolish religion from so long ago, a dead legend, fools who worshiped a carpenter's son who even the rabbis of the God he claimed to be the son of denied. This compulsion to control all drove him back to Jerusalem within the week. He called all to a new throne he had built for it stood higher than the temple he built. He now had the recordings of the massacres of so many Jews who had been persecuted throughout the ages. He had the Jews watch as they had been persecuted worse than any other had in history. He then told the masses, actually all the world for when he gave a public address all had to stop and listen, lest they shall die. He told those in Israel that if it had not been for him, Israel would be ruled by Gentiles and not by him, a Jew. All who came across the name of the Lord came to destroy and persecute you. I came to my name and gave you a new homeland, free of war and a modern temple where you may show the world your love and worship of me. I demand the same loyalty from my chosen people as I do for all who walk upon this Earth, for none shall walk without me. I stand free from the lusts and poison of women since I shall not travel down the dark alley to my doom. I give myself to my Empire as my Empire shall give themselves to me and only me. I was once lost as you are now, yet from the heavens came to me a great one who knew the true word from the gods. He gave me that word, and now we are gods. Behold your new mighty prophet who shall rule and live within the holy of holies in my temple. Look at the great things I have given you, for in history has never one man ruled the entire Earth. This is my Earth, and you live upon my Earth. Have you not seen my great works since I am the only man in history to rule the complete Earth? No man can do this, nevertheless, a god can. His Empire now flooded the world with the new digital copies of the United Roman Bible. As the Great One returned to Rome, he heard reports that brought him great anger. Too many people around the world were angry that he had declared himself a god and refused to worship him. He ordered all his armies and police agencies to seek anyone who refused to say he is god and to beat them to death in front of all. This turned to being time-consuming and many just confessed these words while in secret worshiping Jehovah. This could not be. He had to have a way to mark those who worshiped him, so he could easily kill those who did not. He ordered his great thinkers to find a way for him. Then a demon appeared before him and worshiped him. This Great One enjoyed this to the extreme of becoming fanatical. The demon then said, "Oh Great One, your solution to his problem is perfect." The Great One looked around and asked, "What solution did I give?" The demon said, "Oh Great One, naturally you said the way to determine who worships you is to have them deny Jehovah and curse his bible and take upon their forehead your number, the number of Nero." The Great One now took a slow drink of wine and said, "Of course I mentioned that my mark would have microchips placed inside them, so that if one has not this chip, they shall neither trade nor receive any good or service. Those who are caught trading with them, the chip will report." The demon looked at the Great One and said, "Oh yes; I remember you adding that detail." The Great One, now thinking this to be his idea called in all his courts and made this new law. They could implant these chips throughout the entire world within only a few days. The Great One told his armies, give our mark to those who are eager for it. If any display, even the least bit of remorse, beat them on the spot, then remove their eyes and cast them into the mobs. His ability to communicate throughout the entire Earth only continually improved. His word became deeds almost as fast as the words came into his head. Nevertheless, as he weakened his enemy, the Heavens released a new punch, as the seals had not worked. The book now appeared, yet this time it was surrounded by a multitude of beautiful angels who was singing praises to the throne. The book now opened itself and began to read Revelations 11:3-6 "And I will give power to my two witnesses, and they will prophesy for 1,260 days, clothed in sackcloth." These are the two olive trees and the two lamp stands that stand before the Lord of the earth. If anyone tries to harm them, fire comes from their mouths and devours their enemies. This is how anyone who wants to harm them must die. These men have power to shut up the sky so that it will not rain during the time they are prophesying; and they have the power to turn the waters into blood and to strike the earth with every kind of plague as often as they want." Heaven had now had enough. This time man had gone too far, actually it was two unholy men, so Jehovah would strike back with two holy witnesses. It then came two great prophets screaming through the streets, "Take not the mark of the beast, for those who do shall be cast into the everlasting lake of fire." I could see anger in the Great One's heart as he tried to turn off the television broadcasts of these two witnesses. They appeared to be in Israel one minute, then far Asia subsequently the Americas. All on the Earth could see them, and as they passed those with the mark the cursed them with a plague. I could now see so many running into the sunken hills and mountains hiding from the armies of the Great One, who I shall currently call the Antichrist. I saw many of his planes begin to crash. Then I saw legions of demons rushing from inside the Earth to save this Antichrist. I now heard two saints talking beside me saying, "Blessed are they who take not the mark, for they shall spend eternity in the heavens. They must stay strong for Enoch and Elijah are among them now, and nothing can stop them. As they walked into the temple, the false prophet escaped into the tunnels under Jerusalem and when to Babylon, the set up a new temple. I heard Enoch cry out as he approached the new temple, "I appear in the strength of His might from the heaven of heavens, and all shall be smitten with fear. The Watchers shall quake, and great fear and trembling shall seize them unto the ends with the earth. And the high mountains shall be shaken, and the high hills shall be made low, and shall melt like wax before the flame. And the earth shall be wholly rent in sunder, and all that is upon the earth shall perish, and there shall be a judgment upon all (men). However, with the righteous, He will make peace, and will protect the elect, and mercy shall be upon them. And they shall all belong to God, and they shall be prosperous, and they shall all be blessed. And He will help them all, and light shall appear unto them, and He will make peace with them. And behold! He cometh with ten thousands of His holy ones. To execute judgment upon all, And to destroy all the ungodly: And to convict all flesh of all the works of their ungodliness which they have been ungodly committed, and of all the hard things which ungodly sinners have spoken against Him." I found myself so impressed with his great words. I now told the book, "Are these words from the Bible, for I have never heard of them?" The book told me, "The foolishness of mankind took out the holy words of one who walked with Jehovah for more than 300 years." I then asked the book, "Who are the watchers?" The book told me, "They are the ones for whom came forth the false prophets and Antichrist. They have worked every sense the days of Enoch to destroy humankind and falsely accuse all who walk upon the Earth. Listen while I disclose you the name of the other witness who is now ministering up the coast of the Dead Sea. Mal.4:5 Behold, I will send you Elijah the prophet before the coming of the great and dreadful day of the LORD: (Matt. 17:11). Jesus replied, "Elijah is indeed coming first to get everything ready." Elijah and Enoch are the last hopes for humanity. I now see one small village in the bottom of South Africa where the soldiers of the Antichrist gave them the mark of the beast in their arms, many without their consent while asleep. The villages have currently fought and defeated the small garrison of soldiers, and those with the marks are standing in a long line having their arms chopped off. This is no game now. The war is on, and the Antichrist for the first time has two saints roaming the holy land, giving hope to the people of Israel. Elijah now tells the world that the Messiah came 2000 years ago and that Jesus Christ is Lord. This is clearly the first time since the rapture that so many people are once again showing hope in a future. Elijah tells them, "Those who confess the Lord, take not the mark of the beast, shall join the Lord when he returned to setting up his kingdom on Earth. These days are numbered. If the false Christ demands your life for not taking his mark, know you that on the day, you lay down your flesh you shall be with our Lord. Know you that even though I came from Heaven to save our Saints, which I would gladly die a thousand deaths just to see our Lord's face once more." Those who had the mark were now at risk no matter where they were, for Elijah and Enoch would appear in any place at any time. It was as if something was guiding.

Now angels stood on my side, humming peaceful heavenly songs and removing the fear that was trying to reside inside of me. They revealed to me a reality that I had not yet noticed. The Earth appeared to have no more blind, crippled, or other manors of handicapped people. I now wondered where they all went. I searched through all the remaining hospitals I could find, and they were all empty. I have never known of hospitals being empty. Just to be safe, I would explore a few more. Hospitals after hospital were not only empty; they were closed. Most medical equipment lay in ruins, and the ripped, torn, blood-soaked empty nursing uniforms. The Antichrist had emptied the hospitals and destroyed any who was handicapped. He declared that those who were not perfect nor could contribute to his cause with full bodies must not live. This had been done while all others were in hiding. He justified this by telling the world that it was God who did this to them, since he created them that way, he did so only to promote human suffering, which like the blood spilled from the poor lambs he watched being sacrificed to him gave him pleasure. He had written over the doors to the closed hospitals, "No other gods shall see my people suffer." The greed in people plus the desire of this generation not to be burdened by caring for the old and crippled generated much public support to this policy. They actually found comfort in these words, as if a mighty one was willing to save them from pain and suffering. Even though all long to live old, the suffering, and loneliness that flood each empty day, took away and glitter to the golden years. The Antichrist was making life great on Earth for the chosen people. Naturally, some ethnic groups and religions were wrong about the day they were introduced by the gods of old, only to trip humankind, and put them on the false roads to war and hatred. The Antichrist had all the answers for every question. One thing was certain; those who belonged to him had a solid future ahead of them. They all had plenty of work, nice homes, and a safe world to live within, for those who were citizens of the United Roman Empire. Any who even yelled at them was severely punished. They all had large white stars of David sown on the outside garment that covered their left arm. The world laughed at how less than one century ago, those who wore these stars were confronted with a short life of prodigious pain. At present, those who wore them were the true 'stars.' The world was now so much better with all those who thought different no longer here to argue and fight over-all things. All those who were living now were so glad that the wrong had been removed. Everything had been going so well; all the right people were receiving the things they desired, until, that terrible day. The day when he had to bite the hand, that had been feeding him, he destroyed it all. His people now were put in the middle of two diverse at present enemies. Before, this did not matter in the past, since the enemy had no ability to fight back. This is not the case now, for when he sat on the temple of a living god all who saw it knew trouble would be ahead. That is the sad point about greatness, and that is the higher you are, the farther you can see, which unfortunately reveals how much more you do not have. When these foolish slaves of greed stand high and say, "This is mine, this is mine." They cannot see all the ones who hang their heads in servitude, yet only see those who possess what they do not have, freedom. This Antichrist, had given up any ounce of freedom because of greed and lust, put in the trap by the demons who gave him his power. Once again, his back was to the wall and he, once again; he had a solution. He would produce false witnesses and have them destroy those who appeared without marks. This quickly reduced the hope of those who did not have the marks had previously enjoyed. Actually, it was not a factor of being enjoyed; it was a factor of survival. Those without the mark had one benefit, and that was their days were numbered. Some few hidden Bibles and biblical commentaries spoke of Daniel's seventieth week, so enduring until the end was a hope knowing that the end is just around the bend. Each day of suffering led to a day closer to eternal life with the Lord. Life would have been so much better if they had only taken seriously the warnings that they saw around them everywhere. It just had been so difficult for so many young people to choose life for the Lord as it clashed with what they thought to be cool. The traditional generation divides now occurred beyond philosophical boundaries, being further compounded because of technological advances, which took advantage of younger minds having better eyesight and flexibility. The generations currently could clash beside each other, each not knowing the difference, nor even what the other was doing.

The Antichrist also developed another technology to advance the evolution of humanity. He now mass produced diet aids and supplements. Obese people would be obsolete within a few short years. All the wasted resources history had consumed in feeding the flesh with an organic bulk was an atrophy. It was nothing more than the glorification of death to maintain life. How much death would it take to maintain a life, which was an existence that could give no more but pleasure to the spirits by suffering? The new healthier creatures would be so much easier to identify than those who still feed from the Earth. So much more had to be done until this new Earth was blessed by his new Super-human beings. The first thing that had to be done was to stop the unmarked from flooding to the witnesses. His false witnesses would accomplish this. These false witnesses walked along the rural routes waiting for the unmarked to approach them. Once they were in the open, guards who accompanied them in hiding would kill the unmarked, keeping a few for public tortures in the cities. The unmarked formed into small groups not trusting larger groups, considering how the false prophet always had spies enter the groups. The Antichrist had to know what they were doing and often, allowed small groups of overlooked to exist so he could learn their living habits and patterns. This way he could determine what they will need to survive and in the future ensure that these resources were not available. I now witnessed something I had never seen in any prophesy and that was a spirit, which looked as if it were Moses dropping manna from the heavens to the forests. I could see people, who now looked much as if pre-historic Neanderthals came out crawling through the trees, such as farm animals rejoicing at feeding time. I asked the angel beside me, "Who is the one that feeds the unmarked?" The angel said, "It is Moses who asked the Lord for permission to feed the children of God manna as the heavens once feed him." I noticed another strange thing and that was an accumulation of the strongest angels as they were fighting to keep the demons out of heaven. I asked the angel that was with me, "I always believed that the evil angels were permitted in the heavens to accuse people of their sins. Leastwise that is what my mother always told me so I would avoid being bad." The angel now told me, "That was true; however, a new Lord now rules the end times and she with her daughters bound Lucifer and all his demons, yet since humanity continued to sin and the prophecy is fulfilled; they were released giving mankind the final spiritual test before the end of Earth's time." I noticed the angel said 'she', nevertheless; I understand in English, while the angel is speaking in Semitic so anytime something is translated pronouns and such become confused. I can see, by the way, that they keep on fighting and tempers have been flared.

My angel now tells me that I am safe and thus should, "Search the Earth for visions to add to the Patmos," As she, who has long blond hair also adds, "You may discover the others in your group, for all are still upon the Earth." I now looked at her and said, "Let us go and search."

We float over the ruined cities that cover the Earth. The Antichrist builds all his structures underground, understanding that nuclear weapons still exist. It is as if these ruins invite one inside to share with their new nakedness, now being bare within nature. I can hardly visualize these former homes bustling with routine arguments and joyous holidays. At one time, cars rushed up and down these streets, as those from away had to go here, likewise, those who were nearby had to go there. I wonder why could not those who were here stay here and those who were there stay there. All the hopes and dreams that went to the building of this little part of a larger world, which with technology became smaller by the day. Some of the buildings have large parts of their face remaining while others were smashing extremely hard with little remaining. No two buildings resemble each other. Much of the wood, which once divided the rooms and sheltered the roofs from rain are now piles of useless splinter covering the mashed concrete. Any wood left now could only be used for fire in some isolated rooms deep within these skeletons that scar the face of the Earth. A village or one specific area could be comprehended, conversely this everywhere, an Earth with a face of scars. This evidence of a once worldwide civilization may be erased as the Earth's crust continues to shift. I decide to scroll over to Russia and China, to see what curse now plagues them. Russia is checkered with destroyed buildings, as if they were plucked meticulously. My angel tells me, "The Antichrist ordered that all the great Bear of the North to be destroyed, as they continue to raid even to this day. His agreement with Israel was to destroy the Bear. The raids were so serious that many Russians moved into Babylon and enter the Roman Empire through Europe. They brought all their precious valuables with them to buy their entrance, and as anything that has not is offered what they have not, they will close their eyes. That power of greed, lust, and envy left many self-claimed righteous to be left behind. They tried to justify their deeds as 'standard business practices.' I was rather surprised when my angel gave me the list of famous ministers who were left behind. Anytime anything touches money, their hands lose their innocence. These are the seven years that the ones who escaped the meteors, plagues and wars, receive one more chance to escape eternal damnation. China looks much different. Many of the buildings in the smaller communities are still standing. The major cities are completely demolished. World War III, one of the shortest wars in history, left its mark here. The rice fields are now covered with weeds, as China gave up most of her remaining men trying to invade Israel. The main reason they hit Israel, outside of the false-pact with the bear, was punishing them for their long alliance with the Eagle. What is even more troubling is that when the Dragon attacked the Eagle, they were destroying their export markets, which within itself would have created a financial crisis, as their banks were now receiving a rich return for their loans. The eagle had the smallest brain of the large beasts, and proved it by so many of its actions. The Eagle would actually give money to the countries they were borrowing that money. The heavens marveled at how the Eagle almost made it until the seventieth year of Daniel. I can see no life in this vast surface below me. My angel tells me that much life does exist, yet most only come out in the dark. She takes me down to one of the small-unmarked clans. They have twelve in this group. Asia probably has sixty percent of the unmarked people on the Earth today, yet they remain unmarked not for Christianity, but from their consolidated belief that the Antichrist is evil, and they want no part of evil. The Antichrist still raids all parts of Asia; however, not with the force he does in the middle east and the Americas, citing they are the most likely to receive hope from this false independence and initiate traitorous actions against the Empire. All the members of this group sleep under car hoods. They lay a car hood on the ground floor of the apartment they hide in and dig under it. Car hoods appear to conceal the body heat that the Antichrist uses to determine potential targets. His lasers will rip apart human flesh, however reflect straight back when shooting at car hoods. After losing a few invaders to reflect shots, which come straight back to the shooter, the invaders move on quickly. This little quirk in the human lasers was accidentally discovered during rain raids, when car hoods offered protection from the rain. Car hoods and trunk hoods can rarely be discovered now, as most have been hidden for protection. Ironically, all in this group wears solid black. Only small parts of the face are left uncovered. This is for protection from any rogue radiation from World War III and from partially destroyed nuclear facilities. Anything that produces energy has now been destroyed. The Antichrist loves dropping chemicals from planes to help force out these clans. Biological warfare is now on the rise, as the mobility of most nations no longer exists. Biological is dangerous in that it can come back on the distributor. The Antichrist has used it extensively on Japan, Australia, middle and southern Africa and South America. These areas have no land forces stationed, and are raided only by air. I asked her if we could fly over Japan and she told me, "Yes, George, however we must be quick for a great event is about to happen that the Patmos cannot miss." I actually was excited by whatever this is, yet also wanted to see Japan. Off we went to Japan, first seeing Mount Fuji, Mount Haku, and Mount Tate. We then scan the countryside, which ironically still has many small buildings in place. The big cities, such as Tokyo are leveled, nevertheless the dark patches of this black that hover over this land is something I have never seen. My angel tells me, "You are now seeing the billions of insects that are feasting on all the dead corpses that flood this island. No one will enter this place because of the plagues feed by the biological warfare." A land covered by the dead, isolated and forever to be slowly consumed by the ugliest of beasts, the insects. We now head back to the book, which now reads to me, (Revelation 7:1) "After this I saw four angels standing at the four corners of the earth, holding back the four winds of the earth, so that no wind would blow on the earth or on the sea or on any tree. Jehovah is now informing his angels not to harm the Earth until he has preserved the 144,000 unmarked. Revelation 7:2 And I saw another angel ascending from the rising of the sun, having the seal of the living God. And he cried out with a loud voice to the four angels to whom it was granted to harm the earth and the sea, (Revelation 7:3) saying, "Do not harm the earth or the sea or the trees until we have sealed the slaves of our God on their foreheads." Do not harm the earth, the sea, or the trees until we have sealed the slaves of our God on their foreheads. (Revelation 7:4) And I heard the number of those who were sealed, one hundred and forty-four thousand sealed from every tribe of the sons of Israel. (Revelation 7:5-8) From the tribe of Judah, twelve thousand were sealed, from the tribe of Reuben twelve thousand, from the tribe of Gad twelve thousand, from the tribe of Asher twelve thousand, from the tribe of Naphtali twelve thousand, from the tribe of Manasseh twelve thousand, from the tribe of Simeon twelve thousand, from the tribe of Levi twelve thousand, from the tribe of Issachar twelve thousand, from the tribe of Zebulun twelve thousand, from the tribe of Joseph twelve thousand, from the tribe of Benjamin, twelve thousand were sealed." The angel now told me, "The Tribe of Dan did not survive as so many elected to take the mark and turned over their families to torture and death. Joseph's son, Manasseh is named instead as Joseph's tribes held fast to the words of the Two Witnesses. Now let us go unto Israel and watch the 144,000 arrive to the mounts where Enoch and Elijah wait for them. I saw a different Israel as I looked down. The Armies belonging to the Antichrist lay in ruins. His airplanes could not fly, because of the turbulent winds in the skies. I now could see twelve large masses approaching the two mounts, as Enoch moved to another mount because the saved ones were so many. I am still so stunned that this many survived here. The angel tells me that all we see not only refused to take the mark but accept Jesus Christ as the Messiah and the Lord. It was too difficult to deny him this rightful title as the greatest of prophets, as Elijah never saw his death, going into the heavens by horses of fire in a chariot and whirlwind, and Enoch, whose grandson, Noah, helped save his small family, the only from Adam and Eve's children. Enoch had also visited the heavens and was of a great benefit this time because of the fear the watchers had concerning him. This made the watchers force the Antichrist away from the fruitless attempts to hinder their great work. The watchers feared that they could be forced again to ask Enoch to negotiate their punishment. One thing that was for certain, no demons took upon themselves the daughters of men. They would never foster that activity again." The angel now stopped talking, turned around, and bowed, as did I, more out of shock than knowing why. I could feel a deep warmth such as never before have I experienced. Our complete surroundings were now in total strobe like flashing warm light. I looked over and saw the greatest creation I had ever seen. He walked by us, and stopped and looked at me. I was now paralyzed, knowing that something was going to happen. His lights now became dimmer, and I could something that I can only describe in parts, first I saw seven golden lampstands, and among the lampstands was someone like a Son of Man, dressed in a robe reaching down to his feet and with a golden sash across his chest. His head and hair were white like wool, as white as snow, and his eyes were like blazing fire. His feet were like brass glowing like a furnace, and his voice was like the sound of rushing waters. In his right hand, he held seven stars, and out of his mouth came a sharp double-edged sword. His face was like the sun shining in all its brilliance. I shall later thank my angel for giving me the words to describe the greatest whatever I ever saw. He extended his left hand for me to shake, which I gladly surrendered to him. I looked in his hand and could see a hole in it that must have been made with a large nail. I then looked at his eyes and immediately said, "I confessed you to be Lord even without seeing, yet now that I had touched the hand who was nailed upon the cross for my sins, and my faith is now my vision. You are the greatest of all Lords, and you are the Messiah and Lord." He looked at me and smiled, saying, "George, make sure you add this to my Patmos for now you shall see the Son of Man, coming with the clouds of heaven, to gather my 144,000 who chose me over the Antichrist." I then said, "Thy will have been always my greatest command." He then continued as the other heavenly creatures prepared to welcome the 144,000 unmarked and tested Saints, which would bring great joy to Abraham, Isaac and Jacob or Israel. I had touched the hand of God and seen that hand had a mark, which forever would display the evil and foolishness of my species, which brings shame to me. As I look around, I see that this place is greater than anything I could have ever dreamed, and is nothing more than a nuclear love-producing mountain, if I must use words to describe this. My angel now guides me back to look at the two small mounts that are flooded with 144,000 white-robed saints. Jesus is now descending to them, and has now changed his heavenly appearance back to his human form. I wonder if that is the same body, he wore 2,000 years ago, for such a thing would be possible by our God. To think that I touched the same hand who doubting Thomas touched. The shouts of praise from the 144,000 circling Enoch and Elijah were thundering through Heaven. I asked my angel, "How can sounds of the Earth be so loud here in Heaven?" She told me, "Anytime a human praises our Lord; that praise is celebrated also in heaven as also are all prayers." I then asked, "You mean, every time I prayed; that prayer was heard in heaven!" She then smiled and revealed to me, "Absolutely, since every prayer is sacred to our God." I now, for the first time during my life, understood that the greatest miracle of all is how our prayers radiate throughout heaven, and are received as sacred from our heavenly father. Our father knows what we are doing. I am glad the Holly, and I have yet to consummate our marriage, not wanting to do so until we hear these words, "What the Lord has joined, let no man put asunder." I now feel much better about this Patmos Paradigm, knowing that our Lord knew about it. I previously had some hidden reservations that Aunt Rita could be involved with Indian spirits. I now understand why this must be done, so that the Patmos is filled with the visions and stories with humanity. I could currently see Jesus talking with his new Saints, and they were now preparing to come to their new home, "Return, O backsliding children," says the Lord, "for I am married to you. I will take you . . . , and I will bring you to Zion." As they ascended, a warm light spread from within them as they gave up their flesh, which the angels quickly collected and put on the moon. The Heavens did not want the flesh to reappear on the Earth, as the Antichrist would use them as evidence supporting his claim that Jesus is from evil. I know one thing, and that is the hand I shook is greater than the Antichrist is. I would dread being the Anti to my Christ. My angel told me to look back down on the Earth. The Antichrist was announcing that all treaties with Israel were no longer valid. He was ordering his planes to level everything, including the temple he built. The war was on, as now only his United Roman Empire and a puppet state in Babylon that the false prophet was holding fast on behalf of the demons who supported him. The Antichrist was even killing those in the Middle East that had his mark. He was going to show his might to what little was left to the world. The demons of Hell were eagerly swallowing the marked souls as they fell into their domain, nevertheless, I could see some souls ascending into Heaven receiving a hero's welcome. So much was going on now; I knew my angel, and I still had so much more work to do for the Lord.

CHAPTER 05

The woman clothed with the son

After George jumped into the open Patmos, we all somewhat stared at each other, knowing what had to be done. It was my turn to jump; therefore, I stood up and walked over to the opening. Jennifer rushed over beside me and said, "Aunt Rita, I will jump now." I brushed her to my side and told her, "You need to go last in case someone does not go." I looked at the children and said, "Have no fear, for you shall have a guardian angel to guide you. I can hear mine calling now, so see you in a few minutes." I jumped into the Patmos to find myself, now a spirit high above the heavens and sinking fast. Then casually an angel came and caught me saying, "Welcome to your Patmos, Aunt Rita." I then asked him, "What visions shall we get to fill our Patmos?" He smiled and said, "Soon the book will be here and speak unto us." As I looked around, I saw what appeared to be a person covered by a large star. I called out, "Is that you Uelanuhi?" I received no answer except for my angel, "Sorry Aunt Rita that is not Uelanuhi." I now answered back, "Oh, sorry, I thought she was my sun goddess." The angel now said, "Remember, you are in the final days of humanity and you are in what you call the white man's heaven." I then told him, "I have always been faithful to the white man's God in spiritual matters, and only giving reverence to my Indian spirits who also work for our Lord, after all, am I not here now?"

The angel then cooled down and said, "I do believe we shall do very well together, now let us introduce you to the book which shall give you your mission for the Patmos. The book now appeared in front of me. It is naturally the absolute most amazing book I have ever seen, being made from gold, pages of silver, and words constructed of diamonds. The book now began to speak, (Revelations 12:1-2), "Now a great sign appeared in heaven: a woman clothed with the sun, with the moon under feet, and on her head a garland of twelve stars. Then being with child, she cried out in labor and in pain to give birth. . . ." I rather floated here, completely shocked at what I had just seen. The book now spoke again, "I can see that this mystery is confusing you, which is nothing to fear, for here it is your visions that are being recorded for the Patmos. Listen to these words, (Genesis 37:9-11) And he dreamed yet another dream, and told it his brethren, and said, Behold; I have dreamed a dream more; and, behold, the sun and the moon and the eleven stars made obeisance to me. And he told it to his father, and to his brethren: and his father rebuked him, and said unto him, what is this dream that thou hast dreamed? Shall your mother, your brethren, and I indeed come to bow down ourselves to thee to the earth? And his brethren envied him; however, his father observed the saying." I then said, "It appears that both Jacob and Joseph knew who the sun was and what was to happen, such as rebuked this asking if he and Rachel shall bow before him. My books have words, which mean so many different things, and are made to accommodate so many situations. The sun covering Jacob or Israel and the moon is Rachel as the sun in the New Testament as the moon, which receives its light from the sun, is the Old Testament or even Jewish law. These symbolic renditions become less viable with the next phrase, "on her head a garland of twelve stars represents the altered twelve tribes of Israel, with Joseph receiving two and Dan zero." I now could see the woman, divided into twelve parts with 12,000 each standing on the moon, which was in truth the earth, except dark now with the false doctrine of a new world leader. The sun was the mighty one in heaving clothing these people, giving them protection against the evil that was all over the face to the darkness. The book now spoke saying, (Revelations 12:2-8), And she, being with a child cried, travailing in birth, and pained to be delivered. And there appeared another wonder in heaven; and behold a great red dragon, having seven heads and ten horns, and seven crowns on his heads. And his tail drew the third part of the stars of heaven, and did cast them to the earth: and the dragon stood before the woman who was ready to be delivered, for to devour her child as soon as it was born. And she brought forth a man child, who was to rule all nations with a rod of iron: and her child was caught up unto God, and to his throne. And the woman fled to the wilderness, where she hath a place prepared of God, that they should feed her there a thousand two hundred and threescore days. And there was war in heaven: Michael and his angels fought against the dragon; and the dragon fought and his angels, and prevailed not; neither was their place found any more in heaven." The book now leads me back to Genesis, so that the beginning would tell the end, In the beginning God created the heaven and the earth. And the earth was without form, and void; and darkness were upon the face of the deep. And the Spirit of God moved upon the face of the waters. And God said, Let there be light: and there was light. (Isaiah 14:12-14) "How you have fallen from heaven, O star of the morning, son of the dawn! You have been cut down to the earth, you who have weakened the nations! But you said in your heart, `I will ascend to heaven; I will raise my throne above the stars of God, And I will sit on the mount of assembly In the recesses of the north. I will ascend above the heights of the clouds; I will make myself like the Most High.' (Ezekiel 28:14-17) "You were the anointed cherub who covers, and I placed you {there.} You were on the holy mountain of God; you walked in the midst of the stones of fire. "You were blameless in your ways from the day you were created until unrighteousness was found in you. "By the abundance of your trade you were internally filled with violence, and you sinned; Therefore, I have cast you as profane From the mountain of God. And I have destroyed you, O covering cherub, From the midst of the stones of fire. Your heart was lifted up because of your beauty; You corrupted your wisdom by reason of your splendor. I cast you to the ground; I put you before kings, that they may see you." My angel now spoke to me saying, "This truth I tell you, for all that is Holy there must also be that which is unholy. Look now at the throne that sits upon Rome, and the wonder that sits high upon his throne and around him is seven spirits, each with a crown as they rule through the evil one who sits upon the flesh throne before all humankind. The horns spoken of are the combatant ways he uses to kill all who have not his mark. As the horn of a bull kills so does he. He sharpens his horns so that he may take the death back to his throne and feed it to his seven spirits that surround Lucifer who rules through him. All kingdoms now have fallen, yet each day he still seeks to find that which is not his. The spirit, which only the leader of the earth may see, once ruled on the highest throne below heaven, then one day ascended and with one-third of all angels tried to sit upon the throne of God. His world was in the days between the first two verses of Genesis, for after God created the earth, he destroyed it for the first time. The planets that are now labeled as in this solar system, once all shared the same few orbits, and were flooded with the beasts and beauty of trees and gardens. His anger erased all life for this sun and scattered the planets into their own orbits. He almost destroyed the Earth the second time yet did not destroy it, as Lucifer did not have a throne upon the Earth, yet the third time he shall make the Earth no more and create a new Earth. His promise was with the man not to destroy the Earth again, yet when Lucifer once again rules the Earth; with only those who have his mark, living this promise between men was no more, as the Heavens have called home the saved to live in the image as their father. Lucifer was cast out of the heavens, only to return to bear the light of his darkness in humanity. You were upon the Earth as the first rapture took place and heard the testimony given by Jessica and Floyd. This sun covers the woman. She shall trice more return into the Earth to feed her son, first collecting the 144,000 saved from Israel and for the great battle at Mount Megiddo. Lucifer fought as hard as possible in the days of King Herod trying to kill the baby Jesus, although no one could touch the firstborn of Egypt, who had, in history tried to kill Moses, in spite of this failed. Israel gave forth the man-child who was our Lord. No greater Empires in the History of the Earthmen existed as those who were founded on Christianity. The Eagles rod of iron once controlled the ways of man, yet slowly the rust weakened her rod and World War III destroyed it. Israel, through being deceived, made a pact with Lucifer allowing the United Roman Empire to once again rule in the Holy Land. As those who walked upon the Earth learned how Elijah and Enoch had taken heavens, many 'unsaved, yet still unmarked,' migrated from all lands into the former Holy Land. They came begging for crumbs from the masters' tables. The Saints, being moved by this great act of faith upon the Earth called upon the throne to have mercy on those who seek the Lord. The petition alleged that these were not wicked people; they were clean souls seeking the salvation that was promised through the Lord on the cross, and that his blood covered them. I marveled that any could petition this great throne and asked my angel, "How can a petition be put forth before a King?" My angel then reminded me that the greatest aspect about this creation is that man was created in the image of God, thus that image could expand the great power of the throne through such reverent petitions. This leads to a perfect existence and the enforcement of the justice, which our father desires." I then asked, "Are you telling me our heavenly father listens to these petitions?" The angel now revealed to me, "Look, our father has listened."

Therefore the Lord, seeing that the Antichrist had broken his pact with Israel and was now mounting a terrible war against her, gave sanctuary to all who would come to his new lands. The masses were so great that the Lord drove from Jerusalem and all lands to the sea for fifty miles and built therein-great temples so that all on the Earth could see their worship. This angered Lucifer as he now fought a greater war against the heavens, which would last until the end of days. This new war took away the demonic power that the Antichrist held, which now lead to increased mechanical and technological errors. He could no longer monitor the world as he had before, for as Lucifer fought in the heavens, he fought in the Holy land, building great temples in Babylon so that all could see worship of him. Many feared worshiping in these temples as they continued to fall killing many. Every inch of the invisible border around the holy land sanctuary, which went on for hundreds of miles, was covered with the Antichrist's soldiers, four men deep, was covered fire from tanks. The Antichrist stopped bombing the Holy Lands, as these bombs would only roll off, and kills his soldiers. He cried in torment each day that he could see these 'traitors of mankind' worshipping. He tried so hard to get spies into the sanctuary, yet all who had his mark that tried to enter fell to their death immediately. This wilderness sanctuary was now the home on Earth for the unmarked, as all from the world struggled to Moab, Ammon, and Petra to this new heaven on Earth. They would wait here until the Lord returns." We now looked down upon the war torn Earth, the aftermath of World War III. Even I wondered how Townsend had escaped so much of this horror, only to be tortured in misery by the land raiders, who fed and lived off the blood taken from their victims. We now zoomed down on a small clan of twenty Koreans hidden under the remains of their former apartment building that fell to the earthquakes that had shaken the Earth after the large nuclear bombs the Eagle unleashed upon China and the rogue fool who ruled the northern part of this peninsula. This group was mixed from many different families who once lived in this large apartment building. They would walk the shattered stairways and sleep in the few open areas in the middle of the gutted apartments. They had to sleep high and stay high in order to avoid the thick radiation that soaked into the surface. They would only descend to the ground on the windy days and scavenge any canned or bagged food items, including candy and pastries. Bread was no longer available and any meat could not be eaten. Food shipped in plastic was edible, and rice could no longer be cooked as any electric or gas was available. However, some butane stoves were discovered and butane cylinders were collected which helped some, yet cooking was done scarcely due to security reasons. The smell of cooked food could produce an unwanted visit from many gangs who routinely searched areas for survivors. This group only had four men, one old and three young. Chin Ho was the group leader, and Bae, Dong-sun, and Du-Ho were the young men who worked hard to protect the sixteen women who were with them. All the women were young. The old women, for the most part elected to die with their families. The young girls were the ones who feared their lives as when the gangs would raid a family, they would rape and kill the young women first, as a bounty for their victories. This is why Chin Ho wanted his clan to stay high in out of sight. Those who stayed on the surface were now plagued with lung disorders from the radiation and were covered with terrible skin blisters. Their moaning or at least someone within their group moaning gave rise to their detection and quick death. Chin Ho and selected women from the group would pay particular attention to any ground movements during the day as all slept and did very little during the day. The nighttime was when they came alive. Chin Ho knew that the gangs were quickly taking everything of any life sustaining value from this area. In addition, that the plagues from Japan would soon cross the sea, so he told his group they would have to travel the mountains up the coast then have a goal to move towards the west, staying in the mountains as long as they possibly could. One of the women found a student atlas of Asia and another found a compass. He carefully and decided the best route would be to stay in the lower parts of the mountain up this peninsula and then cross due west through Mongolia staying clear of the Himalayas going to the Caspian Sea then circling the northern part of it, going into the Holy land from the mountains of Turkey to settle in Jerusalem. The group, which only had three former Christians now questioned, "Why should we go to the Holy Land, for is that not into the trap of the United Roman Empire, which hates the people from South Korea for their long time association with the great Eagle? If we are to die, why not die here?" Chin Ho told them that he had a dream in which an angel told him that, "All who went there would be saved from the evil one." The group argued about this mad decision, until one of the women, Ae Cha stood up and told them all a chilling story. She spoke of how a once thought to be a crazy woman named Eun lived on their floor. This woman would always preach to everyone she saw every day, begging him or her to join her church and that they need to serve the Lord of Love. She was able to convert her sister, and they would be gone for long hours at a time studying their word. Her sister would always bring home so many papers concerning her new Lord's teachings and prophesies. She spoke of nothing else. My mother feared that she would not be able to pass her college entrance exams, yet my sister did not care. Then one day, both my sister, the crazy woman and all who studied in their group vanished. The news told this same day of so many Christians around the vanishing world. My father looked at her papers and her Bible. It was a Christian Bible, so fear flooded his heart. He searched the places where they studied only to hear of the same stories coming from the other families who also had their members lost. He came home, got my sister's papers, put them on our table, and called all of us around the table. We searched all through them only to discover many terrible things are happening. We are all in danger and I shall follow Chin Ho, for our only hope is through my sister's Lord. Slowly, within the next few days all the members agreed to follow Chin Ho, more for the desire to stay with this group and the consensus that life would not last much longer here. The group continued to scavenge what they could find from the higher floors, as the raiders seldom went to high above the ground, as these buildings were collapsing on a schedule that no one could predict. The rainy season had finished, thus they would rush to the cold lower mountains before moving west which would offer them a slow transgression to warmer weather. In the mountain areas, staying close to the trees they could travel much during the day. Nighttime travel would be dangerous as the terrain was chaotic in places to say the least. However, they would have to work some distance between his port city, before daytime travel would be feasible. What remained from the roads would have to stabilize their nighttime travel, as they would avoid being trapped against a large stream or small river. Bridges were rare, yet they did exist. The open plains and rocky seashores, coupled with the bare mountain sides constricted their movement, yet did not prevent it. They had been fortunate to find small grocery stores along the way, which had yet to be raided. The locals had rushed to the big cities during the first days of the end, fearing that they would have no security in their farms. Oh how so wrong they were. The second day saw the group lose their first member, a woman named Ae Sook, who stepped on a snake the previous night. She had kept it a secret, now wanting to hold up the group and with morning so near hoped that the daylight would enable the others outside the group to save her. She fell dead in front of the group as the sun rose, which was not a good omen for the day to come. The group buried her by covering her with rocks and light dirt. They feared that birds could alert the raiders of new people passing through. The Antichrist did not leave many of his forces to occupy these lands, fearing that the plagues he released in Japan would harm his forces. A few planes attacking were enough to keep the fear alive. He would attack any gang activity when spotted, as he refused to share any form of power with any other.

Sharing power now led Chin Ho to call another meeting and to scold his new family. He started by lecturing all in this group, "If we were only to die, then we should have died where we began. We are not on this journey for only a few to live. This is a journey of faith, and as such; we must be led by a heart of compassion. No one among us knows what misfortune may approach us, nor even what fortune. If we divide the fortune, then we should also divide the misfortune. I know that if we enter the holy land with the same hearts as those you wish to do harm to us we will perish beside them. I lost three daughters in this war. I could not save them, yet I might be able to save other men's daughters. If I were only concerned about myself, I would have only brought young men. If our ways are too hard for you, let us know. Furthermore, make sure that you conceal your monthly ways for any blood on the Earth will attract beasts we do not want to meet. I ask the young men with me to remember, that as they loved their mothers, someday a young man shall love one of these women as their mother. Do not think that we are without hope, for if we were without hope, we would lay beside our loved ones rotting in the soil. We have the hope of my dream, and the hope of a dream is greater than any treasure upon our world. I have heard some of you say, we have no tomorrow. I heard you say that last month, last week, and even yesterday. Can you all not see the error in what you said, for today is yesterday's tomorrow? Each member of this group has a gift that we will need to survive. I know a couple of you women are nurses. The next empty hospital or any pharmacies that we pass, please get what we need in the care of our feet. Anyone who does not care for his or her feet now will surely die. Each day, I shall check the feet of the boys, and they shall check your feet. Everyone must have his or her feet checked each day. We must now, as most have already, select a special friend. You and your friend are to check each other daily. People, it is the stupid little things that will kill us now. Most of these things we can prevent. If you think, something is wrong, have your friend check it, then one of our nurses. We play this game either together or not at all. We shall be doing most of our travels now by day, as the normal population for this area is low. Be on the lookout for small farms." Then one of the girls said, "Our Chuseok is past, what harvest can we find?" Then Chin Ho said to them, "My dear, we can find all the harvest. We shall be looking for vegetables that are from roots, including onions, radishes, and carrots. These have a habit of growing larger the longer they stay in the ground, thus our food supply is waiting for us to harvest it. Also, be careful around farms in which they appear to have been harvested, as these may still have residents. We will cover any hole we dig, so that the spies in the skies will not become suspicious. I am also on the lookout for swords and bows with arrows. Many farmers prefer these for their protection, as I fear a gunshot could ring for miles. Remember, when walking across the grass, look for holes and snakes. We have about another three years before we make it to the Holy Land. This is based upon my extremely conservative progression estimate. We need not to rush into our deaths, but wisely live into our future." With this, the gang once again began their long journey. Their day had only one sticky part. While walking along an urban road, one of the boys heard the sound like a truck struggling to make it up the hill before them. The group easily slides into the concealment of the roadside brush. They were feeling safe as the trucks rolled by until one of the dogs on the second truck began barking uncontrollably. The guards motioned the convoy to keep on moving claiming, "The stupid thing must have smelled a critter." They all laughed about it and continued. This added a variable which the group had not considered, and that was hunting dogs. Chin Ho surmised that no place would be safe from the dogs, yet for the same reason the additional time in the far backwoods would result in the same risk. The important variable would be food, and other items needed to survive. The large fear the group new shared was the terror of looking through the eyes of the raiders. They had the eyes of bitter hate and the voices of the rivers of gargling death. Everything about them was surreal, and clearly not from this world. Any noises that come from them came from lost graves. We just wanted to know what right they had to take so much life from the world, which had become more home centered than any other time in the modern ages. So much would be possible as advances in technology were increasing the quality of life even within third-world countries. Large world bloodbaths had decreased as so much work towards world peace was in the works. What was so special about now to destroy humanity? Why could we have not been destroyed during one of those horrible wars and during a tremendous plague outbreak? Either way, now the only form of socialization was the evening talks before the cold night hours approached, which gave warning of a winter ahead in the mountains. Chin Ho hoped that the movement away from the ocean would help, yet even he could not predict any abnormal winters, as such were common throughout history. Extra garments would have to be carted on their backs, as a horrendous storm would kill them. The extra garments could be used as tents during the rainy seasons, so not all would be lost. The harder soils were making it harder to find food, as the northern part of the peninsula had a different taste for vegetables, tuned more for trade with neighboring China. The group now formed into their smaller clans to discuss that day's events and talk about some of their former days. They all agreed now how the hunger for knowledge, and to pass exams had forbidden them to enjoy the socialization treats that the older ones enjoyed. Any discussions of love always ended up with the movies, and talking about the deep love their legends had for each other, willing to cast aside their thrones to have the one who ruled their hearts. The thrills of seeing one sacrifice everything for the honor and love of one so dear to his or her heart. The modern lives of this generation in Korea had followed suit with that of the other booming Asian nations, as their women were slowly doing more things, yet not as much as the west. Few really tormented over this, still preferring the traditional roles and feeling that men even though were not able to manage a home or raise children. The men were in no rush to trade these roles, so all was fine. This group was also such an example, as the men protected the women, and the women protected their health and other personal areas, such as hygiene. Chin Ho had talked with the group that since none would live in Korea again, all that was Korean would have to be put asunder. This was not only globalization it was spiritualism. Their goal was to fly away and never return. The things of old are gone and may only be enjoyed helping to reduce the pain and misery that would accompany this long journey, which was not only a journey of land, but also a journey of transition. By our journey's end, we would all be new people. We all agreed to this, as all see changes within ourselves. Just a few glimpses of the horror that walked around in human shells without any doubt currently united them as knowing who the real enemy was. The only joy in life now was during those so very rare times that one of those warriors dropped dead. We had seen a few of them along the way, and noticed they had chunks of their forehead cut away. We were shocked, yet Chin Ho said the defenders had done that to remove the chips they had in their heads because that is how their leaders tracked them. We wondered how Chin Ho knew this, and he told me one of his friends saw them put a chip in his son's head when he joined our enemy. He joined to buy some time for his parents to escape. When his mother discovered the sacrifice, he made, she jumped out of their window landing on some of the occupying raiders. He felt that she did this so the loss of her son produced deaths among the enemy, which she did get three of them. They tended to be less aggressive toward the apartment raids, so this may have also allowed others to escape and by Chin Ho knowing about the chip deal, could be a factor for the success of their journey. That night, they discussed the twelfth chapter of revelations, and the woman clothed in the sun. Chin Ho now explained to us that this was the hope we were searching, for the wilderness sanctuary that would be opened for those who came in faith, and we would unquestionably be a testament of faith. Bong Cha now joked that she would praise the Lord just to see a woman clothed with the sun. The sun was the life to the world. It was one of the four great elements, and without the sun, life would not exist. As the woman gives life, the sun sustains it. The sun also defeats the dark and changes anything it contacts turning it into a light, even as the death and dark the covers the moon. We now discuss what we had learned about the other planets in this solar system and how they had no life on them and how this world would soon be the same, if the God in heaven had any mercy, considering those who walked on the Earth killed those who were hiding and crawling. Each day, this group passed the starving remains of those who passed before them. Chin Ho could not understand why these people starved, as we were eating plenty and supplementing our vegetables with vitamins and other such enhancements, the nurses found in the pharmacies for the group. We had retained a lot of our body mass, and thus could almost pass as a raider, if not for those marker chips. Our group was now getting a little loose on our security, and soon we would pay with another death. The group traveled through rural areas for many weeks now, only seeing an occasional farmhouse. Chin Ho now taught his group about other wild roots and leaves that could be eaten. In his younger days, he had served as the military as a Ranger and learned how to live on the land. In only a few months, he was now the father whom all followed. We would all enjoy nice swims in any ponds we would come across, even when the weather was cold, as the nurses stressed hygiene. While walking one day, Dong-Sun stepped on an old newspaper that was lying on the road. When he did so, a mortal went off, blowing his body completely apart. Chin Ho had the group bury the body parts, which was sickening indeed. He then mixed some of the unidentifiable parts in one of his furs he tore and placed it on the exposed hole. He warned all in the group not to step on anything that they could not see underneath if possible. Furthermore, try to stay in a straight line stepping the same as the one ahead of them, still of course avoiding paper, cans, and such. He now led his group about 100 feet from the small country road. Once they passed through Mongolia, the small group began to notice angels following them. This brought a new hope in the group as food also began to appear in strange places. They avoided any city ruins fearing that regional gangs may still be defending their lost cause. The angels now would give warning signs, such as having ambushes detected by mechanical malfunctions of their weapons and flocks of birds betraying their location. This group currently would spend extra time each day reading the Bibles they had found along the way. Though they would walk through the shadow of death, they would fear no evil. The Earth was their shadow of death, for the days when the woman was not clothed in the sun were long gone. They could now reflect about all the times they had watched TV or a fresh movie while a 'foolish neighbor went to church; alternatively, it bought some new makeup and a new dress to look in fashion, while their foolish neighbor went to church; bought more makeups or a video game, while their foolish neighbor gave to the poor. The tides had changed as no foolish neighbors filled the churches now, for they were now wearing the best of makeup, dressed to the best of fashions and eating the best that a spirit could eat. The only thing that would get this group to the other end now was an attitude of gratitude and thanks, even giving praise for the weeds they ate, as these kept them alive and not starving as those who chose not to eat thereof. Nowadays, as they were passing through Turkey or what was at one time Turkey angels would walk among them at night and talk with them. The angels now told Chin Ho's group that all the unmarked Jews had been offered this additional sanctuary, yet refused to accept it. We could not understand that by them being able to see the miracles that they still refused to walk into this sanctuary. This was especially strange, as the blood had flowed deep in Israel, as around ninety-eight percent of the Jews had returned. Those who now lived in the Holy Land held fast to messiah's return, believing that Jesus was a false prophet and the greatest deceiver of humankind. They had the Bible to support their view, and they would endure for the true Lord to arrive. Chin Ho's group grieved that now twice the Messiah had returned, and the next time was the last time. This group was a good example, in that they believed without seeing or knowing, but just based on the common sense logic of it. They claimed themselves to be Christians now. Within a couple of months, be under the sanctuary of the Lord, and wanted to worship in the ruined temple at Jerusalem. The angels now warned this group that the journey ahead would now be harder than originally planned. The Antichrist and false prophet were now releasing all demons in hell to stop anymore to enter the sanctuary. The tide shifted quickly. The angels told Chin Ho's group that those who held fast to the Lord would spend eternity in heaven. Now a great storm has passed through where they were hiding. After three days of this storm, the sun returned. Now the raiders covered the area day and night. Finally, one of the women, who now had the flu, released a large cough. Once, they found her, the area was scoured in detail until all eighteen was captured. They immediately beat the three men who the women, now stripped and tied to poles so all could see. This was for two purposes, the first being a special reward for those who served the Antichrist and second as a sign to identify and track any unmarked who may pass by, as they would naturally give the women, some respect by not penetrating them or even worse, by not looking at them. The three men were strapped to tables outside and blinded, then tongues cut out, then each finger removed at each joint. They would chop on the first person, move into the second, then third, beginning again on the first. They had large-screen televisions on site so all who were in attendance could enjoy each chop and hear their horrendous screams, and as they would beg for mercy. This slow torture process continued to the toes, and then their private was removed. The final stage was driving long nails in their arms and legs and afterwards let them bleed to death.

A new mysterious change in the heavens was now secretly unfolding during this time of elevated war in the heavens. With all-out war raging around the throne, captured demons were now placed inside unmarked people when they were being tortured and the spirit of the dying Saint being returned to Heaven's throne. The demons could not capture angels and take them to hell, as hell could not receive them and would instead cast them back to the throne. So strange the wars in heaven, as the demons fight against a giant, they cannot defeat, nor are they trying to defeat, having only one goal and that is to occupy the throne. The throne is the power, and any who sits upon the throne has all the power. The throne also has one other thing that the demons forgot about, and that is God. Even if the demons made it to the throne, they would perish at the sight of God. None, not even Lucifer has seen Jehovah, for any who looked at him are blinded. The throne has special cells, which a spirit can hide in while talking to him who sits on the throne. These cells heat up while the voice from the throne speaks, which ensures that the audience is listening. Those who have been within the inner boundaries of this throne report that it has a power, which defies anything else, which could be comprehendible, a sinew that appears as millions of lodestones fighting with the chaos of mass voltage being swallowed into a single point. Their immediate comprehension fills like a socket too massive to transfer this amalgamation of pure power and love. I fear and tremble at the thought of ever being in one of those cells. My angel, who is always beside me, at times I know not if it is her will, because I hold on to her hand with all my might, never letting go. I do believe she gives me a new sense of hope in saying, "You have no fear sense your soul is covered with the blood of Calvary, and therefore, the son to the throne will speak in your behalf. I then began to remember how my Indian spirits always talked to me about the great son. I know the Bible has been translated through so many languages, yet I also suspect that English, a language still has its seeds merging from Angles, and Saxon/Jules, and Viking, that only a deity would use it to its full potential for creative manipulation to double verify prophesy. An example the quickly comes into my mind is how I am hiding behind the protection of the son as my intercessor to the throne of creation and all life. Could the woman have clothed with the son, and not the sun? I would have only introduced what I feel as this truth sitting here seeing the war in heaven, and the comfort of feeling the wisdom of our father, as he can collect his foolish enemy on his porch steps rather than depending on other methods. My angel told me that not long ago, the new Lord of the Earth, who serves Jehovah through her penance could use the powers of evil to capture these demons. Considering that the card has been tossed across the table, this time the father must actively participate in the final disposal of the evil that has tormented the hearts of his humankind creation. Humanity has always tried to escape death as the punishment of sin. This great mystery has been revealed throughout the ages that being absent from the body is to be present with the Lord under specified conditions revealed through the word. I look over the heavens now and can see the multitudes that escaped death through the rapture. They are working with the 144,000 that came with Elijah and Enoch preparing for the final war in which the son shows the light of his power received from our father.

I keep thinking of the woman clothed with the
sun as the angel now sings a song to me,
"Why do the heathen rage and the people imagine a vain thing?
The kings on the earth set themselves, and the rulers take counsel
together, against the Lord, and against his anointed, saying,
Let us break their bands asunder, and cast away their cords from us.
He that sitteth in the heavens shall laugh: the
Lord shall have them in derision.
Then shall he speak unto them in his wrath,
and vex them in his sore displeasure.
Yet have I set my king upon my holy hill of Zion.
I will declare the decree: the Lord hath said unto me,
Thou art my Son; this day have I begotten thee.

Ask of me, and I shall give thee the heathen for thine inheritance,
and the uttermost parts on the earth for thy possession.
Thou shalt break them with a rod of iron; thou shalt
dash them in pieces like a potter's vessel.
Be wise now therefore, O ye kings: be instructed, ye judges of the earth.
Serve the Lord with fear, and rejoice with trembling.
Kiss the Son, lest he be angry, and ye perish from the
way, when his wrath is kindled but a little. Blessed
are all they that put their trust in him.

My soul now remembers parts of the original message for my Patmos, "And she brought forth a man child, who was to rule all nations with a rod of iron: and her child was caught up unto God, and to his throne." She brought forth a man-child who would rule all nations with a rod of iron.

The son will rule with a rod of iron. The woman brought forth the son, thus the woman appears to be Israel, especially with her crown of twelve. The twelve have been argued to be the twelve apostles or the twelve tribes of Israel. I cannot tell for sure from where I am looking, in that I see one score and four thrones, yet my mind now is flooded with this thought, "I will declare the decree: the Lord hath said unto me, Thou art my Son; this day have I begotten thee." I wonder now, who gave birth to the son, as this song the angels were singing came from Psalms chapter two. The son was begotten from the father or from this throne, I can see before me. This wonder creates questions which I feel can no longer feed my perception of the truth. The truth is in reality all that is not false as the light is all that is not dark. Things that mattered before do not matter now. Sure, the son had flesh for thirty-three years; however, he was before as John adds in his first chapter, "In the beginning was the Word, and the Word was with God, and the Word was God. The same was in the beginning with God. All things were made by him; and without him was not anything made that was made. In him was life; and the life was the light of men. And the light shineth in darkness; and the darkness comprehended it not." As my recent redemption was in knowing that the son protected me from that which begot him, so figure it out anyway you want to, for when you see what is before me, not all mysteries have their value. I like the way that John adds how the light shines through the darkness, and the darkness does not comprehend this. How the demons can continue to fight this kamikaze war against the throne defies all my logic. I can see the impossibility of this futile war yet they keep flooding into the garbage disposal that empties into the hells below us. Even so, on Earth now the Antichrist continually tries to dim the light of this throne, yet finds himself always facing one more hurdle. He cannot hurt the ones protected in the wilderness, nor can he take away the hope that so many are fueled by as they trek to this land. I can see Chin Ho, Bae, Dong-sun, and Du-Ho being welcomed by the Heavens. From a hidden cavity inside a wrecked apartment building in Pusan, South Korea, they lead sixteen women for over three years based upon a promise they had heard their lost loved ones speak about the return of the only true God, and now they are covered with the blood of the lamb to have eternal rest. I can only see two of the women, Ae Sook and Dong-Sun, who died during the voyage. Their steps in faith have taken away all their pain for eternity.

The plight of the other women still finds them on the Earth, however they are with the others now in the wilderness, and in the sanctuary they searched for living among those who are guided by faith, love, hope, and charity. After watching their male counterparts being ground through the meat grinders for the world to enjoy, these women were raped by the followers of the false prophet as a reward for serving him for several months. After this, their feet were cut off and their faces soaked in acid, so that they could portray the beast all the evil ones believed they could be. Their shamed bodies were laid in the desert for the carnivorous birds to feed upon their flesh. During the first night of their death wait, angels appeared and delivered them to the sanctuary. These women now saw how hideous their faces were and having no feet saw no possible hiding place. They soon discovered that the lust, envy, greed and all other manners in which people use to either upgrade themselves or downgrade others had no home in this divine place. No one cared if others had feet, or a face that was destroyed. The only thing that mattered was another one joined this group and would be able to enjoy an eternal home, free of the misery, which the dust of the Earth could only give to its former dust that walked and talked. The sooner their flesh could return to the dust from whence it came the better. The next stage was the stage in which they were created in the image of the father. The crying of those in the wilderness was only from the pain of waiting to go home, to fly away from the misery of Daniel's seventieth week, a truth that was available on every device they previously had that was connected to the world wide web and the uttermost parts of the earth for the Lord's possession. This was having more truth as Lucifer had been removed as the Lord of this world and ironically, his converted spouse placed in charge, one who had even previously been chosen to be the mother of Adam's children. When my angel told me this, I could only shake my head knowing that with God all things are possible. Now, my angel showed me a site that these sore eyes thought they would never see again, for now beside me was the viewer of the first half of this tribulation. As our angels met with each other, they agreed to pour our visions into the Patmos and return us to our little hidden sanctuary in the mountains of the Rockies. George and I now began to prepare for our return. Surprisingly, we were put into a nice protected see through the capsule. I asked my angel, "Why are we here?" Our angels both told us, "To help the others in your group if they need such help." George and I agreed, now relaxing while watching the war. George now looked at me and said, "The value of

Christian parents is worth more than all the gold in heaven, especially once you see the truth about righteousness and wickedness." I just shook my head and agreed, feeling true love flowing through my soul. We both now realize that are arguments in the Patmos are not for those of this world, but those in the depths of time and space. This is the way and this is the truth.

CHAPTER 06

The mother of harlots and seven bowls

We watch George and Aunt Rita rushing into the Patmos portal, and we are now questioning the reason for having Jennifer wait until last. We currently ask her if she trusts us, as we all give her our oaths that we will seek this new adventure in which destiny has given us. We are actually hoping for anything to get us out of here, and feel that by making Jennifer go last, we are stripping her of her rightful honor. She agrees to tell Floyd, "Take care of these girls." She then kisses each of us, and into the portal, she submerges. This is the vision given to Jennifer.

Into the unknown, I now ascend. I know from the years of enjoying the word to my mother who going up is much better than going down. Then slowly appears a tall strong angel who welcomes me to my Patmos. I feel rather shy being with a male angel, yet look into my soul and see myself being neither male nor female. This now creates a structure of bewilderment in my mind as I wonder, "How do I know this angel to be male, as no visible signs distinguish a gender." I know I cannot be in that many dangers as my parents, George, and Aunt Rita are up here somewhere. I would also hope that with the being the land of the righteous than I would be in no danger." This angel approaches me and declares, "Fear not Jennifer, for I have been sent to help you with your

Patmos vision." I ask this angel, "What is your name?" He answered me, "I am Sachiel, an archangel of the order of Cherubim." I now thought to myself, "This one must be important." Sachiel quickly answered, "In these days no angel is more important than the other. We now know about the importance of the Patmos, as our Lord spoke into your brother George. Therefore, we shall ensure that your spirit receive what it must to feed your Patmos." I then asked my angel, "Sachiel, what is my Patmos?" Sachiel then spoke, "The mother of harlots, and seven bowls." I then questioned, "Is not the seven bowls close to the last big war between the heavens and the Earth. Have George and Aunt Rita covered all before me." Sachiel then informed me, "No Jennifer, for you were to go last, yet you went third. The way you fill your Patmos does not matter, for all your Patmos shall be combined as one for the ages, a Patmos created by those who still dwelt in their flesh." I then looked at myself and questioned, "I am a spirit now, and how can I still be in my flesh?" Sachiel answered, "Believe me; you are still in the flesh, as you shall return to your flesh within only a few seconds of absence, less than a few breaths at most. Being absent from your body, you need not to obey the laws of time nor space. Let us now listen to the holy book of heaven as it reads what it gave to the Earthmen to feed their souls with the word of our God." Now descending before me was the book with the word, as I could see if was completely protected by so many legions of angels, and before me, with pages the size of Jupiter the book opened itself to Revelation chapter 17. The book began to speak, "Then one of the seven angels who had the seven bowls came and said to me, "Come; I will show you the judgment of the great whore who is seated upon many waters with whom the kings upon the earth have committed fornication, and with the wine of whose fornication the inhabitants on the earth have become drunk." So he carried me away in the spirit into a wilderness, and I saw a woman sitting on a scarlet beast who was full of blasphemous names, and it had seven heads and ten horns. The woman was clothed in purple and scarlet, and adorned with gold, jewels, and pearls, holding to her hand a golden cup full of abominations and the impurities of her fornication; and on her forehead were written a name, a mystery: "Babylon the great, mother of whores and of earth's abominations." And I saw that the woman was drunk on the blood of the saints and the blood of the witnesses to Jesus. When I saw her, I was greatly amazed. But the angel said to me, "Why are you so amazed? I will tell you the mystery of the woman, and of the beast with seven heads and ten horns that carries her." The New Testament now closed as the Old Testament appeared, opening to the second chapter of Daniel, "As you looked on, a stone was cut out, not by human hands, and it struck the statue on its feet of iron and clay and broke them in pieces. Then the iron, the clay, the bronze, the silver, and the gold, were all broken in pieces and became like the chaff of the summer threshing floors; and the wind carried them away, so that not a trace of them could be found. Even so, the stone that struck the statue became a great mountain and filled the whole earth. And in the days of those kings, the God of heaven will set up a kingdom that shall never be destroyed, nor shall this kingdom be left to another people. It shall crush all these kingdoms and bring them to an end, and it shall stand forever." I now asked Sachiel, "Why the old and new testaments are in separate books, and is the Patmos supposed to be a ministry?" Sachiel then said, "The books are separate yet they are one, coming from the same throne. That which is in the New was spoken afore and revealed in the old. The Patmos is not a ministry. We reveal the word so you may know what to search for in your Patmos. Let us now look upon the Earth." I now saw the Earth before us, unlike the world I had known. Such a short time has changed so much, and I could hear the angel speaking to the holy one who was writing what would later be known as the book of Revelations. Sachiel reminds me that, "The ten horns do not yet have a kingdom and tell me this is the news I had heard on my radios." I look upon the Earth and see the things I could not see beyond the mountains of Montana. Here I can see the nuclear holocaust of World War III. This war was instigated by the tremendous influx of releasing demons who, unlike before in history, no longer played a silent role. They now returned with a great revenge to unleash upon those whom they considered had taken away their right to enjoy the fruits of the great throne. Humankind has throughout history sought to have what he had not. Even in the times of Enoch, the daughters of man joined with the angels and created what almost destroyed the Earth, a race of giants who stood as tall as mountains.

The main outcome of World War III is that is removed the Eagle, Dragon and Bear, and crippled Muslims from world power. The new power in Europe was now able to put the final nails into the claws of the Bear and prevent this bear from destroying Israel and receiving the promise of a sea of oil. With horns in so many European nations supporting this new leader, who had powers as never before seen in humanity, a new United Roman Empire emerged. The one who sat on this new throne was an incarnate Lucifer and known by Christians as the Antichrist. He may have used the Roman Empire in his name selection, as this empire in its history provided peace in the Middle East, a peace that died when it died. He immediately removed the temple mound as his sign of ultimate power over what few Muslim's remained, as they also with the Christians and converted Jews were found missing from the Rapture. He now had a new form of technology beyond what the Earth had previously seen. He used this technology to rebuild the temple in Jerusalem, causing many who remained in the Holy Land to declare him the messiah. He creates a new power in his inner circle as the minister of religion in the new world, now that all that 'Jesus' crap was no longer valid, declaring that the demons had taken them into the hell that they deserved and that his religion would save them. He found comfort with the Jewish faith as he was born and lived as a Jew, and the minister he selected was Jewish. Lucifer then convinced him to make Judaism the official language of his Empire, enabling him to easier control his empire for why would the heavenly throne punish him, after all he was caring for Jehovah's chosen people. The Antichrist saw the logic in this, thus declared the world language to be Judaism and sent his religious minister to Jerusalem to lay the foundations for this. His religious minister came to be known in Bible language as the false prophet. The false prophet was received with great praise in Jerusalem as the city swelled with almost the whole nation wanting to honor him in person. This was the advantage the Antichrist needed as he used his great-unchallenged power in the skies to search for and destroy as much life as he could in the fallen Eagle and Bear. He did not worry so much about the Dragon, as the Bear had delivered a 200 million-soldier army for him to slaughter. He quickly repaid this gift with the final nails to keep the bear in the northern wastelands that he deserved to stay. The use of Judaism as the official language kept it close to the Bible, enough slowly to fine-tune it enough to promote his false religion. Lucifer had millennia to study every little trick that the Old Testament could provide him, that the conversion of so many, not only from the Middle East, but also within his European stronghold as the resistance by any Christians left behind slowly dwindled. The new doctrine would offer a human sacrifice in the new temples each Sabbath. These people were easy to collect from the Americas, Africa, Asia, and Australia. The world had a new god, and this was the Antichrist. I looked over and saw another woman clothed with the sun. This harlot was so different, for she loved to drink blood, and the United Roman Empire feed her all the blood she could handle; she was so filled with unworthy motives. We could see that so easy for where we were sitting, yet the people trembling upon the Earth were seeking a life past World War III. History had taught them that as the world changed so did its rulers and those who were ruled. At least, this ruler kept the Bible in their hands, so how could it be false. After all, the Christians had been removed from the Earth, not going to Heaven as they were told, but going to Hell as he told us, and he was the one who was doing the miracles. The Rabbis were quick to show how the Messiah was yet to appear on the Earth. This made it so easy to phase out the teachings of Jesus, who had talked about coming back, yet never had. They also pointed out that the word Rapture was not in the Bible and was part of this false doctrine. They also quoted Sam.15:22-23, And Samuel said, Hath the Lord as great delight in burnt offerings and sacrifices, as in obeying the voice of the Lord? Behold, to obey is better than sacrifice, and to hearken than the fat of rams. For rebellion is as the sin of witchcraft, and stubbornness is as iniquity and idolatry. Because thou hast rejected the word of the Lord, he hath also rejected thee from being king." This proved that to obey the Lord was better than sacrifice; however, when you fail to obey, then you must sacrifice and that disobedience was the sin of witchcraft. This proved that sense all knew that the Christians had not always obeyed they should have sacrificed, and considering that, they had not; they indeed were witches. The Antichrist and false prophet promised to remove this witchcraft from the world. The religious Babylon of the time of Peter the Apostle and the End Times of Revelation is a city. This harlot sits in a city that has a Christian religious heritage, has the blood of Martyrs and Saints on her hands clothed in purple and scarlet. She is located near the Mediterranean Sea and sits on seven mountains or hills, has religious influence throughout the world, is full of abominations, primarily idols, and now influences world political leaders because of her religious power. The Antichrist received a mysterious visitor one night, which introduced himself as Nimrod. Nimrod warned him about giving the Jews too much freedom and suggested that he rebuilt Babylon to show them his great power. Thus, he immediately rebuilt Babylon, which gave rise to many complaints from Jerusalem. This angered the Antichrist as he would deal with no one on matters that we his to control, thus he broke the treaty with the Jews and moved his false prophet to Babylon. He then, in a sign of power built a larger temple next to the Jewish temple and visiting it, sat upon his throne he had built in the Jewish temple and pronounced himself the one true god. Babylon and Rome were not both spiritually and physically one now. The days of peace in Israel only lasted for three and a half years. The world drank her wine and enjoyed it. Those who were of the new Babylon nation, and the United Roman Empire complained how the Middle East was ungrateful for all the wonders their god had given them, while others in unclaimed lands throughout the Earth suffered daily, and gave their blood as sacrifices. The Jews agreed and participated in drinking this blood. The Jews had accepted the false prophet, fulfilling the prophecy given by Jesus revealed in (John 5:43), "I have come in my Father's name, and you do not accept me; if another comes in his own name, you will accept him." The false prophet was clothed in purple and scarlet and adorned with the choicest of jewelry the world had to offer, most of them from the former kings and queens of great empires. This fit the false prophet who now sat in Babylon as blood was flowing into Israel as it did elsewhere. Technologically advanced now allowed for the citizen of the Antichrist and servants outside the borders to be marked. This mark was large, an immediate tattoo of himself that was laced with a series of computer chips, which allowed for market activities, passing empire law and military officials and all personal activities. Intruders were easily captured and sacrificed in the temples. The Antichrist had no prisons as he had destroyed all prisons on the Earth setting all prisoners free. He used these prisoners as part of his punishment on the populations.

Sachiel now guided me to another mighty angel who told us that he would send fourteen plagues to the earth in a succession of events during the Great Tribulation. "The seven trumpets and the seven bowls are judgments from God. The seven bowls containing the wrath of our God's full strength will be poured out on the people who have chosen to worship the false prophet and his master. These Seven Bowls would produce abhorrent sores that would appear to people who have the mark. The oceans and rivers become red, and all the Ocean creatures die. The days of the boiling sun appear again scorching people causing the rivers to dry up. As those in Babylon now grow angry at the false prophet for allowing the great river Euphrates to dry up, leaving only a red muddy riverbed with the stench of dying dried-up sea life. Sachiel now took before the throne of the almighty as he declares, "It is done'. We looked upon the earth and saw that there were noises, thunder, lightning, and the greatest earthquake that the Earth had ever experienced on Earth. Every island and mountain was moved. Giant building and road crushing hailstones fell around or very near to those who had the mark. The United Roman Empire was now once more facing decline, as their darkness becomes pain. They believed that no other would be greater than their Empire, because they were the true ones and the false ones had to be destroyed, in favor of their true God did who came forth from the original Testament, being the new Noah, saving the Earth from the disasters of World War III. During the fifth trumpet, they invaded the earth and tortured people for five months to remove as much of the war mongrel that tried to destroy the Earth with nuclear weapons. Only those who worshiped the Antichrist had the right to exist a life without constant torture. The rebellious, many now connected in another reality quickly adapted to this new reality, which had the promise of an easier life and more technology to play. During the sixth trumpet, the United Roman Empire had the pleasure of killing one-third of the remaining people. They justified this as removing threats to the citizens of the Empire and as mercy killings, removing those who suffered irreversible damage from the last World War and in stopping uncontrollable plagues. This brought peace to the hearts of the righteous in the Empire, for why would an evil world allow those with permanent radiation defects steal from those who were trying to protect the Empire's interests and security. The Antichrist stressed in the world that the security of the United Roman Empire lay with forces he had outside the Empire, for now foreign force could ever occupy his land inside the Empire's borders. He demonstrated patience and the lack in greed during his world conquering by stopping at the Ural Mountains, when all of Asia lay helpless before him. He stopped six hundred miles from the Mediterranean in Africa to ensure the secure sea as an exotic playground for those who served his Empire with profits. He was greedy with the Middle East takes all of Egypt and the Babylonian and the holy lands to include all of ancient Mesopotamia. Lucifer told him that when the seventh trumpet was to sound, the time after his victory would be near, for then the war would intensify in the heavens. He would not lose his second bid for the throne, as his victories on Earth would lead him to his final destination. The demons now sat in stunned silence relishing how they had won the worship from every marked human being. After the seventh trumpet comes the last set of judgments known as, the seven bowl judgments released before the battle of Armageddon is set up the messiah returns for the second time.

The Heavens are making another final attempt to try to get some of the hardened sinners to repent and turn from the Antichrist for salvation.

Although hardened against the oldest form of Christianity that almost destroyed the world with its wars and destructed the new religion that still had a foundation in the old. It was like riding the same horse that was simply painted a new color. As they refused to be marked, their freedom had been won with great sacrifice, and they had no desire to be burned again by the false doctrines that had put humankind through so much misery for the previous two millennia. They still refused to repent and turn to God, as they had done no wrong and had no desire to return in a world where a few rich received everything, and the masses worked like a dream that ended with the nuclear holocaust that finished everything. These "disasters that God will throw at them will be so supernatural, which these people will know, without any shadow of a doubt, that it is God doing all of this, yet they shall still blaspheme God and refuse to repent. These judgments are severe and extreme. Jehovah shall no more be blamed for what Lucifer did and the lies that he feed the foolish minds of his servants, who believed them, so they could hold on to this new world power. Jehovah would now release his anger and wrath with full force in this world that has now become extremely wicked and evil. These last judgments are unyielding and intense. Jehovah is now fully releasing his wrath on this world that has now become extremely evil and wicked. Sachiel now told me that the revealing of thoughts and reasons no longer mattered. So much had been done to show the unmarked the truth, a rapture, a recalling of 144,000 by Enoch and Elijah and a sanctuary in the Holy Land in which the United Roman Empire could not penetrate.

Those who had the mark now had to suffer, as the weakening of individuals marked could give more leeway for the unmarked. Then one of the four living creatures gave to the seven angels seven golden bowls filled with the wrath of God, who lives forever and ever, to pour upon the whore of Babylon. The group of angels now reads from Revelations. (Revelation 16: 1-2) "Then I heard a loud voice from the temple telling the seven angels, "Go and pour out on the earth the seven bowls of the wrath of God. So the first angel went and poured his bowl on the land on the earth, and a foul and painful sore came on those who had the mark of the beast and who worshiped its image." This plague was introduced first to exemplify a repeat as Moses gave to Pharaoh, as shown in the Old Testament, Exodus 9:10 "So they took soot from the kiln, and stood before Pharaoh, and Moses threw it in the air, and it caused festering boils on humans and animals." This was to verify who the right was, and who the wrong was in this final phase of days. As I looked around, I saw the soldiers and warriors now covered with smelly boils and other such ugliness that many now wrapped their faces in colored rags. I could now see the unmarked appear in public more often now, as the marked could not chase them because of the sores on their feet. The bear on the north was now reforming her armies, for her third raid on the holy lands, and since she was not marked, the Antichrist supplied all the state of the art military supplies. Now a solid argument could be advanced in the fallacy of the official religion, as only a certain sector suffered this very foul and loathsome sore or boil that clings to all the people who have the mark of the Beast. I noticed that this plague was not released on any who had not the marks that were still living in this time. The verse also tells us that these "bowl judgments" are the wrath of God being poured out, therefore, the word "bowl" judgments. I can hear all the cries coming from the marked, yet none in heaven have any sorrow, for these people caused so much more grievous pain on the unmarked that revenge was justified, yet sores could not balance the scales of justice. In line floated six more angels with six more bowls. The Second Bowl now was poured upon the Oceans. (Revelations 16:3) "Then the second angel poured out his bowl on the sea, and it became blood as of a dead man; and every living creature into the sea died." This next bowl judgment, God causes the entire oceans to turn to blood, and every living creature in the oceans is killed as a result. The blood was actually a discolored coagulated form of oil that was reacting with underground gas from the earthquakes being dumped into the ocean. This oil was blood made from life before Adam walked the Earth, yet fittings that even the first of beasts to roam the Earth were here now to promote the end. Just try to imagine the magnitude of such an event, not to mention the stench that will probably be in the air from all the rotting fish and sea creatures who have now died and who may be floating on top of the ocean waters.

The Third Bowl is emptied upon the Earth focusing upon the rivers. In this next judgment, Jehovah now comes after all the rivers and springs and transforms them into blood. An angel then makes the statement that the reason God is doing this is to pay back with vengeance those who have killed his prophets and saints. He says that God is now giving them blood to drink since these people spilled the blood of His saints and that this is now due. (Revelation 16:4-7) "The third angel poured out his bowl on the rivers and springs of water, and they became blood. Then I heard the angel responsible of the waters say: "You are just in these judgments, you who are and who were, the Holy One, because you have so judged; for they have shed the blood of your saints and prophets, and you have given them blood to drink as they deserve." And I heard the altar respond: "Yes, Lord God Almighty, true and just are your judgments." I can see a red planet below me, as the oceans changed from blue to red and now all of the oceans, rivers, and springs on earth are now nothing except pure blood. Another repeat between Pharaoh and Egypt (Exodus 7: 17-18) Thus says the Lord, "By this you shall know that I am the Lord." See, with the staff that is in my hand, I will strike the water that is in the Nile, and it shall be turned to blood. The fish on the river shall die, the river itself shall stink, and the Egyptians shall be unable to drink water from the Nile.'" This was the message that everyone felt, as even water springs and wells produced a smelly red thick liquid that instead of giving life, it took life. All the blood that the Antichrist spilled, and the blood from World War III, which he orchestrated on the sidelines, was now screaming for revenge wanting to know how much longer before something was to be done and their blood avenged. The pouring of the seals has so far hit the flesh, covering them with sores, destroyed the oceans which trapped them to their homelands and the skies, with their airplanes, although the skies now had large flocks of birds who were currently unpredictable, and now the revenge had entered their homes as all running water was foul. Their sores would now grow worse with additional biological infection as new insects feasted on this fresh blood supply. Even the snow and the rain were at present an acidic red, which burned the skin when touched. Thus, now for the marked, days of rain were days of no gain. The children also suffered from this, as these marked were quick to broadcast the horror suffered by the children as evidence the unmarked were evil. Hence, they quickly forgot how they brutally killed all the children of their enemies. Children were a valuable booty in the great wars, for they could be used as individual sacrifices for the wealthy, so they would not have to sit in a large congregation, and be cleansed by the temple sacrifice. With a child, they would beat him or her making them confess the sins of their new master. This made for a personal sacrifice for Lucifer, although he would accept the blood either way. The lavish beaches of the Mediterranean, the private pool of the United Roman Empire were now a cesspool of filth and stench. Dead fish, snakes, snails and so many ugly sea life washed ashore. The sand seems to work great in holding this new sea blood, almost turning into quicksand if the depth supported it. Ordinary steps were met was a great struggle. The other prevailing factor in this pandemonium was the billions of insects, which of course flocked to anything that moved, which decreased both the wild life and domestic animals. Many of these animals became crazy, as insects would be logged in their cavities, especially their ears that removed any sense of balance and drove them to attack anything that might jar their heads. The special treat was how the insects were attracted to the mark people's sores. They bit and dug at them nonstop, opening the wounds, which then made it possible to lay their eggs. The larva would grow inside the sore and when strong enough journey to through the swollen sore escaping from its nursery. Water is life; the lack of water quickly brings life to a stop. I was amazed at how many were still alive and packing the temples; however, the sacrifices now had a mark, as those who were unmarked were living within their communities, which were now becoming social once more. One thing that changed was the unsaved unmarked people who had argued the end-time God was not righteous. One look at all the marked with all their sores proved justice was on the way and with the newly reformed end time ministry available, the numbers of unmarked unsaved were few and far between. The groups would not let them live among the saved, for fear that Jehovah would become angry. Their small churches were spit shinned as not one speck of dirt could be seen. The house of this God of justice was to be kept perfect; a sign of their great love in this might source of salvation. Salvation was a concept easily to understand as each of them had many close encounters with the marked, which almost lead to capture, nevertheless, something pulled them into safety and then filled them with the seven true spirits of Jehovah. These saints now understood the value of being washed with the blood, and they had no desire to be cleaned. Back to the marked, water was a serious issue; however, through careful allocation of the vegetation and fruits, plus meat they could get some moisture. Coconuts and cactuses almost became obsolete within just a few days. Then the military discovered the oceans were returning, having only stayed infected, like their sores for ten days. The last few days after the land water infection were eased as the salt water was brought in for human waste disposal as most people had blocked the blood from staying in their toilets as the stink and insects took away any benefit. The government sets up emergency salt-water treatment facilities to generate fresh water, which now had the value of gold as those who drank it would be able to continue. The Antichrist also saw an opportunity to strike some unmarked people as they were now disregarding their security as if to suggest he could no longer kill. He would hit them once again, if not for a little surprise as Jehovah had different plans.

The next angel poured the fourth bowl onto the sun, as the land, sea and rivers had already had their special treat. The heat from the sun was used to scorch marked men with great heat. (Revelations 16:8-9) "Then the fourth angel poured out his bowl on the sun, and power was given to him to scorch men with fire and men were scorched with great heat, and they blasphemed the name of God who has the power over these plagues; and they did not repent and give him glory." Nothing so far had weakened the evil beasts who ruled the Earth, for their hearts were hardened, as were Pharaohs. Knowing that all the oceans, rivers, and springs being turned into blood, these people still refuse to repent and turn to God. These people are cursing and blaspheming God through all of this instead seeking salvation and asking God for forgiveness. This intense heat did a number on the military hardware belonging to the United Roman Empire. The planes stopped as the electrical circuits melted and fuel became unstable. Homes have now been without electricity. The sky above this empire at night looked like most of the world, except for the pockets of saints waiting to go home, and of course, the sanctuary in the Holy Land, which remarkably was unguarded now. The guards had fled back to their homelands to die with their families, as the Antichrist no longer had a hold on his stubborn people. Electric lines were down, burned into thousands of small sections. Many buildings, at least over one-half burned, leaving many inhabitants to seek shelter in the wildernesses or packed government buildings. Some of the Empire's scientists try to report that the ozone layer was destroyed, yet reports flooded in how the unmarked were living life as usual. If this was a malfunction of Earth's environment, then its effects should be felt by all and not one select groups, the group that had tried to defeat evil. Oh, the false prophets and his priests openly cursed and blaspheming God and blaming him for all the unjust punishments the one true faith had endured. This boiling heat even melted car tires against the road, as their constant explosions sounded like a battlefield. The skin sores now returned yet were of no value as the sunburns were actually cooking their flesh. The vegetation completely dried and burned. Water evaporated so fast that the dirt turned into brittle sand. Glass windows exploded shooting razor-sharp knives to cut into the marked one's burned bodies. This intense heat even completely dehydrated the deceased sea life and burned it, leaving any small specks of dust behind. The Antichrist made no public appearances, for if the people saw him with sores, he would lose his power. Lucifer told him to stay inside, and he would have some demons do some tricks to reassure the people that he was still in control. The official statement was that as a god, he went to the heavens to complain of the evil his holy empire was suffering. He would fight for the justice they deserved. This gave his people some more hope to hang as the miracles around his palace proved they were on the correct side. As with the Pharaoh in the times of Moses, this god among men would never give up. (Exodus 10:27) "However, the LORD HARDENED PHARAOH'S HEART, AND HE WOULD NOT LET THEM GO." HE WOULD FIGHT TO THE END, AS LUCIFER TOLD HIM THAT HIS DEMONS WERE WINNING THE BATTLE FOR THE THRONE AND THAT SOON THEY WOULD RULE THE THRONE TOGETHER. WHEN WE HEARD HIM SAY THIS TO HIS BODY ON EARTH WE ALL LAUGHED, FOR ALL IN HEAVEN KNEW THAT LUCIFER WOULD NEVER SHARE HIS THRONE, NEVER HAD, AND NEVER WOULD.

Promptly, the fifth angel poured out the fifth bowl. We listened to the book as he gave us this message, (Revelation 6:9-10) When he opened the fifth seal, I saw underneath the altar the souls of those who had been slaughtered for the word of God and for the testimony they had given. They cried out with a loud voice, "Sovereign Lord, holy and true, how long will it be before you judge and avenge our blood on the inhabitants on the earth?" (Revelation 16:10-11) The fifth angel poured his bowl on the throne of the beast, and its kingdom was plunged into darkness; people gnawed their tongues in agony, and cursed the God of heaven because of their pains and sores, and they did not repent of their deeds." These are one of the millions of examples where prayers are answered in heaven's time and not man's time. The fifth bowl answers the prayers of the fifth seal. In this seal, Jehovah goes after both Rome and Babylon, more specifically the throne of the Beast. New Babylon had not played many roles yet in the Antichrist's plans, yet would be the future capital, since he no longer felt a need to impress the holy land but a need to depress them, and he believed that with the help of Nimrod, he would be able to do that best in Babylon. He hated Rome in that he was landlocked with just the narrow Strait of Gibraltar and even narrower Suez Cannel. Although air power had been his punch, he needed vast supplies and materials for his divine projects. Babylon offered this to him, plus a feeling of being closer to the center of his new world's trade routes as he would someday rebuild the dragon and the bear. He had no desire to see the Eagle fly again, yet needed quick routes to either shore to collect his ransoms and bounty. Now Jehovah was striking headfirst at the Antichrist in that if he wanted to rule in darkness, then darkness it would be. He had used this with some success against Pharaoh for his ninth plague, (Exodus 10:21-23) "Then the Lord said to Moses, "Stretch out your hand toward heaven so that there may be darkness over the land of Egypt, a darkness that can be felt." Consequently, Moses stretched out his hand toward heaven, and there was dense darkness in all the land of Egypt for three days. People could not see one another, and for three days they could not move from where they were; however, all the Israelites had been light where they lived." Once again, the unmarked had lights and now began to sing great praises to the heavens. Jehovah causes total darkness to fall upon his kingdom. He even blocks out the stars, and the moon refuses to share her received sunlight. The people are still being plagued by the boils and sores from the first bowl judgment, and that they are in extreme pain because of all of this. If only they had not prepared to mount a fight. On top of their sores, they had the severe sunburns, which would not let them sit or lay down. I remember one time in Montana when I was swimming in Canyon Ferry Lake, that the cool afternoon breeze deceived me concerning the true impact of that day's sunrays. After swimming and enjoyed this recreational day, I collected my brothers and sisters, and we went back to our Christian home. That evening I discovered, through pain, that I had burned myself. I plastered myself with salves, gobbled some pain pills, and tried to sleep. When I hit my matrices,' I rose twice as fast as I had laid down. The night increased my pain from the sunburn. I do not even want to know how bad these burns are raging tonight among them, yet I do know that they would be gnawing their tongues in agony because of their pain. Burns gives a special sort of agonizing pain, as the body will not let you escape its new imperfection. Yet, now seeing that their Antichrist was not successful, they still would not, and for those who were marked could not, repent. Some who were marked have such severe burns that the marks were barely visible, yet some of the chips remained in them. A few of the chips had been pulled or pushed out by the larva, notwithstanding the Lord or themselves made their hearts hard. The darkness also invited the mass revival of rodents who now roamed the Earth, as they desired, with no limits as previously confined by the light. Their new freedom also allowed them to share diseases, and enjoy large feasts on any foodstuffs, what they could now easily invade in groups if need so. The shock of being eaten while still alive caused some tongues to gnaw in agony. Especially when a bite cuts into a burned skin with liquids that pressure the swelling pains reaches a new level. A tongue that gnaws does so with persistent anxiety and distress. Fear of the unknown now becomes known but not seen. This additional component affects the hidden recesses of the mind filling it was death. Egypt suffered for three days, yet this darkness would not relent. The knowing that the unmarked had light made this situation excruciating, yet did nothing more but add to their belief, that as the true martyrs, their suffering was for a reason and that endurance would see victory, as the unmarked would spend their days in blindness after losing their eyes. There is no fat woman singing yet, for repentance was a concept he or she only now held to define the unmarked, as they would beg for their lives once again. The mercy in allowing them to keep their lives was forever subjugated.

Now the next angel stepped up and released the sixth bowl her bowl, (Revelation 16:12) "The sixth angel poured out his bowl on the great river Euphrates, and its water was dried up to prepare the way for the kings from the East." The Euphrates River is gone, as even the water behind the Ataturk Dam was boiled away from the scorching sun. This River represents more than just water draining, in that Adam and Eve drink from this and three other rivers. Even life evolving from aliens who settled on the Earth selected this area to begin, as Neolithic villages, depicted by the ushering in of pottery in the early seventh millennium BC, are known throughout this area. The circle of man's life can now be attributed to this area, as life began here, it would end here. The main impact was felt in the loss of sea trade with Babylon and the world. Transportation by trucks and planes had ground to a stop because of the scorching sun; however, special train tracks were opening the flow of blood throughout the veins of his Empire. The Antichrist saw one excellent advantage to having the Tigris and Euphrates Rivers dried up. He wanted to avoid the trap that the Dragon fell into when trying to move her large 200 million warrior armies is supporting the Bear's earlier attempt to conquer this region. The Dragons Armies, heavily augmented by women, struggled to cross the two rivers, which had given the Antichrist his opportunity to destroy them and collect the massive loads of military hardware they had to leave at the riverbanks for his future operations. The Antichrist now wanted to provide an avenue for the Dragon to move straight to the Holy Land. He had been casually monitoring the Dragon's movements, as she had control of India and the Far East, plus much of Siberia, which the Bear had abandoned. She once more had a 200 million plus army with plenty of reserves to defend in case of another surprise like the one they had before. (Revelation 9:14-16) saying to the sixth angel who had the trumpet, "Release the four angels who are bound at the great river Euphrates." So the four angels were released, who had been held ready within the hour, the day, the month, and the year, to kill a third of humankind. The number to the troops of cavalry was two hundred million; I heard their number." The Antichrist gave them access to the Holy Lands, telling the Dragon that this area was the source for all the recent plagues. This judgment paved the road for two things to happen. The Euphrates River is allowed to dry up and to prepare the way for the kings from the east to come for the last and final battle on planet earth, the battle of Armageddon. (Revelation 16:16) "And they assembled them at the place that in Hebrew is called Harmagedon." The kings from the east are China and several other Asian nations, with the fighting spirit of the Mongol Empire of old. These nations were angry that they had to suffer all these punishments, plus the persecutions from the United Roman Empire, citing that they had only requested to remain unmarked and neutral. Sadly, neutral meant unsaved, which left them unprotected. They were now fighting for revenge. (Revelation 16:13-14) "And I saw three foul spirits like frogs coming from the mouth of the dragon, from the mouth of the beast, and from the mouth of the false prophet. These are demonic spirits, performing signs, who go abroad to the kings of the whole world, to assemble them for battle on the great day of God the Almighty. Lucifer had now once again enabled the Antichrist, the Beast, and false prophet to do great wonders as the time for war on Earth was at hand, since he was not winning the wars in heaven.

This next judgment is the last and final of the fourteen judgments. The last angel came forth and poured the seventh bowl, (Revelation 16:17-21) "The seventh angel poured out his bowl into the air, and out of the temple came a loud voice from the throne, saying, "It is done!" Then there came flashes of lightning, rumblings, peals of thunder and a severe earthquake. No earthquake like it has ever occurred since man has been on earth, so tremendous was the quake. The great city split into three parts, and the cities of the nations collapsed. God remembered Babylon the Great and gave her the cup filled with the wine of the fury of his wrath. Every island fled away, and the mountains could not be found. From the sky, huge hailstones of about a hundred pounds, each fell upon men. And they cursed God on account of the plague of hail, because the plague was so terrible." I shiver as the words, "it is done," are shouted out. Jehovah has decided it is time to let this rebellious Empire have a taste of his punch. I know that in my life, I have seen big boys who were kind, and how little people who were bullied to enjoy pushing their luck. The push and push, defying any fear they previously held, until that last time with the wrong button was pushed, and the kind big boy settles the account instantly. However, the small bullies have that taste of blood and look for another kind person to torment. This kind tormented suffering big person decides it is time to settle the score. This had previously changed from a, "do not do that" to a "you must do this" and this is to change sides. No more serving two masters, for now a road had to be chosen and the journey taken to its finish line. Jehovah releases a great earthquake, which changes to face of the Earth. No building is left standing. Old Rome is crumbled, and Babylon lay in disaster. The great army to the east now finds itself hiding behind rocks and trying so hard to live through the hundred-pound hailstones, whip drop as bombs over all the face of the Earth. The women and children suffer the greatest as the men of the Earth now struggle only to protect themselves. Curses and blasphemy's rage throughout the world against both Heaven and Hell. The United Roman Empire or Babylon to the Heavens was no more. Airplanes were bashed into pieces, as even the hangers could offer no protection. Vehicles also were no more as the bridges and road and all public places destroyed, even the stadiums of old in the Eagle, which had been preserved by the Antichrist for future government operations. The foolish kings or national heads that were in alliance or occupation of the Antichrist now declared their new freedom, (Revelation 18:9-10) "When the kings of the earth who committed adultery with her and shared her luxury see the smoke of her burning; they will weep and mourn over her. Terrified at her torment, they will stand far off and cry, "Woe! Woe, O great city, O Babylon, city of power! In one hour, your doom has come!"" Their shattered nations now felt that they had travelled the false road far too long and only chance of survival lay in fighting the heavenly forces that had tormented them so. Thus, they currently prepared to revenge the Holy Land, for at least they had to exact some revenge. This is also the time, when we see so many of the unmarked separating themselves and repenting. The end is near, yet they did not travel the road of evil, thus at present did a fast turnaround to the road of righteousness. This was also possible by the fact that the large armies that controlled most of Asia now lay in hiding in their way to the last Great War. Whatever between the millions of reasons they refused the mark, there was now one great advantage to being unmarked, and that was the option to repent. The darkness that still covered the Earth made escaping from the hailstones virtually impossible. When the sun did return after the terrible Earthquake, the marked could not believe that a destruction worse than twenty World War IIIs had scoured the Earth forever. Trees were uprooted along with underground pipes and cables. The heavy winds began once more as the Earth's surface no longer had anything to hold it fast, thus the skies would turn pitch black with dirt and dust sweeping it clean from anything made by man or nature. As we look down upon the Earth we wonder, "What is that below us." There are no more islands as Hawaii and Great Britain are gone. The old mountains are gone; nevertheless, in their place are new mountains. Just about the only thing that moves upon the Earth, besides the marked crawling, is the sanctuary in the Holy Lands, as their great rejoicing is flooding this heaven with wells of elation. The great city that was divided into three parts is Jerusalem, as three great faiths sprang from the God of Abraham. The voice from the temple of heaven shouting, "it is done" is Jehovah, as all of heaven shook when he spoke. His Son Jesus said, "It is finished" right before dying upon the cross. Now Jehovah is going to say the exact same words as His last and final judgment is thrown onto this earth. After this last judgment has passed, the only thing that will be left is for all the kings on the earth to march foolishly towards the battle of Armageddon. The last bowl was emptied into the air. As the hailstones continued to crash into Earth's surface, Sachiel pulled me to his side and suggested that we move on, for the final war would soon be at hand. He took me to where George and Aunt Rita were. I saw a giant gold basis, in which Sachiel told me to release my Patmos. I saw my visions blending in such a way to form the story, which still had four more empty holes, thus our Patmos has a lot more to digest. I simply sit down with George and Aunt Rita still digesting what I have just seen. Hard-nosed fools pushed the wrong button, and the blood of the martyrs is now rightfully demanding their day of justice as the Great Final war is being staged.

CHAPTER 07

Seven Seals

The four of us now stood looking at each other, a mind game of does a boy or girl jump in now, after two girls have gone through. I could only think of finishing early so I could be with George, so I casually walked over to the Patmos portal and jumped, before Floyd or Little Running Eagle had a chance to figure out what I was doing. I knew that if I were going to be a strong mate for George, I had to start showing leadership and bravery. Actually, by this jump I was hiding how afraid I was. What if George, Jennifer, and Aunt Rita were dead or had been tortured beyond recognition. Then as I was somewhere that was very dark, then many lights started appearing before me, and I saw a big strong angel. The relief of this site instigated me to ask, "Is that you George?" The angel looked confused and said, "Holly, fear not child, for I am the Archangel Zadkiel, and I shall help and guide you through your visions for the Patmos." I then asked him, "What visions will I be given?" Zadkiel told me, "Holly, you will be shown the seven seals which are the first seven judgments against the evil ones on Earth." I looked over behind him, saw four horses, and said, "Oh wow, look at those pretty horses, can I ride one of them?" Zadkiel answered, "Oh no Holly; Holly, you do not ride those horses. Follow me, and you can see why. First sit here beside me and we will discuss what has happened and what you need to watch for your Patmos. Many of these things had already happened as told to you by Jennifer." I then asked, "Zadkiel, why is Earth really being judged? I did not go into Christian churches that much, as my parents took us to the Indian spirit meetings. They made us do most of the same things that the Christian kids did and my father always told me to think of the spirits as different faces of heaven. He always told us the Jehovah had seven spirits. I feel rather awkward being here since I never went to church that much." Then Zadkiel told me, "Many who went to church and stood on corners praying loud so all could see they did not make it here in the rapture. You worshiped the true God, so you were covered in Jesus's blood." I then told him, "Zadkiel, I remember my father having us all baptized the way the Bible said to, and we had to declare that Jesus was the Lord and Messiah." Zadkiel now smiled and said, "Holly this is why you are here. The visions you record shall be part to the history of humanity. The first rapture has already happened and the leaders who will fight World War III are currently being deceived. Not all hope is lost for those who repent and serve our Lord, as death without being marked and belonging to the number 666 will give them eternal life. In addition, Enoch and Elijah will bring 144,000 home, and then for the last great battle of Armageddon, those Saints still living will be raptured to the Lord. You shall see how hard Jehovah and Jesus are working to save as many children of Adam and Eve as possible. Any alien children who were living upon the Earth were removed through disease through the last couple of centuries so that only Earth people would remain. You will see the celebrations here in Heaven each time a soul is saved." I then told him, "I know it is hard to save people, as I have seen some people work so assiduously even going to people's houses only to be cursed. I know that had to hurt, and I always felt sorry for them. I know that things, which involve love, can hurt and so much of Christianity engrosses love. I remember how hard I worked to get George to notice me. All the other boys were always staring at me with no exceptions, yet he just would walk with me like a Gomer Pyle." Zadkiel now told me, "Do not worry Holly, you and George will always be together, as this Patmos will give you some advantages if we get busy on it." I then told him, "Do not get mad at me, I am the girl here, and you are supposed to be guiding me, so guide me." Zadkiel now laughed and said, "I never could figure out what the watchers seen in you women?" I just looked at him, having no idea, which the watchers were simply saying, "Zadkiel." He then continues, "Jehovah is dealing with what may be among the most stubborn and determined Earthlings, especially those who believe that science is the answer to everything. Some may have even been hurt by false ministers and evil Christians. The list goes on and on for reasons yet all of them combined does not equal one excuse for not repenting. I cannot understand why, after being hit so hard, they would still refuse to repent; however, the reason for that is beyond the scope of your vision. It is important that you understand why these judgments are being so severe, intense, and will be happening worldwide. Another reason why this must be is to shake up the faith and loyalty that all the hardened and rebellious sinners have in the Antichrist, the False Prophet, and the Beast. The seven seals contain hidden judgments known only to Jehovah and Jesus, as none other may open these scrolls and look into the contents. "A book that is sealed" is that which has its consequence hidden (Isaiah 29:11) "The vision of all this has become for you like the words of a sealed document. If it is given to those who can read, with the command, "Read this," they say, "We cannot, for it is sealed." The first four signs have transpired many times in the last two millennia. Nevertheless, they never happened, as they shall this time around. These seven seals occur before the Antichrist breaks his pact with Israel. Life is not as terrible for the Jews as it is for the other nations who have the full wrath of the Antichrist. Even knowing how the Antichrist betrays those who trust him, as he did to the Dragon, and she laid down her first 200 million-soldier army, they still revere him as a prophet greater than Jesus and Solomon, for he rebuilt the temple and removed the Muslims, officially denying them any claim to the holy lands. Something must be done by the heavens to pull back the lost ones before the markings become mandatory in a few years.

Zadkiel told me to behold the rebirth of the Roman Empire, now called the United Roman Empire since the Antichrist also had conquered the barbarians, Hungarians and made the bear too weak to fight. Zadkiel now called to the book to appear and read the scriptures, (Revelation 6:1-2) "Then I saw the Lamb open one of the seven seals, and I heard one of the four living creatures call out, as with a voice of thunder, "Come!" I looked, and there was a white horse! Its rider had a bow; a crown was given to him, and he came out conquering and to conquer." I had seen this as World War III had begun. The nuclear bombs exploded everywhere as the new United Roman Empire conquered all of Europe and the Middle East, not wanting anything else. The Middle East was to deceive Israel and cash in on some blessings from the heavens, a strategy that Lucifer gave to the Emperor. No other government is left standing, as any other kings lay down their crowns. I looked up and saw the book open again and start to speak telling me about the signs of the end of the age (Matthew 24:3-8) "When he was sitting on the Mount of Olives, the disciples came to him privately, saying, "Tell us, when will this be, and what will be the sign of your coming and of the end of the age?" Jesus answered them, "Beware that no one leads you astray. For many will come in my name, saying, 'I am the Messiah!' and they will lead many astray. And you will hear of wars and rumors of wars; see that you are not alarmed; for this must take place, but the end is not yet. For nation will rise against nation, and kingdom against kingdom, and there will be famines and earthquakes in various places: all this is but the beginning of the birth pangs." Sure, history had many famines and earthquakes, yet the ones from the judgments were massive and introduced death to an unprecedented scale. His colossal air forces coupled with all the oil he can use from the Middle East allows him to conquer as if going to a turkey shoot. To add more territory would only add to his administrative burden and require him to trade for the resources he took from their lands. This way was better, raid, take what he wanted, butcher some to show his power and concentrate on his power base. There was only one monetary system, his, making all others of no value. Trade with him, the way he wanted, or no trade at all, and most likely your life gone. He is portrayed as the rider on the white horse. He now rules the holy lands with peace and diplomacy. He can solve all problems, especially since the entire world obeys him. He built the new temple. To put the absolute icing on the cake, he is bringing all Jews back, without charge to the Holy Land and giving them former Muslim lands plus gainful work as he is rebuilding Israel into a showcase on the Mediterranean. He has the largest air force and navy and only army in the world. His white planes represent all his great victories over the Bear, Dragon, and Eagle. His advanced military equipment is the bow that caused all the other kings of the world to lay down their crowns at his feet. Lucifer had ordered some of his special demons to reveal to the Antichrist great secrets in technology as evidenced in how fast he could remove the temple mount and build the new temple twice the size as the one Solomon had his demons build.

Zadkiel now points me back over where our Lord is standing as he is about to unlock the next judgment. (Revelation 6:3-4) "When the Lamb opened the second seal; I heard the second living creature say, "Come!" Then another horse came out, a fiery red one. Its rider was given power to take peace from the earth and to make men slay each other. To him was given a large sword." A judgment that revealed what had happened so fast on the Earth. Every day, so many bombs were being dropped, and land armies were going into small villages, such as Townsend from what Jennifer told us, and pulling people into the open so that all could see them die. The individualism and cruelty of these murders are what made them so bloody. The bombs were intended to force people into the open by destroying any structures that could give them shelter. His name is death, as I remember what Jennifer saw him do in our hometown. He now no longer presents the image as a peacemaker, not even in the holy land, as his heart is now jealous as he sees the Jews sacrifice to Jehovah each day. He begins by declaring himself a god to all those who live outside the holy land. This causes division within his Empire as threats of a Civil War surface. He handles this swiftly by destroying the source of the threat and all around it. One threat came from the former King of Denmark. He had his armies march in, kill every man and child, and sold every woman into slavery, with one special touch first. He had all these women blinded. This gave me some security, in case they were to lay the seeds for a future rebellion. It also forced all future rebels to operate in small areas with few contacts. The risk of large operations being detected was too great. The joy of being worshiped creates an ecstasy for greater than that of the love with a woman, which he hates considering it degrading and a primary reason for leaders to lose their power. Even so, he does not want anyone else beside him when he is being worshiped. Of course, Lucifer cannot pass up this threat as he possesses his Antichrist and displays great miracles for those worshiping him. Lucifer now talks his Antichrist and False Prophet to demand human sacrifices. They even talk Jerusalem into offering human sacrifices in the temple, giving them Arabs to sacrifice instead of animals. The priests fall for this, remembering not that this is murder, and that sin cannot cover sin. Arguments abound as the weather this Caesar is divine and how to allocate the limited resources that are now available because of the massive worldwide slaughters, to the extent that people start killing one another. Life slowly was becoming a precious gift that must be fought in order to maintain. Now, in the United States, Asia, Australia, and Africa, people came out of hiding to fight guerrilla style. One or two people could slowly chip away at the large forces as they marched or rode past them. Trucks and planes could be booby-trapped, such as delayed-triggered bombs, on the planes to have them explode into the air, and brake lines cut in vehicles. Detail in planning was communicated to make sure the hidden population was well removed from the ambush areas, as the raiders would first comb an area where an ambush had been attempted and torture the local population. The goal was to remove the total confidence these raiders had in their security. They had to feel the fear of not knowing if death was around the bend.

Zadkiel now called for me to look again at the Lord as he opens the next seal. (Revelation 6:5-7) "When the Lamb opened the third seal; I heard the third living creature say, "Come!" I looked, and there before me was a black horse! Its rider was holding a pair of scales in his hand. Then I heard what sounded like a voice among the four living creatures, saying, "A quart of wheat for a day's wages, and three quarts of barley for a day's wages, and do not damage the oil and the wine!" "His unexpected civil war now brought famine and a depression throughout his Empire and the world. The available food supplies were the targets of attacks and counterattacks. The rebels believed that by making the Empire's armies starve they could win, which unfortunately was the same strategy of the Antichrist. He could control the money supply. Nonetheless, he lost the ability to control the prices, as low prices on foodstuffs resulted in them being immediately liquidated, and high prices allowed the extremely rich to eat, of which he believed many of them were supporting the war against him. His system was failing and starving citizens do not produce the security and production he needed. Something had to be done, and someone had to pay. The only available food supply was in the Holy Land, and he had to take it out. Lucifer had a plan. Simply break the pact, take the food, declare himself the god of Israel, sit on the throne in the temple, and demand they worship him. The Antichrist considered this only for a short time, as his empty belly forced him to take advantage of what was, in reality, already his. I mean to think about it, if you rule the world and the world has food, who eats first? This was childhood logic.

With the shortage in food also came the loss to the people effectively to fight off diseases, which took advantage of this situation. Neighbors did not care if others in their neighborhood were dying, that only meant more food for them. The poor were now very hungry, as the rich grew fatter. A hungry man has no laws, thus the rich became targets, as their booty was too appetizing to ignore. The rich were being hit from both sides. The Antichrist had to feed his military, which was not only for national defense but also for civil defense. The poor had nothing else to pay in support of his military, as it is tough to get blood from a turnip. The only source he had was to tax the rich, and he needed a lot of revenue, just to feed his standing military. The taxes kicked in, forcing many wealthy to stop production as they no longer have the available cash to finance day-to-day operations. Life in the United Roman Empire was as bad as in the unclaimed lands.

Zadkiel now called for me to look again at the Lord as he opens the fourth seal (Revelation 6:7-8) "When the Lamb opened the fourth seal; I heard the voice of the fourth living creature say, "Come!" I looked, and there before me was a pale horse! Its rider was named Death, and Hades was following close behind him. They were given power over a fourth of the earth, to kill by sword, famine, and plague, and by the wild beasts on the earth." This was after World War III since WW3 could not be attributed to the Antichrist as others participated of their own free will and greed. These are the people, such as in my hometown in Townsend that died. All lots of people were dying now as this civil war was spreading worldwide. This angel rides a pale horse, the color ascribed to a person near death. Prior to the current disposition, actually before the cross, those who did go straight to hell or Hades, which had two parts, one part for God's people or Abraham's Bosom (Luke 16:22) "The poor man died and was carried away by the angels to Abraham's bosom and the other for the condemned." In preparation of the Daniel's seventieth week, Abraham's bosom was officially moved to heaven, as the mansions were now prepared. They needed to be in place to welcome those who arrived because of the rapture. Therefore, Hades now was Hell. Most of those who died were servants of the Antichrist, as the Saints and what was currently called the stubborn were in deep hiding. They were now referred to as the headstrong, because they were pretty well able to justify their view based upon scripture, which was of course in dire need of correction. This is where the active ministries were gaining results daily. Many people will die because of plague or pestilence. The Antichrist used biological warfare as a test on Japan, and although he could wipe out the population, he could not send his forces in order to collect any booty because the island was covered with disease-infested corpses. Later, when Japan fell into the ocean, these plagues manifested themselves to kill once more, this time his people and at a very inopportune time. Zadkiel now reminded me that many other events were also taking place at present, yet we need not to worry about those, as they are being viewed by others in our group. The key point about the killing of twenty-five percent in the population, most of which belonged to the United Roman Empire is that now, a possibility existed for the lost to become saved. Before, even a sneeze could result in immediate capture. More breathing room also enlarged the roaming groups' sizes, which made it possible for more views and ideas to be exchanged, which during these times did not consist of local movie reviews but primarily discussing world events as they were fulfilling prophecy. Christianity was not a boring subject now, but a plan, a method, and a procedure to join the others in Heaven. Heaven was not a concept, which required faith to believe; it was a reality, and the ultimate route to bypass the Antichrist, and the Bible was the 'get past the Antichrist card.' The pale color denotes death. He who stays on the horse is the Antichrist, who will be the one responsible for organizing and developing all the events to occur to feed his thrust for blood. The thing that puzzles me is how Jehovah is allowing this. The anger starts to fill my soul and as my Archangel notices this, he pulls me to the side and reveals to me, "Holly, those who are dying are the ones who killed the innocent and have blood from their hands. The righteous and those who are not evil are being protected; however, those who are not evil will have to choose their road soon. Again, notice that this power is given to him. God is "allowing" evil to kill itself." Happiness returned to my soul as I marveled at the seven spirits of Jehovah and the deep wells of wisdom that spring eternal astuteness throughout the heavens.

Zadkiel now called for me to look again at the Lord as he opens the next seal. (Revelation 6: 12-17) "When he opened the fifth seal, I saw underneath the altar the souls of those who had been slain because of the word of God and the testimony they had maintained. They called out in a loud voice, "How long, Sovereign Lord, holy and true, until you judge the inhabitants on the earth and avenge our blood?" Then each of them was given a white robe, and they were told to wait a little longer, until the number of their fellow servants and brothers who were to be killed as they had been was completed." The spirits of the righteous in heaven see the release of the four horsemen, and know the start of the end-times are at hand. They want to know if their blood is being acknowledged as it cries from the Earth and needs to grasp where they fit in relation to the priorities and knowing they have been wronged want to recognize when they receive justice. They are not being Jehovah to revenge, just to judge, as they want to know when they will have their day in court. "How long will it be until you judge those who murdered us?" Nevertheless, the end is not at hand for life on Earth, as more are being saved each day, and for the justice to be just, all must receive it as still more believers are to be martyred. I now ask Zadkiel, "Why are these Saints under the Altar and not with the righteous? Have they sinned?" Zadkiel reassures me, "Oh no, Holly; they are martyrs they do the sacrifice they gave for the forgiveness of their sins was themselves, thus they are being treated with the great honor of being a sacrifice as commanded by the word, listen to the book while it reveals this gift to you. (Exodus 29:12) "And shall take some of the blood of the bull and put it on the horns of the altar with your finger, and all the rest of the blood you shall pour out at the base of the altar. (Leviticus 4:7) "The priest shall put some of the blood on the horns of the altar of fragrant incense that is in the tent of meeting before the Lord; and the rest of the blood of the bull he shall pour out at the base of the altar of burnt offering, which is at the entrance of the tent of meeting." "Now can you understand why the souls of sacrificed martyrs are under the altar in heaven?" Consequently, as Israel poured the sacrificed animal blood on the base of the altar, so now the Lamb pours the blood of those who died in his namesake before his father's great altar. The giving of white robes to the souls beneath the altar denotes that this one was the golden altar of incense, for the priest kept these garments in the Holy Place under the Law of Moses. I can feel that the heavens are getting ready for some wrath to pour out from the throne. Revenge is a dish best served cold; the throne is going to fish with Lucifer a little longer, giving him the false perception that he is getting away with killing those who have not the mark. I see his prideful boasting walk, as he is now ordering his legions to attack the throne, hoping to take advantage of perceived opportunity to take possession of the throne. The pot is boiling, and the steam will be blowing its lid. Holding back one's temper can cause shaking and trembling.

Zadkiel now called for me to look again at the Lord as he opens the next seal. This is the seal that began to have the unbelievers to start rethinking and move their spiritual debates to physical actions such as repenting, which is not really that big of a deal. It is not like having to win a big court battle, or pay a horrendous administrative fee or even undergo initiation rituals. Unlike those who belong to the Antichrist, no mark is required. Therefore, no one will be monitoring where you are or listening to your conversations. This show is now beginning again, (Revelation 6:12-17) Zadkiel told me that, "It is now time in the fall upon the church of the United Roman Empire." The book began talking once more, "I watched as he opened the sixth seal. There was a great earthquake. The sun turned black like sackcloth made of goat hair; the whole moon turned blood red and the stars across the sky fell to earth, as late figs drop from a fig tree when shaken by a strong wind. The sky receded as if a scroll, rolling up, and every mountain and island were removed from its place. Then the kings on the earth, the princes, the generals, the rich, the mighty, and every slave and every free man hid in the caves and among the rocks on the mountains. They called in the mountains and the rocks, "Fall on us and hide us from the face of him who sits upon the throne and from the wrath of the Lamb! For the great day of their wrath has come, and who can stand?" Every mountain and island was moved and rearrange, which was caused by the surface plates on the Earth shifting. It was impossible to identify the surface markers. Rome and Babylon were shaken severely. As the Earth's surface shifted so many volcanoes erupted the sky turned dark because of so much dust, which made the sun black, and the moon red. The earth atmosphere disperses light coming from the sun but the longest wavelength of red color passes through the atmosphere as it causes the red-colored shadow of the moon. This change in color also occurs when very large volcanoes erupt, which releases a huge amount of dust particles and smoke in the atmosphere. Because the martyrs begged for justice at the fifth seal, God judges the marked inhabitants of earth as guilty. The spilling of innocent blood has stained the earth blood red. At that time, the entire world, to include every mountain and island, shakes. God punctuates this event with a worldwide earthquake, likely caused by meteorites slamming into the earth, one after another; similar to how figs drop in the ground from a fig tree when shaken by a strong wind. These meteor showers, or balls of fire from the heavens had been waiting for ages to hit the earth, yet Jehovah had diverted them. This time, he let them run their natural course as they do between Mars and Jupiter. The dust into the atmosphere provides additional friction as more particles are released into the terrifying dust storms that are now moving dust from Arizona to the Sahara. Marked People now say the great day of wrath has come. The Antichrist is cursed by many now as an imposter. Those with his mark try everything to become free of it. Many of the first to get the mark received it in their arms, until Lucifer later had the Antichrist change it to the forehead. Those who were marked in their arms have now sawed off their arms and lay in hiding beside those who not long ago they were trying to kill. Accordingly, some were trying to find a mystical way to bypass this wrath, as the demons were so busy performing miracles trying to keep as many people as they could so that they could exist beside humankind on the Earth. However, so many people still do not repent. Another religious sect is telling those with the mark of the Antichrist that if they repent and curse Lucifer, they might be saved; conversely, they must immediately commit suicide. We are still waiting for the judgment on these cases, as this is the period of saving unbelievers, and if all these earthquakes do not prove that time will soon end as well as evil, then they shall perish in the lake of fire. You can lead a horse to water, but you cannot make him drink it. You can give sight to the blind, yet if he refuses to open his eyes, he will not see. My view here is not meant to save them, but to look at their situations and verify if enough is being done to justify a guilty verdict for their judgment. So much is being done, I mean mountains are crumbling, islands to include; Japan, Great Britain, and even Australia is no more. An earthquake, at least ten times worse than any in history were proving that something else is at work here. Even caves are no longer safe, except those who are being occupied by believers, who do not care if they are protected in the cave, for if they die, they will be along with the others who were saved by the rapture. Their race will be finished, and that finish was on the high road that leads to the great throne. The Antichrist and false prophet had led most of the world astray, yet the road they were traveling is no more. This road now has a detour sign. That detour sign has the directions to the high road, and the ones who take it are rejoicing, as they are welcomed home. Sure, the ones who believed without seeing went first; however, even as doubting Thomas made it; the doubters that needed those extra pushes are rolling in. They laid down starved, beaten bodies and put on nice white robes, not as white as the ones for those under the altar; however, both had been washed with the blood of the lamb, and that is the credit card up here that is accepted everywhere. The Lord showed mercy so many times in history and Lucifer is playing with this repeat action, after all did not Jehovah have mercy on him when he made his first attempt for the throne. If only his second attempt was not failing so badly with all the war, he is creating in heaven. Lucifer must decide if he should continue taking a beating for the throne, or as he is allowed to exist with humanity now, he could reap a greater harvest of souls. His false prophet and Antichrist are failing terribly. The fools tried to sit upon the throne in the temple in Jerusalem. How foolish, as Lucifer told them, we will get more souls by standing on the corners praising the Lord, yet they would not listen to him. Lucifer now was wondering if this time something might be different. That last earthquake was an actual punch from the Lord and not the usual sissy slap. He wondered now if he should give himself up and plead for his salvation. (Jeremiah 18:7-8) "At one moment I may declare concerning a nation or a kingdom that I will pluck up and break down and destroy it, but if that nation, concerning which I have spoken, turns from its evil, I will change my mind about the disaster that I intended to bring on it." He was too close to a victory, fighting in the heavens and on Earth. Consequently, God protects selected believers, specifically who is known as being "the servants of our God." (Revelation 7:1-3) After this, I saw four angels standing at the four corners of the earth, holding back the four winds of the earth so that no wind could blow on earth or sea or against any tree. I saw another angel ascending from the rising of the sun, having the seal of the living God, and he called with a loud voice to the four angels who had been given power to damage earth and sea, saying, "Do not damage the earth or the sea or the trees, until we have marked the servants of our God with a seal on their foreheads." At the time, Jehovah provided his servant's protection in the holy land, which had remained unharmed by end-time events. The land and the sea are unharmed, even the trees have not been harmed. This was the only nation on Earth, which had not received its surface destruction. This gave Enoch and Elijah a chance to save many souls, and to add to the authority of their message.

(Revelation 7:4) "And I heard the number of those who were sealed, one hundred forty-four thousand, sealed out of every tribe of the people of Israel." (Revelations 14:1) "Then I looked, and there was the Lamb, standing on Mount Zion! And with him were one hundred forty-four thousand who had his name and his Father's name written on their foreheads." (Revelation 7:13-14) "Then one of the elders addressed me, saying, "Who are these, robed in white, and where have they come from?" I said to him, "Sir, you are the one that knows." Then he said to me, "These are they who have come out of the great ordeal; they have washed their robes and made them white in the blood of the Lamb." Zadkiel saw how heavy my eyes were as I now saw even the Holy Lands, without their 144,000 saved saints began to turn as the rest of the Earth. Zadkiel said, "Unto each was given a choice. He showed me those who had chosen the Lord and survive this great ordeal (Revelation 7:9) "After this I looked, and there was a great multitude that no one could count, from every nation, from all tribes and peoples and languages, standing before the throne and before the Lamb, robed in white, with palm branches in their hands." Asian, black, white, Indian, it is as Red and Yellow, Black and White; they were all precious in his sight. So many had made it home, notwithstanding I did not want to see what was in Hell, for the numbers were now so great that Lucifer had to call his legions from the war in heaven to initiate and indoctrinate his new flock, who now would trade all they ever had on earth for one drop of water.

Zadkiel now called for me to look again at the Lord as he opens the next seal, telling me this was the last seal. (Revelation 8:1-6) "When the Lamb opened the seventh seal, there was silence in heaven for about half an hour. And I saw the seven angels who stand before God, and seven trumpets were given to them. Another angel with a golden censer came and stood at the altar; he was given a great quantity of incense to offer with the prayers of all the saints on the golden altar that is before the throne. And the smoke of the incense, with the prayers of the saints, rose before God from the hand of the angel. Then the angel took the censer, filled it with fire from the altar, and threw it on the earth; and there were sounds of thunder, rumblings, flashes of lightning, and an earthquake. Now the seven angels who had the seven trumpets made ready to blow them." Zadkiel now told me that scholars through the ages have tried to discover a great secret in the silence for one-half an hour. He reminded me that John estimated about one-half an hour, which was a comfortable time to prepare the altar with its candles and incense. The incense from the golden censer takes some time to intensify to a level, which Jehovah finds pleasing. He reminded me that the Lord was slow to anger, and thus when drawn to wrath used his wisdom and patience always hoping to save one more soul. The spiritual logistics in mountain such campaigns require some formation. This is a transition between the seven seals, prayer offering, and then seven trumpets. The initial phase of punishment on behalf of the martyrs had occurred, yet Jehovah had fourteen more judgments for his nemesis of the ages. This quiet is just before the next rounds of eruptions. Like the quiet that sometimes occurs before a thunderstorm or in the middle of a hurricane. After Jesus breaks the seventh seal, the scroll can be read and put into effect. This next and final seal judgment is another direct move from Jehovah. This seal then ends with an angel throwing a censer, which is filled with fire, to the earth. When he does this, the earth is hit by thundering, lightning, and another earthquake! I now must ask Zadkiel, "Why are my visions so complex and destructive?" Zadkiel looks at me and says, "The complexity is only in relation to the stubbornness of the Earthmen and the great love that our God has for those who dwell upon the Earth. This era must end and thus Jehovah can have his Saints, created in his image to share his heavens with them for eternity. These Saints had survived an expunging process, or as metals are boiled and remixed to add to their power, such are his Saints. You saw deception as Israel enjoyed its favored status, yet that wolf in sheep's clothing soon grew hungry. You saw war upon war, with a rebirth of an ancient Empire to replace the great Bear, Dragon, and Eagle is conquering the world, as once did the eagle. (Deuteronomy 28:49) "The Lord will bring a nation from far away, from the end of the earth, to swoop down on you like an eagle, a nation whose language you do not understand. You saw the world suffer from famine, as the new Empire lost its power, as did his father by becoming that which the Lord hates. (Proverbs 6:16-19) "There are six things that the Lord hates, seven that are an abomination to him, haughty eyes, a lying tongue, and hands that shed innocent blood. Hearts that devise wicked plans, feet that hurry to run to evil, a lying witness who testifies falsely, and one who sows discord in a family." This caused so many to die and death covered the lands. His wicked plans gave birth to the cries of the martyrs who wanted the Lord to avenge what Lucifer had taken from those who walked the Earth. The days of great judgments are upon the Earth now." Zadkiel then asked, "What message do you take from this Holly?" I then told him, "Zadkiel, I take from it a father who believes in his children that may not be good, yet he continually tries to save his children as they run through so many dangers. I see a thief sneaking into homes, taking from them all he can. I also see others who climb mountains of challenges and sail high into the sky. I see the power of love and the death of hate." Zadkiel then told me, "Our father shall be pleased with your work, and we shall now pour your bowl into the Patmos vessel." I then poured my bowl into the vessel and saw my visions blend into to the truths that were already within. I sat my empty bowl into one of the remaining four holders. Zadkiel then said, "Let us take you to those who have also traveled on this great road through time and the heavens. I now looked over and saw Aunt Rita, Jennifer, and George. Aunt Rita scooted away from George making a space for me beside George. I looked at that open space between them and realized; this is my place, and I could not be happier to be the one that united them. All three were great heroes in my heart. As I sat down in my place, Sachiel and Zadkiel now gave us the good news. Zadkiel then asked George and me to stand up. When we stood up, we heard a voice from above, below, inside, and outside say, "I have joined you together as one." Sachiel came over to congratulate us, as we both were confused as to what had happened. Zadkiel now went over to the Patmos and dropped a scroll into the pool that revealed what had just happened. Aunt Rita and Jennifer currently began to shout for joy. I looked at George, and he looked at me. Sachiel now said to Jennifer, "Please reveal to them the gift they have just received." Jennifer yelled out, "George and Holly wake up Mr. and Mrs. Miller." I looked at Zadkiel and said, "Is that true?" He smiled and said to me, "Mrs. Miller, it is veritable for eternity. You two have found favor with the Lord, and he has joined you. I hope you can understand the lack of an appropriate ceremony, as we are in the process of finishing the ages of humanity." I then looked at him and said, "I so understand and am in awe that our heavenly father knows so much about our needs." Zadkiel now reminded us, "Holly, did not you see those of the United Roman Empire suffering from famine, yet those who gave themselves to the Lord had food. He knows their needs and as he feeds the birds about the sky he cares about the needs of his children." I then repeated over and again, Thanks so much my heavenly father." My mission was completed, and now for a season I can relax with my husband.

CHAPTER 08

Little Running Eagle and the Seven Trumpets

Our group is getting smaller, and I know it is time for me to go. The choice is between Floyd and me, and I want to keep Floyd here a little longer to protect my little sister, Flying Dove. I know there is a reason for us doing this so that does not worry me, because I feel comfortable around Aunt Rita. She acts so much like my parents. My ancestors discovered how to blend the spirits of God with their spirits. They were all on the same team. I remember shaking my head at school when those kids whom I saw going to church on Sunday with their parents, would brag each day about all the bad things that they had done. I screwed her; I stole this pen from the dime store. Oh, well those days are gone; however, those kids are not. My parents told me that in all things we had to do fairly, for any bad thing we would do, all the Indians would be blamed. My people had to fight the difficult demons of hate for what the white people did to us. They learned how to forgive, because of this, I could be friends with George, and my sister could have Floyd as her boyfriend. The road of Love is the hard way, with both sides filled with tears. Oh well, into the Patmos portal I went and am now floating in some sort of dark space. I will have to lay back and show my great patience; either way, at least I am not suffering so I must be going the correct way. There is a light, and it is getting closer. The light is white, so I was always told the white lights were the good lights. I can make the light out now. It is an angel. My heart, wait, where is my heart? I am in a spiritual form now, which I guess since this place is, empty space, which must be good. The angel currently says to me, "Little Running Eagle, I am the Archangel Raguel, and I wish to welcome you to your Patmos." I then say, "Thank Ruguel, may I ask you questions." Raguel answers, "Of course, ask me anything since this is your Patmos." I ask him, "What is my purpose and reason for my Patmos, have I done evil?" Raguel answers, "Oh no, Little Running Eagle, you have done no wrong, quite the contrary; you are being given a great mission, and that is to view and report on the seven trumpets during the tribulation so that possible other people may learn about what happened to your species." I then thought to myself for a second and asked Raguel, "I am from the Indian faith, and should I be here when so many real Christians are available?" Raguel later said, "Have no fear, Little Running Eagle, it is our father who art in heaven that determines who is holy and who is not. Now, look to the throne and see the angels of the heavens so that you may know that our father is here and the grief that humanity has placed in his heart." I could see angels celebrating, and I asked Raguel, "Why do those angels celebrate?" He told me, "They are celebrating another Saint who defeated evil and is now coming home." When I looked closer at these celebrations, I felt love and peace flow through my soul. They were truly as happy as one on Earth would be when their son came home from a deadly war. I afterwards asked, "Raguel, I can see so much power here, why does the father just not take his Saints and bring them home?" Raguel then said, "Little Running Eagle, he did during the Rapture. These are those, which have been saved since the Rapture. Our father had protected the free will of man until their sins became too great and much blood of the saints now cries from the ground. He shall take his Saints, yet for now the wicked must be punished, and you shall receive much vision concerning seven of those judgments. These trumpets do, in some ways bear a resemblance to the seven seals, and seven bowls, with the bowls being more severe as they are the last push by the crown to release these vials on a battle ready spiritual and dying soma world. The seven bowls will be the final judgments upon the Earth as abhorrent sores appear on those who wear the Beast's mark and have his number (666), all the oceans turn to blood and all the living things about the sea die, followed by the water from the rivers, and springs turning into blood. Subsequently, the sun searing people, the United Roman Empire becomes painfully dark, the Great river

Euphrates drying up allowing the second great 200 million warrior armies from the Kings of the East to march towards Mount Megiddo. Then Jehovah declares, "It is done." He has finished trying to save the children of Adam and Eve. Now there is rackets, thunder, lightning, and the ultimate earthquake ever. The islands and mountains are moved. Hailstones drop from the heavens that weigh over a hundred pounds each. These things are to come. At this point, the seven seals have been released, the first four being the four equestrians followed by cries of martyrs under the altar of justice, the initial earthquake of the judgments followed by a short silence in heaven and the preparation for the seven judgments that we shall review for your Patmos. The function of the seven trumpets is to animate each one with the Earth. All have had the great news of the gospels shown to them as commanded by our Lord, (Matthew 24:14) But before He comes again the "gospel of the kingdom will be preached in the entire world." Matthew 24:14. "And this good news (gospel) of the kingdom will be proclaimed throughout the world, as a testimony to all the nations; and then the end will come. The circumstances now are that those who ministered the true gospel have been raptured; nevertheless, the unbelievers have given birth to believers." Messages with words have dulled the unmarked unbelievers that now dwell upon the Earth. Jehovah is now going to give them a clearer vision of his word, so that they may know his power and glory. At present, during this age, each person will resolve whether to worship Jesus or Lucifer. After the last person was making his or her final decision, then probation will close and Jesus will come the second time with his might to Mount Megiddo and time for the United Roman Empire shall be no more.

Those who were too busy to receive the gospel will have time during these judgments to select. Traditions are no more, as a new form a life has formed on Earth. The unmarked hide and run from the marked. The marked now suffer from the wrath of God as they steadily lay their bodies on the Earth and their souls in the Hells below us God will interrupt the lives of people on earth and challenge their paradigms. Their minds will be opened, as so many now search for any who know the words of the heavens so that when they die, they will be saved. The invisible God is making himself visible as they see those of the United Roman Empire suffer. Now they search for the unmarked to beg that they ask the heavens for forgiveness." Raguel now pauses, thus giving me a chance to look below us. I see individuals that walk on the surface or should I say for those marked, crawling on the surface. I hear one old man crying out, "If only he would not have sat in the temple of the God of Israel, and say he was a god. That is when everything started going wrong. Now all in our once, for a very short season, powerful Empire became the fools of the Earth, that the heathens may now call us mislead and pity us. Before each day was filled only with the challenge of enjoying the great pleasures, yet now each starving day only gives the torment that yet tomorrow will be the same. The poor cannot steal, for there is nothing to steal as the rich have given all for barely enough also to suffer one more day. So many have tried to kill the fool that sits on our throne, yet his demons protect him." I turn away from this old man and look at all the hells that burn below the surface and see how the four horsemen of the apocalypse have fed them well. It is such a foolish thing to fall into the hands of an angry God. I see the first angel preparing to sound his trumpet as Raguel tells me the first four will go fast, yet he will slow them down for me so I can capture the events in excellent detail for my Patmos. I now feel a great earthquake. Raphael tells me that, "Outside approximately one year, humanity will be no more and that this great earthquake's mark the beginning and a greater one will mark the time to fight the Great War. This is now the time of the Great Tribulation. This earthquake is felt among all the world, as with it comes strange noises and great thunder, louder than the nuclear bombs that men released upon the Earth and lightning. Jehovah is showing the world his power is greater than that of the United Roman Empire, even at its height a few years earlier. Now there is a short silence in heaven as the seven angels with their seven trumpets prepared for this mission. The first four will sound almost as one. Your hour is now at hand."

Raguel now said, "Stand beside me as the word of God speaks to us through his message to mankind, (Revelation 8: 6-7) "Now the seven angels who had the seven trumpets made ready to blow them. The first angel blew his trumpet, and there came hail and fire, mixed with blood, and they were hurled to the earth; and a third of the earth was burned up, and a third of the trees were burned up, and all green grass was burned up." This was so much greater than that of World War III. Moreover, it was so fast, that none of the United Roman Empire's security network detected this invasion. Many of the standby or reserve nuclear arsenal exploded in their launch pads underground. Their leader, who Raguel calls 'the Antichrist "is on his national emergency broadcast network telling giving this speech, 'my great people, fear not for we are being invaded by aliens from another world. They invade us because the god of Israel has made them angry. They have told me that as long as the unmarked live among us, we shall suffer. We must kill them so that we may live. I also know, through the wonderful angels who love only our empire has told me we shall once again rule the earth. They have given us permission to feed upon the flesh of the unbelievers. Eat now to live and feast later from our future over abundance. Those who go hungry tonight do not love their Empire for they allow the unmarked to eat the food that has been given to us. My angels tell me that until we destroy the unmarked, we shall suffer great tribulations. You make the choice on who lives, do you live, or do the unmarked live." Raguel now shook his head and told me, "He has deceived the world too many times. Now he will have them believe that the unmarked are causing this. They may now believe that since the hail is falling with fire from the sky that none of this world can be doing this." Hail and meteors will be hurled to the earth. Fires will be ignited all around the world and one-third of the trees and forests will be burned. All the green meadows, crops, and grass will be charred. This devastation may be caused by meteors that rain down on earth. Volcanoes may begin erupting. The earth now appears brown as green I cannot find. One third of the crops are no more. This will cause greater problems because the Empire's reserves for grains were exhausted during the occupation wars since the Antichrist needed everyone for his militaries. The unmarked have no grain reserves for they have been in hiding for the previous six years and any fields that were discovered were harvested and returned to the Empire. I look, rather surprised, at the unmarked how their flesh is still strong, yet the marked looked very much starved. Raguel explains this by telling me, "Our heavenly father feeds those who have repented." I now asked him, "How can he feed them when there is no food for them to eat?" Raguel discloses to me, "He feeds them in their dreams and when they pray." At first I wondered how this could be, yet simply looking around at all this glory in his heavens tells me that with him, all things are possible. If he can feed our minds in dreams, why could he not feed our bodies or give to the dust that, which the dust needs to continue functioning. This first trumpet caught the marked by surprise, causing terror in all humanity as never before seen. Raguel tells me that many thought the seven seals were their punishment and that this age had passed. Now they look and see so many of their factories, schools, military establishments, shopping markets and hospitals burning. The hospitals were disposable as most were completely empty and only used as Empire storage areas. The Antichrist forbids any to seek hospitals for medical attention. He said hospitals were for the unmarked. His 'angels' would heal their illnesses, which in the beginning did hold true. In an effort to lay the final foundation for an Empire-perishing move, all the provinces devalued the currency of Rome, which lost the Antichrist his hold on the financial markets. The individual provinces now traded with own precious metals and gold reserves. Paper and computer backed financial tools were no longer used. Credit to Rome was terminated and tax revenues not forwarded. With his military now standing not to be paid, they went back to their home provinces and joined the local militaries. This opened up Asia, Australia, Africa and the Americas as the occupational forces returned to their homes. Asia did not worry the Antichrist, as he had not really had any dealings with them during his world conquests. He has weakened Japan with a plague, which most of the Asians appreciated and any war with Russia, he used Israel as the front, by flying their flags and having them handle the surrender terms. The Russians now hated the Jews so much that they had refused to let the Russian Jews return to Israel and banned them to Siberia to live a short life. The great bear of the north now had a thirst for Jewish blood, and the Antichrist had created it. Now that his military was collapsing, he could only see a Holy Land that had to be destroyed. This tormented him day after day, for he had to think of a plan to reunite in the Holy Land for one more war. If he went down, so would Israel, as Sampson took down the temple filled with his persecutors, he would take Jacob down with him. All his financial markets had collapsed, as so did all production. His people had only one thing now and that was time to die. Fierce competition now to trade for whatever food staples could be found among the burning trees and storage areas now give those who held this unprecedented power. Now, they could decide who ate and who starved to death. In spite of this, no matter how much they received for this food, they could do nothing with the bounty, for what good is a truck of gold, when tomorrow they would have to give three trucks of gold for their food. The world leaders can find no way or plans for coping with this apocalyptic emergency. Rampant civil unrest will be unleashed in all cities of the United Roman Empire, as people suddenly realize that many of them will die of hunger in places, which have never faced food shortages. This was something they never even dreamed possible, for that is why they killed the unmarked, to reduce the world's population so that those who lived could eat and have great pleasures. A complete breakdown of the United Roman Empire and its law and order now only witnessed people stampede to secure their food by any measures. The new pilot Empires could offer no remedy except to blame their former Caesar. Raguel now pointed to the book as it now began to speak, (Luke 21:25-26) "There will be signs in the sun, the moon, and the stars, and on the earth distress among nations confused by the roaring of the sea and the waves. People will faint from fear and foreboding of what is coming upon the world, for the powers of the heavens will be shaken." I simply shook my head in amazement for what was now unfolding in the Earth.

Raguel now said, "Remain beside me as the word of God speaks to us through his message to mankind concerning the second trumpet, (Revelation 8:8-9), "The second angel blew his trumpet, and something like a great mountain, burning with fire, was thrown into the sea. A third of the sea became blood, a third of the living creatures in the sea died, and a third of the ships were destroyed." I then told Raguel that, "I had recently completed a school report on Meteors, especially since many believe they killed the dinosaurs. I learned that small rocks enter Earth's atmosphere just about every day, but burn up unnoticed. NASA claims that an object the size of a car should hit Earth each year and larger asteroids on the scale are expected to hit once every 2000 years. The most damaging meteorite strike in recent times was the Tunguska event, a large-scale explosion that destroyed a strip of Siberian forest in 1908. An asteroid known as Apophis, which is about 1,000 feet wide and has the potential to wipe a nation off the face of the planet in a direct hit, is expected to come within 20,000 miles of Earth within this generation.

The United States had methods developed to deflect this; however, the United Roman Empire destroyed NASA and all its resources. An asteroid could only be described as a mountain in a great ball of fire. I am very much surprised that it only killed thirty-three percent of the ocean life and the ships. The massive tsunamis would destroy most ships in the sea or even in dock and lift much of the nuclear waste that had been secretly disposed in the ocean. A starving world could now only witness at least 33 percent of the salt-water red as like blood. This, ocean bed was already very fragile from the giant earthquake that shook it recently, thus now the ocean bed must have been cracked releasing the mysterious contents from earlier ages into the ocean. Who is to deny that Jehovah put them there for this day?" Raguel then told me, "This is only thirty-three percent, nevertheless if they do not repent, a bowl will be released that will leave not one drop untouched." I then added, "The marked people, who were already starving, just lost about the only source of food to feed parts of their society. The loss of the sea life and much of the sea vegetation is a solid blow to any attempt to feed themselves, as they now do not have enough ships to search the oceans for new species to consume." Raguel then looked at me and said, "You are very observant Little Running Eagle." He continued by asking, "Why were you named Little Running Eagle, for do not Eagles fly?" I told him that, "My father had a vision when I was born that the Eagles would someday fly no more." Raguel then smiled and said, "Your father had a true vision indeed. Are you finished with this trumpet?" I told him the only thing that would be of any value would be to record all the death in the oceans, which I am sure that when any would see Apophis hit the ocean they would know that the price to be paid would be high. Let us move on."

Raguel now said, "Stand beside me as the word of God speaks to us through his message to mankind concerning the third trumpet, (Revelation 8:10-11) "The third angel blew his trumpet, and a great star fell from heaven, blazing like a torch, and it fell on a third of the rivers and on the springs of water. The name of the star is Wormwood. A third of the waters became wormwood, and many died from the water, because it was made bitter." I then answered, "I never heard of a star named Wormwood, what does wormwood mean?" Then Raguel answered saying, "Humanity has named very few of the stars, yet wormwood has appeared many times in the Bible (Deuteronomy 29:18 Proverbs 5:4 Jeremiah 9:15; Jeremiah 23:15, Lamentations 3:15, 19 Amos 5:7; Amos 6:12, and now in Revelation 8:11). The word "wormwood each time is linked with bitterness, poison, and death. Wormwood was a well-known bitter herb not only in the Bible times but also in China and so many other places, its effect will be to embitter the waters of the earth, so much, so that the water is undrinkable." And the book opened again saying, (Jeremiah 9:13-15) "And the Lord says: Because they have forsaken my law that I set before them, and have not obeyed my voice, or walked in accordance with it, but have stubbornly followed their own hearts and have gone after the Baals, as their ancestors taught them. Therefore thus says the Lord of hosts, the God of Israel: I am feeding this people with wormwood, and giving them poisonous water to drink." Raguel continues, "If the Lord made the water of his children poisonous for worshipping Baals, then would he not do the same to the United Roman Empire for worshipping one of more evil than Baal? The great bear got its taste of wormwood as their word Chernobyl means Wormwood. In Chernobyl, Ukraine, the worst nuclear accident for humanity exposed six point six million people to lethal radiation. This prophecy specified, "Many men died of the waters, because they were made bitter." This is exactly the case in Chernobyl. The massive nuclear tragedy contaminated the surface rivers and waters and underground water tables for hundreds of miles. One of the main reasons people have become sick and died is because of the radiation in the waters, polluting the Dnieper reservoir and River, which among Europe's largest water systems. There have also been accounts of poisonous gases and radiation emitted from small meteors that have previously hit the earth. Rivers and lakes all over the world now contain contamination from, acid rain, radiation, erosion, pesticides, and pollution. The giant earthquake and global reaction to the large meteor coupled with so many underground volcanoes spurred by the movement of the mantel tectonic plates, which actually cracked sealed plates from earlier ages, released poisons into the underground water tables. As the former European territory has now been under the decaying United Roman Empire, they knew the Chernobyl that had returned for another visit. Jehovah had now given them some more bitter water to drink. Bitter water also carries with it death for without water, life does not last long. The Earth was now receiving its long overdue portion of the solar system's asteroids, as the surfaces of other planets reveal scaring their empty worlds.

Raguel now said, "Stand beside me as the word of God speaks to us through his message to mankind concerning the fourth trumpet. (Revelation 8:12) "The fourth angel blew his trumpet, and a third of the sun was struck, and a third of the moon, and a third of the stars, so that a third of their light was darkened; a third of the day was kept from shining, and likewise the night." I divulged to Raguel, "I learned in school that the dust storms in Middle America were blamed for the year that had no summer. I remember reading the theories about the dinosaur's extension that the meteor had caused the dust to darken the sky causing all vegetation to die. What makes this trumpet appear as divine is that only four hours during the day and four hours during the night are darkened instantaneously. This will naturally dim hope for a speedy agricultural recovery and add to the increase in carbon-dioxide in the atmosphere, as the green vegetation is no longer producing oxygen, as we have long known that pollution particles reflected some sunlight which most likely will prolong this judgment, as the plants must have sunlight." Raguel then confided with me, "Little Running Eagle, these four trumpets were not to destroy men, they were to show the power of Jehovah and give them a chance to repent before he takes both gloves off for the seven bowls." I looked down over the Earth now and could see some green returning to the American Midwest and even some in Montana. If the Antichrist would have known his leaving would create blessings he would have, for his evil reasons, remained. I am now glad he left my home state, as maybe my newly converted neighbors will prepare for his next coming, which will not be as a thief in the night.

Raguel now said, "Stand beside me as the word of God speaks to us through his message to mankind concerning the first woe. Now the book appeared and spoke as follows, (Revelation 8:13) "And I beheld, and I heard an angel flying through the midst of heaven, saying with a loud voice, "Woe, woe, woe to the inhabitants of the earth by reason of the other voices of the trumpet of the three angels, which are yet to sound!"

Raguel now said, "Listen now for the time of sorrows shall continue so that all may know, this is from God's holy word to all through his message to mankind concerning the fifth trumpet. (Revelation 9:1-12) Moreover, the book began speaking once more, "And the fifth angel blew his trumpet, and I saw a star that had fallen from heaven to earth, and he was given the key to the shaft of the bottomless pit. He opened the shaft of the bottomless pit, and from the shaft rose smoke like the smoke of a great furnace, and the sun and the air were darkened with the smoke from the shaft. Then from the smoke came locusts on the earth, and they were given authority like the authority of scorpions of the earth. They were told not to damage the grass of the earth or any green growth or any tree, but only those people who do not have the seal of God on their foreheads. They were allowed to torture them for five months, but not to kill them, and their torture was like the torture of a scorpion when it stings someone. And in those days, people will seek death but will not find it; they will long to die, but death will flee from them. In appearance, the locusts were as horses equipped for battle. On their heads were what looked like crowns of gold; their faces were like human faces, their hair like women's hair, and their teeth like lions' teeth; they had scales like iron breastplates, and the noise of their wings was like the noise of many chariots with horses rushing into battle. They have tails like scorpions, with stingers, and in their tails is their power to harm people for five months. They have as king over them the angel of the bottomless pit; his name in Hebrew is Des, (Destruction) and in Greek, he is called Apollyon. (Destroyer) The first woe has passed. There are still two woes to come." I looked at Raguel and stated to him, "I think you will have to do some explaining to me on this one, first, show me the star that had fallen from heaven to earth, since I did not see a star fall." Raguel then explained, however asked for the book to introduce what he was to say." In addition, the book appeared and spoke as follows, (Isaiah 14:12-15) "How you are fallen from heaven, O Day Star, son of Dawn! How you are cut down to the ground, you who laid the nations low! You said in your heart, "I will ascend to heaven; I will raise my throne above the stars of God; I will sit on the mount of assembly on the heights of Zaphon; I will ascend to the tops of the clouds, I will make myself like the Most High." But you are brought down to Sheol, to the depths of the Pit." Raguel now told me, "The star that had fallen is he that you call Lucifer. He took with him one-third of heavens angels. Those who were determined to be the most evil were locked into the bottomless pit." I could now see what was like unto a giant volcano shooting a great hot burning smoke into the sky. Then I could see legions of demons escaping into the earth. This was the invasion of these demons, which was so great and dense that the sun and atmosphere was darkened throughout the Entire Earth. These demonic locusts afflicted humans by stinging them with their tails, and the symptoms were analogous to the sting of a scorpion's poisonous venom. Scorpion sting symptoms may include, muscle cramping, twitching, difficulty speaking and forming sentences, burning pain, a feeling of suffocation, rapid breathing, numbness, and weakness. They were given bodies that was befitting to their mission, the appearance of these demons from the bottomless pit had the face of men, hair of women, teeth of lions, tails of scorpions, breastplates of iron and like airplanes, they made a great noise when they flew. The smoke of a great furnace darkened most of the areas over the complete Earth for the mission of this trumpet was to increase the number of people who would have the mark of the Lord on their head. Ironically, all the grass was permitted to grow. I wondered how they could change their appearances so easily. The book now opened and began to speak, (2 Corinthians 11:14-15) "And no wonder! Even Satan disguises himself as an angel of light. Therefore, it is not strange if his ministers also disguise themselves as ministers of righteousness. Their end will match their deeds." At least they did not have the power to kill, but only to torment. When roaming the unmarked people's lands they searched for those who were not saved and stung the living daylights out of them, yet would not touch or harm the saved people. It did not take long for Bibles to start opening and the ministers to capitalize on this proof of the need to repent. Many of those who were stubborn soon realized that this prolonging pain was not to be desired. I actually could see people repenting and as they repented, the Lord's mark would appear on their heads and the pain from the scorpion like sores would vanish. It is easy to get converts when you look around you and see these hideous creatures looking for the unsaved. The Antichrist was now in serious trouble, for his people could not work, or even harvest the new vegetation that was around them, begging to be consumed. I could see many large rebellions now, as the people quickly discovered that nothing could kill them. The Antichrist, the Beast, and False Prophet now lived in their war butchers. Rome was now vacant as the people fled to the caves in the mountains, which did not offer much hope. Some found the saved and chained themselves to them, yet even this had little value, as the demons would attack them and not the saved. I could see people having the United Roman Empire's 666 logo burned from their foreheads and the chips dug out and with bandaged heads rushed to any of the now famous ministers who would show them how to become saved. Even with so much death and wars reducing the number of humans alive on Earth, these five months saw the greatest recruitment of lost souls. If it had lasted longer, the entire world would have been saved. These converted Romans escaped into Asia and Africa, as Africa is the easiest if they could find something to float across the Mediterranean. I noticed that some people, when they tried to remove the Roman mark, the mark would return. I asked Raguel to explain this to me and he spoke, "Little Running Eagle, this is because they cursed the Lord when they took the mark, swearing forever allegiance to the fallen star. The ones who can keep this mark off are those who were deceived or honestly believed they were a righteous people, which was because of Lucifer's great ability to deceive. For no man or woman can escape Lucifer's deceptions least he have the word of God inside of him or her." The angels throughout heaven were celebrating as so many were accepting the truth now on Earth. Notwithstanding, the five months ended and a new tribulation was to unfold before my eyes.

Raguel requested that I look upon Jerusalem. I saw that Jerusalem was again divided, for the Antichrist had united this city, yet when he lost his power, the new kings rushed to control Jerusalem, somehow feeling that this could be used as a bargaining chip in the plagues sent from the Heavens. I saw where the new temple that the Antichrist had built in Jerusalem was destroyed, ironically by the Jews for they considered it defiled by the Antichrist when he declared himself a God. As the Antichrist saw how those who had the Lord's mark on their heads were not tortured, yet those who had his mark was tortured he decided to add another mark, this one being called "The Mark of the Beast by the Christians" and the "Mark of the Reborn Roman Empire" by the Antichrist. This mark was the removal of the receiver's left hand if they were right handed and a new high biological-technological hand, which was intertwined with the brain in such a way that if it were removed, the person would go crazy. If the person was left-handed, the opposite hand was replaced. Lucifer wanted these people still to be able to sign their name with their original flesh, in the advent they wished to sell their soul to him. With no deaths for five months, he was very stressed out, since he had so much extra space in the bottom of his pit, he wanted to put some more souls in there while he still had the key. Raguel lets me quickly view the divine work of Enoch and Elijah as they had saved twelve thousand from eleven of the twelve tribes, with Dan remaining and Joseph getting an extra twelve thousand, and ascended into heaven, the second time for Elijah, as he was the perfect candidate for this mission. I asked Raguel, "Why had they only saved Jews?" Raguel now showed me Elijah and Enoch preaching to the Gentiles and many being saved. The Gentiles accepted these Saints as if they were of their own blood. Even though they saved many, it was not their appointed time to depart from the Earth. This was for those Jews who would not accept anything as being from God until the messiah returned. They treated the two witnesses as the ones who were crying, "Prepare for the coming of the Lord." Jesus did return to Elijah and Enoch and bring Jacob's seed home. Once they ascended into heaven, Israel currently came exclusively under the laws of the New Testament. They could only be saved, as with the Gentiles through the Lord Jesus, who is the Christ.

Raguel now called for me to stand before the book as the second woe or sixth trumpet sounded and the book began to talk once more, (Revelation 9:12-21) "The first woe has passed. There are still two woes to come. Then the sixth angel blew his trumpet, and I heard a voice from the four horns of the golden altar before God, saying to the sixth angel who had the trumpet, "Release the four angels who are bound at the great river Euphrates." So the four angels were released, who had been held ready for the hour, the day, the month, and the year, to kill a third of humankind. The number of the troops of cavalry was two hundred million; I heard their number. And this was how I saw the horses in my vision: the riders wore breastplates the color of fire and of sapphire and of sulfur; the heads of the horses were like lions' heads, and fire and smoke and sulfur came out of their mouths. By these three plagues, a third of humankind was killed, by the fire, smoke, and sulfur coming out of their mouths. For the power of the horses is in their mouths and in their tails; their tails are like serpents, having heads; and with them they inflict harm. The rest of humankind, who were not killed by these plagues, did not repent of the works of their hands or give up worshiping demons and idols of gold and silver and bronze and stone and wood, which cannot see or hear or walk. And they did not repent of their murders or their sorceries or their fornication or their thefts." I could only ask Raguel, "Is it true that one-third of those remaining will die, the way I see it that could be one billion?" Raguel then answered, "That is true, yet remember that before World War III and the tribulation, the world had six billion. The only ones who are happy with this are the four released demons, who is grabbing these souls quickly and giving them to Lucifer to lock in the bottom pit where they have been bound." I inform Raguel, "The book said four angels, not four demons. Why do you say demons?" Raguel then calmly said to me, "Angels are not bound my friend, only fallen angels are bound. Would you think that the God of Love would put into prison his righteous angels?" I then thought about and told him, "Your words are true. Thanks for showing me this." I could see at large army marching in from the East. Raguel told me, "They march for two things, the oil from the middle east and to find women to take as wives." I asked Raguel, "Why do they not marry the women from their nation?" Raguel then said, "Their numbers were too great so each family could only have one child, and the parents wanted a son so their name would live on, thus girls were aborted. They did not realize that for their nation to live on they would need mothers and mothers only come from the girls. They march to the Middle East for the oil that is needed now for them to win back what they lost, which really was not that much, so they truthfully have in their heart the desire for expansion. The Antichrist learned of their march to the west through some of his spies. He sent diplomats to ask them for a treaty. He agreed not to occupy any land in Asia if they would not march on him. He was later filled with anger when he learned that they were originally ordered to march upon the Middle East, and take Babylon and the Holy Lands. Strangely, they only wanted the Holy Lands for the potential brides wanting some Jewish blood in their nation's genetic pools with the hope of mercy on future plagues. The Antichrist could not bear the thought of another nation, not in his league occupying Jerusalem. Lucifer warned him that if he lost the Holy Lands, he would find a new ruler for the Reborn Roman Empire." I now looked upon the Earth and saw so many war jets roaming the skies one more time, looking for any invaders into the Holy Lands. When the Antichrist discovered that the Dragon's army had deceived him and that they were planning to march upon the Middle East, he launched all his planes against this army, with little success. The soldiers, who were all on foot simply hid in trees and spread out so that any attack would use up too much resources to give any benefit. The Antichrist now turned his attack upon the Chinese Nation, bombing their cities and any place that may have people. The Antichrist used his favorite type of chemical warfare bombs on this nation, wanting to keep the infrastructure intact so he could have it for food and war production. These chemical bombs actually started their slow detonation while in midair. This was to obtain a secondary, or delay effect, as when the initial smoke would begin to clear, this layer would backfill it. I can see how this looked like fire, smoke, and sulfur coming out of their mouths. I can understand who one would say these horses had head like lions. Having no technology in 70 AD how else could you explain something going very fast, for only horses when fast and no creature had the stunning power and agility as a lion. I even noticed Nostradamus had trouble explaining the wars that were only 600 years ahead of him, so how can one describe something almost two millennia ahead of him. That is also a problem with me now, how do I explain what I see here in heaven, except to say magnificent, wonder, unbelievable. I can now understand why people are dying to get here. Okay, maybe that was a tasteless joke, created by the extra peace of comfort that comes from having an Archangel helping me. I know that when I return to my flesh in Montana, the jokes will go away. The first thing I shall do is make sure I have the Lord's mark on my head." Raguel, who can read my mind quickly answers, "I will make sure you all get that mark so have no fear, for now just look around and tell you Patmos what you see." I nod my head yes and notice that these killings are happening very fast. I guess this one is not going to last for a long time. I also notice that the Americas, Africa, and Australia are pretty much working and studying the Bible. Asia and Europe are being pounded very well. The demons are still searching for those who do not have the new Roman Mark. All who removed the old Roman mark had it replaced, most against their will, when they had their hand replaced with the new bio mark. No person may engage in any public, private, or financial activity without using the marked hand to gain his or her approval. What little food that was emerging was being tightly controlled. The Bear would not let any who had the marked hand to enter their territories as these marked hands had special sensors that would activate and most times explode with a blast hard enough to destroy everything within a 500 feet radius. The Russians border guards would shoot any entering their territory who had the marked hand. I can also see so many souls being pulled into the Euphrates pit as other demons are chaining them to ensure they do not escape. The Antichrist now ordered that all who had his mark to go to the temples to worship the new idols, of himself of course, and for the woman to have sex with the horns of his idols. He also ordered a mass hunt for the unmarked and for them to be brought to his temples and to be sacrificed. Within one week he ordered these sacrifices to be stopped, because these "Christians would sing and praise the Lord that they were being saved from this horrible Earth and would soon be walking streets of Gold." So many Romans now refused to be in the temples when these Christians were being sacrificed fearing that the temples would collapse. Even the Antichrist now feared some of his temples would be destroyed so he began to execute the Christians in private. I now shifted my view back to the Chinese homeland where the chemical warfare was killing so many. The government sent messengers to their armies to return home and defend the fatherland. The commanders and soldiers refused, saying that there was no reason to return. The government even gave them permission to raid India for their wives, yet the soldiers also wanted any protection that might come with a Jewish wife so they refused and continued to march, mostly at night in the total darkness towards the holy land. I can also clearly see many demons teaching the priests the secrets of witchcraft and wizardry so that they could conjure up more evil to keep control of those who worshiped in their temple. I now told Raguel that I had enough watching these thieves and asked that he bring the book back to read.

Raguel now informed me that the book would be reading many packages as the seventh trumpet calls forth the seven angels with the seven bowls of God's wrath, which will be coming shortly. The book began with (Revelation 11:14), "The second woe has passed. The third woe is coming very soon." (Revelation 11:15-19) "Then the seventh angel blew his trumpet, and there were loud voices in heaven, saying, "The kingdom of the world has become the kingdom of our Lord and of his Messiah, and he will reign forever and ever." Then the twenty-four elders who sit on their thrones before God fell on their faces and worshiped God, singing, "We give you thanks, Lord God Almighty, who are and who were, for you have taken your great power and begun to reign. The nations raged, but your wrath has come, and the time for judging the dead, for rewarding your servants, the prophets and saints and all who fear your name, both small and great, and for destroying those who destroy the earth." Then God's temple in heaven was opened, and the ark of his covenant was seen within his temple; and there were flashes of lightning, rumblings, peals of thunder, an earthquake, and heavy hail." Raguel told me that before the third woe, the last seven bowls were emptied in which meant that time had ended and as the heavens celebrated the time for the last war for almost one millennium was at hand. This shows the great faith that the saints had in victory over evil. (Revelation 15:1-8) Then I saw another portent in heaven, great and amazing: seven angels with seven plagues, which are the last, for with them the wrath of God is ended. And I saw what appeared to be a sea of glass mixed with fire, and those who had conquered the beast and its image and the number of its name, standing beside the sea of glass with harps of God in their hands. And they sing the song of Moses, the servant of God, and the song of the Lamb: "Great and amazing are your deeds, Lord God the Almighty! Just and true are your ways, King of the nations! Lord, who will not fear and glorify your name? For you alone are holy. All nations will come and worship before you, for your judgments have been revealed."

After this I looked, and the temple of the tent of witness in heaven was opened, and out of the temple came the seven angels with the seven plagues, robed in pure bright linen, with golden sashes across their chests. Then one of the four living creatures gave the seven angels seven golden bowls full of the wrath of God, who lives forever and ever; and the temple was filled with smoke from the glory of God and from his power, and no one could enter the temple until the seven plagues of the seven angels were ended." (I Corinthians 15:51-52) "Behold, I show you a mystery; We shall not all sleep, but we shall all be changed, In a moment, in the twinkling of an eye, at the last trump: for the trumpet shall sound, and the dead shall be raised incorruptible, and we shall be changed," I now just sat back and looked upon the Earth. I saw the saved running with great happiness as the angels stood before them praising the Lord. The Saints demanded they worship the Lord with them to ensure they were not demons. For the first time in so many years, the radios were broadcasting again, telling all about the fall of all the kingdoms on Earth. The Reborn Roman Empire was no more. The remnants of China's government were no more. All the kings of the small nations were no more. Jesus now ruled even his holy land. The new colonies in the America's claimed Jesus to be his king, as also in Africa and Australia. Australia now had a large population of saved Saints as when so many ships were destroyed leaving only small ships the masses jumped through small rafts or whatever they could get on, from Island to Island from the Far East to Australia, where the Antichrist did not raid because he claimed it was not cost effective. To waste one jet fighter for a whole day, to maybe get one old lady or many times nothing was no value, for Lucifer forced him to the population dense areas of India and China and now some life that was escaping. Australia was strange in that it first disappeared under the sea to reappear after the meteors. Even though the Battle of Armageddon was so soon to be, I mean like in about one week, Jesus was ruling the nations on Earth without appearing, for he was preparing for the battle to come. The nations that had repented only needed some protection from the demons and beasts of the Antichrist so they could serve the Lord in the open. God opened his temple in heaven, which now means those who were raptured and the Saints of the ages could now worship along with the twenty-four elders. Many righteous had done great works for the Lord through the ages and they would soon be rewarded. The end of time would be soon announced and time would be no more. The Battle of Armageddon and judgments were now to be. Those who hated the Lord would not spend their eternity with Lucifer. The tree of the knowledge of good and evil would now be destroyed, as the Saints would take on the image of God, as Adam was created. The tree of eternal life was placed in the middle of the temples for all to freely eat thereupon. Those who were not saved upon the Earth and were not to fight in the Last Great Battle lay down their body's to rot among the dust and their souls were bound into the bottomless pit as Lucifer soon would lose the Lord's keys. Those who had suffered to be Saints now tasted heaven as the angels were telling them about it. The Saints knew they had not suffered for the Lord, but that the Lord had suffered for them and for their foolishness in not making the rapture. They had been wrong, yet the mercy of the Lord had given them a second chance. Second chances were no more as those who served Lucifer were now going to discover. The human who turned his cheek while they nailed him to the cross was now on his way with the greatest Army ever to be seen in the short history of humanity. My Patmos was now signaling that I had completed my mission. Raguel now took my bowl to the pouring container and watched me empty my bowl. My visions quickly merged with the others as I put my empty bowl in one of the remaining slots. I could only see two more slots that are open. I would guess that they are for Floyd and Flying Dove. Raguel now looked at me and said, "You have done well, and the Lord is pleased with your works." Those made me feel good, that while he was preparing for his second battle with Lucifer, he had enough love to examine my work. I actually did not consider it work, for I was only watching others struggle to live. I could have easily been among them if not for the loving leadership of my father, Flying Eagle. We shall soon once again fly. As I was floating along with my head in the clouds, I almost crashed into the capsule that held my friends. I know, this is not the time for jokes, yet there are clouds here in heaven, so get over it. George and Jennifer start jumping for joy as I enter in the capsule with them. They both are so excited to see me. I understand George since he has been my friend since the first day we met in kindergarten in good old Townsend K-12 School District. I feel for Jennifer, as she actually has no one else to be with as the other two boys are her brothers and they think she is the best thing ever created. She has had some hard times with potential mates so she instead became the super tomboy sister to her three brothers. I know that if I hurt her in any manner, George would destroy me. That is why I must handle her with delicate hands, like now. She now tells George, "Holly is looking somewhat put out by you not being with her now." He does not get the message and instead claims that she is with her Aunt Rita. I can see what Jennifer is up to, yet George has no idea. Jennifer finally gives up for now and returns to be with the girls, yet is monitoring George and me waiting for her chance to replace him putting him back beside Holly, where he belongs. George tells me that they are married now. I think to myself, "This guy needs to wake up. Maybe Aunt Rita will jump in and save the day." As for now, we are waiting for Flying Dove and Floyd to come drifting into our capsule and then see what our next mission, if there is to be one will entail.

CHAPTER 09

Flying Dove and the Beasts

Floyd and I now stood staring at each other. We could read what was on each other's minds. Something was wrong, because no one had returned. Was Aunt Rita involved with this deception? Why would she do this to us? I told Floyd, "We are not going in there until we get some answers. Just because they blindly went in, does not mean we will do the same." I stood in front of the Patmos portal and yelled in, "If you want us, show yourself so that we may approve you. At this time, we heard a noise such as thunder and our cave shook mildly. Floyd then let slip, "I think you made someone mad." I told him, "It is better for them to be mad, than for us to wish we had looked before we leaped." Now a voice spoke through the portal, "Do you not trust in your God?" I yelled back, "I trust in my God and I know he has many demon enemies who would try to deceive me. A voice from a strange portal does not make you God." Then an angel come through the portal and spoke saying, "Then I will have to trust in you to get me back to my home." I asked, "Who do you think you are that we should go where our friends do not return?" He answered saying, "I am the Archangel Haniel." I looked at him and said, "Prove to me that our friends are safe." He ordered me to call their names that they may answer me. I called my brother and he answered me and told me he was safe. I then told my archangel that I would go now, and he said, "Flying Dove, hang on for a minute, and Floyd can go with his Archangel." Floyd then said, "I will go at the appointed time or now if

Flying Dove wishes me to go first." I told him, "You stay put; I will go with my Archangel." I took hold of his hand and we jumped into the portal as one. Once through I told him, "Wow, this is beautiful, now can you tell me why I am here?" At this time, Haniel told me, "You are to collect visions from humanity's ending days and store them in your Patmos, which when completed will be combined with those of your friends. Your mission will be somewhat more expanded than that of your colleagues. You shall share the Prophet Daniel's beasts as they flow through time into his seventieth week." I now told him, "Do not think that when you say beasts that fear comes to my heart, for my father has taught me how to capture and kill many castes of beasts." Haniel then answered, "These visions are not to bring fear to you, but peace to your heart as you see how high he who sits on the throne has worked to save as many of his creations as possible and to bear testimony of this to those who shall receive this Patmos through the ages." I then told him, "I hope you do not think me to be ill-deserved for not knowing much about the Bible, for my parents raised me not only for Jesus but to also love and enjoy the spirits of the world he created that I may also love the Earth." Haniel then told me, "Fear not Flying Dove, for he who sits on the throne has selected you, and his wisdom is far greater than ours. Only he judges and directs the actions of others in his heavens. I will tell you that one of the judgments against humanity will be against those who hate and destroy the Earth. I naturally have respect for how your people have cared for the Earth that Jehovah gave you for your flesh to survive." I then said to Haniel, "Speaking of flesh, where is mine?" He told me, "You shall inherit your flesh again for a short season before time is no more."

Haniel now revealed to me that we would surveying the beasts of Daniel and those in the Revelation. He now waived for the book to appear and read the words from its pages as he began as follows, (Revelation 12:3-9) "Then another portent appeared in heaven: a great red dragon, with seven heads and ten horns, and seven diadems on his heads. His tail swept down a third of the stars of heaven and threw them to the earth. Then the dragon stood before the woman who was about to bear a child, so that he might devour her child as soon as it was born. And she gave birth to a son, a male child, who is to rule all the nations with a rod of iron. But her child was snatched away and taken to God and to his throne; and the woman fled into the wilderness, where she has a place prepared by God, so that there she can be nourished for one thousand two hundred sixty days. And war broke out in heaven; Michael and his angels fought against the dragon. The dragon and his angels fought back, but they were defeated, and there was no longer any place for them in heaven. The great dragon was thrown down, that ancient serpent, who is called the Devil and Satan, the deceiver of the whole world—he was thrown down to the earth, and his angels were thrown down with him." Haniel now directed my attention to the book so that I would know what I was seeing. We see that the great dragon is Satan who has deceived the whole world, and that he was thrown down to the earth with his angels. This red dragon has seven heads, ten horns, and seven crowns. (Revelation 17:1-8) "Then one of the seven angels who had the seven bowls came and said to me, "Come, I will show you the judgment of the great whore who is seated on many waters, with whom the kings of the earth have committed fornication, and with the wine of whose fornication the inhabitants of the earth have become drunk." So he carried me away in the spirit into a wilderness, and I saw a woman sitting on a scarlet beast that was full of blasphemous names, and it had seven heads and ten horns. 4 The woman was clothed in purple and scarlet, and adorned with gold, jewels, and pearls, holding in her hand a golden cup full of abominations and the impurities of her fornication; and on her forehead was written a name, a mystery: "Babylon the great, mother of whores and of earth's abominations." And I saw that the woman was drunk with the blood of the saints and the blood of the witnesses to Jesus. When I saw her, I was greatly amazed. But the angel said to me, "Why are you so amazed? I will tell you the mystery of the woman, and of the beast with seven heads and ten horns that carries her. The beast that you saw was, and is not, and is about to ascend from the Abyss and go to destruction. And the inhabitants of the earth, whose names have not been written in the book of life from the foundation of the world, will be amazed when they see the beast, because it was and is not and is to come." Haniel stops the book here and directs my attention to the beast that was and at the time of this Revelation (95 AD) was not, and that was to come. This beast has seven heads and ten horns and is about to ascend from the bottomless pit and go to destruction. I now asked Haniel, "What is the Abyss?" He waved for the book to reappear and to begin speaking, (Luke 8:27-33) "As he stepped out on land, a man of the city who had demons met him. For a long time he had worn no clothes, and he did not live in a house but in the tombs. When he saw Jesus, he fell down before him and shouted at the top of his voice, "What have you to do with me, Jesus, Son of the Most High

God? I beg you, do not torment me" for Jesus had commanded the unclean spirit to come out of the man. (For many times it had seized him; he was kept under guard and bound with chains and shackles, but he would break the bonds and be driven by the demon into the wilds.) Jesus then asked him, "What is your name?" He said, "Legion"; for many demons had entered him. They begged him not to order them to go back into the abyss. Now there on the hillside a large herd of swine was feeding; and the demons begged Jesus to let them enter these. So he gave them permission. Then the demons came out of the man and entered the swine, and the herd rushed down the steep bank into the lake and was drowned." From this we can see that the Abyss is not a place where they want to go, so it must be like in a prison, as some demons are bound. The book does not tell us how they escaped nor does it explain why Jesus let them remain upon the Earth as they would naturally look for more people to possess." I then asked Haniel, "Are not the Jews forbidden to eat meat from a pig and if so, why would one have such a large herd of swine feeding." Haniel then asked me, "Do your farmers allow swine to graze in the fields or do they give them dirty muddy pig pens? I shook my head agreeing with the pigpens. He then said, "These must then be a wild heard as few were killing them their numbers would increase. Remember that the Romans occupied Israel at this time. The book will now give you a few more passages to clear your mind concerning the Abyss being a spiritual prison. (Jude 1:6-7) "And the angels who did not keep their own position, but left their proper dwelling, he has kept in eternal chains in deepest darkness for the judgment of the great day. Likewise, Sodom and Gomorrah and the surrounding cities, which, in the same manner as they, indulged in sexual immorality and pursued unnatural lust, serve as an example by undergoing a punishment of eternal fire. (2 Peter 2:4) "For if God did not spare the angels when they sinned, but cast them into hell and committed them to chains of deepest darkness to be kept until the judgment." So now the word has shown you where this beast came from, and that they were prisoned, yet they shall be released from the Abyss through the fifth trumpet. (Revelation 9:1-2) "And the fifth angel blew his trumpet, and I saw a star that had fallen from heaven to earth, and he was given the key to the shaft of the Abyss; he opened the shaft of the Abyss, and from the shaft rose smoke like the smoke of a great furnace, and the sun and the air were darkened with the smoke from the shaft." So we can now see that this beast has come, and that he was and for a time while in the Abyss was not. Listen to these words, (Revelation 17:9-11) "This calls for a mind that has wisdom: the seven heads are seven mountains on which the woman is seated; also, they are seven kings, of whom five have fallen, one is living, and the other has not yet come; and when he comes, he must remain only a little while. As for the beast that was and is not, it is an eighth but it belongs to the seven and it goes to destruction." We are told that five kingdoms had fallen, being Egypt, Assyria, Babylon, Medo-Persia and Greece. The one that was living was currently ruling or Rome; the seventh had not yet come but would last only a little while. Now the Red Dragon who at the time was before but now not is the eight, yet of the seven." I looked at him and asked, "Are you trying to confuse me, I was following you with ease, yet now my head is spinning. Haniel now said, "Now, this is why we shall now discover the mysteries as told by Daniel in his second and seventh chapters. In chapter two, Daniel records the dream that God gave King Nebuchadnezzar." And the book came to me and began to read (Daniel 2:28-33), "but there is a God in heaven who reveals mysteries, and he has disclosed to King Nebuchadnezzar what will happen at the end of days. Your dream and the visions of your head as you lay in bed were these: To you, O king, as you lay in bed, came thoughts of what would be hereafter, and the Revealer of mysteries disclosed to you what is to be. But as for me, this mystery has not been revealed to me because of any wisdom that I have more than any other living being, but in order that the interpretation may be known to the king and that you may understand the thoughts of your mind. "You were looking, O king, and lo! There was a great statue. This statue was huge, its brilliance extraordinary; it was standing before you, and its appearance was frightening. The head of that statue was of fine gold, its chest and arms of silver, its middle and thighs of bronze, its legs of iron, its feet partly of iron and partly of clay." Notice the five parts of the beast, head, chest and arms, middle and thighs, legs, and feet. The book began again, (Daniel 2:34-36) "As you looked on, a stone was cut out, not by human hands, and it struck the statue on its feet of iron and clay and broke them in pieces. Then the iron, the clay, the bronze, the silver, and the gold, were all broken in pieces and became like the chaff of the summer threshing floors; and the wind carried them away, so that not a trace of them could be found. But the stone that struck the statue became a great mountain and filled the whole earth. "This was the dream; now we will tell the king its interpretation." Haniel now clarified, "The stone cut without hands is the Messiah and his unveiling the Kingdom of God at his second coming with Floyd shall witness. This stone struck the statue on its feet will exist when the Lord's kingdom fills the whole earth. Now the book will tell you more about the great mountain that filled the whole earth, (Isaiah 2:2-4), "In days to come the mountain of the Lord's house shall be established as the highest of the mountains, and shall be raised above the hills; all the nations shall stream to it. Many peoples shall come and say, "Come, let us go up to the mountain of the Lord, to the house of the God of Jacob; that he may teach us his ways and that we may walk in his paths." For out of Zion shall go forth instruction and the word of the Lord from Jerusalem. He shall judge between the nations, and shall arbitrate for many peoples; they shall beat their swords into plowshares, and their spears into pruning hooks; nation shall not lift up sword against nation, neither shall they learn war anymore." I then asked my archangel, "Why do you have the book read so many words, for if you show me, I shall believe what you say?" Then Haniel said unto me, "That what you say is true, for with this vision requiring many pieces of the puzzle placed in position. Our father, who art in heaven wishes that the Patmos reveal to those who see it that he had revealed these mysteries and that humanity could have changed its destination." I then told him, "I do know that so much information concerning these prophecies was available even on the World Wide Web that could share it with whomever was seeking to find it." Haniel now pointed to the book as it was preparing to read once more. (Daniel 2:37-38) "You, O king, the king of kings—to whom the God of heaven has given the kingdom, the power, the might, and the glory. Into whose hand he has given human beings, wherever they live, the wild animals of the field, and the birds of the air, and whom he has established as ruler over them all—you are the head of gold." Haniel now asked me to tell him what I thought about this. I told him, "Well since a king naturally would represent its kingdom, then the king he was talking to would rule the head of gold. We know that this was Nebuchadnezzar so this must be Babylon, thus would be the top of the statue, and end at its feet, which I would think would be the mother of the harlots in the end times. I know that Egypt and Assyria had fallen long before this so they would not be able to come and thus not included this prophet's beast." I looked over at the book as it prepared to read once more. (Daniel 2:39) "After you shall arise another kingdom inferior to yours, and yet a third kingdom of bronze, which shall rule over the whole earth." Haniel showed me the Medo-Persian Empire that fell to Alexander the Great's Greek Empire that stretched from India to Europe in the short thirty plus years of his life. The book began yet again, (Daniel 2:40) "And there shall be a fourth kingdom, strong as iron; just as iron crushes and smashes everything, it shall crush and shatter all these. Rome with its well-trained armies conquered every part of its known world, making the Mediterranean their private sea. As this statue had two legs, the Roman Empire split into eastern and western empires as each leg eventually walked its own path, dragging the other half in its memories. Constantinople ruled the eastern half longer than Rome held its territories. The book began to read aloud hitherto once more. (Daniel 2:41-43) "As you saw the feet and toes partly of potter's clay and partly of iron, it shall be a divided kingdom; but some of the strength of iron shall be in it, as you saw the iron mixed with the clay. As the toes of the feet were, part iron and part clay, so the kingdom shall be partly strong and partly brittle. As you saw the iron mixed with clay, so will they mix with one another in marriage, but they will not hold together, just as iron does not mix with clay." Haniel now revealed, "The final empire will be a combination of spirits (iron) and human (clay) as they cannot mingle. Lucifer has ruled all these empires, thus we can now see the seven heads of the beast in Revelations 17, as all of these have ruled over Israel. The book now continued. (Daniel 2:44-45) (And in the days of those kings the God of heaven will set up a kingdom that shall never be destroyed, nor shall this kingdom be left to another people. It shall crush all these kingdoms and end them, and it shall stand forever; just as you saw that a stone was cut from the mountain not by hands, and that it crushed the iron, the bronze, the clay, the silver, and the gold. The great God has informed the king what shall be hereafter. The dream is certain, and its interpretation trustworthy." Haniel directed my attention to the stone that was not made from hands crushing the iron, bronze, clay, silver and the gold. I now asked him, "When are the days of those kings?" The book now answered, (Daniel 7:24) "As for the ten horns, out of this kingdom ten kings shall arise, and another shall arise after them. This one shall be different from the former ones, and shall put down three kings." (Revelation 17:12) "And the ten horns that you saw are ten kings who have not yet received a kingdom, but they are to receive authority as kings for one hour, together with the beast." Haniel then alerted me that this represented, "The period of the kingdom characterized by feet of clay or iron. The Lord shall bring his kingdom (the stone) and smash the feet thus reigning in his kingdom on Earth. The ten kings are the ten toes to the feet that are to be smashed." The book was now flashing his pages wanting to add to my confusion. (Revelation 17:12-18) "And the ten horns that you saw are ten kings who have not yet received a kingdom, but they are to receive authority as kings for one hour, together with the beast. These are united in yielding their power and authority to the beast; they will make war on the Lamb, and the Lamb will conquer them, for he is Lord of lords and King of kings, and those with him are called and chosen and faithful." And he said to me, "The waters that you saw, where the whore is seated, are peoples and multitudes and nations and languages. And the ten horns that you saw, they and the beast will hate the whore; they will make her desolate and naked; they will devour her flesh and burn her up with fire. For God has put it into their hearts to carry out his purpose by agreeing to give their kingdom to the beast, until the words of God will be fulfilled. The woman you saw is the great city that rules over the kings of the earth." Haniel now directed me to look into the Earth as I saw a false religion as they cried out, "Let us destroy him who sits upon the throne." I saw saints in hiding saying to their brothers in the faith, "Behold Lucifer is deceiving as did Nimrod trying to deceive those who love the Lord." So many things were happening, yet I now saw another beast come from the Abyss, as the book again flooded my now feeble mind with its words. (Revelation 13:1) "And I saw a beast rising out of the sea, having ten horns and seven heads; and on its horns were ten diadems, and on its heads were blasphemous names." (Daniel 7:1-7) "In the first year of King Belshazzar of Babylon, Daniel had a dream and visions of his head as he lay in bed. Then he wrote down the dream. I, Daniel, saw in my vision by night the four winds of heaven stirring up the great sea, and four great beasts came up out of the sea, different from one another. The first was like a lion and had eagles' wings. Then, as I watched, its wings were plucked off, and it was lifted up from the ground and made to stand on two feet like a human being; and a human mind was given to it. Another beast appeared a second one, which looked like a bear. It was raised up on one side, had three tusks in its mouth among its teeth and was told, "Arise, devour many bodies!" After this, as I watched, another appeared, like a leopard. The beast had four wings of a bird on its back and four heads; and dominion was given to it. After this, I saw in the visions by night a fourth beast, terrifying, dreadful, and exceedingly strong. It had great iron teeth and was devouring, breaking in pieces, and stamping what was left with its feet. It was different from all the beasts that preceded it, and it had ten horns." Haniel now told me we would view time for a while and allow me to record my visions of the seven world kingdoms. The book would tie this into scripture for me. I now looked at Revelation 13 and 17 and the seven kingdoms appeared in this order, "Egypt, Assyria, Babylon, Medo-Persia, Greece, Rome and the Antichrist. I now looked at the statue we had just tried to assemble from Daniel 2 and how they fell into Daniel 7, 8 and (11-12), which was confusing me. I saw the head of gold from (2) and a Lion with Eagle's wings from (7) representing Babylon. I now saw the Breast and Arms of Silver in (2) matching the Bear raised up on one side and three ribs for its three conquered kingdoms (7) flowing into the Ram with two horns (8) and the four kings in (11-12) identifying Medo-Persia. I now looked at the belly and hips of bronze in (2) matching the Leopard with four heads with wings (7) flowing into the he goat with the Great horn and little horn (8) and the mighty king in (11-12) representing the speed and might of Greece and Alexander the Great. I now looked at the two divided legs of iron in (2) flowing into the fierce beast of (7) and the Little Horn from the four horns of (8) and the kings of the north of (11-12). I now looked at the feet of iron and clay, this time seeing how it played out on Earth in (2) to the divided kingdoms with ten horns and one little horn (7) flowing into the little horn waxed great in (8) and the kings of the north in (11-12). Now the interesting part, which we will discuss after the stone that fills the whole earth, yet for now the stone, which was not cut by hand, smashing the ten toes in (2), flowing into the judgment scene in (7) and the cleansing of the heavenly sanctuary in (8) and the time of the end of (11-12) signifying judgment. The final kingdom, which will be forever and ever, the stone that fills the whole earth in (2) to the kingdom given to the saints in (7) flowing with the executive judgment in (8) and Michael stands up in (12) discloses our Lord's Kingdom. Haniel now tells me simply to say what I see and we will let the book talk more, for we need not give prophecy as those who see this Patmos will be able to verify what happened, if they need to do so. I can see the False Prophet and Antichrist in their newly created Earthly Kingdom. Though they can have all, they wish only to take what pleases the underworld or the commands from Lucifer. The empire is called the United Roman Empire for ancestral bragging rights only and to gain favor over the holy land, such as to say, 'we have returned' rather than say, 'we now take you." They have nothing to do with the original empire, except the Antichrist took all of Europe pushes to the Ural Mountains to prevent any future barbarian or Asian attacks. He burned the lands from Moscow to Russia's old border to establish a solid buffer zone in the event an invasion from Asia was to happen. He raided and looted the entire world. He just did not want to occupy it, for fear of diluting the impact of his worldwide military. Any way I saw it, his rule was horrible and without mercy as all in the world trembled him. At first, he had a peace agreement with Israel sealed with a new temple he built for them. Later, when he declared himself god, only to witness Enoch and Elijah to snatch 144,000 from his grasps, he went after Israel with the same hate as with all others who suffered on the Earth because of the Lucifer in the flesh. He watches humanity suffer through twenty-one judgments as he marches those few remaining to the final acts of humanity in the flesh. To me, knowing if the ten toes matched the ten horns was of no value. It only confused me, which I felt was not faith enhancing, however it is not my will but he Lord's will that must be done. Bottom line, the Earth does not look good now and I can hear so many cries from the martyrs asked for justice. I can prophesy that they will get their justice. Nevertheless, I can understand why a God that is so slow to wrath and tried so hard so save his creation now must call the game. If only our species would not have been so evil. Why did we hurt each other so much in our greed? I have always asked that question when I hear the whites and blacks scream about discrimination and prejudice. They should be thankful they were not born Native American. We were massacred for having lived here first. I consider myself one of the lucky ones in that George and his family, especially Floyd has always treated us as if we came from inside their hearts. Hate is such a terrible word. Why has humanity built their legacies on killing that, which is different, yet at the same time hate those who are the same? I can see so much outright hateful murder all over the blood stained Earth. I can understand why Jesus said that if this time had not been shortened, all would die. I see so many newly converted Saints going to their deaths cheering. They have that same fever that the early Christians did in the dead Roman Empire. I looked at Haniel and motioned for the book the begin talking once more, (Daniel 7:8) "I was considering the horns, when another horn appeared, a little one coming up among them; to make room for it, three of the earlier horns were plucked up by the roots. There were eyes like human eyes in this horn, and a mouth speaking arrogantly." I see this as the Antichrist, filled with Lucifer, coming forth deceiving the world. He now had all the power on Earth, for his power was only over whom he could see, for the Saints were in hiding. If they only knew what was ahead. They would beg those who had the Lord's marks to save them. I cannot understand where he who sits on the throne gets all his patience. As I hear, the Antichrist speaks about how he shall give humankind the mysteries of the ages for the god of old had betrayed humanity I become sick in my stomach. Lucifer had the foundation his demons needed to evolve evil to heights he only could dream of previously. His long separated kings who had been bound under the Euphrates were proving to be of more value than he originally believed. I guess around 10,000 years of burning would bring out the worst in anything. I looked over at the book as he now continued talking about the judgment before the Ancient One. (Daniel 7:9-10) As I watched, thrones were set in place, and an Ancient One took his throne, his clothing was white as snow, and the hair of his head like pure wool; his throne was fiery flames, and its wheels were burning fire. A stream of fire issued and flowed out from his presence. A thousand thousands served him, and ten thousand times ten thousand stood attending him. The court sat in judgment, and the books were opened." This is what brings closure to all this horror, and that is this final judgment. The wicked will pay for their evils, as I have enjoyed glancing at all the hells that burn below me. The books of life were opened. No fancy attorney would get them off the charges now put before them. I cannot cry as I watch them fry. The wicked seem to expect so much mercy when they are under the guillotine, yet refuse to give it when the victim's heads are under the same guillotine. Those, who before were tall and proud and without mercy now crawl low begging as if to think someone will spare them. Evil depends on mercy while the righteous defends mercy. The book now flashed its pages again, which means it is time for me to pay attention and for it to read. (Daniel 7:11-12) "I watched then because of the noise of the arrogant words that the horn was speaking. And as I watched, the beast was put to death, and its body destroyed and given over to be burned with fire. As for the rest of the beasts, their dominion was taken away, but their lives were prolonged for a season and a time." The Antichrist is assassinated, and his body burned by fire. His followers knew that the time was quickly ending and were hoping to buy some time, which now was not for sale. They were spared to their appointed time, which was very soon as the final Battle was nearing. The book once again continued its message, (Daniel 7:13-14) "As I watched in the night visions, I saw one like a human being coming with the clouds of heaven. Moreover, he came to the Ancient One and was presented before him. To him was given dominion and glory and kingship, which all peoples, nations, and languages should serve him. His dominion is an everlasting dominion that shall not pass away, and his kingship is one that shall never be destroyed." The one who sits upon the throne now gives the Lord dominion over all that he created forever and ever. Haniel tells me, "The peace and joy that was now flowing among the heavens had not been felt since the days before Lucifer tried to steal the throne. The wars, miseries, and sufferings were to be no more, unless you are in one of the pits." The book once again started sharing his words with me as I could tell these were among his favorite passages, as we now would talk about Daniel's visions being interpreted. (Daniel 7:15-16) "As for me, Daniel, my spirit was troubled within me, and the visions of my head terrified me. I approached one of the attendants to ask him the truth concerning all this. So he said that he would disclose to me the interpretation of the matter." I now felt relief knowing I was not a strange one for not knowing what these words meant. I was really getting confused until I simply looked at the visions and put the pieces in the appropriate places. I can attest to how nice it is to have an angel nearby to ask questions and get an appropriate direction. As I was thinking this, I could see Haniel's spirit begin to glow. Moreover, why not, he had helped me so much. I am now curious as to how this angel explains this to Daniel. Our book ended his temporary pause. (Daniel 7:17-18) "As for these four great beasts, four kings shall arise out of the earth. But the holy ones of the Most High shall receive the kingdom and possess the kingdom forever—forever and ever." This prophecy is between Daniel and Jehovah revealing Israel. From the time of Babylon until the end of time, thousands of nations have existed on Earth. The focus is on Jacob, is even with Abraham, Ismael and Esau, the Elder would have to be considered. The Antichrist had looked at this book while originally making the Old Testament the Bible of the Empire. This was one of the reasons for him to name is Empire, the United Roman Empire and thus try to sway the high Rabbi's that we were truly in the days of old and that the Christians were so far off on their scare tactics that their doctrines should be completely dismissed. The four beasts are four kings of the Earth. Each king is a kingdom and shall be connected with Israel (Holy ones). History reveals that Babylon, Persia, Greece, and Rome ruled over Israel. The book now reappeared. "(Daniel 7:19-22) "Then I desired to know the truth concerning the fourth beast, which was different from all the rest, exceedingly terrifying, with its teeth of iron and claws of bronze, and which devoured and broke in pieces, and stamped what was left with its feet; and concerning the ten horns that were on its head, and concerning the other horn, which came up and to make room for which three of them fell out. The horn that had eyes and a mouth that spoke arrogantly, and that seemed greater than the others did. As I looked, this horn made war with the holy ones and was prevailing over them, until the Ancient One came; then judgment was given to the holy ones of the Most High, and the time arrived when the holy ones gained possession of the kingdom." Daniel ignored the first three and asked about the fourth beast. This kingdom was different in that I was exceedingly terrifying, which could in no way favor Israel. He now asked to know more about this last beast. (Daniel 7:23) "This is what he said: "As for the fourth beast, there shall be a fourth kingdom on earth that shall be different from all the other kingdoms; it shall devour the whole earth, and trample it down, and break it to pieces." This fourth kingdom shall conquer the whole earth through bloodshed, and that would be from what one could know from Israel's view. (Daniel 7:24) "As for the ten horns, out of this kingdom ten kings shall arise and another shall arise after them. This one shall be different from the former ones, and shall put down three kings." Out of these ten, shall arise another after them. This little horn (Antichrist) is different, as Lucifer dwells in him. (Daniel 7:25) "He shall speak words against the Most High, shall wear out the holy ones of the Most High, and shall attempt to change the sacred seasons and the law; and they shall be given into his power for a time, two times, and half a time." Alternatively, until the time the Antichrist's final desecration of the Jewish temple he built them or the Abomination of the desolation. I now saw three years and six months or the first half of Daniels week, or the time of his power over Israel as the children of Jacob continued to defuse the claims coming in throughout the world of the danger that would confront them because of their alliance. The events of these three and one half years are revealed in chapters six through nineteen in Revelation. To better understand the beast we just viewed the book suggests. (Revelation 13:1) "And I saw a beast rising out of the sea, having ten horns and seven heads; and on its horns were ten diadems, and on its heads were blasphemous names." At this time, Haniel revealed to me, "Time for the one that left Daniel sick, Chapter 8." I then thought that if a divinely skillful interpreter of dreams and visions cannot recognize this, even with Archangel Gabriel explaining this prophecy to him, what chance I could have with my Archangel Haniel. Haniel then told me, "Flying Dove, you can look before you and see the prophecy unfold before you, so why try to solve it when it is solved before you? We shall now explore Daniel's vision of a ram and a goat." (Daniel 8:1-2) "In the third year of the reign of King Belshazzar a vision appeared to me, Daniel, after the one that had appeared to me at first. In the vision I was looking and saw myself in Susa the capital, in the province of Elam, and I was by the river Ulai." (Isaiah 21:2) "A stern vision is told to me; the betrayer betrays, and the destroyer destroys. Go up, O Elam, lay siege, O Media; all the sighing she has caused I bring to an end." I saw one who was named Abradates who was prince of the province of Elam revolt and join Cyrus the Persian, becoming a province of Persia and then with the Medes to conquer Babylon. (Daniel 8:3-4) "I looked up and saw a ram standing beside the river. It had two horns. Both horns were long, but one was longer than the other was, and the longer one came up second. I saw the ram charging westward and northward and southward. All beasts were powerless to withstand it, and no one could rescue from its power; it did as it pleased and became strong." Haniel tells me that the ram is identified a few versions ahead. (Daniel 8:20) "As for the ram that you saw with the two horns, these are the kings of Media and Persia." Haniel reminds me that Daniel is writing this during the declining days of Babylon. The ram has two horns, the kings of Media and Persia, with the Medes being the weaker. This empire enjoyed many conquests, including modern day Turkey, Iran, Syria and many more nations, excluding Egypt, which Babylon, Greece, and Rome included in their conquests. King Ahasuerus also deposes Queen Vashti creating a world dominating empire. No one could stand before them. (Esther 1:1) "This happened in the days of Ahasuerus, the same Ahasuerus who ruled over one hundred twenty-seven provinces from India to Ethiopia." No other nation could stand escape their rule when they conquered these one hundred twenty-seven provinces. Now we are looking at the next beast as the book reveals. (Daniel 8:5-8) "As I was watching, a male goat appeared from the west, coming across the face of the whole earth without touching the ground. The goat had a horn between its eyes. It came toward the ram with the two horns that I had seen standing beside the river, and it ran at it with savage force. I saw it approaching the ram. It was enraged against it and struck the ram, breaking its two horns. The ram did not have the power to withstand it; it threw the ram down to the ground and trampled upon it, and there was no one who could rescue the ram from its power. Then the male goat grew exceedingly great; but at the height of its power, the great horn was broken, and in its place there came up four prominent horns toward the four winds of heaven." I now saw Alexander the Great, coming out of the west and conquering all nations. He was young and fast in his raids conquering everything from Macedonia to India and south to Egypt, marching over 5000 miles in twelve years. He was waxed great in that he completely destroyed the Medes and Persians and conquered more territory than they had held. Although not related, he brought with him the Greek language, which made it possible to spread the gospel and western culture. Alexander, who died at thirty-one as also did all natural heirs. His empire survived thirty-six warring generals eventually to be divided into four empires. This is the four horns, one to the east, west, north, and south as the four winds. The book reappeared; as I am sure, it shall many times, and continued with its heavenly words. (Daniel 8:9-11) "Out of one of them came another horn, a little one, which grew exceedingly great toward the south, toward the east, and toward the beautiful land. It grew as high as the host of heaven. It threw down to the earth some of the host and some of the stars, and trampled on them. Even against the prince of the host it acted arrogantly; it took the regular burnt offering away from him and overthrew the place of his sanctuary." This kingdom came out of one of the four winds, thus it did not come out of the goat, it came out of another land. It came after the division and it was much more powerful, as this one was *exceedingly* great. They conquered the south (Egypt), east (Syria) and the Holy Land (beautiful land). Rome crucified Christ and in 70 AD overthrew the temple, which not one stone was left unturned. (Daniel 8:12) "Because of wickedness, the host was given over to it together with the regular burnt offering; it casts truth to the ground, and kept prospering in what it did." The "little horn" changes before our eyes, from a mortal man to an incarnation of Lucifer himself. The focus shifts from the Israelites, Israel, Jerusalem, and the temple, to the "host of heaven" and the "stars of heaven." We are now in Daniel's seventieth week. (Daniel 8:13-14) "Then I heard a holy one speaking, and another holy one said to the one that spoke, "For how long is this vision concerning the regular burnt offering, the transgression that makes desolate, and the giving over of the sanctuary and the host to be trampled?" And he answered him, "For two thousand three hundred evenings and mornings; then the sanctuary shall be restored to its rightful state." "I saw these to be almost six years and four months on the lunar calendar, which would be most of the Tribulation, less the time they the Jews worshipped in the new Temple. Now Gabriel interprets the vision (Daniel 8:15-18) "When I, Daniel, had seen the vision, I tried to understand it. Then someone appeared standing before me, having the appearance of a man, and I heard a human voice by the Ulai, calling, "Gabriel, help this man understand the vision." So he came near where I stood; and when he came, I became frightened and fell prostrate. But he said to me, "Understand, O mortal, that the vision is for the time of the end." As he was speaking to me, I fell into a trance, face to the ground; then he touched me and set me on my feet." Daniel had been watching the Empires of Old, and now seeing the end times became bewildered as any would seeing jets as compared to chariots. Gabriel placed him in a trance so he could bring him to the time of his vision. It is rather strange that he is not standing far from me, although our archangels are keeping us separate. I now think if the roles would have been reversed then there would have been a book in the Old Testament called 'Flying Dove.' Haniel directs me to listen to Gabriel. Three times in chapter 8, the vision relates to the seventieth week. Building a stronger foundation for this vision and beast, the book feeds me concerning the persecutions being foretold and the desolating sacrilege, bringing tribulations such as the world has never seen. (Matthew 24:9-21) "Then they will hand you over to be tortured and will put you to death, and you will be hated by all nations because of my name. Then many will fall away, and they will betray one another and hate one another. And many false prophets will arise and lead many astray. And because of the increase of lawlessness, the love of many will grow cold. But the one who endures to the end will be saved. And this good news of the kingdom will be proclaimed throughout the world, as a testimony to all the nations; and then the end will come. "So when you see the desolating sacrilege standing in the holy place, as was spoken of by the prophet Daniel (let the reader understand). Then those in Judea must flee to the mountains; the one on the housetop must not go down to take what is in the house; the one in the field must not turn back to get a coat. Woe to those who are pregnant and to those who are nursing infants in those days! Pray that your flight may not be in winter or on a Sabbath. For at that time there will be great suffering, such as has not been from the beginning of the world until now, no, and never will be." (Daniel 8:19-26) "And he said, Behold, I will make thee know what shall be in the last end of the indignation: for at the time appointed the end shall be. The ram which thou sawest having two horns are the kings of Media and Persia. And the rough goat is the king of Grecia: and the great horn that is between his eyes is the first king. Now that being broken, whereas four stood up for it, four kingdoms shall stand up out of the nation, but not in his power. And in the latter time of their kingdom, when the transgressors are come to the full, a king of fierce countenance, and understanding dark sentences, shall stand up. And his power shall be mighty, but not by his own power: and he shall destroy wonderfully, and shall prosper, and practice, and shall destroy the mighty and the holy people. And through his policy also he shall cause craft to prosper in his hand; and he shall magnify himself in his heart, and by peace shall destroy many: he shall also stand up against the Prince of princes; but he shall be broken without hand. And the vision of the evening and the morning which was told is true: wherefore shut thou up the vision; for it shall be for many days." Gabriel informs Daniel that this vision is the 'last end of the indignation.' The "horn" is granted a period to rebel against God and to succeed, not because he is stronger than God is, but because his rebellion is a part of the aspiration of God. His reign is divinely permitted so that Jehovah's righteous anger may be poured out on a sinful people and this time is needed so that more may be saved, as they individually emerge victorious over evil. Because of transgression, the host will be given over to the horn along with the regular sacrifice; and it will fling truth to the ground, perform its will, and prosper. Later in the reign of these kings, the little horn emerges from one of the four kingdoms. From a human perspective, he arises because of his own power and greatness. From the divine point of view, he is raised up and given power because the "when the transgressors are come to the full." As the iniquity of the Amorites was not yet full and the Israelites would have to wait over 400 years to possess the land of Canaan, thus the "little horn" was not permitted to rise to power until sin had run its complete progression, and the time for God's anger to be poured out through this king had come. The sins of the Jews are in this vision. This is against the Jews and against Jerusalem that this king lashes his wrath. Through this king, God gives His people exactly what they justify. Arrogant, cunning, and deceptive, he is powerful, but "not by his own power." He is so wicked and evil that it becomes apparent someone is backing him, Lucifer who is greater than he is, granting him power and expanding his pride. The book now supplements this for me by reading. (Isaiah 14:5-6, 12-15) "The Lord has broken the staff of the wicked, the scepter of rulers, that struck down the peoples in wrath with unceasing blows, that ruled the nations in anger with unrelenting persecution. How you are fallen from heaven, O Day Star, son of Dawn! How you are cut down to the ground, you who laid the nations low! You said in your heart, "I will ascend to heaven; I will raise my throne above the stars of God; I will sit on the mount of assembly on the heights of Zaphon; I will ascend to the tops of the clouds, I will make myself like the Most High." But you are brought down to Sheol, to the depths of the Pit." This dictator has the same pride, which symbolizes Lucifer. He will deceive and destroy greater than any before him was, being the master of destruction. His destruction will be all the greater with nuclear, chemical, and biological weapons in his arsenal. Being greater in deception than even Hitler was, he can bring about their destruction when they least expect it. His destruction will come upon him even more surprised than he brought to others, but not by any force of humanity, but because of the martyrs crying under the altar of the Most High. As the ram was subdued by the goat, this "horn" will be destroyed by our Lord, which Floyd will talk about following my Patmos. Then Gabriel told Daniel that these visions would take place in the future, long after his death and asked him not to make these visions known during the remainder of his days. The book now lit and told us. (Daniel 8:27) "And I Daniel fainted, and was sick certain days; afterward I rose up, and did the king's business; and I was astonished at the vision, but none understood it." I looked at Haniel and asked, "How much longer before my mission is complete?" He told me, "Keep your spirit strong for you shall endure." I then asked, "Why did Gabriel ignore us? I have seen his name in the Bible and would have enjoyed meeting with him." Haniel said, "We serve the one appointed to with our utmost abilities. He was appointed to Daniel. You will have plenty of time to visit with him when time is no more." I then commented, "The vision made him sick for many days and he was not allowed to reveal it. That appears strange to me." Haniel now showed me some more visions that I may understand the truth, "True prophets have always told men what they needed to hear, and the time was not at hand for the people to need this message. False prophets tell men what they want to hear, thus a danger of misleading and deceit lay at hand. Revelation was given after the Lord died and to a prophet, even though Jesus spoke much about this. Humanity, when deciding they wanted to hear these words would then receive them and no prophet would be punished for telling this. The message is so period related that too much symbolism would confuse the masses as it did Daniel. Haniel then added, "'Understanding dark sentences', Daniel also mentions that they would not understand the language, and this is true of the Latin that enveloped the world under the Roman conquests. The Greek, Persian, and Chaldean languages were all known in Palestine, but Latin was unheard of until the Roman legions started controlling world affairs. 'But he shall be broken without hand,' is a reference to the final destruction of the wicked at the coming of Jesus which will destroy all those who oppose God and his chosen. This corresponds to (Daniel 2:34), "Thou sawest till that a stone was cut out without hands, which smote the image upon his feet that were of iron and clay, and brake them to pieces." Destroying the last earthly kingdom and establishing the eternal kingdom of Christ. "He shall also stand up against the Prince of princes," was both the crucifixion and the Battle of Armageddon." Now one of the spirit of wisdom guided the word to me that they may provide additional visions and scrolls that I may see that which is to come and the truth, which even Daniel had suffered so to understand. "The end-time Antichrist, the "little horn" of Daniel's Seventh Chapter vision, emerges from among the ten kings that manifest from the fourth beast. The "little horn" of the from Daniel's Eighth Chapter vision comes out of the third beast, the Greek kingdom. Hence, these two "little horns" cannot be the same. One is the Antichrist and the other is the type of the Antichrist. This distinction is clearly established in Daniel's Eleventh chapter. We move through the Greek period in detail leading to the time of Antiochus Epiphanes, one "little horn" (Daniel 10:20-11:35). Then we caper to the end-times to see again the other "little horn," the primary end-time fulfillment, so this designates the first one as a manner of the second. Likewise, the words highlighted by Jesus in Mathew 24:15 "So when you see the desolating sacrilege standing in the holy place, as was spoken of by the prophet Daniel, let the reader understand", "abomination" and "desolating," are used in Daniel 11:31, "Forces sent by him shall occupy and profane the temple and fortress. They shall abolish the regular burnt offering and set up the abomination that makes desolate," in describing the final king of the third kingdom, yet they are not used in the original vision of Daniel 8:13, "Then I heard a holy one speaking, and another holy one said to the one that spoke, "For how long is this vision concerning the regular burnt offering the transgression that makes desolate, and the giving over of the sanctuary and the host to be trampled?." In so doing, it establishes this as a type for the original vision. With these words in Daniel 9:27, "He shall make a strong covenant with many for one week, and for half of the week he shall make sacrifice and offering cease; and in their place shall be an abomination that desolates, until the decreed end is poured out upon the desolator." And its application in the end-times in

Daniel 12:11, "From the time that the regular burnt offering is taken away and the abomination that desolates is set up, there shall be one thousand two hundred ninety days." We shall now look at the Mid-Tribulation Crisis, as our book reads about the Time of the End. (Daniel 11:40-45) "At the time of the end the king of the south shall attack him. But the king of the north shall rush upon him like a whirlwind, with chariots and horsemen, and with many ships. He shall advance against countries and pass through like a flood. He shall come into the beautiful land, and tens of thousands shall fall victim, but Edom and Moab and the main part of the Ammonites shall escape from his power. He shall stretch out his hand against the countries, and the land of Egypt shall not escape. He shall become ruler of the treasures of gold and of silver, and all the riches of Egypt; and the Libyans and the Ethiopians shall follow in his train. But reports from the east and the north shall alarm him, and he shall go out with great fury to bring ruin and complete destruction to many. He shall pitch his palatial tents between the sea and the beautiful holy mountain. Yet he shall come to his end, with no one to help him." Be you not confused, for attempts to link these details to Antiochus IV Epiphanes have great merit, yet they are not at the appropriate time. "At the time of the end" clearly places this prophecy in the Tribulation Period. This prophecy begins at the middle of the Tribulation since the King will invade the Beautiful Land (Israel) after setting up the abomination that causes desolation as the Dragon fights again on Earth (Revelation 12:13-17). "So when the dragon saw that he had been thrown down to the earth, he pursued the woman who had given birth to the male child. But the woman was given the two wings of the great eagle, so that she could fly from the serpent into the wilderness, to her place where she is nourished for a time, and times, and half a time. Then from his mouth the serpent poured water like a river after the woman, to sweep her away with the flood. But the earth came to the help of the woman; it opened its mouth and swallowed the river that the dragon had poured from his mouth. Then the dragon was angry with the woman, and went off to make war on the rest of her children, those who keep the commandments of God and hold the testimony of Jesus." The historical boundaries of the King of the North reached as far north as Alexandria Eschata (Leninabad, Russia), thus Russia and the nations surrounding the Black Sea are involved in the battle against the Antichrist. Edom, Moab, and Ammon (modern Jordan) will be delivered from the hands of the United Roman Empire. Physically, this land is an advantageous place for the inhabitants of Israel to flee. Petra and the lower canyons of Moab and Edom are natural fortresses. They might well be the prepared desert place when the dragon fights again on Earth (Revelation 12:13-14) So when the dragon saw that he had been thrown down to the earth, he pursued the woman who had given birth to the male child. But the woman was given the two wings of the great eagle, so that she could fly from the serpent into the wilderness, to her place where she is nourished for a time, and times, and half a time. The fleeing Israelis will be protected for the final three and one-half years of the Tribulation." Daniel's eleventh chapter has so much more prophecy, however for your Patmos it would add to confusion, so we shall finish by discussing what happens after Israel is no longer protected. The book began talking about the resurrection of the dead (Daniel 12: 1-3). "At that time Michael, the great prince, the protector of your people, shall arise. There shall be a time of anguish, such as has never occurred since nations first came into existence. But at that time your people shall be delivered, everyone who is found written in the book. Many of those who sleep in the dust of the earth shall awake, some to everlasting life, and some to shame and everlasting contempt. Those who are wise shall shine like the brightness of the sky, and those who lead many to righteousness, like the stars forever and ever." At the time relates to the 'time of Jacob's trouble' as our Lord spoke (Matthew 24:15-21) "So when you see the desolating sacrilege standing in the holy place, as was spoken of by the prophet Daniel (let the reader understand), then those in Judea must flee to the mountains; the one on the housetop must not go down to take what is in the house; the one in the field must not turn back to get a coat. Woe to those who are pregnant and to those who are nursing infants in those days! Pray that your flight may not be in winter or on a Sabbath. For at that time there will be great suffering, such as has not been from the beginning of the world until now, no, and never will be." I looked out upon the Earth and saw great suffering, unequaled from the beginning of the world and that shall never again be equaled in Israel. The other nations had suffered like this ever since the beginning of World War III. Michael now appears to give the protection that is required for Israel to flee into the mountains and deserts of Moab and Edom. Two-thirds of Israel will die during this crazed revenge attack by the Antichrist as he struggles to keep them from the protection of Michael and the ministry of Enoch and Elijah. (Zechariah 13:8) "In the whole land, says the Lord, two-thirds shall be cut off and perish, and one-third shall be left alive." To Daniel he was told to once again (Daniel 12:4), "But you, Daniel, keep the words secret and the book sealed until the time of the end. Many shall be running back and forth, and knowledge shall increase." Yet at Patmos John was told (Revelation 22:10) "And he said to me, "Do not seal up the words of the prophecy of this book, for the time is near." Therefore, both books could be opened at the appointed time to open had come. Many shall run back and forth attest to air, ship, train, bus travel. Knowledge has indeed increased with mass computers and the World Wide Web. The key here does not pertain to all knowledge, but specifically to that knowledge that could appreciate and understand this sealed knowledge, although all knowledge increased tremendously. Computers and advanced libraries do not guarantee understanding prophecy, (Amos 8:12) "They shall wander from sea to sea, and from north to east; they shall run to and fro, seeking the word of the Lord, but they shall not find it." Having eyes some cannot see and having ears, they cannot hear. As Pharaoh's heart was made hard, so will be the heart of the wicked. During the Tribulation Period, Daniel and Revelation will become open books. There predictions will be unsealed because of their fulfillment. These prophecies will become clearer to those living through the events as so many saved will use these words to save others for Christ. The wicked will deny these words, yet the wise will treasure them, to the extent that so many march to their horrifying death with their hearts belonging to the Lord. Haniel looked at me and asked if I was ready for Gabriel's revelations. I begged Haniel if he could spare me this, and with a large laugh, he told me, "Your work is done for now child, let us take you to be with the others in your journey." Soon, as we dashed around so much activity around the throne as the ages were unfolding I saw Aunt Rita. As we were approaching I noticed a large group of angels celebrating and I asked Haniel, "May I witness this?" We stopped as he took was within the group. Archangels have a special privilege, which allows them to go and come in peace and ease. I saw humans, with destroyed flesh covered in blood walking on a golden path and they were smiling. They formed a line as their flesh became no more and their spirit's appeared. I then saw other spirits join them. Haniel told me they were their family members. They were singing praises to the Lord as angels began to guide them to the altar, where they were staying until they had received justice. These spirits, which joined them who had not lived during the Tribulation returned to their stations. I asked Haniel, "Do all Saint's arrive in heaven in their flesh?" He told me,

"No Flying Dove, only those who die during the tribulation at the hands or by order of the Antichrist so that their flesh may not be a part of the eternal dust of the Earth. Sin had killed them and as such, death could not have a grip on their flesh." I could see they were filled with great joy, so I motioned for us to continue to my destination. Soon, I heard my brother start to shout for joy. I was soon standing before the Patmos pool as Haniel handed me my Patmos to pour into the basin. I saw its contents go into the basin and that which was in it turned bright yellow. I asked Haniel, "Why did my Patmos change the color of that within the basin?" He told me, "Because yours included the victory of the righteous from Daniel's twelfth chapter." I then put my container in one of the two remaining slots. I would guess the remaining slot is for Floyd. I now joined my group as Haniel bid me farewell. He was a good tour guide and patient with my confusion. I now began telling my group about all the beasts that I had witnessed throughout the times of my Patmos. I had received a challenging Patmos, yet with the help of Haniel I felt good about that which our Patmos would be able to show those in the far future. My message was how Jehovah had warned humanity so many times about the things, which were to come. I am just so happy that the one who sits on the throne knows the hearts of man and judges accordingly. Now I wondered, after Floyd arrives what would happen next. I should have asked Haniel.

CHAPTER 10

Floyd in the Valley of Jehoshaphat

Even though it has only been a few minutes since everyone has been gone, it might as well have been years. I am all alone in this crazy empty hole in the ground. I cannot believe that this is really happening. That hole is staring at me wanting to pull me deep inside of it. Each little chilly creek in this place sends chills up and down my back. Unlike George, I have seen what these evil killers are doing up on the surface and like a plague, I feel that they can creep in through any possible hole, then if not physically possible then by some form of magic, especially since these woods are so packed with mystics and enchanters. I should jump in now or should I? I really do not know for sure. I know that Flying Dove and Jennifer are in there and those are my two greatest loves in my life. I hope that my mission is a success so that Flying Dove will be proud of me. We still have not gotten used to being able publicly to reveal our relationship. However, with her parents gone and Little Running Eagle best friends with George, I felt it was time for me to start taking care of her. She is so smart and strong. She did not scream as some of the other girls did when the soldiers were raiding Townsend. Some of the junk we saw in our small town was terrifying. When they would pull people's eyes out and squash them with their feet even made me quench. Yet Flying Dove would remain calm, more concerned about staying safe and calm.

She was strong by helping Jessica when we made our journey to Aunt Rita's cabin. I see something moving in our Patmos portal now. I guess it is time for me to jump, so if this is the end, so be it. If it is . . . Wow, there is an angel waving at me. I am a spirit. This is cool as soon as I figure out how maneuver my soul. Got it, now I shall see what that angel wants, "Excuse me, can you help me?" The angel looks at me and says, "I am the Archangel Chamuel and I have been sent by the most high to serve you during your visions for your Patmos. I shall guide you so that the truth may be known for the ages by the ages." I then said, "I am Floyd and what truth do I search for?" Chamuel now told me, "You shall learn the truth about the end of humanity and enemies of he who sits upon the crown. We shall justify for the ages what had to be done and why it had to be done." I then asked Chamuel, "Will you tell me how it ends?" Chamuel said, "The book will tell you and the visions will show you. You must forget all that you have heard about the end of Age of Good and Evil. Tell no being who has flesh what you have seen, for if you do, many will persecute you." Watch as the book from the most high, which he has shared with humanity, shall tell us its holy words. A saw a giant beautiful book with living words inside it and wells of love cooling its pages as so many angels did bow as it passed them saying, "Glory to the Word of the Most High." The book appeared and opened up and I heard these words concerning the end times, (Matthew 24:21-22) "For at that time there will be great suffering, such as has not been from the beginning of the world until now, no, and never will be. And if those days had not been cut short, no one would be saved; but for the sake of the elect those days will be cut short." I then spoke to Chamuel, "I believe the times of suffering have already begun, I do have comfort in knowing that some will be saved; however, that also says that because of the time it took some were lost." Chamuel now suggested that we take the first of so many looks at what was to come concerning the end of Age of Good and Evil, as the book began again in a rather joyous tone. (Revelation 16:12-21) "The sixth angel poured his bowl on the great river Euphrates, and its water was dried up in order to prepare the way for the kings from the east. And I saw three foul spirits like frogs coming from the mouth of the dragon, from the mouth of the beast, and from the mouth of the false prophet. These are demonic spirits, performing signs, who go abroad to the kings of the whole world, to assemble them for battle on the great day of God the Almighty. "See, I am coming like a thief! Blessed is the one who stays awake and is clothed, not going about naked and exposed to shame." And they assembled them at the place that in Hebrew is called Harmagedon. The seventh angel poured his bowl into the air, and a loud voice came out of the temple, from the throne, saying, "It is done!" And there came flashes of lightning, rumblings, peals of thunder, and a violent earthquake, such as had not occurred since people were upon the earth, so violent was that earthquake. The great city was split into three parts, and the cities of the nation's fell. God remembered great Babylon and gave her the wine-cup of the fury of his wrath. And every island fled away, and no mountains were to be found; and huge hailstones, each weighing about a hundred pounds, dropped from heaven on people, until they cursed God for the plague of the hail, so fearful was that plague." I then asked Chamuel, "Should that not have said Armageddon as it is written in the Bible." Chamuel now answered, "No Floyd, the word Armageddon does not appear in the Bible, although that does not make this false, for there shall actually be two battles during that hour, one end humanity and the other to bind Lucifer and his followers. The site where the "Battle of Armageddon" will take place is called the Valley of Jehoshaphat, because it was there that God destroyed Israel's enemies (2 Chronicles 20:20-26). Ironically, the Antichrist will set out in a great rage to destroy and annihilate many, but his army will be struck down by a sharp sword out of the mouth of the rider on the white horse, (Revelation 19:11-16) "Then I saw heaven opened, and there was a white horse! Its rider is called Faithful and True, and in righteousness he judges and makes war. His eyes are like a flame of fire, and on his head are many diadems; and he has a name inscribed that no one knows but himself. He is clothed in a robe dipped in blood, and his name is called The Word of God. And the armies of heaven, wearing fine linen, white and pure, were following him on white horses. From his mouth comes a sharp sword with which to strike down the nations, and he will rule them with a rod of iron; he will tread the wine press of the fury of the wrath of God the Almighty. On his robe and on his thigh he has a name inscribed, "King of kings and Lord of lords." Chamuel revealed, "Floyd notice these are the armies of heaven and the nations he will strike down in will rule them with a rod of iron. He is fighting Lucifer and the demonic kings that rule under him, that he unlocked their prison with the key, freeing them from under the Euphrates when the sun dried it. From all that is known of eternity for the Saints in Heaven, he will not rule with a rod of iron, but with love and peace. The bottomless pit will be ruled with the rod of iron. Humanity will be no more, as Lucifer destroys all who follow him as his kingdom's search the Earth for saints, which are all with the Lord in White Robes riding white horses. God remembered great Babylon and gave her the wine-cup of the fury of his wrath. Nimrod's Babylon is the mother city of evil, (Revelation 17:5) "and on her forehead was written a name, a mystery: "Babylon the great, mother of whores and of earth's abominations." She receives God's wrath. And a loud voice came out of the temple, from the throne, saying, "It is done!" Every island fled away, and no mountains were to be found. All land on Earth is islands. The continents are islands, thus land is no more, not even the mountains. When it is done, the Age of Good and Evil is no more for those who know evil are kept in the kingdoms at the four corners of the Earth. The Saints are under the love of He who sits on the Throne, as the kingdoms at the four corners of the Earth may never harm or touch until the appointed time. There are so many versions and details that so many great men of God have advanced through the ages; however, it all boils down to evil lost and evil is punished as they may not share in the fruits of He who sits on the Throne. The Saints merely enjoy what Jehovah has created for them, as he now lives with the test and true images that he created. We will review that for the Patmos when you are with your group. Now, we shall hear some more from the book about humanity's end and see some more visions." I asked my archangel, "How can the book be so joyous when it reveals this wrath?" Chamuel divulged to me, "When you have seen the suffering through the ages caused by Lucifer, you also would rejoice when learning that evil will now agonize." I then questioned Chamuel, "Why did you not show me the spiritual battle between the Lord and Lucifer?" Chamuel now told me, "Lucifer assembled his entire kingdom, and he who rode the white horse was called The Word of God, which of course was our Lord, only with one modification. God had given him the power of his word, thus Jesus simply spoke the word, and Lucifer and the remainder of his unholy trinity were bound for 1,000 years in the bottomless pit. All those whom they had deceived, including and all the devils, and all the demons, and all evil souls, and in fact, any soul, even if still in the flesh, that did not have the mark of God on its forehead were given to the four kingdoms on the corners of the Earth and Gog and Magog. The Lord gave the key back to He who sits on the Throne. The Word imprisoned all evil." I looked and now saw the book preparing to give us some more words concerning the reaping the Earth's harvest (Revelation 14:14-20). "Then I looked, and there was a white cloud, and seated on the cloud was one like the Son of Man, with a golden crown on his head, and a sharp sickle in his hand! Another angel came out of the temple, calling with a loud voice to the one who sat on the cloud, "Use your sickle and reap, for the hour to reap has come, because the harvest of the earth is fully ripe." So the one who sat on the cloud swung his sickle over the earth, and the earth was reaped. Then another angel came out of the temple in heaven, and he too had a sharp sickle. Then another angel came out from the altar, the angel who has authority over fire, and he called with a loud voice to him who had the sharp sickle, "Use your sharp sickle and gather the clusters of the vine of the earth, for its grapes are ripe." So the angel swung his sickle over the earth and gathered the vintage of the earth, and he threw it into the great winepress of the wrath of God. And the wine press was trodden outside the city, and blood flowed from the wine press, as high as a horse's bridle, for a distance of about two hundred miles." Chamuel now directed me to these words, "was one like the Son of Man," telling me that this is the famous Battle of Armageddon that humanity fancies. There is not really much of a fight here; any human in this battle for Lucifer was nothing more than grapes being harvested. Chamuel now asked me to view, "swung his sickle over the Earth, and gathered the vintage of the Earth." I marveled at what I was seeing and asked Chamuel, "Where is all this blood coming from?" Chamuel spoke, "I will tell you a great mystery. Starting with Abel, every person who ever died because of evil their blood was saved inside the depths of the Earth. Jehovah brought this blood up to the surface and oceans for some of his judgments, then returned it to his throne collecting every drop to destroy his enemies in the flesh in the Valley of Jehoshaphat. Look now at that area, which is the distance from Dan to Beersheba. The height of the initial flow of blood will be astonishing. Most likely, the flow of blood will not taper down as it flows from the Valley of Jezreel, into the rift of the Jordan Valley, and onward to the Dead Sea and then will flood to the west, once again turning the Mediterranean Sea to blood. This blood shall remain so that it may avenge the rotten dead flesh of the evil, so that the wild beasts may be feasting at the appointed time. First, the blood taken back by he who sets upon the throne, so that he may never forget the love and suffering that his images endured for his root." Chamuel now said, "The appointed time is at hand," and the book spoke. (Revelation 19:17-18) And I saw an angel standing in the sun; and he cried with a loud voice, saying to all the fowls that fly in the midst of heaven, Come and gather yourselves together unto the supper of the great

God; That ye may eat the flesh of kings, and the flesh of captains, and the flesh of mighty men, and the flesh of horses, and of them that sit on them, and the flesh of all men, both free and bond, both small and great." This is the end of humanity, as he became food for the birds. I now beheld more visions, as I heard the sixth trumpet sound and the war began. I saw all nations gathered against Israel. I saw all the dead saints resurrected and fighting the spiritual war in the heavens. The living saints were given their heavenly bodies and joined the resurrected to watch the Word be spoken by him who rode the white horse. The son of man then directed that the Seventh trumpet be blown and Armageddon was in a flash fought and won by Jesus Christ. I saw no Saints fighting with him. Chamuel then reminded me that the Bible never spoke of Jesus placing his Saints in a fight. Jesus then cast the Beast and False Prophet and all his kingdoms into hell. I now beheld another vision as the book began to speak, (Zechariah 14:2-9) "For I will gather all the nations against Jerusalem to battle, and the city shall be taken and the houses looted and the women raped; half the city shall go into exile, but the rest of the people shall not be cut off from the city. Then the LORD will go forth and fight against those nations as when he fights on a day of battle. On that day his feet shall stand on the Mount of Olives, which lies before Jerusalem on the east; and the Mount of Olives shall be split in two from east to west by a very wide valley; so that one half of the Mount shall withdraw northward, and the other half southward. And you shall flee by the valley of the LORD's mountain, to the valley between the mountains shall reach to Azal; and you shall flee as you fled from the earthquake in the days of King Uzziah of Judah. Then the LORD my God will come and all the holy ones with him. On that day, there shall not be either cold or frost. And there shall be continuous day (it is known to the LORD), not day and not night, for at evening time there shall be light. On that day, living waters shall flow out from Jerusalem, half of them to the eastern sea and half of them to the western sea; it shall continue in summer as in winter. And the LORD will become king over all the earth; on that day the LORD will be one and his name one." Chamuel now told me, "I noticed you looked strange when I said the Lord would fight this battle, as the message reveals, "Then the LORD will go forth and fight against those nations as when he fights on a day of battle." The world will avenge Jerusalem, however the Lord will win the battle, and into eternity as on that day living waters shall flow out from Jerusalem, there will only be day and one season. As Babylon is no more, so her curse shall no more be upon the Saints as all will speak the heavenly language as once did Adam and Eve, (Zephaniah 3:8-9) Therefore wait for me, says the Lord, for the day when I arise as a witness. For my decision is to gather nations, to assemble kingdoms, to pour out upon them my indignation, all the heat of my anger; for in the fire of my passion all the earth shall be consumed. At that time I will change the speech of the peoples to a pure speech, that all of them may call on the name of the Lord and serve him with one accord." At the time all the earth is consumed he will change to speech of the peoples to a pure speech so they can serve him with one accord. The book now adds. (Psalm 46:9-10) "He makes wars cease to the end of the earth; he breaks the bow, and shatters the spear; he burns the shields with fire. "Be still, and know that I am God! I am exalted among the nations; I am exalted in the earth." He will stop the wars at the end of the Earth and will be the exalted one. Chamuel now asked me if I thought we should review this with some more detail. I agreed and began by asking him about the battle of Armageddon and what happens afterwards. The book began by adding, (Revelation 16:16) "And they assembled them at the place that in Hebrew is called Harmagedon." (Revelation 20:1-10) The thousand years and Lucifer's doom. "Then I saw an angel coming down from heaven, holding in his hand the key to the bottomless pit and a great chain. He seized the dragon, that ancient serpent, who is the Devil and Satan, and bound him for a thousand years, and threw him into the pit, and locked and sealed it over him, so that he would deceive the nations no more, until the thousand years were ended. After that, he must be let out for a little while. Then I saw thrones, and those seated on them were given authority to judge. I also saw the souls of those who had been beheaded for their testimony to Jesus and for the word of God. They had not worshiped the beast or its image and had not received its mark on their foreheads or their hands. They came to life and reigned with Christ a thousand years. (The rest of the dead did not come to life until the thousand years were ended.) This is the first resurrection. Blessed and holy are those who share in the first resurrection. Over these, the second death has no power, but they will be priests of God and of Christ, and they will reign with him a thousand years. When the thousand years are ended, Satan will be released from his prison and will come out to deceive the nations at the four corners of the earth, Gog and Magog, in order to gather them for battle; they are as numerous as the sands of the sea. They marched up over the breadth of the earth and surrounded the camp of the saints and the beloved city. And fire came down from heaven and consumed them. And the devil who had deceived them was thrown into the lake of fire and sulfur, where the beast and the false prophet were, and they will be tormented day and night forever and ever." I then asked, "Did not we say that the Saints of the Tribulation would be in heaven with the other saints?" Chamuel then said, "We have simply divided the good from the evil, they all end up together as we shall listen once more. "They came to life and reigned with Christ a thousand years. (The rest of the dead did not come to life until the thousand years were ended.) This is the first resurrection. Blessed and holy are those who share in the first resurrection. Over these, the second death has no power, but they will be priests of God and of Christ, and they will reign with him a thousand years." Blessed are the holy who share in the first resurrection for they will reign with him a thousand years. The rest of the dead did not come to life until the thousand years were ended. Coming to life is dwelling in the New Jerusalem (Beloved City) and the camp of the Saints. The evil trinity is released. Lucifer now must collect his kingdoms Gog and Magog from the four corners of the Earth and once more deceive them, taking them into battle against the Lord. Lucifer would have only one reason for war and that would be to win the throne of God. He will first try once more to prove that his species is greater than Adam's, yet of course fail again. When they went to attack the Saints, fire came down from heaven and consumed them. The unholy trinity is cast into the bottomless pit for eternity. Consumed is defined as, "to do away with completely." They were as numerous as the sands of the sea and are no more, which contradicted so much doctrine that was on the Earth. This should not have mattered in that the real punishment sees the Saints being blessed in which by being at the four corners of the Earth they absolutely did see them. The book now wished to add some more clarity to the great mysteries that were unfolding also considering that I do not know all the factors that may be at play in this apocalyptic period. The book now changed its cover as Chamuel told me, "Fear not Floyd, you shall hear another version of the holy words so that your understanding will be greater." The book now made known, "(Revelation 16:12) "The sixth angel poured out his bowl on the great river, the Euphrates; and its water was dried up, so that the way would be prepared for the kings from the east." As we had just seen in Lucifer's final defeat, he gathered the kings from the four corners of the Earth. They also had been active in the ending of the Age of Good and Evil. The Euphrates also had to be dried so the kings who had been bound in the pit could be released. The book spoke again. (Revelation 16:13-14) "And I saw coming out of the mouth of the dragon and out of the mouth of the [Leopard] beast and out of the mouth of the false prophet, three unclean spirits like frogs; for they are spirits of demons, performing signs, which go out to the kings of the whole world, to gather them together for the war of the great day of God, the Almighty." This is the unholy trinity gathers the kings for the spiritual battle of Armageddon, just as they did at the end of the 1000 years against the Saints. It is amazing to me that after 1000 years they would use the same strategy. They must have done some amazing signs to get these fallen angels to challenge the throne again. Their deception was so great they believed this time would result in a victory. The book asked me to reconsider this passage again, "(Revelation 16:16-17) "And they gathered them together to the place which in Hebrew is called Har-Magedon. Then the seventh angel poured out his bowl upon the air, and a loud voice came out of the temple from the throne, saying, "It is done." We see here that the seventh bowl was dumped into the air. The last three were directed towards the unholy trinity, Air, Euphrates River, and the Throne of the Beast. This allowed them, like their earlier Trumpets to be executed without regard to the constraints of time. The first four were against the Earth as they were poured on the land, sea, rivers, and sun. The argument that the sixth bowl was poured to allow a human army to cross the Euphrates has no bearing, for the River would have been low because of the scorching sun, which is hot even during normal cycles, yet to intensify the sun would have drained it the from Turkey to the Tigris. In addition, two of the four against man involved blood, which is life in the flesh.

The book now continued (Revelation 17:12-13). "The ten horns which you saw are ten kings who have not yet received a kingdom, but they receive authority as kings with the beast for one hour. These have one purpose, and they give their power and authority to the beast." The ten spiritual kings will have a kingdom only for the last battle and only for the purpose of this last battle.

The book has now added an event that was not related to this final battle, but would be one that I would know, (Zechariah 14:12) "Now this will be the plague with which the LORD will strike all the peoples who have gone to war against Jerusalem; their flesh will rot while they stand on their feet, and their eyes will rot in their sockets, and their tongue will rot in their mouth." This was World War III that I had lived through. Even though the United States had not went to war against Jerusalem, we had failed to protect them as we had in the past and been blessed for doing so. As Israel was chastised in the past for backsliding, the United States ended up in a nuclear war with China, which allowed the newly quickly, almost if by magic, United Roman Empire to conquer with ease. The news that I had seen, and pictures in the newspapers documented this scripture as people did indeed have their flesh rot while still standing. I now looked at Chamuel and said, "I think the Patmos needs to know some more about the Lord returning?" Chamuel looked at the book and said, "Tell him about the son of man returning. A professes that Jesus will return. (Acts 1:11) "They said, "Men of Galilee, why do you stand looking up toward heaven? This Jesus, who has been taken up from you into heaven, will come in the same way as you saw him go into heaven." (Luke 13:35) "See, your house is left to you. And I tell you, you will not see me until the time comes when you say, 'Blessed is the one who comes in the name of the Lord.'" (Matthew 23:39) "For I tell you, you will not see me again until you say, 'Blessed is the one who comes in the name of the Lord.'" I then looked at Chamuel and asked, "Why can you not just tell me?" Chamuel then said, "Before a complete record of both the old and new testaments are included in the Patmos. It will have evidence that humanity had these available at the end times and that they were exceptionally readily available on many platforms. When those judges of the other empires review the judgment of humanity, they shall see that the wrath was slow, the mercy was great, and that is not only the righteous, but evil was given so many attempts to repent and accept the ways of the righteous in a legal system that complied with the divine laws of the universes. The righteous always comply while the wicked always deny. The wicked deceive with the righteous grieve. The righteous cleave to believe, while the wicked misconceive to achieve. All understand that He who sits on the Throne may do as he wishes and needs to permission to do so and more importantly has no fear in doing so. This is, as humanity would say, to satisfy for eternity the consciousness of the seven spirits of He who sits on the Throne." I now saw the value of this in that it is concerning eternity. I now asked, "Will there be a sign of our Lord's return?" Chamuel answered, "Yes, Floyd he will appear in Heaven and the earth will see him." The book revealed, (Matthew 24:30) "Then the sign of the Son of Man will appear in heaven, and then all the tribes of the earth will mourn, and they will see 'the Son of Man coming on the clouds of heaven' with power and great glory." While swallowing my visions I noticed two white horses. The book as with Chamuel can read my mind, therefore the book shared, the words concerning the last rider on the White Horse (Revelation 19:11) "Then I saw heaven opened, and there was a white horse! Its rider is called Faithful and True, and in righteousness he judges and makes war" and then white horse from the sealed scrolls. (Revelation 6:2) "I looked, and there was a white horse! Its rider had a bow; a crown was given to him, and he came out conquering and to conquer." The seals are broken to the scrolls by the Lord who releases the white horse to conquer as this white horse is ridden by the great deceiver. The rider called Faithful and true for he judges thus is our Lord. Two separate horses and directions. He continues to offer the unsaved grace. (Revelation 2:16) Repent then. If not, I will come to you soon and make war against them with the sword of my mouth.) I subsequently wanted a review concerning what this mighty sword was. (Ephesians 6:17) "Take the helmet of salvation, and the sword of the Spirit, which is the word of God." (Revelation 19:13) "He is clothed in a robe dipped in blood, and his name is called The Word of God" and the word became flesh (John 1:1) "In the beginning was the Word, and the Word was with God, and the Word was God." (John 1:14) "And the Word became flesh and lived among us, and we have seen his glory, the glory as of a father's only son, full of grace and truth." I now have one-half of both of these wars identified; yet still wonder what manner this 'word' will come. (Luke 9:26) "Those who are ashamed of me and of my words, of them the Son of Man will be ashamed when he comes in his glory and the glory of the Father and of the holy angels." (Luke 21:27) "Then they will see 'the Son of Man coming in a cloud' with power and great glory."(Mark 13:26) "Then they will see 'the Son of Man coming in clouds' with great power and glory." (Matthew 26:64) "Jesus said to him, "You have said so. But I tell you, From now on you will see the Son of Man seated at the right hand of Power and coming on the clouds of heaven." I now asked, "Chamuel, I somewhat have the understanding that the Lord fights his battles through his power, as it would be foolish to match Saints against demons, devils, or even humanity, nevertheless I keep remembering always being told that he comes with his saints." Chamuel then recommended that we listen to the book and then discuss afterwards. I nodded in agreement and the book began. (Revelation 19:14) "And the armies of heaven, wearing fine linen, white and pure, were following him on white horses." Concerning Saints, (Zechariah 14:5) "And you shall flee by the valley of the Lord's mountain, for the valley between the mountains shall reach to Azal; and you shall flee as you fled from the earthquake in the days of King Uzziah of Judah. Then the Lord my God will come, and all the holy ones with him." (Jude 1:14) "It was also about these that Enoch, in the seventh generation from Adam, prophesied, saying, "See, the Lord is coming with ten thousands of his holy ones."(2 Thessalonians 1:7) "and to give relief to the afflicted as well as to us, when the Lord Jesus is revealed from heaven with his mighty angels." So we see the Lord come with his mighty angels, saints, all the holy ones, and the armies of heaven, wearing fine linen, white and pure, were following him on white horses." They are with him, yet the Lord has the key to their victory which flows through the double-edged sword in his mouth and that is the Word.

Chamuel now showed me the wrath of the Lord and the book told me where this was given to man so that he or she may know these things, and not be caught naked, least all see his or her shame. Moreover, our scene begins with the Seventh Trumpet (Revelation 11:15). "Then the seventh angel blew his trumpet, and there were loud voices in heaven, saying, "The kingdom of the world has become the kingdom of our Lord and of his Messiah, and he will reign forever and ever." During the time the trumpet sounded, the kingdom of the world was now the kingdom of our Lord. The Earth had only one Kingdom of the Lord, as he was the promised deliver (Messiah). Moreover, this was so. (Revelation 11:18) "The nations raged, but your wrath has come, and the time for judging the dead, for rewarding your servants, the prophets and saints and all who fear your name, both small and great, and for destroying those who destroy the earth." Since Earth had only one Kingdom and that was the Kingdom of the Lord, these nations were the ones from the four corners of the Earth. This is a spiritual verse, as humanity is no more as they are all, both great and small being judged. Those who destroy the Earth cannot be of the Lord, thus they must belong to the destroyer and deceiver for they are destroyed. War one, and war two was finished the same way. (Psalm 46:6) "The nations are in an uproar, the kingdoms totter; he utters his voice, the earth melts." His word melts the Earth, both humanity and evil ones, spirit or flesh. The flesh tremble and the spirits create violent disturbance, only to hear that their words have no power. This disturbance reminded me of a wild animal in a cage fighting to escape. The Kingdoms new they were defeated thus they trembled while the nations who were no longer kingdoms for they had no power, thus they could only bluff having power in the hope of escaping their consummation or destruction. (Isaiah 42:14) "For a long time I have held my peace, I have kept still and restrained myself; now I will cry out like a woman in labor, I will gasp and pant." His word will have all his wrath giving it great power. He will immediately judge Israel, which has a covenant with He who sits on the Throne.

The Coming of the Son of Man (Matthew 24:29-30) "Immediately after the suffering of those days the sun will be darkened, and the moon will not give its light; the stars will fall from heaven, and the powers of heaven will be shaken. Then the sign of the Son of Man will appear in heaven, and then all the tribes of the earth will mourn, and they will see 'the Son of Man coming on the clouds of heaven' with power and great glory." I see that the powers of heaven are shaken and the stars will fall. The evil is defeated and then the Son of Man appears in heaven as humanity now sees that the Son of Man is coming to Earth with his power. He brings his glory with him. The heathen was also judged at Armageddon. (Joel 3:12-14) "Let the nations rouse themselves, and come up to the Valley of Jehoshaphat; for there I will sit to judge all the neighboring nations. Put in the sickle, for the harvest is ripe. Go in, tread, for the wine press is full. The vats overflow, for their wickedness is great. Multitudes, multitudes, in the valley of decision! For the day of the Lord is near in the valley of decision." (Jude 1:14-15) "It was also about these that Enoch, in the seventh generation from Adam, prophesied, saying, "See, the Lord is coming with ten thousands of his holy ones. To execute judgment on all, and to convict every one of all the deeds of ungodliness that they have committed in such an ungodly way, and of all the harsh things that ungodly sinners have spoken against him." The evidence that this judgment was foretold, as early as the seventh generation from Adam reveals that humanity had time to save themselves. The Lord will destroy the sin in man suddenly as all the riches in the world will be of no value. (Zephaniah 1:18) (Neither their silver nor their gold will be able to save them on the day of the Lord's wrath; in the fire of his passion the whole earth shall be consumed; for a full, a terrible end he will make of all the inhabitants of the earth." (Proverbs 11:4) "Riches do not profit in the day of wrath, but righteousness delivers from death." I now asked Chamuel, "Should we also not include proof that humanity was warned?" Chamuel agreed and looked at the book, yet first added, "The danger with these signs is that signs were given to warn about both wars, thus must be studied to determine which end is being referenced. The choice of war has no bearing, except for only a few minutes at most that the end is at hand. It is not required, nor has it ever been recorded that all things mark the end. In addition, another problem that we have seen believes all prophecy will be fulfilled in the same age. Some prophecies about the same ages are given as to prove the righteousness of the prophet. A prophet is known by his prophecies, as a baker is known by what he bakes. Let us look at the increase in knowledge and if it pertains to the end of times.

(Daniel 12:4) "But you, Daniel, keep the words secret and the book sealed until the time of the end. Many shall be running back and forth, and evil [a] shall increase."

Footnotes:

a. Daniel 12:4 Chaldean Compare Gk: Heb knowledge

Man has always obtained increases in knowledge from disobedient angels as Enoch introduced to us by revealing the watchers. Daniel wrote this book in Chaldean, which was later translated to Greek, which used the Hebrew word knowledge. Daniel must keep his prophecy sealed because of an increase in evil. Evil means, wicked, immoral, sinful, etc . . . . The increase in evil did result in the increase in the enchanting, magic, witchcraft, and supernatural. Man's advances were not due to science, they were due to the spiritual sharing of knowledge through the kingdoms at the corners of the Earth." I now sat back and looked at the history of humanity. I watched the angels in Enoch's time that took upon themselves the daughters of men as their wives and saw them teaching how to do abortions and the art of makeup for their faces, and so many other things. I could see humanity riding on horses for over 6000 years then in less than one century walking on the moon. I cannot explain why this did not happen during any of the earlier ages as they had great minds, if not greater. Therefore, the end time increase was in evil, which produced the knowledge. That would explain why the technology would break down, as its sole goal would be in some way to get some human blood in trade. As I think about it, if something works, it should always work, as long as maintained within the parameters that it was designed. It would be hard to criticize an airplane for not flying under water, yet for some small electrical device that had been regularly inspected to malfunction causing the plane to land in the ocean and kill all those aboard it would appear to be evil demanding its sacrifice. Drugs always scared me, especially coke and alcohol, as they destroy the flesh it has its chains tightly wrapped. Another good one is tobacco, as more Americans were dying each month from smoking related deaths than in some of the wars that the Eagle had fought. As they were dying, I wonder if they understood that the politicians who were claiming to be working so hard to guarantee the pursuit of happiness understood they lived from the tax revenues collected so the government would give these people permission to kill themselves. If knowledge had truly increased then why were the plagues that humanity faced gaining power? Also, if humanities technology was really so superior that they could create small chips to control gigantic tasks, then why could they not replace a kidney, liver, a long term heart, or for that matter a human body, which cannot be as complicated as some advances that were functioning as everyday luxuries. I like this one; an invisible beam comes into a home and displays a choice of programing on a thin black TV. The TV talks and performs the same as every other TV watching that channel. Wow, humanity did well on that one, now how do I get rid of this cold? I guess everything begins with a thought. An empty mind creates a thought and then an action. I know that I night of intense study for an exam can produce negative results when the thought that contains an answer is sidetracked. Now, here is an example of information that was packed inside a mind that does not produce a thought. Hence, how can a person, without effort, produce a thought about something unseen when that, which was seen, cannot emerge in a thought? Therefore, it must be from our subconscious or existing in the mind but not immediately available to the consciousness. This then causes me to ask what, and who that consciousness is my mind. Who is that person I am talking too when I talk to myself? I am supposed to believe that minds such as mine were able to design advanced technologies. I do not want to think about this anymore. Anyway, why would I be thinking about something like this when I have heaven in my view, an Archangel, and the holy book of He who sits on the Throne to feed my mind? Sometimes, I can understand why humanity was such easy pickings for Lucifer to deceive. The next thought that appears in my mind is the end time sign of the Beast to enforce his mark. The book, who is rebooting himself from the long delay in my short mind now reveals, "(Revelation 13:17) "so that no one can buy or sell who does not have the mark, that is, the name of the beast or the number of its name." The first thing that comes to my mind with numbers and names is the holocaust and how the Germans assigned a number to each prisoner that would remain on their flesh for the remainder of their days. I had an Asian friend who told me that all the people in his nation had cards that proved them their citizens. I know that in Montana, we all had to have social security numbers and any time someone would want to get a loan or a credit card, they would have to reveal their social security number. Now, most states issue electronic debit cards that are used as food stamps. Electronic deposits for paychecks are so common today. My father told me that when he was in the military, they would be issued pay from a paymaster, then be given time for "payday activities." Now, the pay is electronically deposited and most bills are paid on the internet through the banks, or lenders bill pay options. Go home, a few minutes later bills paid, and now the one sad disadvantage of technology. Idle time on hand, becoming the devil's workshop, one click gambling or visiting one of the millions of porn sites, as if each of them has discovered something new, and another candidate to miss the rapture. These are just a few examples. To replace cash, which is actually has many benefit's that improve the quality of life, and does at times a life a little harder for thieves, who now instead of cash, go for the debit card and pin number. Hence, evil evolves discovering new opportunities. The point here is that a debit card or mark system can easily be implemented and justified. A citizenship mark would help identify illegal aliens, so crafty politicians, and especially the great deceiver can easily guide his kingdom or nation into a system that would enforce a mark, if not only to guarantee that those who were entitled to certain privileges received them.

Now I am going to analysis all these false Christ's and prophets as the book again reveals. (Matthew 24:4-5, 11) "Jesus answered them, "Beware that no one leads you astray. For many will come in my name, saying, 'I am the Messiah!' and they will lead many astray. And many false prophets will arise and lead many astray." This warning is not a new warning, yet one as old as humanity, as the Sadducees, Pharisees, Essenes, and Zealots were on their corners warning about the same thing in Jerusalem that age. The amazing thing is that they were right about all the prophets at that time except for Jesus. If they had studied the word of God, they would have known. Knowledge would have set them free and bound all the gentiles, as they would not have had the Messiah to save them. Therefore, their ignorance created Christianity, and luckily, through the paradigm of the printing press, the Christians were able to have the word of God in their hands to study and decrease the possibility of being deceived, although not all escaped from this sign. This sign was for those who were listening to him speak at that time, hold on to his words and you would be going in the correct direction. You will fall into the hands of the deceiver when you add to or take away from his word. Cults are less dangerous today that at other times throughout the ages due to, "That which is done in the dark being revealed in the light." Names such as Jim Jones and David Koresh created so much awareness that such cults found themselves being choked. We have yet made it to the stage as Sodom and Gomorrah, and only now in Daniel's seventieth week compete with the flood. False teaching is not something new, has always been around beginning with Lucifer as the snake in the garden and being critically injured at the Battle of Armageddon and permanently destroyed at the end of the 1000 years.

Chamuel now directs me to the vision concerning wars and rumors of wars. Moreover, the book revealed another great truth. (Matthew 24:6-8) "And you will hear of wars and rumors of wars; see that you are not alarmed; for this must take place, but the end is not yet. For nation will rise against nation, and kingdom against kingdom, and there will be famines and earthquakes in various places: all this is but the beginning of the birth pangs." Okay, as I hear this and watch it unfold I realize, wars and rumors of wars have been and always will be. I look back into Genesis and see, (Genesis 6:11) "Now the earth was corrupt in God's sight, and the earth was filled with violence." Violence and war go hand and hand with the love of evil. The time to worry is when there is NO rumor of war, as in the first half of Daniel's seventieth week. The Lord tells us here, "See that you are not alarmed; for this must take place, but the end is not yet." The end is not yet hey, I have an idea. Should I show the Lord that I am smarter than he is, and go ahead and worry about these wars, even though he told me not to worry? What part of do not worry is confusing. Famines and earthquakes are only the beginning. The delivery is still in progress so hang on to some more birth pains. The Lord ties all three of these, famines, earthquakes and rumors of wars into the same category.

I marvel at what the Theological literature would have revealed if he had told us to worry about them. Famine is a function of a paradigm. The scientists at the beginning of the twentieth century calculated that humanity would not be able to feed themselves and would soon fall into deep famine with mass starvation. Technology, tractor now large farms, and people feed, with the Earth now having more people living than all of humanity combined in history, until the rapture, World War III and the twenty-one judgments and the Great Battle. I called for the book to reveal again this time from Luke (Luke 21:9-11). "When you hear of wars and insurrections, do not be terrified; for these things must take place first, but the end will not follow immediately." Then he said to them, "Nation will rise against nation, and kingdom against kingdom; there will be great earthquakes, and in various places famines and plagues; and there will be dreadful portents and great signs from heaven." Now here, we also have another witness to what the Lord said, "do not be terrified . . . the end will not follow immediately," and you hear of wars . . . Nations will rise against nation . . . famines and plagues. If a nation rising against nation does not qualify for war then I must be a monkey's uncle. So here also, everything is tied together with the do not worry as there will be great signs from heaven. Therefore, I must now ponder, will these great signs come from the internet or from heaven? Well, maybe since this verse said the signs would come from heaven, and then I should select heaven. Amazing how seeing, hearing can result in selecting. To think some people appreciate the intelligence of Einstein when they could be reading this. Now, I am going to look at the causes of famines. I see that the vast majority of them are related to wars either directly or indirectly and the rogue actions of governments who take from their people. Situations created by the evil in men, so evil caused these famines. I am only going to brush over earthquakes as two to of the twenty-one judgments deal with big earthquakes. I can see where the closer we get to the end times, the more likely we will have more earthquakes, as those who destroy the earth can have a hand in this. I know that the nuclear bombs of World War III shook the heck out of our small town, and I have always been told that if you shake it too hard, you could break it.

When I heard the book read from Mathew, something hit me that this Patmos should address so I asked Chamuel if the book could read that for me again. I just still have some reservations concerning talking to books, especially when it belongs to He who sits on the Throne. (Matthew 24:7) "For nation shall rise against nation, and kingdom against kingdom: and there shall be famines, and pestilences, and earthquakes, in divers places." I want to look at the word pestilences, which are devastating like bubonic plague. Now this is something that should catch our eyes, although not new as they have ravaged humanity greatly in the times since Christ, especially with the Black Death almost wiping out Asia and Europe. That demon is still waiting to reappear which along with the other plagues should be a motivator to join those who join the rapture. I really place this more in the human sacrifices that the demons are demanding in return for their revealing the great secrets of technology. We must pay and they do not accept visa, as they only bank at the blood bank. The design of these microscopic monsters and their ability to wage war and destroy our body's ability to continue is like an ant killing a dinosaur. As we tackle the destroyers of yesterday, such as leprosy in Christ's time, we face new destroyers such as HIV/AIDS, although it did not make the daily headlines in the last few years it was whipping through Asia and Africa, just to name a few more places. I was always so amazed how so much attention had been given to Hitler and Stalin as great killers, when the Spanish flu that struck at the end of World War I go more people than World War I, Hitler and Stalin combined. A person's chances of surviving a bullet were greater than those small creatures of Hell. I shiver when I think how they just float into a home, decide who they want to kill and how many, then look for new victims.

Now I will look at people being lovers of themselves. The book reads about Godlessness in the last days (2 Timothy 3:1-5) "You must understand this, that in the last days distressing times will come. For people will be lovers of themselves, lovers of money, boasters, arrogant, abusive, disobedient to their parents, ungrateful, unholy, inhuman, implacable, slanderers, profligates, brutes, haters of good, treacherous, reckless, swollen with conceit, lovers of pleasure rather than lovers of God, holding to the outward form of godliness but denying its power. Avoid them!" Even though I will contend that these sorts of people or type of deaths occurred throughout all the ages, I even noticed a marked increase during our last days. This passage tells us to avoid these type of people in the last days. I will add some spice to your lives and tell you to avoid them period. I know it was so terrible during the last few years as all advertisements were flat out lies, salesmen were treacherous, police were abusive, politicians were reckless, and pleasures emptied the churches. This is the basis for the power of my love for Flying Dove. She actually hates the power that money has over people and is grateful for everything. She will sing all the way to school in the mornings because of life. She has never boasted a day in her life and her entire world is built around respect for her parents, who in turn have much respect for her and Little Running Eagle. I have discovered that anyone who is swollen with conceit falls into the grips of evil never to escape. Flying Dove's complete family and relatives would give their lives immediately to save others. They also live the Christianity they have been making it internal and personal. It lives in them and combines them with the Earth. I fear sometimes that Flying Dove would walk in mud not to step on a leaf. I feel so happy knowing that she and her brother are here in heaven waiting for me to join them.

Another End Time sign I have heard repeatedly is that the gospel will be preached to the whole world. I looked at the book and heard (Matthew 24:14) "And this good news of the kingdom will be proclaimed throughout the world, as a testimony to all the nations; and then the end will come." The gospel had been preached throughout the world ever since Saul converted to Paul, and it has not slowed down since. Many ministries preach to the complete world and others have established missionaries. This means that so many souls in other remote countries have a selection of ministries to learn from and many a living missionary available to help not only with the things of the soul, but also with other needs. I remember that sometimes when one of my parents was ill and we did not go to church, they could turn on the TV, allowing our family still to enjoy an excellent sermon. That is a plus for all churches; they all were trying so hard. I never was too hung up on denominations, especially since there were just a few churches in Townsend. Most people selected the church they attended based upon the one their grandparents attended.

I rested my soul for a second to think about all that I had collected for the Patmos. I glanced over at Chamuel who gave me a positive nod. The book then closed and peacefully ascended as if anticipating another question. My mission was to reveal this great battle, which was barely a flash for the spirits and the last of humanity. The earth currently has no mountains or islands. A new shaped continent covers maybe one-fifth of the surface, as the rest is water. I can see green covering all the lands with a few trees spotted here and there. I see no ruins from any structures built by man nor do I see any roads. I have no idea where Montana is nor can I imagine that if we were returned to Earth where we would go. Chamuel now offers to guide me back to the group that I am a member. I ask Chamuel if I will once again live in my flesh and he tells me that the Lord will determine all things. I think that if we did get our flesh back, we would be the only members of humanity existing. Chamuel guides me to my Patmos where I must empty my bowl. As I pour mine in, I see the liquid all turn red for a few seconds and then pure white. My mission is almost complete as I place my bowl in the last remaining hole. All the holes are filled with bowls, so I would believe that should mean that we all completed our mission. I now see a clear capsule with my partners inside smiling at me. Chamuel guides me to the door and enters with me. He is the only angel with us, so I ask him, "Can we help you?" He speaks to our group, "Hello great Saints, I am the Archangel Chamuel. I have spoken with those who hosted you throughout your mission. The twenty-four elders are very pleased with the Patmos you have assembled and they wish to meet with you. I shall escort you there, where after meeting the twenty-four elders we will discuss your wonderful futures." With that, he sat down and we all smiled at each other. We had a sense that we were given such a high mission and by some miracle, a group of rural hillbilly mountain kids danced in the heavens. They had truly saved the last dance for us, as evil now exists in only three beings and they are burned. If I were to have a concern, it would be over the dormant cells that exist as the sands of the seas, on the four corners of the Earth. I scoot in beside Flying Dove as we naturally reveal our special relationship. I almost wonder if we will ever be apart and on a different subject, when will be meet our parents and other siblings. The Age of Good and Evil has ended.

CHAPTER 11

Evidence of the warnings and rewards

I am so glad to see all my friends and family collected once more. We have been through a lot, yet each one of us has matured precipitously. Although we do not have wool hair, as did Moses, we do have that far off stare in our eyes. As Holy sits so content beside me, I discern that all in this group has no anxiety or worries. We appear to all remember that a return trip home was promised after this mission, yet none of us truly desires to return. Even though we were among the blessed ones in Aunt Rita's sanctuary, it just did not feel right or natural. Food mysteriously appearing, everyday hungry, and feeling the tremendous pressure that something evil is outside, more like knowing the big bad wolf is clawing at the walls. It was a thin wall holding out darkness, hate, sin, unrighteousness, sorrow, discord, and mountains of death. We were able to hold off the darkness with candles, which as with all things physical do not last long. We were lucky to have the strong leadership of Jennifer to keep us in accord with Aunt Rita. I just felt so sorry for her; she was living alone with no one within miles of her home. Notwithstanding, even in this remote area, the beasts were drawing near. Under ordinary conditions, such as having to replace our wood for hear and food, time would be on their side. We would have to go into their traps to obtain what we needed to survive. Fortunately, with spiritual intervention we received our food and wood to burn. All I can see anywhere down there is thirst, hunger, boredom, anxiety as if we were waiting until we were caught and guilty because we were free. We have now tasted freedom from sexual immorality, idolatry, adultery, prostitution, sexual offenses, theft, greed, drunkenness, slander, swindling, impurity, witch craft hatred, discord, jealousy, fits of rage, selfish, ambition, dissensions, factions and envy, abomination, lying, cowardice, unbelief actually un everything, murder, sorcery. Even in our small town and school, we saw these seeds being planted. Most times the sexual offenses resulted from outsiders sneaking into our town. Way, it still hurt the victim, and took away some more of our freedoms as freedom refuses to live beside evil. I had never noticed the appalling grip of evil that destroys everything around it. Chamuel is now motioning for our capsule to stop and we all glide out, as if being pulled, into two rows in front of twenty-four thrones. There are none sitting on these thrones. Now a species I have yet ever to see are forming around us. Chamuel tells us not to fear, for they are the guardians of the twenty-four thrones. From every direction I see an appearance which is gold looking and crimson, and with the form of fire. Then I looked downward, and I saw a place inconceivably pleasant. I saw the trees in full flower. Their fruits were ripe and pleasant-smelling, with every food in yield and giving off abundantly a pleasant fragrance. We rested while the pleasant-smelling told us no danger awaited for us here. Chamuel now guided us back into our capsule, which now had the head of a lion and the tail of a crocodile. I asked him what had happened to our capsule and he told me that it had been taken away along with our previous spiritual bodies. I now behind the beautiful new bodies that we were inside, as Holly's beauty was greater than that of the angel's I had seen so far. I could see that Holly, Flying Dove, Jennifer, and Aunt Rita looked different from Floyd, Little Running Eagle and myself. I now told Chamuel, "I am glad that we are as male and female, yet I see no others who are as we." Chamuel then told me, "You appear to the others and they appear to you, yet you appear to each other as the vision in your mind reveals to you." I further asked, "Why are we in front of twenty-four empty thrones?" He then told us, "The Judges are before He who sits on the Throne now, and therefore we may advance, for I shall take you to the special place that has been prepared for the Spirits of the Patmos. Your judgment may be postponed." Jennifer then cried out, "We must be judged?" Chamuel then said, "Oh, fear not for judgment simply removes any claim that sin may have on your book of life. You all have no worries; it is merely a requirement of the heavens that all who enter must be judged. You entered while still in the flesh and we were working on your Patmos when time ended, and still having flesh while all flesh was made no more, and being protected by your capsule, your journey will be different." Flying Dove now asked, "Will we return from that which we departed?" Chamuel now answered, "Flying Dove, that place is no more for all that was has passed away as are things are being made new." I now asked, "Will all flesh be no more?" Chamuel then answered, "Only to that of this creation, which saw the Earth be created, destroyed, created again, flooded and then destroyed. Flesh will appear again on the neighbor of Earth Venus, as the Lord that saw the Earth become no more, shall see a new Venus be born, as also is a new Earth now born with a new beautiful city enjoyed her fruits." I somehow get the feeling that every question I ask is being answered honestly, yet my spirit cannot eat these words or take these answers to cover the questions. I now ask Chamuel, "Why could we not travel back into time to where we departed through the Patmos Portal?" Chamuel then said, "George, time, and space are no more. Heaven exists outside the dimensions of both space and time, as they were on created for that life which was in the flesh so that a connection can be made between an action and the appropriate reaction, such as no heat producing cold for that time and place. You are now where you were and where you will go." I just felt a few circuits blow on that answer. I feel no reason why I should worry about anything now, I have no hunger, I am not too cold or hot, I have love in my heart and love around me, so it may be time to toss my oars and go with the flow of this calm river. As we glad along with this what Chamuel now calls 'the chariot', it slows down and he bids us his farewell. I ask him, "Where are you going, like I mean we are somewhere, I think, and doing I have no idea and now we are being abandoned?" Chamuel told us, "Eternity shall never find you alone for you live in He that sits on the Throne, and He lives in you." Holly now asks, "Is he out here also?" Chamuel smiles and says, "If you are." Then he slowly fades away and our chariot is both moving and staying in place. Sometimes I think the stars are around us, and then they disappear. Now the color of the space that surrounds us begins with changes as if they were the colors of the rainbow. Even this rainbow does not want to give me a reassurance of stability as its colors are dancing to a rhythm that has never before invaded my mind. We are all looking at each other wondering if we have ever before met, or are we all enjoying a new type of dream. I wish I knew which way up was and which some other way was. I seriously can find no resolution in my mind, yet by the same path, I can find no dissolution. I look into the hungry eyes of those around me and try to define the thought of nothing being hungry in heaven. I can see our hunger is to know our destiny. We went from being a happy small clan in a town protected from the world to the recorders of our species' demise and the representatives therein for eternity lost in the universe. Now, after our victory we wonder, "What did we win?" We feel neither victorious nor defeated, we feel empty yet full. I can only hope the path of this chariot will find these things for us.

The revolutions of the luminaries of heaven, accordingly evading their respective classes, their respective powers, their respective periods, their respective names, the places where they commence their progress and their respective times are as the mumbled rainbow that tries to blend within them. The whole account of them, according to eternity shall be effected, which we pray also to be.

Now a new spirit emerges before us saying, "I am he who is to guide you so that you shall not be lost. Listen to my words so that you may know that where you now exist. The sun and the light arrive at the gates of heaven, which are on the east, and on the west of it at the western gates of heaven. See the gates from where the sun goes forth; and the gates where the sunsets; and the gates the moon rises and sets; and I behold the conductors of the stars, among those who precede them; six gates were at the rising, and six at the setting of the sun. All these respectively, one after another, are on a level; and numerous windows are on the right and on the left sides of those gates. First proceeds forth that great star, which was called the sun, the sphere of which is as the ball of heaven, the whole of it being replete with splendid and flaming fire and where it ascends, the wind blows. The sunsets in heaven, and, returning from the north, to proceed towards the east, are conducted to enter by that gate, and illuminate the face of heaven. In the same manner, it goes forth in the first month by the great gate. It goes forth through the fourth of those six gates, which are at the rising of the sun. These are the leaders of the chiefs of the thousands, who preside over all creation, and over all the stars in heaven. That they might rule in the face of the sky and twelve gates. We beheld in heaven, at the extremities of the earth, through which the sun, moon, and the stars, and all the works of heaven proceed at their beginning and ending. Many windows also are open on the right and on the left. We saw likewise the chariots of heaven, running in the emptiness above to those gates in which the stars turn, which never set. One of these is greater than all others are. We saw every support respecting these, which takes place at all times under every influence, at the arrival and under the rule of each. All things shall we I reveal to you. You see the conduct the stars of heaven, which cause all their operations and return. Heaven shall shine more than when illuminated by the orders of light. At that time we beheld the Ancient of days, while he sat upon the throne of his glory, while the book of the living was opened in his presence, and while all the powers which were above the heavens stood around and before him. The holy ones assembled, who dwell above the heavens, and with the united voice petition, supplicate, praise, laud, and bless the name of the Lord of spirits. There our eyes beheld the secrets of the heavens, a mountain of iron, a mountain of copper, a mountain of silver, a mountain of gold, a mountain of fluid metal, and a mountain of lead. The saints shall exist in the light of the sun, and the elect in the light of everlasting life, the days of whose life shall never terminate; nor shall the days of the saints be numbered, who seek for light, and obtain righteousness with the Lord of spirits. Peace is to the saints with the Lord of the world. Darkness has passed away. There shall be light interminable; nor shall they enter upon the enumeration of time; for darkness shall be previously destroyed, and light shall increase before the Lord of spirits; before the Lord of spirits shall the light of uprightness increase forever combining power, voice, and splendor like fire. They shall all speak with united voice; and bless, glorify, exalt, and praise, in the name of the Lord of spirits. The Cherubim, the Seraphim, and the Ophanin and all the angels of power, and all the angels of the Lords shall unite their voice. Their united voice shall bless, glorify, praise, and exalt with the spirit of faith, with the spirit of wisdom and patience, with the spirit of mercy, with the spirit of judgment and peace, and with the spirit of benevolence. All shall say with a united voice; blessed is He; and the name of the Lord of spirits shall be blessed forever and forever; all sleep not and shall bless heaven above. All the holy in heaven shall bless it; all the elect who dwell in the garden of life; and every spirit of light, who is capable of blessing, glorifying, exalting, and praising his holy name more than the powers of heaven, they shall glorify and bless his name forever and ever. We now beheld the sons of the holy angels treading on flaming fire, whose garments and robes were white, and whose countenances were transparent as crystal. We saw two rivers of fire glittering like the hyacinth. In the midst of that light, a building raised with stones of ice, and in the middle of these stone vibrations of living fire. There were rivers full of living fire, which encompassed it. With them was the Ancient of days, whose head was white as wool, and pure, and his robe was indescribable. We found some new life flow through our spirits as the vibrations calmed our confusion. Now we beheld the sun become dark and the moon no longer reflects its light. Our host spirit, who had bounced us through this realm we travel, now also bid his farewell, telling us before leaving, "You shall now receive visions so that you may understand the mysteries that surround you." I do believe that what has most of us on the uneasy side is the absence of the Earth and now no sun or moon. Any sight of those would give us a perspective of positioning and familiarity. We keep reassuring ourselves that Chamuel told us we were not to be punished. The Earth had represented to us both friend and enemy. It gave us what the flesh needed to survive, yet at the same time tried to take it back. We now have a vision before us that has the Messiah sitting on a throne inside a gigantic cube of gold reigning as king. A voice now tells us, "Behold, New Jerusalem." This is rather eerie that a voice is speaking yet no speaker is visible. Having survived the onset of World War III, we can see the value of a city inside such a large cube. The world that it sat upon would have trouble harming those in this city, if that world were to do such a thing, which would not be in the line of behavior we would expect from an eternity in heaven. We see so many spirits with bodies such as ours are playing and enjoying life in this world, with its dark green grass and bright multi-shaded blue sky. A blue sky without a sun is new for us, as Jennifer delights that sunglasses would no longer be needed while lying outside in the bright sky. Lion's sleep beside deer, as the deer and giraffe graze in peace, without that constant listening to every little noise for the split second advantage to avoid painful bitter death while the attacker eats bite by bite. The lion looks at peace also chewing his grass, now probably wondering why he never took advantage of this diet before and would instead kill trying to fill a stomach that had eaten nothing for many days, if not even a week. This peace and constant diet are creating fatter deer and lions. Flying Dove asks, "Why are there so many spirits? Jennifer looks at her and answers, "Cannot you see, they have a lot of children?" Flying Dove says, "Exactly." We all look at her strangely, then Aunt Rita replies, "Oh . . ." The rest of us look at each other, and then the light comes on. I say, "Good question, this is heaven, so why are they having children, if only we have the females and males." Then the voice answers, There are two species, the Tolna and Encsi.

The Encsi are married couples who remained together and were saved, shall have new children. It was the marriage at the time of death, which is the final one God joined. For what God has joined cannot be separated. The Tolna are all who were single or spouse remarried following their death. They shall neither marry, nor be given in marriage, but are single like angels in heaven. Floyd now asked the voice, "What about Flying Dove, and myself?" The voice said, "All here are married, as Aunt Rita's husband died saved and shall join you all soon." Flying Dove, who is always meticulous in the details asked, "Am I married to everyone in this group?" The voice said, "Only with Floyd, if you so desire and your brother with Jennifer if she so desires. When you speak it you will be married." She smiled and said, "I do, as also did Jennifer, who would not have her rightful position beside Little Running Eagle."

All who receive their new heavenly bodies lose their Earthly memories. Since knowledge of evil has been forever erased, all knowledge had to be forever erased. The former things will not be remembered or come to mind, as pain and sorrow are no more. Your new bodies are actually the original body designs of Adam and Eve. They are made in the image of the Almighty and thus do not decay or give way to small monsters who bring forth plagues. The unconsciousness and consciousness unite as one, which means your thoughts are your words. Thus, you are who you are. There shall be no more deceit and or bearing false witness. All shall enjoy protected eternal life, while also being served by the angels and other creations as the Holy One will make known. Darkness is no more, as light rules all things. Floyd looked around and asked, "How can we have light as there is no sun?" The voice said, "All light comes from the Holy One." Holly then commented, "If our thoughts are our words than nothing can be corrupted." The voice agreed and added, "Only righteous pleasure and worship and dreams coming true." Flying Dove asked, "When will we dream, as I thought we would never sleep? What would we dream concerning?" The voice said, "True, you shall never need to sleep. Dreams are your hopes and desires as some want to live within certain terrain features. The list shall never end when the heart is filled with peace and hope. No eye has seen, no ear has heard, no mind has conceived what God has prepared for those who love him. Jennifer then commented and asked, "I notice that we are all asking different questions at different times. Will we keep our differences such as in personality?" The voice said yes. This was a bit of good news to us, to go along with the angels serving us. I did not care if they serve us or not, I just always dreaded the thought of being a robot for eternity. Holly now asked, "How does our age progression develop here?" The voice said, "Zero when born, progress till thirty then stops. No one shall age or grow past thirty." Holly then added, "That is why my Aunt Rita looks so much younger. Maybe we should start calling her Rita?" We all agreed as that placed a smile on Rita's face. Now Rita commented and asked, "I notice everyone is wearing white robes, is white our only color?" The voice said yes, and then added, with the white shorts and blouses underneath for more recreational activities. Your thrill of existing will be enhanced by games and learning new things plus traveling to new parts of our galaxy. I then asked, "Are we allowed leaving this galaxy and if not, how far may we travel and explore?" You may travel wherever you wish; we just recommend that you still within our galaxy, as travel outside the galaxy can be dangerous. If you wish to explore outside the galaxy, you may request the escort and protection by some of our armies. Your happiness is an expansion of your life experiences, not its end. Your eternal environment is designed with your individuality in mind and actually mirroring your uniqueness. One good example is commanding a ship through a terrible storm. You will be given clone angels for your experience. The clone means they appear, as you desire. Many mountain climbers reach new heights in their climbs, as the risk of injury is no longer a factor in the risk of the climb. You are all smaller images of He who sits on the Throne. No eye has seen, no ear has heard, no mind has conceived what He has prepared for those who love him. We looked at the Earth with the giant golden cube, which extended high in the firmament above it, as what land we could see had no mountains and we could only see the one large continent. The voice knowing my mind answered, 'The time for the new heaven and earth has not come." I wondered, why the delay. The voice said, 'for the time on Venus has not finished, and both Venus and Earth will be remade at the same time as this will give Jehovah two creations in his image that shall easily join him for eternity as he will reign from inside your golden cube.' I then asked, "Is that why that large golden cube is on the Earth that is now?" The voice affirmed that the golden cube would be moved to the New Earth where it will descend. We now went with a spirit to a mountain great and high, and he showed us the holy city, Jerusalem, coming down out of heaven from God. It is shown with the glory of God, and its brilliance was like that of a very precious jewel, like a jasper, clear as crystal. It had a great, high wall with twelve gates and with twelve angels at the gates. On the gates were written the names of the twelve tribes of Israel. There were three gates on the east, three on the north, three on the south, and three on the west. The wall of the city had twelve foundations, and on them were the names of the twelve apostles of the Lamb. The angel who talked with me had a measuring rod of gold to measure the city, its gates, and its wall. The city was laid out like a square, as long as it was wide. He measured the city with the rod and found it to be 12,000 stadia [1400 miles] in length, and as wide and high as it is long. He measured its wall and it was 144 cubits thick [200 feet], by man's measurement, which the angel was using. The wall was made of jasper, and the city of pure gold, as pure as glass. The foundations of the city wall were decorated with every kind of precious stone. The first foundation was jasper, the second sapphire, the third chalcedony, the fourth emerald, the fifth Sardonyx, the sixth carnelian, the seventh chrysolite, the eighth beryl, the ninth topaz, the tenth Chrysoprase, the eleventh jacinth, and the twelfth amethyst. The twelve gates were twelve pearls, each gate made of a single pearl. The street of the city was of pure gold, like transparent glass. I did not see a temple in the city, because the Lord God Almighty and the Lamb are its temple. The city does not need the sun or the moon to shine on it, for the glory of God gives it light, and the Lamb is its lamp. He will create all things new. To him who is thirsty I will give to drink without cost from the spring of the water of life . . . And the Spirit and the bride say, "Come!" Moreover, let him who hears say, "Come!" Whoever is thirsty, let him come; and whoever wishes, let him take the gift of the water of life.

We now saw another vision. We looked, and beheld, a great multitude, which no one could count, from every nation and all tribes and peoples and tongues, standing before the throne and before the Lamb, clothed in white robes, and palm branches were in their hands. Moreover, they cry out with a loud voice, saying, "Salvation to our God who sits on the throne, and to the Lamb." In addition, all the angels were standing around the throne and around the elders and the four living creatures; and they fell on their faces before the throne and worshiped God. And I saw a great white throne and Him who sat upon it, from whose presence earth and heaven fled away, and no place was found for them. And I saw the dead, the great and the small, standing before the throne, and books were opened; and another book was opened, which is the Book of Life; and the dead were judged from the things which were written in the books, according to their deeds . . .

If anyone's name was not found written in the Book of Life, he was thrown into the lake of fire. The voice spoke again, "During your individual Patmos, while viewing the damnation of the holy trinity, we rather eluded the damnation of all others, electing to discuss it in detail here for the entire group, therefore after it is recorded into your Patmos, this information will be forever sealed. Your chariot shall now visit the lakes of fire." This puts a damper on our moods very fast. We are in the middle of searching for our homes in eternity and then all of a sudden we are dropping fast. I asked the chariot to pause, and when it did so, I called for Chamuel. Chamuel appeared and I asked him if he would join us on this Patmos, to ensure we pleased the Lord. With this, he agreed and entered our sealed chariot. Once again, we descended. We all felt much better having him with us, at least we would have someone who knew how to get out and guide us back. Chamuel now guided us into a larger chariot, thus we would have room to move around and obtain more information. Then a friend that we all knew reappeared. Before us now was the book from He who sat on the Throne. Chamual also gave us peace by telling us that the book also had the 'word' that would save us, if need be. Holly asked Chamual if we could be in danger and Chamual answered casually, "Not with **The** book with us." They then recommended that we first let the book show us where humanity had been warned about this punishment for the Patmos. We all agreed and told the book to read away and send a visible frame with each saying while reading it allowing any who research this ease in connecting the words with the proof. The book agreed and began, "Wherefore if thy hand or thy foot offend thee, cut them off, and cast them from thee: it is better for thee to enter into life halt or maimed, rather than having two hands or two feet to be cast into everlasting fire. Likewise, if your eyes offend thee, pluck it out, and cast it from thee: it is better for thee to enter into life with one eye, rather than having two eyes to be cast into hell fire. Then shall he say also unto them on the left hand, Depart from me, ye cursed, into everlasting fire, prepared for the devil and his angels. Even as Sodom and Gomorrah, and the cities about them in like manner, giving themselves over to fornication, and going after strange flesh, are set forth for an example, suffering the vengeance of eternal fire. And they shall go forth, and look upon the carcasses of the men that have transgressed against me: for their worm shall not die, neither shall their fire be quenched; and they shall be an abhorring unto all flesh. Whose fan is in his hand, and he will thoroughly purge his floor, and gather his wheat into the garner; but he will burn up the chaff with unquenchable fire. Moreover, if thy hands offend thee, cut it off: it is better for thee to enter into life maimed, than having two hands to go into hell, into the fire that never shall be quenched, where their worm dies not, and the fire is not quenched. Additionally, if thy foot offends thee, cut it off: it is better for thee to enter halt into life, than having two feet to be cast into hell, into the fire that never shall be quenched, where their worm dies not, and the fire is not quenched. Also, if your eyes offend thee, pluck it out: it is better for thee to enter into the kingdom of God with one eye, than having two eyes to be cast into hell fire, where their worm dies not, and the fire is not quenched. These shall go away into everlasting punishment: but the righteous into life eternal. In flaming fire taking vengeance on them that know not God, and that obey not the gospel of our Lord Jesus Christ. Who shall be punished with everlasting destruction from the presence of the Lord, and from the glory of his power? Likewise, fear not them, which kill the body, but are not able to kill the soul: but rather fear him, which is able to destroy both soul and body in hell. The wicked shall perish, and the enemies of the Lord shall be as the fat of lambs: they shall consume; into smoke shall they consume away. For, behold, the day cometh, that shall burn as an oven; and all the proud, yea, and all that do wickedly, shall be stubble: and the day that cometh shall burn them up, says the Lord of hosts, that it shall leave them neither root nor branch. Behold, they shall be as stubble; the fire shall burn them; they shall not deliver themselves from the power of the flame: there shall not be a coal to warm at, nor fire to sit before it. When the Lord shall have washed away the filth of the daughters of Zion, and shall have purged the blood of Jerusalem from the midst thereof by the spirit of judgment, and by the spirit of burning. Moreover, the sight of the glory of the LORD was like devouring fire on the top of the mount in the eyes of the children of Israel. Besides, the LORD will create upon every dwelling place of mount Zion, and upon her assemblies, a cloud and smoke by day, and the shining of a flaming fire by night: for upon all the glory shall be a defense. Behold, the name of the Lord cometh from far, burning with his anger, and the burden thereof is heavy: his lips are full of indignation, and his tongue as a devouring fire. For the Lord thy God is a consuming fire, even a jealous God. For our God is a consuming fire. The sinners in Zion are afraid; fearfulness hath surprised the hypocrites. Who among us shall dwell with the devouring fire? Who among us shall dwell with everlasting burnings? Still in hell he lift up his eyes, being in torments.

The book paused then continued with (Luke 16:19-28) The Rich Man and Lazarus "There was a rich man who was dressed in purple and fine linen and who feasted sumptuously every day. And at his gate lay a poor man named Lazarus, covered with sores, who longed to satisfy his hunger with what fell from the rich man's table; even the dogs would come and lick his sores. The poor man died and was carried away by the angels to be with Abraham. The rich man also died and was buried. In Hades, where he was being tormented, he looked up and saw Abraham far away with Lazarus by his side. He called out, 'Father Abraham, have mercy on me, and send Lazarus to dip the tip of his finger in water and cool my tongue; for I am in agony in these flames.' Nevertheless, Abraham said, 'Child, remember that during your lifetime you received your good things, and Lazarus in like manner evil things; but now he is comforted here, and you are in agony. Besides all this, between you and us a great chasm has been fixed, so that those who might want to pass from here to you cannot do so, and no one can cross from there to us.' He said, 'then, father, I beg you to send him to my father's house—or I have five brothers—that he may warn them, so that they will not also come into this place of torment.'"

Likewise, shall cast them into a furnace of fire, there shall be wailing and gnashing of teeth." Then he will say to those at his left hand, 'You that are accursed. Depart from me into the eternal fire prepared for the devil and his angels. I was hungry and you gave me no food, I was thirsty and you gave me nothing to drink, I was a stranger and you did not welcome me, naked and you did not give me clothing, sick and in prison and you did not visit me.' Anyone whose name was not found written in the book of life was thrown into the lake of fire. For just as Jonah was three days and three nights in the belly of the sea monster, so for three days and three nights the Son of Man will be in the heart of the earth. They will also drink the wine of God's wrath, poured unmixed into the cup of his anger, and they will be tormented with fire and sulfur in the presence of the holy angels and in the presence of the Lamb. Concerning Self-Deception, "Not everyone who says to me, 'Lord, Lord,' will enter the kingdom of heaven, but only the one who does the will of my Father in heaven. On that day many will say to me, 'Lord, Lord, did we not prophesy in your name, and cast out demons in your name, and do many deeds of power in your name?' Then I will declare to them, 'I never knew you; go away from me, you evildoers.' Likewise, the smoke of their torment goes up forever and ever. There is no rest day or night for those who worship the beast and its image and for anyone who receives the mark of its name." For what shall it profit a man, if he shall gain the whole world, and lose his own soul? Alternatively, what shall a man give in exchange for his soul? Moreover, just as it is appointed for mortals to die once, and after that the judgment. Upon the wicked, He will rain snares; Fire, brimstone, and burning wind will be the portion of their cup. You will make them as a fiery oven in the time of your anger; The Lord will swallow them up in His wrath, And fire will devour them. "The Son of Man will send forth His angels, and they will gather out of His kingdom all stumbling blocks, and those who commit lawlessness, and will cast them into the furnace of fire; in that place there shall be weeping and gnashing of teeth. "So it will be at the end of the age; the angels shall come forth, and take out the wicked from among the righteous, and will cast them into the furnace of fire; there shall be weeping and gnashing of teeth. If anyone does not abide in Me, he is thrown away as a branch, and dries up; and they gather them, and cast them into the fire, and they are burned. Moreover, the tongue is a fire, the very world of iniquity; the tongue is set among our members as that which defiles the entire body, and sets on fire the course of our life, and is set on fire by hell. Just as Sodom and Gomorrah and the cities around them, since they in the same way as these indulged in gross immorality and went after strange flesh, are exhibited as an example, in undergoing the punishment of eternal fire. He also will drink of the wine of the wrath of God, which is mixed in full strength in the cup of His anger; and he will be tormented with fire and brimstone in the presence of the holy angels and in the presence of the Lamb. And the smoke of their torment goes up forever and ever; and they have no rest day and night, those who worship the beast and his image, and whoever receives the mark of his name. Nevertheless, as it is written, "What no eye has seen, nor ear heard, nor the human heart conceived, what God has prepared for those who love him"—God has something far better than words can describe for those who love Him. And the beast was seized, and with him the false prophet who performed the signs in his presence, by which he deceived those who had received the mark of the beast and those who worshiped his image; these two were thrown alive into the lake of fire which burns with brimstone. And the devil who deceived them was thrown into the lake of fire and brimstone, where the beast and the false prophet are also; and they will be tormented day and night forever and ever. And death and Hades were thrown into the lake of fire. This is the second death, the lake of fire. Likewise, if anyone's name was not found written in the book of life, he was thrown into the lake of fire. "And the smoke of their torment goes up forever and ever; and they have no rest day and night, those who worship the beast and his image, and whoever receives the mark of his name." The Son of Man will send forth His angels, and they will gather out of His kingdom all stumbling blocks, and those who commit lawlessness, and will cast them into the furnace of fire; in that place there shall be weeping and gnashing of teeth. And the devil who deceived them was thrown into the lake of fire and brimstone, where the beast and the false prophet are also; and they will be tormented day and night forever and ever. "But for the cowardly and unbelieving and abominable and murderers and immoral persons and sorcerers and idolaters and all liars, their part will be in the lake that burns with fire and brimstone, which is the second death. And if your eye causes you to stumble, cast it out; it is better for you to enter the kingdom of God with one eye, than having two eyes, to be cast into hell, where their worm does not die, and the fire is not quenched. And these will pay the penalty of eternal destruction, away from the presence of the Lord and from the glory of His power and then I will declare to them, 'I never knew you; depart from me, you who practice lawlessness.' And behold, they cried out, saying, "What do we have to do with You, Son of God? Have you come here to torment us before the time?" "And if your hand or your foot causes you to stumble, cut it off and throw it from you; it is better for you to enter life crippled or lame, than having two hands or two feet, to be cast into the eternal fire. "Then He will also say to those on His left, 'Depart from me, accursed ones, into the eternal fire which has been prepared for the devil and his angels; "And these will go away into eternal punishment, but the righteous into eternal life. Likewise, in Hades he lifted up his eyes, being in torment and saw Abraham far away, and Lazarus in his bosom. And he cried out and said, 'Father Abraham, have mercy on me, and send Lazarus, that he may dip the tip of his finger in water and cool off my tongue; for I am in agony in this flame.' I have five brothers that he may warn them, lest they also come to this place of torment.' Therefore leaving the elementary teaching about the Christ, let us press on to maturity, not laying again a foundation of repentance from dead works and of faith toward God, of instruction about washings, and laying on of hands, and the resurrection of the dead, and eternal judgment. The Lord knows how to rescue the godly from temptation, and to keep the unrighteous under punishment for the Day of Judgment. Just as Sodom and Gomorrah and the cities around them, since they in the same way as these indulged in gross immorality and went after strange flesh, are exhibited as an example, in undergoing the punishment of eternal fire. And the smoke of their torment goes up forever and ever; and they have no rest day and night, those who worship the beast and his image, and whoever receives the mark of his name."

"Enter by the narrow gate; for the gate is wide, and the way is broad that leads to destruction, and many are those who enter by it. Truly, truly, I say to you, he who hears my word, and believes Him who sent me, has eternal life, and does not come into judgment, but has passed out of death into life. Truly, truly, I say to you, if anyone keeps my word, he shall never see death. Therefore what benefit were you then deriving from the things of which you are now ashamed? For the outcome of those things is death. For the wages of sin is death, but the free gift of God is eternal life in Christ Jesus our Lord. What if God, although willing to demonstrate His wrath, and to make His power known, endured with much patience vessels of wrath prepared for destruction? For the sorrow that is according to the will of God produces a repentance without regret, leading to salvation, but the sorrow of the world produces death. For many walk, of whom I often told you, and now tell you even weeping, that they are enemies of the cross of Christ, whose end is destruction, whose god is their appetite, and whose glory, is in their shame, who set their minds on earthly things. Still, these will pay the penalty of eternal destruction, away from the presence of the Lord and from the glory of His power, then when lust has conceived, it gives birth to sin; and when sin is accomplished, it brings forth death. We know that we have passed out of death into life, because we love the brethren. He who does not love abides in death. Nevertheless, the present heavens and earth by His word are being reserved for fire, kept for the Day of Judgment and destruction of ungodly men. As also in all his letters, speaking in them of these things, in which are some things hard to understand, which the untaught and unstable distort, as they do also the rest of the Scriptures, to their own destruction. 'He who has an ear, let him hear what the Spirit says to the churches. He who overcomes shall not be hurt by the second death.' And the beast was seized, and with him the false prophet who performed the signs in his presence, by which he deceived those who had received the mark of the beast and those who worshiped his image; these two were thrown alive into the lake of fire which burns with brimstone. Blessed and holy is the one who has a part in the first resurrection; over these the second death has no power, but they will be priests of God and of Christ and will reign with Him for a thousand years.

Moreover, the devil who deceived them was thrown into the lake of fire and brimstone, where the beast and the false prophet are also; and they will be tormented day and night forever and ever. In addition, death and Hades were thrown into the lake of fire. This is the second death, the lake of fire. Likewise if anyone's name was not found written in the book of life, he was thrown into the lake of fire. Nevertheless, for the cowardly, unbelieving, and abominable, murderers, immoral persons, sorcerers, idolaters, and all liars, their part will be in the lake that burns with fire and brimstone, which is the second death. Son of man, take up a lamentation over the king of Tyre, and say to him, 'Thus says the Lord GOD, "You had the seal of perfection, Full of wisdom and perfect in beauty. You were in Eden, the garden of God; every precious stone was your covering: The ruby, the topaz, and the diamond; the beryl, the onyx, and the jasper; the lapis Lazuli, the turquoise, and the emerald; and the gold, the workmanship of your settings and sockets, Was in you. On the day that you were created, they were prepared. You were the anointed cherub who covers, and I placed you there. You were on the holy mountain of God; you walked in the midst of the stones of fire. You were blameless in your ways. From the day, you were created, until unrighteousness was found in you. By the abundance of your trade, you were internally filled with violence, and you sinned; therefore, I have cast you as profane from the mountain of God. Moreover, I have destroyed you, O covering cherub, from the midst of the stones of fire. Your heart was lifted up because of your beauty; you corrupted your wisdom because of your splendor. I cast you to the ground; I put you before kings, that they may see you. "By the multitude of your iniquities, in the unrighteousness of your trade, you profaned your sanctuaries. Therefore, I have brought fire from the midst of you; it has consumed you, and I have turned you to ashes on the earth in the eyes of all who see you. Moreover, the beast was seized, and with him the false prophet who performed the signs in his presence, by which he deceived those who had received the mark of the beast and those who worshiped his image; these two were thrown alive into the lake of fire, which burns with brimstone. He seized the dragon, that ancient serpent, who is the devil, or Satan, and bound him for a thousand years. He threw him into the Abyss, and locked and sealed it over him, to keep him from deceiving the nations anymore. Moreover, the devil, who deceived them, was thrown into the lake of burning sulfur, where the beast and the false prophet had been thrown. They will be tormented day and night forever and ever. Likewise, I saw a great white throne and Him who sat upon it, from whose presence earth and heaven fled away, and no place was found for them. Additionally, I saw the dead, the great and the small, standing before the throne, and books were opened; and another book was opened, which is the book of life; and the dead were judged from the things, which were written in the books, according to their deeds . . . Moreover if anyone's name was not found written in the book of life, he was thrown into the lake of fire.

Do you not know that wrongdoers will not inherit the kingdom of God? Do not be deceived! Fornicators, idolaters, adulterers, male prostitutes, sodomites, thieves, the greedy, drunkards, revilers, robbers—none of these will inherit the kingdom of God. Now the works of the flesh are obvious: fornication, impurity, licentiousness, idolatry, sorcery, enmities, strife, jealousy, anger, quarrels, dissensions, factions, envy, drunkenness, carousing, and things like these. I am warning you, as I warned you before, those who do such things will not inherit the kingdom of God. However, as for the cowardly, the faithless, the polluted, the murderers, the fornicators, the sorcerers, the idolaters, and all liars, their place will be in the lake that burns with fire and sulfur, which is the second death.

Indeed, true companion, I ask you also to help these women who have shared my struggle in the cause of the gospel, together with Clement also and the rest of my fellow workers, whose names are in the book of life. He who overcomes will thus be clothed in white garments; and I will not erase his name from the book of life, and I will confess his name before My Father and before His angels. All who dwell on the earth will worship him, everyone whose name has not been written from the foundation of the world in the book of life of the Lamb who has been slain. The beast that you saw was, and is not, and is about to come up out of the abyss and go to destruction. In addition, those who dwell on the earth, whose name has not been written in the book of life from the foundation of the world, will wonder when they see the beast, which he was and is not and will come. Also, nothing unclean, and no one who practices abomination and lying, shall ever come into it, but only those whose names are written in the Lamb's book of life. Moreover, I saw the dead, the great and the small, standing before the throne, and books were opened; and another book was opened, which is the book of life; and the dead were judged from the things, which were written in the books, according to their deeds. Moreover, if anyone's name was not found written in the book of life, he was thrown into the lake of fire, nothing unclean, and no one who practices abomination and lying shall ever come into it, but only those whose names are written in the Lamb's book of life. I tell you the truth; whoever hears my word, and believes him who sent me has eternal life and will not be condemned; he has crossed over from death to life.

Hell bound is all fornicators, idolaters, adulterers, homosexuals, sodomites, thieves, covetous, drunkards, revilers, and extortionists. Those who are sexually immoral in any way, or malicious, or envious, or murderers, or whisperers, or backbiters or haters of God, or violent, or proud, or boasters, or inventors of evil things, or disobedient to parents, or undiscerning, or untrustworthy, or unloving, or unforgiving, or unmerciful or lewd, or unclean, or contentious, or jealous, or selfish, or dissentious, or revelries, or angry or foolish, or disobedient, or deceived, or hateful, or lawless, or offensive, or insubordinate, or unholy, or kidnappers, or liars, or perjurers, or lovers of themselves, or lovers of money, or blasphemers, or unthankful, or slanderers, or without self-control, or brutal, or despisers of good, or traitors, or headstrong, or haughty, or lovers of pleasure, or cowards, or unbelieving, or sorcerers, or those who practice witchcraft, or soothsayers, or whoever interprets omens, or conjures spells, or a medium, or a spiritist, or one who calls up the dead, or diviners, or one who practices magic, or whoever loves and practices a lie." Chamuel then said, "They were warned."

So also is the resurrection of the dead. It is sown a perishable body, it is raised an imperishable body; it is sown in dishonor, it is raised in glory; it is sown in weakness, it is raised in power; it is sown a natural body, it is raised a spiritual body. If there is a natural body, there is also a spiritual body. For behold, I create new heavens and a new earth. Then, the former things shall not be remembered or come to mind. Nevertheless, according to His promise, we are looking for new heavens and a new earth, in which righteousness dwells, for the Lamb in the center of the throne shall be their shepherd, and shall guide them to springs of the water of life; and God shall wipe every tear from their eyes. Likewise, we saw a new heaven and a new earth, for the first heaven and the first earth passed away, and there is no longer any sea. In addition, the new city has no need of the sun or of the moon to shine upon it, for the glory of God has illumined it, and its lamp is the Lamb. Additionally, there shall no longer be any night; and they shall not have need of the light of a lamp nor the light of the sun, because the Lord God shall illumine them; and they shall reign forever and ever. Thou dost light our lamp; The Lord our God illumines our darkness. For with Thee is the fountain of life; In Thy light we see light. Thy word is a lamp to my feet, and a light to my path. He is the light of the all; and they who follow him shall not walk in the darkness, but shall have the light of life. Likewise, this is the message we have heard from Him and announce to you, that God is light, and in Him, there is no darkness at all. What is more, he showed us a river of the water of life, clear as crystal, coming from the throne of God and of the Lamb. Also, it will come about in that day that living waters will flow out of Jerusalem, half of them toward the eastern sea and the other half toward the western sea; it will be in summer as well as in winter. From your innermost being shall flow rivers of living water. You shall hunger no more, neither thirst anymore; shall the sun beat down on you, neither nor any heat. On each side of the river stood the tree of life, bearing twelve crops of fruit, yielding its fruit every month. The kingdom of God is not eating and drinking, but righteousness, peace, and joy. The renewal in which there is no distinction between Greek and Jew, circumcised and uncircumcised, barbarian, Scythian, slave and freeman, but Christ is all, and in all. The Lamb in the center of the throne shall be their shepherd, and shall guide them to springs of the water of life; and God shall wipe every tear from their eyes. Nevertheless, you have come to Mount Zion, to the heavenly Jerusalem, the city of the living God. You have come to thousands upon thousands of angels in joyful assembly, to the church of the firstborn, whose names are written in heaven. You have come to God, the judge of all men, to the spirits of righteous men made perfect, to Jesus the mediator of a new covenant, and to the sprinkled blood, that speaks a better word than the blood of Abel . . . Therefore, since we are receiving a kingdom that cannot be shaken, let us be thankful, and so worship God acceptably with reverence and awe, for our God is a consuming fire. However, in keeping with his promise we are looking forward to a new heaven and a new earth, the home of righteousness. However, just as it is written, "Things which eye has not seen and ear has not heard, and which have not entered the heart of man, all that God has prepared for those who love him." Moreover, I heard a loud voice from the throne, saying, "Behold, the tabernacle of God is among men, and He shall dwell among them, and they shall be His people, and God Himself shall be among them." In addition, I looked, and I heard the voice of many angels around the throne and the living creatures and the elders; and the number of them was myriads of myriads, and thousands of thousands. Nevertheless, you have come to Mount Zion and to the city of the living God, the heavenly Jerusalem, and to myriads of angels, to the general assembly and church of the firstborn who are enrolled in heaven, and to God, the Judge of all, and to the spirits of the righteous made perfect. Moreover, the gates of it shall not be shut at all by day: for there shall be no night there. In addition, there shall be no more curse: but the throne of God and of the Lamb shall be in it; and his servants shall serve him and they shall see his face; and his name shall be in their foreheads (minds). Moreover, there shall be no night there; and they need no candle, neither light of the sun; for the Lord God gives them light: and they shall reign forever and ever. Moreover, he said unto me, these sayings are faithful and true: and the Lord God of the holy prophets sent his angel to show unto his servants the things that must shortly be done. Behold, I come quickly: blessed is he that keeps the sayings of the prophecy of this book. Then the eyes of the blind shall be opened, and the ears of the deaf shall be unstopped. Then shall the lame man leap as a hart (deer), and the tongue of the dumb sing: for in the wilderness shall waters break out, and streams in the desert. They shall build houses, and inhabit them; and they shall plant vineyards, and eat the fruit of them. They shall not build, and another inhabits; they shall not plant, and another eats: for as the days of a tree are the days of my people, and mine elect shall long enjoy the work of their hands. They shall not labor in vain, nor bring forth for trouble, for they are the seed of the blessed of the Lord, and their offspring with them. The wolf and the lamb shall feed together, and the lion shall eat straw like the bullock: and dust shall be the serpent's meat. They shall not hurt nor destroy in my entire holy mountain, says the Lord. For as the new heavens and the new earth, which I will make, shall remain before me, says the Lord, so shall your seed and your name remain. Moreover, it shall happen, that, from one new moon to another, and from one Sabbath to another, shall all flesh come to worship before me, says the Lord. The righteous shall never be removed, but the wicked shall not inhabit the (new) earth. Moreover, there shall not way enter into it anything that defiles, neither whatsoever works abomination, or makes a lie, but they, which are written in the Lamb's book of life. Moreover, there was given him dominion, and glory, and a kingdom, that all people, nations, and languages, should serve him: his dominion is an everlasting dominion, which shall not pass away, and his kingdom that which shall not be destroyed. Then we, which are alive and remain, shall be caught up together with them in the clouds, to meet the Lord in the air: and so shall we ever be with the Lord. Even though I walk through the valley of the shadow of death, I will fear no evil, for you are with your rod; your staff, and me they comfort me. Surely, goodness and love will follow me all the days of my life, and I will dwell in the house of the LORD forever."

Chamuel said unto us, "This you did not witness, therefore now you have witnessed so you understand." The master sent his messengers to humanity, who beat, and killed them saying they were from the deceiver. You all have heard those stories, as those debts have been settled. Humanity was warned and freely rewarded. They merely had to accept the one who created them and enjoy eternity in his image. We now looked at each other knowing we needed some time alone together. We traveled quickly through the multiple hells, you for the most part we kept our eyes closed. The Patmos did most of the viewing. The horrible screams were enough to appall us to no end. They not only were suffering from their individual torments, but also from the demons and devils who added to their misery. I consider this so low because they deceived innocents, trapped them, took them from their eternal reward, and now continue to feast upon them. I can so completely understand the words that the book told us, how if your hand does evil cut it off. The reason to cut if off is not so much that you will do evil again, it is why you will do evil. That reason being that evil has your hand and it will spread caster than a cancer until it controls all your body. It is better to see your hand rot than your soul within the deceiver's grip, which once it took hold never surrendered. We now saw a small capsule arrive beside us then entered within our large capsule. We watched it not being alarmed, as Chamuel appeared not to worry. Then a male spirit got out and walked to the middle of our group representing himself to be of no danger to us. We all just looked at him, figuring that another mission was going to be given to us. To our surprise, Rita cheerfully exclaims, "Richard, is that you?" He smiles and walks towards her shares their warm hug. Rita tells us, "Family, this is Richard, Holly's Uncle." We all then got excited, for finally since we have been here we were able to see someone that we believed would be here. I practically adored the way Rita called us family, as her previous age being far beyond ours give her the title of aunt. This extra member actually rearranged our grouping order now, in that we were four couples now and each couple concentrated on their mate whereas before a few of the couples were rearranged in order to keep Rita from being alone. Our group now felt somewhat like outsiders here, in that we saw just now how much we missed, yet I for one, do not understand why we had to miss it. Either way, something still had to be in the works in that Chamuel was still with us. Somehow, we all had that feeling that our preferential treatment had not quite yet ended.

CHAPTER 12

Temporary home in Midlertidifjem

I painfully ask Chamuel, "Why must we keep the terrifying visions from the underworlds that we have reported, considering the other Saints here in heaven are not tormented by them." Chamuel then looks at us and reveals, "Oh the children of the Ancient One, you are yet to become Saints." Jennifer then angrily questions, "Why do you say that we are not Saints?" I could feel the hurt in her voice. Chamuel then said, "Saints in heaven may no longer have the knowledge of Good or Evil." I subsequently asked Chamuel, "How do we make ourselves free of such knowledge?" Chamuel then said, "Only He that sits on Throne may do that?" Next, in a flash Flying Dove spoke out with fire in her voice and anger in her heart, "Stop with the twenty questions game and tell us what is going on." I look at Floyd, who simply smiles back at me. We all know she had a right to be angry at the game that Chamuel was playing. Chamuel then answers, "I was not playing games, for I answered the question laid before me." Next, Flying Dove, still poised for battle loads another arrow in her mouth and questions, "Later tell us what is going on?" Then Rita added, "Tell us where we are going and why, please tell us all you know about the future plans laid out for us." Chamuel now paused and said, "Have no fear chosen ones, for you are the protectors of the Patmos, and for only one millennium, we shall give to you a world of your choice so that you may live in peace until the Patmos is beyond the reach of any in our heavens. Lucifer shall be released for a short season. After he is defeated once again, our knowledge of Good and Evil will be cast with him, and with those who he lives within their hearts into the bottomless pit for eternity with its keys destroyed." Holly now asked, "How can something be locked into a fathomless pit, for this tells us the bottom is not sealed?" Chamuel currently reports, "Holly it has no bottom for it is as a globe, such that the ending is the beginning." We were now able to see how the pit would indeed be bottomless. Little Running Eagle now questions, "Why do you talk about He who sits on the Throne, as being separate from the Heavens, and as such who rules the Heavens?" Chamuel is now answering, "Until Evil will be incessantly imprisoned in the bottomless pit, and the Ancient One must sit upon the Throne. Once the boundless pit is, forever sealed throne will be no more, as the Ancient One and the Lord will forever live inside the Saints so that the original image, and the created images shall reflect from each other being both independent and dependent. Worry not about understanding this, as you shall understand it when you are made one with it. Now, we shall search for your new home for the next thousand years." Flying Dove at the moment shot another arrow, "I thought that time was no more?" Chamuel then clarified, "When the bottomless pit is sealed so shall time." As we continued our search through so many places, I noticed that all the solar systems we were seeing had two stars. I asked Chamuel, "Why do all these places have two stars?" He said, "So that there will only be daylight." Not long thereafter, if such a concept of long now matters, we discovered a world we all loved. This would hand large dark-green lakes that feed into blue, salt-free lakes. We could see many long sand filled beaches surrounded by mountains that had a sharp, almost castle like peaks. The planet was surrounded by many moons, which helped reduce the lights from the suns and thus enabled us to see the millions of stars behind it. The surfaces of the moons were, for the most part, smooth with small mountains and long shallow riverbeds. They were lightly speckled with meteor craters, which gave us some insurance of a stable space to the region. Some of the mountain ranges looked like city skyscrapers made from sand, mixed with both smooth and steep walls. Some even appeared to have steps carved from the winds cut into their sides. We also appreciate how these lakes and ocean side mountain ranges have passes, which lead to large flat Meadowlands. We ask Chamuel to allow us some more time to study this world. Jennifer loves the way the inner moons reflect the sunlight on the mountain ranges as it creates a perception that one touches the other. I enjoy the way in which the moons different orbits allow them to appear stacked on each other. This aids in taking away the emptiness of space and adds to the feeling of not being alone. Holly now asks Chamuel, "How do we make our homes and travel from place to place?" Chamuel answers, "We will have armies of angels on the moons surrounding this world that can protect you and build your cities as you desire. This world is in view of the Throne, as he points to the bundle of burning stars to the right of our sky. As we look into this area, we can now feel the power radiating from it. Concerning your ability to travel, there are two options. First, which will be desirable when exploring, playing, or traveling in groups are the white-winged horses. You will see them traveling through the sky. They will obey your commands as anything, which lives for this world, and its moons must do. Second, you may think of the place, and as you think about it, you shall be taken in that place. A special treat these sky horses can provide is the touring of the mountain peaks even as they tower above the clouds. This world is called Midler-tidif-jem or Midlertidifjem." We now all agreed that this would be our world, and Chamuel lowered our space chariot onto the beach and told us. You may keep your chariot as your home until your cities are completed. At that time, one of you shall guide our angels where you desire to hide it. You will need it when your knowledge of evil cast into the bottomless pit." Jennifer now asked, "Will our children have the knowledge of evil?" Chamuel then answered, "No, for in order to be born from the knowledge of evil, the great deceiver must place it in their soul. The deceiver now being bound, therefore, cannot place this knowledge in their souls. We shall have the Tree of Eternal Life grows twelve different types of fruit on this planet, where you all may eat freely thereof. Flying Dove saw a beautiful mountain range with white ice and evergreens and asked if we could all talk there first as we discussed our new world. We also were hungry for a taste of Montana once more. We held hands as we floated through the soft wind to a congenial rock ledge that overshadowed a amiable tree filled valley. They appear to be taller on this world and able to find more places to grow even though scattered among the mountain cliffs, which are indeed steep. Both suns are shinning now, so the stars are not visible. They slowly emerge as the suns fall to away from each other, with only one being visible, for the most part, of the day. Jennifer believes that is because of the other parts around the world needing sunlight also at all times. We practice using our new bodies on this ledge. I enjoy the ability to jump and hold that position. We can control the gravity, which means that if we jump from this cliff, we can float through the air and control our descent. This is nice, especially when sitting almost in the clouds. We do not feel any heat or cold. This world has no animals. Little Running Eagle and Flying Dove want to create some animals in this world. We all agree that would be a good idea, although we do not know how to do such a task. I wave for one of the sky horses to come before us. When he arrives, I ask him, "How can we create beasts in this world?" The horse looks at me in confusion. Rita then adds, "I think the horse believes you to be foolish" as everyone now laughs. Afterwards a thick light blue cloud appeared before us as a woman with wings walked out and introduced herself, "I am Metetron, the angel and destroyer of the beasts." She was unlike any woman or angel we had ever seen. Her wings were enormous, a wooly white, and very furry. Her hair was the color of coal and extremely long as it flowed under the protection of her wings. Her skin was white and soft. She had black breast cups wrapped with a yielding flowing silk that blended into a large curved horn that came from her back. She had a shoulder plate covering her left shoulder. Her arms, legs, and right side of her chest and stomach were painted in light blue symbols as a language we know not. She was adorned in beautiful braces that had many beautiful stones embedded in her arm highlighting the symbols. The symbols have a peaceful, almost musical rhythm to them. The belts that held up her waist silk had many coin badges not being able to describe it as anything else. In her right hand with a dragon tail shaped knuckle bow, a twelve-pointed tsuba that extended halfway up to her blade followed by a bloodless razor-sharp kissaki with the Boshi at her swords end. Blood was still dripping from the middle part of blade verifying the accuracy of her swing. She held the head of a beast in her left hand as his blood spotted her lower legs and draping silk that lightly covered her left leg. She also had a large precious stone, most likely a diamond hanging from a chain that extended from her belly button. Metetron now lowered her sword, raised her head, and asked us, "How may I serve you today?" Her voice was soft and her lips red as cherries and eyes warm with her eyebrow's coal black. However, even though looked so peaceful we could still see that sword and had to remember she was a fighter. I then asked her, "Metetron, who does that head belongs to?" She answered, "To the beast that I took it from, so now it belongs to me." Flying Dove now fires another one of the famous voice arrows, "Oh goody, another Chamuel. We get to sit here and ask millions of questions." Metetron then looked at her and said, "Subsequently why do you not tell me why you have called for me, instead of asking foolish questions to horses and me?" I was impressed with Metetron's answer as she put Flying Dove back into her place. I then asked her, "Metetron, can you make beasts of this world?" She answered, "Yes, tell me what you want, and we will make them. I then told her, "Metetron, you look so kind and sweet, yet with that beast's head; I can see you are also a great warrior." She then smiled and told us, "Oh, this is part of our training, as we are always preparing for invasions. This is a copy of some beasts whom we have discovered four suns below us. When we find another life form, we must all train so if they attack, they will be walking into their deathtraps." She then released her sword and the beast's head, as they both vanished to include the beast's blood that spotted her body. She now walked casually before us and said, "When you design an animal, you must also tell me where to put in on this world. You should design its feeding habits to match where you put it to live. We only create beasts who eat vegetation, as flesh eaters are no longer permitted. Thus, if you want to make a lion, he will eat the vegetation. I will tell you how many of each breed that an area my support, also accounting for the sky horses that must similarly feed. They will not reproduce, nor will there be male or female. Their function is to serve you and keep the vegetable cleared and kept low. They also will be able to defend you from other beasts, in case some sneak in from other worlds, which I can assure you will be vertically impossible. Fortunately, for your safety, I always deal with the virtually impossible. Little Running Eagle began by suggesting that Metetron create buffalo, elephants, giraffes, and highly bred cattle. Flying Dove suggested next that Metetron creates Doves, Eagles, Rabbits, squirrels and ponies. I suggested dogs, and Holly suggested cats. Rita and Richard suggested Owls and zebras. Metetron now created a globe of our world and asked us where to put these animals. We all agreed that it would be nice if they could live together over our entire world. Metetron currently suggested that we divided the globe now, so her comrades could create the borders. We asked if she could leave the globe so our group could discuss it for some time. Metetron then created the animals, and we saw their numbers as they roamed the globe she had made for us. This globe floated across the sky above us. We could touch a place, and that place would appear before us. We later learned that the image of that place was before us, since we could not determine how so many places could all be here in front of each. We so much enjoyed this gift, as we could all learn so much about this world. Metetron told us, "You may add islands, rivers, mountain, and change the lands anyway you wish to do. This is your world. Rita recommended that we make these changes together and to consider that we would all have children to care for. I then asked Metetron if she could give us some visions of the heavens where most Saints were living, therefore, when we created our world, it would give consistency to our children when we later departed. Metetron then told us, "Of course; however, remember you do not have to give up this world, and since you have claimed it, no other Saints may live here." Jennifer now added, "That is good news Metetron, so it would not be like we were wasting these thousand years, but building a strong foundation for our future." Metetron then added, "Very wise, and make sure you have as many children as possible before the beast is forever imprisoned in the bottomless pit. When the new heavens and new earth appear, all Saints will be given their eternal souls, which shall neither marry nor make children." Holly now asked, "Will I still be married to George?" Metetron then said, "Yes, and you will keep the memories for the one thousand years you have lived in this heaven. You will not remember your days on earth nor your journeys for the Patmos." I then looked at everyone and then said, "If we want to do the things we did in Montana, then we simply create them here, such as our Canyon Ferry Lake and the Helena National Forest, making them exactly as we wish, taking out the bad, ugly, and adding more of what we liked. One example is the briar patch on the north end, plus all that junk that fools have been throwing at it. We can change the water to a soft blue. Everyone agreed, and then Jennifer said, "Tonight, we shall divide the world into five parts, one for each of us, and one for all of us." We all looked at Jennifer knowing she had discovered the perfect plan for us. We all wanted our own lands in the future when our families were large, yet for now, we wanted to live together and enjoy ourselves first. Rita then suggested that we all agreed to wait one year before having children and thus concentrate on making our world exactly as we want and to learn everything we can about ourselves first. We all agreed, as I was happy to have some strong thinking women in our group. Then Holly and Little Dove suggested we broke into our individual couples and discover our relationships. Rita and Jennifer immediately agreed, thus telling us 'males',' we would soon be joining our spouses. Metetron then asked, "Do you desire anything more from me, as I am naturally of no value on your relationship needs?" As I looked at her, I thought, "It is so sad that such a creation of beauty not be involved with relationships." Jennifer then walked over to her and gave her a hug and kiss upon her cheek saying, "You have been such a great help, and I do so much want you to be actively a part of our world." I afterwards added, "Is there someone we could ask to make you the Angel of Midlertidifjem, which you may dwell with us." Metetron then asked, "What about when you go your four ways?" Rita subsequently added, "Could we not make four of you?" Metetron said, "That you may, give me your thoughts concerning me living among you, and if you are all in agreement I will ask my Legion King." She then collected our thoughts and apologized saying, "I am sorry, as one of you does not desire this, my Legion King will not accept this request." We then asked, "Who does not desire this?" Metetron said, "As I must serve all of you, I must accept the desires and wishes of each, therefore, I will not betray that honesty." I then, knowing that we cannot lie, suggest we ask each one to stand and that the one who said no, tell us why." The group agreed and one by one, we stood. Holly had moved to the back of the line. When all confessed to saying yes, with only one remaining to talk, as only Holly remained. I then asked Holly, "Why do you not want Metetron to live among us?" Holly then said, "Because she is so beautiful and immaculate." Jennifer now added, "Holly, we are in Heaven as all things shall always be beautiful and perfect. If you fear beauty and perfection you will not enjoy heaven." Holly later confessed that she was wrong and agreed to have Metetron live among us. Metetron then vanished and within a few seconds reappeared saying, "The King has agreed, thus I shall serve you and your descendants for as long as you desire." I noticed that she had no sword with her and asked her, "Metetron, where is your sword?" She answered, "It is with my Legion, as I shall have no need for it here. If a war must be fought, my Legion will fight it, and my mission will be to guide you to safety." I believe we all felt much more relaxed knowing this side of Metetron would live with us. We also knew that with her around, we would be safe. Jennifer then asked her, "Metetron, is there anything that you need to bring you joy?" Metetron then answered, "I am an angel. We are a different creation from our Lord's images. We neither have a gender nor are we given in marriage. We simply know how to serve." Then Flying Dove said, "For not having a gender, someone puts you together with the perfection that women can only dream of being." Metetron then said, "The body I now have was created by your group. This form brought joy to all within your group. Flying Dove then said, “I can see what brings our men joy and the joy we receive watching them pretend not to be impressed.” I then told Flying Dove, “I do not pretend, not to be impressed yet because of her beauty, I cannot deny her power and the security that she gives us.” Jennifer then added, “Exactly, she is as an older sister whom I never had.” Holly then added, “I guess this is what makes heaven a joy, not to overshadow her being created to help make our lives happier and safer.” We all agreed and individually gave her hugs and kisses along her cheek while welcoming her to our new family. It then hit me, “Wow, Metetron is as the love to our mother and power of our father.” Everyone joyfully agreed. I then asked her, “If we talk about our battles with evil will that place you in danger?” She answered, “Your previous experiences with evil have no effect on me, as I have no knowledge of Evil, thus cannot hear it, cannot see it, and accordingly cannot know it.” Rita then said, “I still have some chills about what we saw in the pits and sure hope we could talk about it, and determine some way to bind it.” I added, “That we must do, especially since Richard does not know it and therefore, cannot help you.” Jennifer then added, “Why do we all not think about how we want our cities to look like and where we want them, thus allowing both Richard and Metetron design them for us. I also recommend that we divide this world into four quarters as we would be an orange and assign the quarters according to seniority in marriage such as North East goes to Rita, South East goes to George; South West goes to Floyd, and North West goes to Little Running Eagle. The suns shine equally in all quarters and if one of the other quarters has an area, you desire simply to make one like unto it in your area. We shall make a small island on the north pole to create our united land, which once we go to our separate lands shall go back to their original owners; however, it is divided between Rita and Little Running Bear.” We all agreed to such a worthy plan since it divided the land equally, accounted for the lack of needed a united land after we divided, and provided an ability to copy what we wanted from the other lands. Thus, Metetron and Richard went around the globe as the rest of us went to another mountain peak that had a nice large plateau that we could show the visions on while we floated above them. Holly asked Rita, “Do you not worry about Richard and Metetron?” Rita then told her, “Holly, you will not have a long relationship if you worry over such things. When your heart is filled with love, you enjoy when the one who you love is also enjoying. Your uncle Richard and I enjoyed so many wonderful years as he suffered hard to give a great life for me. If he were to desire that angel, I would care not. It would not be worth the agony of my fruitless worry. Holly, you must think about what worries you. Thus, your real question is, 'Do I trust an angel with my husband?' The answer to that is yes, and I can only hope to flood him with as many angels as he wishes. If I cannot trust him, then I cannot keep him. He is worthy of a life of trust." Holly looked at her aunt and said, "Aunt Rita; I need you to teach me many things about how to be such a great wife as you." Jennifer and Flying Dove both added, "Please teach us also." I then, being a funny boy added, "Yes, Aunt Rita, teach them." We all laughed, as we currently knew the great value of Rita and Richard, as I knew Little Running Eagle, Floyd, and myself would be talking much with him. Aunt Rita now smiled and said, "Do not rush it; it will come to you naturally over time and time we have so much of. at present, let us prepare to fight the horrors in our minds." We now all joined our thoughts as the descent to the pit once more began. We could now clearly see how it was indeed a globe with a giant rock near the center. This rock was very dense, probably weighing a ton for each grain within it. The rock is large enough that when walking around on it; you do not notice the gravitational pulls, which strangely is the same of that which is on the surface. The closer one goes to its center, the less the gravity. The opposite is true when moving over the surface, for as one goes nearer to the surface the gravity pulls harder making it impossible to leave the pit. The big difference is that the gravity will not throw the spirit that is floating towards its limits to center rock, yet strongly pulls them away as if teasing them to try again. The heat is extreme yet these evil beasts still find enough consciousness to prey upon each other. Jennifer now notices colonies of souls being tormented in the same way. We try to determine how the torments are different; nonetheless, each time close our eyes, after viewing just a few of them. This place is very much packed, as I am able to determine that, their sizes were reduced when placed inside here. We now agree to concentrate on one face at a time and discuss it. The first face we see appears somewhat long gated, as its neck is slightly smaller than its cheeks. Flames burn all around its head, yet it waivers not as its evil eyes are locked solidly on us. A white light replaces most of its lips. The eyes are the demonic feature here, red with a small round black pupil to control the center. These eyes told us why he was in hell, and I suggest that its white lips mean it was a deceiver. I now was beginning the think that as we looked at each one, we could see why they were here. The next spirit we looked at had a face filled with rage as each of its hands was like claws and its teeth showing in its open mouth as if to devour. Whatever should enter its mouth? Fire also blazed around its tilted head and around its evil eyes stared away from us looking upward as if discovering another spirit to torment. Same white flowed through its hands as if to tell us this was a murderer. We now saw a group of fire spirits as they danced around a small white light. We could see specific gender parts for both male and female floating freely in the fire, and white flashing lights, which looked like whips as they beat on the center light. We agreed that this might have been a rapist, who beat and tortured its victims. To think of an eternity of being raped and beaten for this deed while on earth. Those few minutes of evil pleasure, not knowing the pains that its victims felt, are now being lived multiple times repeatedly, with no end ever to come. The next group we saw had its victims wrapped inside swirls of blazing fires wrapped inside some sort of insulation that would not let the heat to escape, causing it to appear with belts of black as they moved around in a circle of a star of David blazing in the middle. The white flowed from them to the star near the middle. Then a voice told us, "These are those who killed my innocent children, without just cause." This region was big as we could see these black swirls, which appeared, as a thick and deep forest. We now saw visions of the Holocaust. I asked this voice, "Do these also include enemies of Israel when Israel attacked them?" The voice then said, "No, for they had just caused." I subsequently asked the voice, "Who are you?" The voice afterwards said, "I am your Patmos, and I want you all to understand why the wicked must be punished, for if you have trouble with it when you first saw it, later other kingdoms shall also have trouble when they see it. What you are doing is noble and shall add so much to our story." Jennifer then asked, "Do you think that the Ancient One will be disappointed in the weakness of our understanding?" Patmos answered, "No, for he recommended that we give you a world where you could search for the truths in your mind. Remember, he created you as a writer writes a book. Should not that writer know what the words are in the book that he or she wrote?" We all were relieved now as I added, "Well, then my comrades, let us give such a great God the Patmos that he deserves." It was as my grandmother always told me, "You catch more bears with honey than you do with vinegar," and this was as good a time as any to spread out the honey, I felt excellent about my last outburst of wisdom as I could see my comrades also enjoyed. We have now watched as large groups gave their terrifying performances. Patmos explained each image with great clarity.

The one thing we never saw was a happy face, as evil can find no joy in tormenting yet only finds torment in not being able to torment more. Patmos explained that the roles were reversed, as those who inflicted the sins would have the memories of their sins in their minds showing how weak and foolish they truly had been, as they could see those, they tormented now living in heaven if they had made it or others living in heaven with their happiness, joy and riches overflowing. Evil also torments over others being happier, richer, or greater than they are. We learned that a lot of the torment in hell is mental as that anguish intensifies the blazing fire and heat around them. We can also see the fallen angels as they search for more to torture, which adds now miseries to the lost souls. Holly wanted to know everything about the security in Hell, so she could put this terror to rest. She saw many horror movies where the beast is killed, only to reappear shortly thereafter. When we start seeing movies with ten plus sequels, any hope of a final death to evil erodes. Patmos then showed us how the pit could never be opened, even if the original Earth was to be destroyed. The dynamics of its design with the profound heat would fire it as a missile through the cold space as it would rise to a point shooting into another star driving straight to its center. Hell's intense density would not be stopped by any object. Patmos afterwards further explained that the Earth could never explode without the throne not knowing about it, thus God would be there immediately and then move it to its new destination, which would be a star and therefore, intensify the heat even more. God made sure that all of Hell knew this, and as a result they should work harder to prevent an increase in their torture. We could see so many Legions of angels surrounding this earth and that these angels were very powerful. Evil was in its pit, and even when it was to be released for a season, it would still be bound upon the old Earth only able to venture to the dormant kingdoms that lay in the clouds. Holly currently asked about those kingdoms, as they would follow Lucifer to attack the holy city. Patmos assured her that these kingdoms were now in a deep sleep. They can only be awakened by the key, which Lucifer will bring to them. We at present each released our visions of the pit into the open Patmos that lay below us, which quickly closed below us. We were at the moment completely free of that terrifying experience and now jumped for joy, until we began to question why we were celebrating. We at this moment in time decided to look for Richard and our guardian angel, as we knew not where they were. We glided around our neighboring mountain ranges as I spotted our big globe and saw someone working with it. I then guided our group back to our globe where we discovered our lost parties. As we landed Richard asked, "Have you all accomplished that which you sought?" Rita said, "I believe we have. So what great works have you done?" Richard told her, "I have added many landscapes features to our new lands, moved some rivers, added a good touch of our Montana to it." We all then walked to our sections and started working on them. One thing that I added to my section was a nice meadow with a copy of Uncle Earl's home covered with new shiny white wood and a amiable strong roof. I did not know what to put inside, as I have never before been inside. I was just comfortable with seeing it in a meadow where it would give me some sense of home. Jennifer was impressed with it, as was Floyd and they both added a copy to their lands, and the three of us added a copy to our temporary united lands. We all enjoyed this activity and found ourselves seeking much advice from Metetron. We all valued her warm input, and were very much surprised with her vast knowledge. She told us that she had traveled many worlds. We then asked her to share some beautiful memories she had seen on these worlds. Each image amazed us so much.

Holly and I decided to add a lake in our lands from her vision. It had deep-blue water in the middle that reflected the forests from the other side. It was shallow along the shores as beautiful meadows allowed easy access. Even the rocks that I could see long the shallow shorelines were laid out in artistic design. I could see us enjoying expanded boat rides on this lake and our children swimming and playing along the shorelines. The open meadows offered us plenty of places to camp on the open as the nearby forests offered a lot of territory for hiking and other forest adventures than with great joy our children will create. The beauty of the white clouds reflecting from the surface is breathtaking, if only I had a breath that could be taken. I still have a spirit that can be inspired as it is now inspired.

Rita and Richard carved out a large copy of a grand canyon. This was grander in that it had way down ridges that towered out into the open canyon. They leveled the top throughout the entire area to create an appearance of what was there before they carved deep into our world. The bottomlands had nice forests with rivers flowing through it. They carved many images along the high cliffs that would promote discovery and even had Metetron flood it with carved images that she liked. This would give them cause to explore through this maze of bewilderment. The suns would chase the shadows inside this canyon world creating another sense of wild movement.

Flying Dove and Floyd selected a beautiful value surrounded by giant steep rock mountains that towered among the clouds, blending the white of the frozen ice that hugged its cliffs with the white as the clouds. The value had nice meadows scattered with tall evergreens that grew closer as they moved up the cliffs. The lake was also a wonder, as it was shallow as far as we could see. It was scattered with rocks that had been shaped into stones. These stones could easily be rearranged in such a way to create small islands, or even seats for comfortable outings as a family in the middle of the lake. The green of the evergreens colored the surface in the area, we were viewing it. We noticed that the far end to the lake was free of shore side trees, thus a deep blue from the clouds colored it. The brown from the lakebed colored the waters before us. The clouds also painted some white on the water. This had a touch of Montana that emphasized its total homeland feeling. I can see them spending much time relaxing and playing here.

Now Little Running Eagle and Jennifer selected their special place. They were more settled in their desires requiring more stability, maturity, and color of their choice. They selected a beautiful spacious slowly sloping valley. This valley was multilayered, as it had layers of different types of trees with so many colors of leaves dancing through it. They only kept a minimal amount of open meadows, which ran as empty rivers through their forests. They also added a few extra tall trees to be scattered that was an excellent special touch. This large value was sandwiched between two solid mountain ranges. Unlike the broken and packed peaks of the other ranges, these mountains had continuous ranges that would glide to a high peak during the middle before slowly dropping to the shallow passes on each side. There were other ranges behind it, which could only be viewed from the passes, thus to leave this valley without the sky horses or flying would require worming through the ranges, which would make for a good, hard thinking mountain adventure. The spaciousness of the valley adds to the majestic view provided by the white spotted mountains. The time they spent so select so many different colors of vegetation add to the wonder of this special place in our world.

Metetron currently asked us for more requests. Jennifer told her that was enough for now, and if we made too many too fast they would lose the special value that we wanted them to have and that is our memories of enjoying them. We all agreed from the images that we saw that she may place some scattered among our lands as special surprises for us, as we have yet to fully explore our lands. This brought her great joy as she asked, "Why do you trust my judgment so fast, as I am a lower creation than you?" Holly surprisingly told her, "Metetron, you are far from being a low creature among us. You are one that we all depend upon and have much respect, and love for all that is you. In the short time, we have known you; you have become the spirit of Midlertidifjem. Midlertidifjem would not be a home without you. The answer for me is always yes for anything you wish to give unto us. Your knowledge of heaven is the only knowledge of heaven we have." With this, she went over and kissed Metetron on both cheeks. Metetron now smiled and said, "Holly, that really means a lot to me, especially knowing that you originally wanted me not to live among you." Holly then fired back, "So you understand why one as foolish as myself would need you even more than the others." At this Flying, Dove jumped in and said, "You do not get her all for yourself. We all want her and thus shall share her until she becomes four when we go to our own lands. I know in my city shall be a large mansion for her to enjoy while I seek her counsel almost daily." Metetron then said, "The wonderful love that you are giving me makes me want to work harder to serve you. I do promise that I shall study your minds and create for you the things you desire. I trust you all do know that your powers are greater than mine?" I subsequently told her, "That may be Metetron; however, we are children of these powers and never had parents to show us how to develop them." Metetron then said, "That brings me much joy, as I can teach these things to my masters, so your joys will be greater." Rita now said, "Metetron, I trust you with my powers and you may use them as you desire." Metetron then added, "I may only use them with your permission as you watch your powers being used. If you turn away for an instant, your powers will go back to you. This is not by my will but by the laws of He who sits upon the Throne." Floyd now asked, "Why would he make a law such as that?" Metetron told us that, "Once an angel abused the powers of other angels and did something very bad taking as many as one-third of the angels as his servants. We all begged that the Ancient One would make it so none among us can ever again abuse the power of another." We all knew this story very well and we knew where the angel and his followers now lived. We also knew that Metetron would not know this as she could know no evil. Floyd now quickly responded, "Okay, I understand now. Thanks for putting my mind at ease. I just foolishly thought another was abusing you and thus wanted to punish whoever may ever abuse you." Metetron then quickly added, "Worry not Floyd, for if one was to abuse me, He who sits on the Throne would quickly obtain justice for on our behalf, as he is always with me. The Ancient One is very protective of his angels and even as I exist with you, he watches us constantly. This is how I get extra powers to create the things, which you desire. He truly only watches us for protection and to ensure we are all happy." I just now had to say, "Metetron, each minute we spend with you we learn so many things. I believe that we will also schedule many classes where you can share with us your great knowledge." Metetron replied, "I can think of nothing that would bring me a greater joy. When do you wish to begin your cities? We can create the shell and then work on the interior designs until you move to your city." Jennifer then countered, "Should we not build a simple city here first?" Metetron then responded, "That would be very wise?" Then as Jennifer was thinking, a bewildered look covered her face and she declared, "I know not what buildings we would need, except for private rooms when we explore the loves the couples share. We have no need for garments, we have no cars, and we do not need hospitals or police officers. We do not eat thus food markets are not needed and we do not drink water nor expel wastes from our bodies, thereby water purification companies are not needed. We only need a large one-room schoolhouse for Metetron to teach us, and a mansion for her to enjoy. Metetron now stated, "I will only have a mansion if each of you with your spouse also has a mansion. I would also recommend that you create a temple so we may sing the songs of heaven and worship the Ancient One and the Lord, as we should also dedicate or tithe our time. Likewise, there are many holy books written by the Saints in heaven that you may have." Jennifer now added, "A temple we shall build first in any city we dwell. We shall have beautiful gardens with all manner of flowers growing within. The inside shall have an altar that we may bring gifts into the Lord. Inside the church will be a separate room with as many holy books that the Throne will allow us to possess. Then each week, we shall ask Metetron to select a book and a message so we may learn much more about the holiness in our heavens." We then all agreed to have an exact copy of our church in Townsend except this one would be made from the best stones on this planet and would have marble floors. Metetron taught us how to seek out the best stones from our lands and how to find and make marble. We enjoyed doing this as it also provided us an opportunity to give some of our time and the best stones in our lands to the Lord. We concentrated totally on our church as Metetron concentrated on acquiring copies of the heavenly books for our library.

We soon had completed our new temple and had many holy books in our library. We were actually surprised about how fast these books were given to our library. Metetron then gave us our first message. She talked about how the Saints requested that the Ancient One allow them to help in building the mansions for the new Saints who were arriving. They agreed that if after creating them and the Ancient One did not like it, he could remove the mansions. The Saints worked hard to add diversity while keeping equality in these mansions. The Ancient One was so pleased that he agreed to allow the Saints to help him with many other tasks. He enjoyed how his creations could add a new touch to what he had envisioned. The Ancient One told them about the Ancient Days when nothing was in this universe. He was actually an atom that was pulled away from the universe or reality that he existed. When he came to this empty universe, his heart becomes lonely, for he was the only atom here. He thus created the heavens and earth. He created many different sorts of life forms only to become sad with them. He then decided to create life forms that would have his image. He next decided to give this image free will, either to serve him or to serve his new enemy. He would work hard to ensure they knew the truth. He would also ensure that they know how to be saved from his enemy. Each image would record their daily deeds in their book while in their deep sleep. He would then open this book at their judgment as review it with them. Those whose deeds prohibited them from entering his kingdom would be given in the one they worshiped to exist in his kingdom. Humanity gave him both his greatest images and his hated images. He would separate the sheep from the goats. When he had permanently removed the goats, he would then dwell with his images who were his Saints for eternity. He would never again be alone, but with others who he had created to his image. This was a wonderful story for us, as we could now understand better some of the emotions that dwelt within us.

We now enlisted Metetron to help us build the temples within our four nations. Rita favored the eastern orthodox style churches from Russia. Metetron then taught her how to build a wonderful orthodox style church. Holly and I favored the Notre Dame, and Metetron taught us how to create it for our future city. Next, she helped Flying Eagle create her copy of the great cathedral of Milan or the Duomo. Little Running Eagle and

Jennifer agreed on the Las Lajas Cathedral and found a beautiful ravine to place it. The beautiful bridge that connected it to the opposite side was also a phenomenon.

We were now ready for our cities. Flying Dove selected a city from Metetron's visions that matched her love of nature and love of towering places, as would any dove. Her city sat at the top of a high mountain with walls that sank great into the bordering cliffs. Inside her city were tall buildings that sank into the deep slope of this mountaintop. She had a beautiful lake that flowed throughout the lower part from the city. She put many sharp steeples on top of her buildings. The buildings on the mountaintop also had grand columns circling them to add support and beauty. They also added many trees in their city.

Holly and I decided to do something different for our city as we selected an image as a city on the sea. We created the large stone platforms with our temple at the center of this city and modern style skyscrapers forming smaller clusters in each of four great platforms that circled the city. The skyscrapers in the center at the city would be our home. We wanted the four satellites so our first four children could live close to us. This would keep our lands as we originally created them and give us the wide-open sea to help us see how big this world actually was.

Jennifer selected a city that resembled Rome. The temple was in the center as she added many museums and enclosed large palaces. The city had many Roman style stadiums and open-air theaters. She also added parks and large playing fields. She told us the palaces were for her children. We counted twelve palaces and jokingly told Little Running Eagle that he would be a busy father. He enjoyed this thought adding, "I shall strive hard to be as great a father as was mine."

Rita and Richard build their city inside their large canyon along one cliff as it rose from the canyon's floor all the way to its top. The city had multiple layers. It was created from the same stone of the adjoining cliff. Hence, many places blended with it, making the determination of where it started and where it ended, very much difficult. That was now the marvel of this city, as it had all the space, our other cities had, yet protected the land it was built upon. I could see window appearing from the mountainside just below the top ridge. It had been wonderful sandy colored steps the ascended the front to the city. They placed their temple on top of this mountain ridge so nothing surrounded it. This temple served as the easily visible marker for this city. They easily gave the Lord the highest honor in this city.

We would now divide into our couples at designated times and work on our cities. It was no hurry, as we did so much enjoy our mansions. We also added a nice park beside our church where we would spend time together with only the suns, moons and sometimes the stars above us.

Metetron depended very much on her globe to help enhance our four lands. She kept it an exact real time replica of our world. She could thus drop into it and still be close enough to respond to our requests. We continued to be very much amazed at her great achievements.

Our year of learning about each other soon had finished. I could see a lot more security in Holly and Flying Dove as Rita was teaching them, along with Jennifer, many things about keeping a relationship strong. When Rita was teaching our wives, we would join Richard, who would teach us how to care and share with our wives. Sharing things did not matter here, because if each wanted it, they would create two. The important thing that Richard taught was concerning sharing time and thought. We warned that our wives might be too eager to please us and thus tell us what she thinks we want to hear. This results in both doing something that neither enjoys, yet pretending that they enjoy thinking the other is gaining happiness from them doing this. He then stressed, we must listen to them, and never assume that they understand anything we are telling them. Always ask them and seek their opinions on everything, especially in the early stages that we were in our relationships. He taught us about pretending not to like something and test if they also claim not to like this. When they fail this test, you must think hard to find the yoke that you have placed around their necks. all then became frustrated not knowing how we would be able to do this. Richard said not to worry about this, for you will, as a couple mold into your relationships, and therefore depend therefore love to give you the power you need. He also added that we were very lucky to have the pure dedicated love of Metetron to help us. We thought about this and then became relaxed as I added, "Where would be without Metetron?" Richard answered, "We would not be in heaven as that is for sure." Richard recommended that we all reproduce at the same time, which would allow all of us to experience this new adventure together. I now asked Richard, "Did you and Rita have children?" Richard told us they had three children, one daughter who died from the flu when she was three years old and two sons. One son died while fighting for the

Army and the other died in a car accident returning home after he had become engaged to his future wife." I then told him how much I marveled his ability to overcome such great challenges. He replied, "It was nothing George, for I knew that we would be given both our original children and new children here in heaven."

This last statement from Richard gave me a new question to ask Metetron as we now went back to join our wives. I asked Metetron, "When shall we be able to see our loved ones?" Metetron acknowledged, "I can show them to you anytime you wish. Remember; however, that when the pit is sealed you will no longer remember them as for eternity all your images shall be as one large family." We now decided to divide into our separate groups for the viewing. Holly would be with Rita and Richard, as Holly's mother was Rita's sister. Jennifer, Floyd and myself formed one group, as Little Running Eagle joined his sister, Flying Dove for their group.

My group asked Metetron to show us our family. She brought before separated images of Dorothy, Lisa, Emery, and Harry with our parents beside them. They were playing what appeared to be football in a wide-open field. They were divided male against female, as these new bodies had no differences in strength between the males and females. We saw Dorothy threw a prolonged bomb that Lisa caught giving them a touchdown. It was beautifully executed as mom protected Dorothy to give her time to throw the long bomb. They had selected a target point allowing Dorothy to throw the ball without waiting to see if Lisa was in the position. Lisa had actually run down the opposite side then moved across the field while also moving closer to her goal. Emery and Harry could not keep up with her as Dorothy's throw dropped perfectly over Lisa's head into her arms. Our family was having a great time as we watched how they did so many things together. Love had a hold on them that not even eternity would break. I could see the longing in both Jennifer and Floyd's eyes as we saw our family for the first time since the Patmos. Jennifer then had the visions terminated and told us, "We now have the peace of mind of knowing our family is together, and they are all merry. We know that each of them would desire that we also be happy. Let us work hard to give them their desire as our family is united and will be united for eternity in heaven." These words revealed to me the selfishness that temped my spirit, for I must, in all things to honestly, and sincerely keep our family first. Jennifer now took each of our hands and said, "We shall go into the temple and thank the

Lord for the wonderful blessings he has given our family." Therefore, we went into the temple and gave our thanks for such a magnificent gift.

Rita, Richard, and Holly first watched Rita's children who had died. All three were in heaven, which proved the righteousness and virtuousness that they had instilled into their children. The three children were in the temple worshiping the Lord thanking him for the great joys he gave them. At that point, Rita suggested that we moved to her sister so Holly could view her family. Richard agreed as we have now seen her mother and two sisters. Holly confessed that she knew her father had not made it, as he had left them just after her youngest sister was married. They now watched how the mother and two of her three daughters were enjoying themselves. Holly could feel their love as it flowed from this vision. The group now decided to close the videos as they had discovered what they had come to find.

Now it was time for Little Running Eagle and Flying Dove to view their families. Their family was somewhat different from our families. Their mother kidnapped, raped, and brutally murdered by a gang of drunk teenagers with rich parents. That was when their father, Flying Eagle took them out of the white man's world and into the forests outside of Townsend. I many times wanted to visit Little Running Eagle; however, he was always engaged, so we became friends at school. Their family actually was busy as Flying Eagle kept them very active in the Native American activities in our local extended area. Floyd was only able to visit with Flying Dove a few times, as they would work on a big school project or presentation together. Floyd told us that when they would show their finished project or presentation to Flying Eagle, he would eagerly display his delight and pride in Flying Dove and his thanks to Floyd for helping. Floyd would bring home, in a big bag, Indian special foods that our family always celebrated. Our mother would give me a thank-you letter for Little Running Eagle to give to his father, as our father would give Floyd, a thank-you letter for Flying Dove to give to her father Flying Eagle. Our parents never questioned Flying Eagle's reluctance in visiting us. Dad always said, "We do not know what monsters have blocked their roads previously, we only know that we shall not block their road now. We know he is a good man from the wonderful friends whom his children are with you. When he wants us to help him fight those monsters, we shall. Now is the time for patience. They are good people; we cannot make them bad people." I never understood why my father said those things nor what he really meant. The thing that I took from his words was that we needed to keep our nose out of their affairs. The raids after World War III found the beasts concentrating on capturing the Native Americans before hitting the communities. They believed the Indians would stay in the forests and thus had to be assembled first. When they attacked their home, their father put them in a special tunnel under the house and stayed at the house for the invaders to kill. He had already stored their clothes and personal items in used Army Duffle bags he had purchased at yard sales. Therefore, he could drop them in his secret tunnel quickly knowing the raiders would search for any signs that another might be living there. They captured him, tied him to the middle post that held up the roof of their home and burned him to death. Flying Dove remembers hearing him scream, as he burned alive. They knew to stay in place, as their lives were so important to him. They joined to Patmos to give meaning to their parent's lives. They have now been able to see their parents together as they were collecting stones from a nearby forest beside their heavenly home. They were happy doing the things they loved the most. Flying Dove felt it was as they had done before they had children. Knowing that their father had found their mother brought peace to their souls, thus they closed their vision.

Holly discussed the details of what she viewed with me as I told her the things we viewed. The only group we did not know was Flying Eagle and her brother. Jennifer and Floyd thus asked them if they could watch their family video as it was also their family now. Little Running Eagle and Flying Dove agreed.

Little Running Eagle then opened their vision one more time. Floyd and Jennifer were horrified when they saw their mother in law beaten to death and those who did it go free. They saw how deep their father in law was dedicated to giving them a good life. When they finished watching how hard, their spouse's father had worked to make a great life for them, and how he gave his life for them, they burst into tears. Little Running Eagle then said, "While the fire burned above us, I saw in a vision God asking us if we served him." We both eagerly agreed. He afterwards told us, "You shall be delivered, and I will guide you to my other special servants as you will travel the heavens and time doing an extreme work that will bring honor to your parents who are with me now." We next saw our parents praising the Lord and thanking him for the pronounced faith he had in us. Jennifer and Floyd told their mates that they had great pride in their in laws. They also thanked them for sharing their family with them. Jennifer then conveyed to Little Running Eagle, that everyone in our group needed to know about the terrible things we did to your family. Floyd then added, "This is a shame upon us and shows how great you two are to allow us to share our lives with you.

When our entire group saw this story, we were all moved. I asked him, "Why had you never told me?" Little Running Eagle answered, "My father told us to leave our monsters locked inside their cages." I then stated to him, "Your father was a very wise man. I want to thank you and Flying Dove for accepting the Patmos with us. Did you know what the Patmos entailed?" Little Running Eagle instantly expressed, "The only thing we truly knew was that if we did this, the monsters would never again leave their cages." I told him that was the reason enough and if the monsters were ever to return let us all know, for your monsters are our monsters. We all decided to go into the temple and have Metetron give us another message. She spoke about how the Lord loved families so much and greatly valued what children would say telling all in heaven that out of the mouths of babes would come wise sayings.

We all agreed to have another year to build our relationships. In our third-year living on Midlertidifjem, we decided to have children. Once we decided to have children, we ran into another problem, and that was how to mate with these bodies. Our bodies were controlled and one with our mind, thus we had no testosterone, estrogen or progesterone in our bodies, so out of sight was out of mind. We called an emergency meeting with Metetron and asked her, "How do we mate?" She told us that she did not know of those things; however, some of the holy books talked about it. We all went to our library and began our scans for 'how to reproduce,' related material. We soon found the book, which explained that as a couple, we had to go before the altar and ask the Lord for a child. If granted, the Lord would merge our souls into one, thus planted the created seed from the male in the womb of the female, then he would separate them returning them to male and female. We now went before the altar, one couple at a time and asked for a seed to be planted. The Lord granted all of us a child. These seeds would grow for about two months, and then the couple had to return to the altar. For this delivery event, the Lord would take the child from the mother's womb and give the child to the father. There was no pain, no strain, just very ordinary and plain. We also discovered that the Lord always gave a female every other child. He did this to ensure that there would be amply females to mate with the males. We all decided that no man and woman should mate within the same family until our numbers were great enough to ensure diversity. We would have Metetron decide which male and female were coupled. We trusted her and knew she would be fair; insuring the next female in line received the next male from another tribe. Our group also decided that the daughter would follow her husband to his homeland. At first, we were saddened over the loss of a daughter, although she was welcomed to return home for visits. Metetron reminded us that when we gave up a daughter, we received another for our sons. We would have to live with this once we departed from our united city. For the first round, we would not have to worry much about this, as we would all be living in the same city.

Nevertheless, the day did arrive when we each took our copy of Metetron and departed for our lands. We knew that the time now was for our individual families. We loaded up our sky horses and started our journey out into Midlertidifjem this time not to return to the united city.

As the centuries flowed past us, we found our memories of the Patmos, and united city fade deep into the recesses of our minds. There had been a time that the Lord had delivered us from the killing hands of evil and placed us among his chosen elect to record his judgment upon humankind.

One morning while returning from our temples, we saw the skies packed with angels with their swords. Our Metetron's told us all the stay inside and to refrain from making noises. The evil one released and was raging war upon the Holy City. I had one more important thing to give to Patmos that being sealed letters we had found on those during the tribulation. I called for Patmos. Patmos appeared, opened his well, and I dropped the sealed letters inside. He closed, and we gave our final farewells. The angels now told us, "It is time to receive your next gift from the Lord; you shall see the new heavens and earth. I witnessed great multitudes of Saints signing praises to the Ancient One as he departed from his throne and became one with the Lord to dwell among his Saints. I thought how wonderful this would be that we could walk to the temple and have our Lord there with us. I remembered how Metetron had told us things would be different once we took our new bodies. We would no longer have children, which did not matter to us, as we had already created enough souls for our lands. She also told us that when we entered our unused bodies, our minds would forget all the things of old. She as well confessed to misleading us about being married in this brand new eternal kingdom. When we received our now souls, all memories would be no more. We would still keep our personality and desires as that was part of our 'image.' I wondered how this would happen. Rita and Richard went first, and as they walked past us, I asked Rita, "Are you ready to return to Midlertidifjem." She answered, "Fellow Saint, why would I ever desire to leave this holy city?" Richard responded the same way. I moved toward the back to this line and walked each one pass me by, not knowing me. Holly even called me her "Fellow Saint." She no longer remembers me, "I went through it."

I am so happy now as my soul is so clean. I am among my fellow saints as also is our Lord. We sing praises and enjoy the billions of stories the Lord shares with us. I sometimes believe he has enough stories to last this eternity. We have all eaten from the Tree of Eternal Life. I look up at the stars and wonder what they look like. The Lord told us that the angels would be glad to give us a tour. A courteous angel named Metetron is assembling a group to tour the stars. She appears to be very wise, so I promise her someday to explore the unknown with her as my guide. I am so happy with all my brothers and sisters around me. I feel so special being with them, as we find so many ways to have fun and get to know each other. I know that happiness has flooded my soul, and that I will be happy for eternity. I so many wishes that all how hear my voice also enjoying the blessings from, 'He who walks and talks between us.'

CHAPTER 13

Letters from the Seventieth Week

Dear dad;

To tell you how sorry I am would be an understatement. I know I should have went to church with mom, sis, and you. It is just that it was so not cool with my friends. We wanted to have some fun in our life and the marijuana and beer made my life so much better. Moreover, Marcie taught me how to love and all the kids were doing this, so I did not want to look old fashioned. I was also afraid that Marcie would tell everyone at school that I was square, instead she is cutting her throat by telling all her friends how good I am. She does not have loyal friends as these girls are tempting me every day. I wonder why God made them look so good and then forbid us to enjoy them. I could never figure your religious stuff, yet I am thankful that you made me go to church with you and mom when I was younger. At least I know what is going on now. Strangely, my friends who used to laugh at me when I talked about Jesus are now asking me millions of questions when we get a chance, which is seldom now. After you all left me in what you always told me would be the rapture, life as changed. China thought we had a new human bomb and started World War III be nuking all our big cities. They got a little jump on us since we were watching Russia. Anyway, we emptied our arsenal on both China and

Russia. The president said, "If we go down so do them." It is clear to see why he was left behind. I am so glad you hated the big cities and made our home in this small town. We listen to the radio to learn how bad things are. There is a new Empire in Europe now and he hates our nation and vows to hunt us down and kill us one by one. He has already started in some nearby towns, so I stay in hiding during the days. I have Marcie and three other girls in our small group. We hiked over to Eldersville to see how these killers operate. They drive up and down the streets shooting gas on the houses, and then another person shoots arrows with fire tips at those houses. We can see the smoke for miles, especially when it ignites the gas lines. I saw a little girl come running out of one house with her clothes on fire. The soldiers shot her in a leg so she could not stand and laughed while she begged them to help her. This waiting each day, not knowing what they are going to do next is killing me. They are now using dogs to track us. We used your old trick of putting pepper on the ground to stop them. We have to make sure not to laugh when they take a big sniff of that pepper.

Today, I am not laughing because Marcie found a pregnancy kit at Walgreens and discovered she is pregnant. I just do not know what to do now. To have a baby when

---

Dear Susan;

To be in such total danger is too much for me to bear. I hate this. This is the bed, which I made. I am so lucky that I have survived for ten weeks now. I saw your old boyfriend Jed today. They had tied him to the stop sign beside the police station. They had beaten him with some horsewhips they found on the Nelson farm. It had the yellow S that he sewed to everything of his. I looked inside the Peterson bar and was surprised to see how empty it was. Even the bottles are all empty. We think the invaders have been there drinking, actually they take bottles outside and turn up the boom boxes and laugh. They look so happy. Old man Johnson has been preaching again. He tells us to stay hidden and strong because these beasts will pay for what they have done to us.

Betty's baby started crying yesterday when she was under the steps at the water plant. Two soldiers heard it and brought the dogs in. They found both of them, and fed her baby to the dogs. It took four of them to put her in the wire cage they had. She was like a crazy animal. Horrendous screams.

She has scratched her fingers to the bones trying to loosen something from the ground to open her cage. They all sat around and laughed the first day she begged, yet when she stopped begging they poured acid on her. She died later that day. She is so ugly; they threw her in the trash bin while still in that cage. When you hear screams like that, a new sense of urgency about being safe and hidden take over. I know to stay away from both kids and older people; because they are caught, the easiest and those with them become trapped also. The weather has been normal for the two freezing months and two burning months. Occupied Forces Radio said they believe the severe alteration was from the nuclear war and things should be back to normal now. We still get the small earthquakes rather regularly now, which make it hard for us to know if it is an earthquake or a large raid from our resident Roman killers.

Oh, by the way, I repented today so I hope to be with you someday soon. I so hope that old man Johnson knew what he was telling us. Just to be safe, I have been asking around. I cannot find any Bibles because the Romans took all of them. They must have read another Bible then we have, because the burned down all the pharmacies in our area. They are worried about us being healed. Old man Johnson told us we do not need pharmacies if we have the Lord. I do not care if I ever am healed; just want to have a house on the same street you live on up there. You are the only thing that gives me hope in the future. You never have to worry about me listening to you again. No more staying out and getting drunk on Saturday night and sleeping Sunday morning, forcing you to go to church by yourself. I will be strong in our love, see you soon, and the sooner the better. Love,

Your husband William

Mom

Why did you do this to me? You were always bitching about how dirty my room was and how you did not like any of my friends. Every time any of my friends came to play with me, you complained and complained. You were all the time complaining and checking all through my things to see if I had any dope. The only break I ever had was Sunday mornings when you were at church with your freaky friends. I hated your friends, because after you were with them, you would come home and act so uppity. Now you and your friends are gone. Damn you!!!! One of my friends told us he went to one of your services. He told us that you all would be crying out how much you loved God and promised to be the lights to the world. However, you come home to your children and turn out that light. Yes, hide the light, complain about my dirty room, and yet keep the important shit a secret. It was not my room that needed cleaned it was my soul. How could you worry about if I was going to college, when that would have only given me maybe forty years, yet eternity if forever? Do you not care about forever? How could you not be concerned about where I was going to spend eternity? My friends are telling us that if we do not repent we could go to hell. Is that where you really want me to spend eternity? My friends are telling me that if we would have repented we could have been in heaven with you people now. Mom, the only thing I think you ever wanted was for me to go to Hell, because that I all you always told, day in and day out. Go to Hell, go to Hell, yet you were with your friends were keeping the going to heaven part a secret. My friend told me that the Bible that you kept with you tells you to spread the gospel to the world. How could you be more worried about saving the world and not your own son? That is so selfish, if really believed the things that church was telling you then why did not you at least try to save those in your in your own house, the ones that you cooked breakfast, lunch and supper for? Instead, you would rush off with your friends to church and lay some money on the table for us to go to McDonalds. Yes, have someone else do your work, have someone else do your job. What a hypocrite. Go to church and pray that someone else come to our house and hope they can save me. Have someone do your work. Save yourself, worry only about yourself. With an attitude such as that, you expect us to respect and follow you. Oh, anyway, I hate to break your heart; however, I gave my heart to Jesus and unlike you, I am telling everyone I see, except for the marked beasts that are trying to kill us, the great news about salvation. I will make it to heaven the grueling way, however tough way is better than no way . . . see you soon.

Sincerely;
The son you betrayed.

Bill;

I still remember the days we were in Army Ranger training. Oh, those were such easy days compared to what is going on now. I am doing so much better than many around me, as I know how to survive off insects and tree bark. There are always strange people popping up around me trying to preach to me. You would almost think the whole world is now nothing but preachers. The way I look at it, if they were really Christians, then why are they here. It seems to me that they want power. They love the power when some fool falls down before them begging God to save them. I actually think some of them think they are god. I remember how we determined that there was no god. That makes me wonder, where you went. Your brother Jeff said you went away with your parents when that Rapture hoax went down. You must be hiding somewhere real fine, so why not let me in on it. I am going to be hiding in forests about one mile from my grandfather's farm. What you say we hook up and slash some throats of those creepy Romans who walk around thinking they are gods. Well not much more going on now,

See you soon
Hoah Rangers always
Sergeant Williams

Liz,

I got the scare of my life again today. I have been hiding in that old empty house at the end of our old street. I have been sneaking into the basement and taking that secret passage we found in the attack. Today when I was sleeping in my favorite corner, I felt something cutting at my throat. When I woke up, I saw a little girl sitting on me and she was going to kill me, so I quickly rolled over on top of her taking her knife and ran it between her eyes. Oh, what has happened to this world? I was so scared that I did this without thinking. I was not even disturbed by her dead body staring at me. I think I am more afraid of live people that I am of dead people. It is the ones who are alive that can hurt. I also heard that the Romans are using children to report where people are hiding. I was horrified when I saw the Romans pulling people out of the house at the end of the other corner. They were all crying as the Romans tied their father to two horses and beat the horses so they would ripe the man apart. I saw his insides splash over his children. Then they made the kids take their mark or they would do the same thing to the mother. After those kids took the mark, they put them in a truck and took them away. Once they were gone, they took and raped her in front of all the houses in this neighborhood. They fed off her pain and begging. The louder she begged the harder they hurt her. I promise someday to kill as many Romans as possible. I wish there was a god, so he would hear the cries of those who suffer as we do. I am going to talk with some of those nutty preachers tomorrow and figure out what I can do. I hate the thought of dying like that man today and that is the end of my existence. If you know of any way to help me, let me know.

Love,
Eddy

Julia

I keep thinking to myself, how glad I am that he declared himself a God in the temple that he made for them in Jerusalem. His roaming killers are quitting. They are now more concerned with finding a way home. They will still kill us if they see us, since it is too much a part of their personality. They will always think of as insects that are trying to hurt them. Most of them have these strange sores on them now. I think that is so great, yet I am still not going to touch anything they have touched. Rev. Anderson says they are being punished by God. I wish God had punished them before they killed both of my sisters. With so many soldiers leaving now, we can now swim in some of the creaks as long as we stay close to the shore, usually under a tree in case an airplane flies over us. Speaking of airplanes, Rev. Anderson told us that the United Roman Empire is having trouble getting enough oil from the Middle East since they have made some deal with China. That is all we need is his guns with all those soldiers. Rumor is that they are marching their second 200 million-soldier army to the west. Hope the Russians kill this one as they did the first one. I guess I should be saving my hopes for another day of life. The last few years have been something else. They only thing that keeps me going is this diary. I still say the biggest disadvantage for us who were dating virgins when the rapture hit was being left without a girlfriend. I still remember all that religious stuff you used to tell me. Rev. Anderson and I discuss it sometimes. If I get any of those sores as the soldiers are getting, I will repent. Rev. Anderson keeps telling me that only the saved people will not get the sores. That is how he knows who is saved and who is not. Strangely, I still am not saved, yet have no sores. I know I will have to do it someday. I just want to make sure a righteous lifestyle fits me. So far, it has been fitting, mostly because I have nothing else to wear. Every day, I write in this diary how much I miss you and for you to say hello to my sisters for me. Today, just like all the other days, I still miss you all. Also, tell my mother I miss her also and that I am still trying to find my father. I am just about convinced now that the Romans captured and converted him. I wonder what he would do if he saw me in his rifle's site. Well, time to crawl among the soldier's garbage cans and find something to eat.

Still Missing You
Mickey

Ms. Josie

I am so sad. I know it is wrong to begin a letter like this, for fear of making you sad, yet since you are not receiving them, I will just pour out my honesty. I just want to thank you so much again, for the wonderful Sunday school classes you taught us. We always had fun with all the cool things you instilled in us. I was so sad when your husband died in that car accident and you started going to a new church. I heard you changed the churches because our church just brought back so many bad memories. They split our class into different classes based upon our ages. That was when I decided to take a small break. That small break never ended, until just last week when my associate found a minister and we now go to his meetings. Under ordinary times, my associate would have been my friend; however, I stopped making friends as the Romans kept capturing them. They always torture them in the open, offering to stop if those who see it will surrender. They do not know for sure if someone is watching, yet they take that chance. I saw a man give himself up, thinking it would save his friend. The liars then tortured both of them. I was tempted the first couple of times, nevertheless I just watched them die painfully and slowly. Now,

I simply retreat to where I cannot hear them. I always feel so helpless in these situations. Yet when you are caught, your life is done. Now, since I found the Lord, if I die I am saved. I feel better about that, and since I have been saved, I have found food in strange places. Yesterday, I found a can of green beans that was tucked underneath a bush. When we find cans such as this we just take it and eat. If the can is here, then whoever put it under this bush is gone. I could feel each bean sliding down into my dilapidated stomach. I ate them slow, so my body could receive them. Anyway, I will save this letter so when we meet in heaven I will remember what I wanted to share with you.

Missing You and God Bless You
Billy

Dear Gloria;

I hate to burden you with my sorrows; however, this is too much for me to bear. People no longer have faces. I can only see their desire to take anything I may need to survive at any cost. Some have a sad face, hoping to get past my first round of defense and drop my guard. I know that when I do, all is over for me. How could a world turned upside down so fast? When our government fell, so did any form of humanity. The greedy ones plowed the stores stripping them of anything they could get and take it back to their dens. I heard of one man who stole all the bread a medium sized bakery had. How foolish, did not he know that the bread would not last? He did not care for all he wanted was to know that since he had it, no others could. This is complete selfishness and greed out of control. I never see girls in public now, for they are the first targets, as gangs will fight over them. I have seen gangs actually chop off one of their arms, or even their feet during a fight when they think they will lose her. This is terrible. Their thinking is that if I cannot have this, and then neither can any other. The other tricky face is the pretending to be afraid of me, so I will think they are an easy target and rush them, only to fall into an ambush. That is why now, if I see someone started at me, I avoid him or her. I saw a group on the corner the other day laughing and celebrating the arrival of a liberation army. Some fools fell for this and went to join them. They gave them food and had them wait on benches, supposedly for the salivation trucks to arrive. They finally had about forty people and then stopped their laughing. They chained the forty people in wagons they pulled out in front and tortured them without mercy until they all died. I felt sorry for those people, however I found a Christian book in a house the other day that said we would have to endure the seven years and that false prophets would try to deceive us. These beasts now must have our lives, as if by them knowing someone else may be alive, tortures them. I have to torture them for seven years, as I stay alive. I pray every morning, afternoon, evening and night. I saw a group put a female in the middle of them and torture her slowly, demanding that she big someone for help. We have seen this one so much that none of us even responded. I cannot save her, and in trying to do so, would only be alongside her dying with her. The basic primitive desire to save one who is innocent and suffering is no longer feasible. Any torture in the street is an ambush. There are no exceptions. I have no friends, for the few, which I did make ended up being captured and tortured. It hurts when someone you know is being tortured in front of you. That is the main reason I left our hometown. I can now see what the Lord has done to humanity, for without him our world would now make those of Sodom and Gomorrah look like angels. I wonder if I shall be blessed with some food today. I found a bag of dry dog food last month. That kept me alive for an entire month. I mean I was so hungry that I have almost to replenish my whole being. I know one thing; never eat dry dog food without plenty of water. This allows it to expand in your belly and get a full feeling making the food last longer. I have been searching hard for some more, yet I almost believe that so many other people are enjoying this life saving treat. I will write you again tomorrow. Please put in a good word with the Lord on my behalf.

A fool forever
Jeremy

Leroy;

I wanted to talk with you about how we behaved in the last war. I was proud of our unit as we focused on the war, and did not hurt innocent civilians. The way we fought freed us from the suffering around us. I remember many times allowing the enemy to crawl away or remain to protect his family. I always marveled how you were able to go see the Chaplain and then return from one of his sermons as if you were a fresh recruit entering into the war. We now have a different breed of soldiers destroying our homeland. They pride themselves in their involvement in the torture, rape, or murder of our former nation's citizens. This should not surprise me. War is ruthless, cruel, painful, harsh, and dehumanizing. Those of us who wish to avoid this anachronistic instrument of foreign policy are aware of the heavy price it extracts. War brutalizes, and the damage it inflicts on us penetrates deep into the social fabric of only the victims of this self-proclaimed genocide of justice. A war such as this cannot build empires; it must destroy them. This dizzying cycle of violence, of retaliation and counter-retaliation, they will find that they were not always the good people they think they are. They can only kill until all are dead. Then whom will they kill? This cycle will end with themselves paying the price for what they did to us. Actually, they will pay the price that accompanies the one they served or killed in and that is that crazy thing that sits on their throne in Rome. The entire world hates him, except for his stepchildren in Israel. I have such a hard time understanding why they adore him so much and how he can be so righteous to build them a new temple and at the same time roam the road killing anyone he and his armies can find. He claims that only the chosen people should inherit this earth and that the gentiles defiled the Holy Scriptures by making a criminal of Rome a deity. He is helping them all to return to their holy land by giving free passage to any Jew who surrenders. We thought he was just collecting them for a private massacre, notwithstanding he broadcast live images of them arriving and being taken to their new homes that he built for them. I saw an old man who lived in the apartment above us report that he was a Jew. I later saw him departing in Israel and going to his new home. I just would not go there if I were them, because a killer is a killer. When a killer runs out of people to kill, he will turn on the ones he has kept and thus kill them. The same is true of a drug addict, as long as he or she has the pills everything is okay, nevertheless when the pills are finished, he or she will do whatever to get the next pill. I guarantee you that you do not want to be around them when that happens. Anyway, I cannot believe I am talking about issues such as this when I have so many more important things to talk about, like will I still be alive tomorrow, and can I find some medicine for the bad cut in have in my leg. I was crawling in the dark the other night and as I was crawling over a piece of glass when it shattered, and a fragment cut into my leg as it was dropping to meet the floor. I went to clean it out in the morning; however, the swelling has sealed some fragments and dirt in it. I just do not know what to do outside of digging into it with needles. Oh well, I have to play with the cards I was dealt.

Someday
Richard

Laura

I do not know why I thought about you today, except to tell you how pretty you always looked when you walked past our house on your way to church Sunday mornings. I always wanted to meet you at your church; however, my dad said that the people in that church were not good. I found another empty apartment last week. It is on the seventh floor, which is about right. Too high and you are almost dead by the time you make it to your floor. Too low is dangerous in that the gang love to terrorize the first three floors. They are worried about ambushes. I wonder what I would do if that were all I had to worry about in my life. This new apartment has a large mattress in one of the rooms. All the other furniture has been destroyed or taken. So many people use the wood for heating. This apartment has a folded car hood in the spare room. I heard that this would hide someone when the raiders start using their human scanners. Anyway, I think our days will over soon as they just keep coming back and back, nevertheless each time they come back they find someone, so with that I look for them to continue on the same routes they have for so long. As I watch the truck park in front of the apartment across the street, I see them running out with a new type of weapon. It is a rifle, with an oval shaped disk on top of it. When they turn it on, I hear a loud humming sound. That sound is like a demon relaxing. They are scanning. They clean out that entire building in one hour, pulling out seven people and beating them to death in the street below us. Now they are coming into our building. I will hide in my car hood and hope it works. That humming sound is getting louder and louder. Now they are on our floor and I hear a door bash down and a woman screaming as they drag her out. I had no idea that someone else lived on this floor. They naturally ask her if she knows anyone else in the building and she denies it, even though they offer her great rewards if she does. She does like the rest of our people have done, deny knowing anything, and have the joy that when you died, you took with you something they wanted and needed. I hear someone wriggling my door handle. My heart stops. How can I endure the terrible beatings the others have? Nevertheless, to my great joy, they leave our floor. I know that they will come back down, so I will stay in this car hood until they pass back through. I finally hear that horrible hum stop and slowly creep to one of my windows and see that they captured twelve people from this building. I honestly thought I was the only one in this building. They have us so divided and afraid that we avoid each other as much as possible. They leave the twenty dead bodies on the street for the wild dogs and other carnivores to feast upon tonight. They want these animals to patrol this area, as if we accidently run into one of them; they will kill us immediately, as they already have the taste of our blood.

Your secret peeping Ed

CHAPTER 14

Council of the Derecske—Létavértesi

The next morning when they awoke, and after congregating, they beheld the most bizarre vision over before even known possible. Emos was gone. His throne was empty. The Patmos, in its safety-sealed shell was also gone. His highest-level warrior angels were guarding his post. Emos had posted an order throughout his realm that all forward exploring worlds were to stop and prepare to return to their home galaxies. The high court of Saints immediately appealed this order to the Council of the Derecske—Létavértesi who was the Council of all the Emos deities. As their request arrived, they were surprised to learn that Emos was already there in a closed season with the Council of the Derecske—Létavértesi. The high court of the Saints then instantly ordered that Emos's call for return to be honor. Something big was going on, and all were in awe about what it could be. Emos briefed the Council on the contents of this Patmos and asked them if they desired to see it. They all assumed their positions as the Patmos began. Throughout the vision, some council members would stand up and demand that this evil thing be destroyed. The head of the council then told all the members, we should study the entire vision before rendering our judgments. As the vision, continued, Council members requested a short pause, and they rushed out of the viewing capsule and sent messages back to their Empires to stop all deep-space explorations and bring our people home.

When the high court (council) of the Saints belonging to the petitioning Emos discovered this universal retreat panic began to run rampant among their people. What could have been in that aged capsule that was of such a great danger? It is as if they had a deadly virus and did not know what was going to kill them. Never, in the history of these aggressive Emosses had a retreat ever been called. They had so many times rushed to each other's aide in the event of danger. This time something this gigantic ever faced them. Nevertheless, it as an aged ball made of material that no longer existed that had a simple message in it. The ball had been scanned for any foreign life forms and any possible weapons in that all these scans returned negative. The Saints now called in both pilots for that episode, Colonel Balatron and Colonel Halitus, and reviewed every detail of that encounter. Nothing out of the ordinary could be found. This frustrated the Saints in that they knew something was there because the Emosses do not retreat without them being faced by an enemy that could defeat them. They would have to wait to discover their doom.

Meanwhile, the Council of the Derecske—Létavértesi reviewed the vision as the individual members were recording their perceived violations and dangers. They soon finished watching the entire vision and now began it again this time citing any violations or dangerous.

The vision began with an atom leaving a dimension in which the Emosses had to destroy at war long ago. They by all their nature bitter enemies as not even an atom remained when they completely erased it from existences. This atom, had managed to enter another dimension before these great wars began. That helps explain why the Patmos Universe is so empty, with only a few other Empires and those are in the area near to the Milky Way. They then saw the atom open from itself and create a great galaxy. This worried the Council in that some hidden atoms could be in this small Patmos Ball. This is why they put it into a very secure capsule, which is if an atom were to open; its expansion would be contained. This was ordinary equipment in that any atom discovered had to be expanded. No one in their history ever found such a small ball with almost an infinite number of whole atoms. The capsule containing the Patmos was being moved through wormholes to put it inside another dimension as far away as possible. They could still control its movements yet wanted it far enough away that if all the atoms exploded the Emosses would be in no danger.

Now the first complaint was filed when this power source declared itself to be lonely and thus create other life forms. There were strict laws against using powers to compensate for personal defects. Deities were never to be lonely as they could create non-life forms to entertain them. Life forms can only be created if they can be secured and protected by their creator. Now, the next couple of cases truly angered them with the destruction of Saturn given the rings of punishment forever to torment those who died there. Then the Jupiter extermination, in which the souls are constantly being sucked into a great Red Spot that is a gigantic storm and pulls them back to the surface, which is deep into the layers of painful gases. The next one, Mars, really made them angry in that the Lord of this planet took one-third of the angels to Throne trying to overthrow it. What angered the Emosses was that he did not immediately punish them as he had on Saturn and Jupiter, whose crimes were far less. Instead, he creates a new species, in his image and allows these rebels to tempt them into sinning, where he can thus punish them with death. The council could not believe this. This was the reason they were so distraught with this Patmos. Any since meets evil will fall. If their people were to view that Patmos, they would come into a contract with evil and thus fall. There is no exception, as they watch Sodom and Gomorrah burn. Next they see all, except a few on a sinking ship that must be repaired by aliens living on the ocean floor, drown in a worldwide flood. Then, within just a few generations, another who shall forever represent evil through his city of Babylon tries to build a tower into the heavens. Such a tower was impossible, and instead of letting them fade out in failure, he gives them seventy-two new languages further to divide them. The Emosses only had one language, and they had never discovered other people, until this small Patmos that spoke another language, yet to put seventy-two on that small world could only have one result, and that would be to keep the people separated making it easier for the evil one to find his prey. It would also make it hard for the Saints to spread his message. This was just so appalling that some of the Council wanted to send a special force to destroy the shell that held all the evil ones for eternity. The Council also agreed that nothing could be guaranteed for eternity, as they had discovered in finding a poison pill that was directed for their happy heavens. They long erased any flesh form of life citing that it was too hard to keep functioning without errors. They watched as the God of this Throne sent his only manifestation in the flesh to his chosen people, just to have them bear false witness and demand that the ruling empire crucifies him. They agreed that this was the event when the species should have been erased. They were furious and now discussed all these killed machines that would destroy innocent lives building such Empires as the Roman, Alexander the Great, Huns, Mongols, to name just a few. They also questioned the justice in a god allowing such an ignorant barbaric evil species continue to exist. No punishments were effective, as those who survived the deadly plagues simply worked harder for evil and rebellion against their divine God. They agreed that the evil of this species was justification for the everlasting fires. They disagreed with the decision to allow them to continue. They argument also advanced that argument that if the rebellion in the heavens before this species was created would have been completely erased, this species may have had a chance. These evil spirits were teaching this weak flesh bound species all the forbidden unlawful carnal knowledge, to include witchcraft, conjuring, enchantment, magic, wizardry, and sorcery. This of course gave them a false perception of having the powers from the gods that they would instead use to torment their fellow beings. When they actually saw some angels come to Earth and take upon themselves the daughters of man as wives this infuriated them. They argued, "How could such a thing happen? To rule ignoring all that is happening around you is the same as committing the crime itself. Even the lowly humanity had laws that associated those who knew about the crime as also being guilty. You cannot sit on the finish line rooting for them to cross and then punish them for crossing. The way you avoid such things is to make it impossible. All the heavenly beings of the Emossess could not touch any of the chosen people as to touch them brought immediate death and erasure from existence. It was that simple, if you do the crime, you would do the time. The next phase really angered them, was the two great wars during the century before their time ended. The second war, which was an extension of the first war proved their lust for war. What shocked them was how one small nation could kill over six million of the chosen people of this world's God. What was worse was the ability of the evil angels to bless his scientists allowing them to rage a war for beyond the world's development since that time, while at the same time requiring the ones who had to stop him to develop everything by pure human mental abilities, which were stretched to their maximum limits. Somehow, they won the war, only to create two more giants, the Russians and the Chinese communist empires that accumulated or controlled much more than the failed Nazis. It was as one fire was still being put out larger fires was burning. This century also saw so many mass genocides as leaders would simply kill as many of their people they did not like as they wished. Anytime a leader steps out of line in the billions of worlds the Emosses ruled; the blood would immediately cry, and justice was served, sometimes even while the killer was still in the act of killing. It was that simple, not like the Ukraine in which Stalin and Hitler competed with who could kill more. They were horrified when the vision showed them that when war came, Roosevelt and Churchill allied themselves closely to Stalin, even though they were well aware his regime had murdered at least 30 million people long before Hitler's extermination of Jews, and gypsies began. However, in the strange moral calculus of mass murder, only Germans were guilty. Although Stalin murdered three times more people than Hitler, to the adoring Roosevelt he remained "Uncle Joe." At Yalta, Stalin even boasted to Churchill, he had killed over ten million peasants. The British-US alliance with Stalin made them his partners in crime. Roosevelt and Churchill helped preserve history's most murderous regime, to which they handed over half of Europe. The Great War indeed focused on one demon while creating two more. This was so sad indeed that a species would have to endure so much injustice. It just never stopped. Now the nation that was supposed to be of the people, the land of the free was no longer released. Money bought politicians as the corruption spread through the complete land. They became the pleasure lovers throughout the world, while other countries starved, and foreign leaders who would not comply became labeled at anti-world leaders and as such found themselves fighting the entire world. Justice was a joke, as to prosecute and put a criminal in jail, drained all the public resources needed to save the honest and suffering. They allowed people to live homeless and die from no medicinal care, while they provided medical care to hardened criminals. Someone or thing had a sick perception of justice. They actually were paying over $35,000 a year to keep an anti-social criminal in prison for life and then placing young good hard-working people in deep debt. Now the activities began where the rebel spirits would no longer hide in the backgrounds while they tripped up the flesh dwellers.

The Council now discussed the perseverance and faith of the Saints. They were given bodies with needs and told to deny themselves. This made them into toothpicks with no flexibility. They either stood straight or broke. There was no leeway or room for flexibility. It was white or black. The great delay in the answering of prayers and the refusal to appear visibly before the Saints, making any contact who was revealed to appear as being insane. The Saints were given the battle of fighting on their own as any support always had other logical reasons. No wonder, the scientists had a heyday with this story. Another, of the so many things that amazed them was how the same story came out with so many extreme versions as with the Buddha's, Hindu's and Voodoo's. Now the real kicker was how three religions from the same God of the equivalent prophet. These three religions received the same Ten Commandments as follows: "I am the Lord your God, who brought you out of the land of Egypt, out of the house of bondage. You shall have no other gods before Me," yet these exact people made a golden calf and worshiped as their god, while still in the desert.

1 "You shall not make for yourself a carved image, or any likeness of anything that is in heaven above, or that is in the earth beneath, or that is in the water on the earth; you shall not bow down to them nor serve them. For I, the Lord your God, am a jealous God, visiting the iniquity of the fathers on the children to the third and fourth generations of those who hate Me, but showing mercy to thousands, to those who love Me and keep My Commandments." They were amazed at the tremendous amount of carved images their places of worship.

2 "You shall not take the name of the Lord your God in vain, for the Lord will not hold him guiltless who takes his name in vain." The Lord's name was taken in vain more times than all other names combined.

3 "Remember the Sabbath day, to keep it holy. Six days you shall labor and do all your work, but the seventh day is the Sabbath of the Lord your God. In it, you shall do no work: you, nor your son, nor your daughter, nor your male servant, nor your female servant, nor your cattle, nor your stranger who is within your gates. For in six days the Lord made the heavens and the earth, the sea, and all that is in them, and rested the seventh day." Therefore, the Lord blessed the Sabbath day and hallowed it. The newest of the three religions

4 "Honor, your father and your mother, that your days may be long upon the land which the Lord your God is giving you." This was the biggest joke ever in the western society as the younger generations forgot about their parents casting them to the side,

claiming them to be such a burden. They are indeed are burdens; however, that was not the reason for this commandment; it was so the new generation could learn from the sorrows of the previous generation and not once again suffer the same sorrows. Nothing, but the same pain continuing generation after generation. As a dog returns to his vomit so shall a fool in his folly. This was one of the laws that he gave to help his people.

5 "You shall not murder. These three religions have fought wars against each other for over one thousand years, killing by the name of the same God. This command also needed so much more clarification, as to kill what and when to kill. According to this command, killing could apply to animals as they are killed and the flesh eaten. Talk about a total disregard for life. Should police officers kill when a citizen is in danger of bodily harm? Should people drive cars, busses, trains or planes as they also kill? Should people kill people from another nation by the name of war only because their nation said they could? If there are reasons or times to kill, then what are they? In addition, the thing that shocked them was that the dead were not allowed to return and report the one who killed them. Without the word on the one who died to accuse their murderer, the danger of placing an innocent being in prison or execute them was very risky. The emphasis had to be on protecting the innocent, as the guilty needed to be accused by the one, they killed.

6 "You shall not commit adultery." The nation that boasted more than any other as being followers of Christ was the leader in adultery and all manners of sex crimes and sex for sale.

7 "You shall not steal." All discovered new ways and things to steal, always seeking profit at another's loss.

8 "You shall not bear false witness against your neighbor.

9 "You shall not covet your neighbor's house; you shall not covet your neighbor's wife, nor his male servant, nor his female servant, nor his ox, nor his donkey, nor anything that is your neighbor's." Coveting became the force behind advertising as they used this tool to make all burn for the same thing. You must want this; you must desire this; it is your crave. Your crave shall be your grave.

These laws impressed the council, yet their enforcement left so desire for any to follow them, just great profit for breaking them. The laws among the Emosses are very simple. If you break one, you vanish. They also demanded that the rich share of the poor, thus the need to steel was removed. The rich who refused to share were made poor to see if they would make better beggars.

They determined the major fault with this Patmos was that the laws were not enforced and the wicked were not made to vanish. No wicked creates a world that leads to fewer temptations.

They now studied the sacrifices and rewards of the innocent who prepared the Patmos. They had indeed performed their tasks as best they could. They should have been better briefed so that they were not in their constant state of fear for doing wrong. In addition, they questioned the decision of touring the pit; as such, a thing need not be recorded in such detail. Punishment was only appropriate when all safeguards had been put in place to deter it. The threat of an eternal punishment in an unending place by an eternal god, of which none had seen pretty much, stretched the line of justice.

Now the concept of heaven came to view. They all agreed that this is the only way that the civilizations needed to be all along. Make one creation that shall live together and forever. If he were to have made a defect or sinner as they all boasted, then remove that image. No need to create eternal punishment or gain love based upon fear.

The council now took their vote and agreed forever to ban the Patmos from this universe. They would place sensors throughout the borders to detect any possible entry of similar objects. They agreed not to destroy it for fear it had a system to communicate back to its source who if they thought, it to be destroyed may send out another one. They also agreed never to let the results of this vision ever to be stored or shared or any part or manner. The final report would simply list the board members and their vote and declare the contents forever destroyed.

They now had to think of a way to report these findings to their empires who were by now almost hysterical. They would simply say that they had suspected that some of the sealed atoms might be destructive powers beyond the various empire's current defenses. The board members were then to report to their thrones and act normal, as they should, since no threat from this near miss existed anymore. The universe wide retreat was to give more time to development exploration equipment that would guarantee the safety of the Empire's citizens and explorers.

The game plan was in play, and the members executed it with style, and soon the aspirations of being closer to their homelands over shadowed any touch of danger they may have faced.

Each of the Emosses returned to their thrones. Emos can in nice and easy, with some fireworks that usually signified celebration then assumed his throne again. His guardian Angel Legion commanders welcomed their master back. The Legion commanders asked Emos if everything was okay. Emos was watching some children play in the world they shared and laughing at the funny things; they did. Emos subsequently looked at the Legion commanders and casually said, "There was a bug and now there is not a bug, so we may all play on the rug." He then said, "You could bring the Council of the Saints in, so I can put them at ease, so they do not bug you to death, as they do me." The Legion commanders asked, "Do you want to see the governors?" Cosmos then said, "No, this is not that important. We can let the council of the Saints tell them, so they can feel worthy." They all began to laugh again. The Legion commanders voiced for their Captions to get the Council of the Saints. They all casually came in while Emos was doing special scale down operations with his Legion Commanders. The Legion Commanders relaxing greeted the Saints and then excused themselves and went upon their way. The Saints noticed this, and started to relax, for when they saw the Legion Commanders leave they knew no danger existed. Emos greeted the Council and then asked them, "What messaged did you have for me when you contacted the Council of the Derecske—Létavértesi. Emos was giving them a chance to wiggle out of getting caught reporting on him. The Saints then said, "We were hoping you would talk with us, as your throne was empty. We know how you so much value our wisdom and loyalty oh great Emos." Emos then reported to them, "That is exactly what I thought, therefore, since I knew you were around my throne that I could spend some fun times with my fellow Emosses. You just can never know how important your wisdom was for me during this short vacation." Actually, the reason is they can at no time know that he was not allowed to tell them, and he was never impressed with their wisdom. Anyway, the mission at hand was simple, 'relax the Empire." Therefore, he would go along with this, as it truly did not matter to him. He knew the higher he swelled their heads the longer they would pester someone else, so a short vacation was indeed ahead for him. He began the briefing by saying, "There was a bug, and now there is not a bug, so we may all play on the rug. Do you understand?" One of the Saints afterwards answered, "Yes, oh great Emos, there was a small problem which you solved so we can go back to normal." Emos then answered, "You never cease to amaze me with your great wisdom and knowledge. I have some catch up work here, as we are all going towards our homes until we can develop stronger planets to send out this deep. There is just so much emptiness that we feel it would be better to have ships that can leap through this boring emptiness much faster. We just can never even remotely chance the loss of a spirit so far out. Can you very wise Saints let the governors know and send Admiral Nidificate, in so we can play around with some options?" The Saints, now completely swelled headed promised to alert the governors, who they always thought were lower than they are, leaped at this chance to act important. They also sent in Admiral Nidificate, who reported with some of his senior officers. Emos greeted the admiral and said, "You did not have to bring your senior officers; however, since you did we might as well let them get their elbows greased also." Emos acted like this was not that important." "Then, all in the group joined him as they also laughed. Emos then told Admiral Nidificate later Admiral, our orders are to return home, however we will head home; however, the way we execute these orders has some flexibility. We can take a straight shot back, or do a bow route or even a way eight. We can expand these last two choices deep or high enough that we should be able to discover new projects and experiences for our scientists. The choice is yours." The Admiral looked at his senior officers as everyone gave two thumbs up. The admiral then looked at Emos and said, "Oh great Emos, I do believe we would like a fat upside down bow for our return journey, as we hope to bring you greater glory." Emos then told the Admiral, "Make it subsequently happen as you desire, just send me a report each day of where we are and where you think we will be the next day. You can send it through our informational links, so it will not be a burden on your staff. To ensure you understand why I am doing this, the Council of the Derecske—Létavértesi only wants to make sure I know what is going on and where we are going. They assume I am determining the routes and missions, which honestly, I do not care. I, as also do you, want to keep them off our backs. I play; you do at least some of what you want to do, and everyone is happy. Can you follow me in this Admiral?" The Admiral answered in the affirmative and asked per permission to resume his duty post. The Admiral told his senior officers, "Gang, we all worried for nothing. At least, we will be able to continue our scientific mission on the way home, so I do believe that things will work out good for us." Emos, after had granted the officers their leave, now went to relax in his holy of holies, which was in a large orange cloud that floated in the upper skies around this spacious world.

The Patmos mission was finished now in this universe, yet would continue in others. One can only image how much evil knowledge it contained and how many civilizations that were filled with sheep would meet their first wolf. Inside this, small ball-sized object was enough darkness to make all the stars across the sky to refuse sharing their light. It contained almost every manner or way to kill and torture. Patmos now wondered if ever again there would be a species as evil and wicked as those who once occupied the old Earth.

INDEX

J

K

L

M

N

P

R

S

T

U

V

W

Z

THE OTHER ADVENTURES IN THIS SERIES

Mempire, Born in Blood
Penance, Genesis or Genocide
Lord of New Venus
Rachmanism in Ereshkigal
Sisterhood, Blood of our Blood
Salvation, Showers of Blood

The Wonderful Ones

Prikhodko, Dream of Nagykanizsai
Tianshire, Life in the Light

AUTHOR BIO

James Hendershot, D.D. was born in Marietta Ohio, finally settling in Caldwell, Ohio where he eventually graduated from high school. After graduating, he served four years in the Air Force and graduated. Magna Cum Laude, with three majors from the area's prestigious Marietta College. He then served until retirement in the US Army during which time he obtained his Masters of Science degree from Central Michigan University in Public Administration, and his third degree in Computer Programing from Central Texas College. His final degree was the honorary degree of Doctor of Divinity from Kingsway Bible College, which provided him with keen insight into the divine nature of man. After retiring from the US Army, he accepted a visiting professor position with Korea University in Seoul, South Korea. He later moved into a suburb outside Seattle to finish his lifelong search for Mempire and the goddess Lilith, only to find them in his fingers and not with his eyes. It is now time for Earth to learn about the great mysteries not only deep in our universe but also in the dimensions beyond sharing these anonymities with you.